ORACLES
OF DELPHI KEEP

ORACLES OF DELPHI KEEP

VICTORIA LAURIE

DELACORTE PRESS

Copyright © 2009 by Victoria Laurie

All rights reserved. Published in the United States by Delacorte Press, an imprint of Random House Children's Books, a division of Random House, Inc., New York.

Delacorte Press is a registered trademark and the colophon is a trademark of Random House, Inc.

Visit us on the Web! www.randomhouse.com/kids
Educators and librarians, for a variety of teaching tools, visit us at www.randomhouse.com/teachers

Library of Congress Cataloging-in-Publication Data
Laurie, Victoria.
    Oracles of Delphi Keep / Victoria Laurie.—1st ed.
        p. cm.
    Summary: In 1938, three orphans—Theo, Carl, and Ian, ages ten to thirteen—lead three teachers through a portal that takes them from Dover, England, to Morocco in their quest to locate six silver boxes before the ancient prophecies therein are found by the evil Demogorgon's offspring.
    ISBN 978-0-385-73572-8 (hardcover)—ISBN 978-0-385-90561-9 (Gibraltar lib. bdg.)—ISBN 978-0-375-89258-5 (e-book) [1. Oracles—Fiction. 2. Prophecies—Fiction. 3. Orphans—Fiction. 4. Orphanages—Fiction. 5. Space and time—Fiction. 6. Gorgons (Greek mythology)—Fiction. 7. Quests (Expeditions)—Fiction. 8. Dover (England)—History—20th century—Fiction. 9. Great Britain—History—1936–1945—Fiction. 10. Morocco—History—20th century—Fiction.]   I. Title.
PZ7.L372792Scr 2009   [Fic]—dc22   2008026438

The text of this book is set in 12-point Goudy.
Printed in the United States of America
10 9 8 7 6 5 4 3 2
First Edition

For my grandfather
Carl Laurie
My first and greatest hero

A NEW ORPHAN AT DELPHI KEEP

Dover, England, September 1930

I an Wigby sat on his cot, staring at the raging storm just beyond his window. It seemed that Lady Lightning and Master Thunder were having another argument, or so the headmistress Madam Dimbleby liked to say.

"That old married couple," she would tell the children, "Lady Lightning and Master Thunder, sometimes have arguments, as married couples often do. Lady Lightning likes to keep her husband, Master Thunder, in line, you see, so she zaps him a good sting every now and again. But the master won't have it, and he roars back at her. Give them a few hours to tire themselves out and they'll soon settle down and let their daughter Mistress Rain have the sky all to herself again."

Madam Dimbleby told the story of Lady Lightning and Master Thunder to all the orphans who came to live at Delphi Keep, to help them adjust to the turbulent weather that often visited their little patch of England. And it worked, if the seven sleeping boys behind Ian were any indication.

But Ian wasn't fearful of the tempest outside. In fact, he'd never been afraid of any storm. Instead, he was fascinated by the brilliant light and the clapping thunder, and he loved storms at night best of all. Yet this squall brought a foreboding to him that he couldn't quite shake, and for some time he'd been less interested in what was happening in the night sky and more absorbed in watching the ground below.

Deep in his five-year-old bones he knew that his life was about to change. Intently, he watched the road leading to the keep, a thin strip of black that he was just able to make out every time Lady Lightning sent a snap to her husband. There had been nothing on the road to call his attention, and yet he couldn't take his eyes off it.

The clock at the foot of the stairs chimed. He counted as the old timepiece gonged eleven times.

Ian sighed. His eyelids were growing heavy and the storm was dying down. Perhaps he should give up his vigil and crawl under the covers. But just as he was about to turn and pull back the bedclothes, Lady Lightning sent a terrific zap across the sky and something on the road materialized out of the darkness. Ian squinted and rested his forehead on the windowpane. The form that had caught his attention appeared to be large.

Ian cupped his hands around his eyes, straining to peer into the darkness. There! Something moved! In fact, it was racing along the road toward the keep! As he watched, he began to put features to the form. It looked like a man on a horse, riding hard through the rain. Ian's mouth fell open. He'd been right! Something exciting *was* about to happen.

He jumped out of bed and trotted on tiptoe to the other end of the long room, past the double rows of sleeping boys.

He paused at the door and placed his ear at the crack. Soon he was rewarded with the banging of a fist on the heavy oak door of the keep.

For a moment the interior of the old fortress remained quiet, but just as he was about to open his door to get Madam Dimbleby, he heard her shuffling down the hallway with her cousin and companion headmistress, Madam Scargill.

"Who could that be at this hour?" he heard Madam Dimbleby ask.

"Whoever it is should be taught some manners!" Madam Scargill complained as more pounding echoed from downstairs.

Ian opened his door a crack and peered into the hallway, catching a glimpse of the back of Madam Scargill's head as she descended the staircase. He waited a beat, then stepped into the hallway and crept to the railing. There was an old table butted up against the wooden slats with a small hole in the back that would give him both cover and a convenient spy hole. He scooted under the table just in time to see the headmistresses open the door and reveal a stranger.

A bony-looking man, soaked to the skin, stood in the doorway. His hair was long and stuck to his unshaven face. He wore a tattered coat and large black boots, and in the dim light he appeared quite frightful. "Please," he said in a deep voice. "I come on a mission of mercy!"

The headmistresses had stepped back as they'd opened the door to the man, and Ian could see their doubtful expressions when they turned to each other in silent contemplation. As they hesitated, the man stepped forward and pulled something out from the folds of his coat. Both women gasped when they saw that it was a small child. "I found 'er not four hours ago," he explained. "She was toddlin' about in this muck, if you can believe it. I took 'er 'ome for a time to wait the rain out, but I don't 'ave any food fit for 'er and up until a bit ago she was frettin' as bad as this storm."

"Oh, my!" said Madam Dimbleby as she hurried to take the child. After hugging the toddler to her chest and pulling the folds of her shawl about the babe, she asked, "Where on earth did you find her?"

" 'Er mum rents the cottage on the edge of me property," the man said. "I found this little one wandering about in the field next to the 'ouse, so I went looking for 'er mum but she's cleared out."

"Cleared out?" Madam Scargill asked in her usual clipped speech. "What do you mean, 'cleared out'?"

"All 'er belongings is gone. 'Er clothes, 'er trunk, all 'er personal things. There was this note, though," he said, and once more he dug around in the folds of his coat, from which he fished a crumpled, damp letter that he held out to the women.

Madam Scargill took the paper, placing her half-glasses onto her nose before she read, " 'I cannot stay any longer. The child would be in danger if she were found with me. Please get her safely to the orphanage at the keep near Castle Dover.' "

"Horrible!" Madam Dimbleby exclaimed as she rocked the small child. "To abandon a helpless child and in the middle of a terrible night like this!"

"And how dreadful of her to leave the job of getting the girl to us up to any passing stranger," sniffed Madam Scargill.

"Did she leave word of the child's name?" Madam Dimbleby asked.

"No," answered the man. "She just left the babe's blanket and . . ." The man seemed about to say something else but caught himself.

"And what?" Madam Scargill asked. Ian knew well she could ferret out the truth from anyone.

"Noffing," the man said with a shuffle of his feet, but Ian, who was watching the man intently, noticed that he discreetly squeezed something in his outer coat pocket.

"Well, I'd best get the girl upstairs," said Madam Dimbleby, turning toward the staircase. "Gertrude, offer the man a cup of tea and a blanket to warm him until this rain lets up."

Ian held perfectly still as Madam Dimbleby walked up to the second floor. He knew she couldn't see him, but the headmistress seemed to have eyes in the back of her head, and often knew when children were in places they shouldn't be. He breathed a sigh of relief as she passed his hiding place on the way down the hall toward the nursery. When she was a safe distance away, he focused again on the man below.

The stranger was now wrapped in a warm afghan and still stood in the entryway, hovering in front of the small coal stove there. Madam Scargill had gone off to make him some tea. The stranger peered down the hallway in the direction of the kitchen, then, seeming satisfied that he was alone, he dug into the coat pocket that Ian had caught him giving a squeeze to earlier, and retrieved something small and delicate.

From where he sat, Ian could just make out that it was a gold necklace with a thin, shiny crystal. The man held the pendant up to the light and let the chain dangle freely. The crystal sparkled and sent small rainbows of color onto the wall behind him. "What do you have there?" Madam Scargill asked, and both Ian and the man started.

"It's noffing!" said the man, quickly closing his fist around the necklace.

"Oh, I think that it is more than nothing," replied Madam Scargill testily. "And I think that it belongs to the child." Her hands found her bony hips, and a cross expression settled onto her face.

"I shall take it as me payment for delivering the babe," said the man, puffing out his chest at her.

Ian smirked. The stranger clearly underestimated Madam Scargill. But Ian knew she would have none of *that* attitude. "You shall take a cup of tea and a warm blanket for your troubles," she said in the level tone that instilled fear in even the most stubborn of children. "Then you shall go to the vicar in the morning and ask forgiveness for your greediness. Now hand it over!" She reached out her hand and appeared to expect no further argument from the stranger in her entryway.

The horseman considered her for a long moment before scowling and dropping the trinket into her palm. From the kitchen the teakettle's whistle beckoned. Madam Scargill gave the stranger a tight smile. "Stay here a moment and I shall get your tea. And try not to relieve us of any further *payment* for your delivery services," she said as she looked pointedly around at the sparse furnishings of the foyer.

When she turned her back and walked away to the kitchen, the man made a face at her retreating figure, then shuffled out of the afghan and tossed it onto a nearby chair. He eased the door of the keep open, paused ever so slightly as the rain poured down, and slipped out quietly into the night.

A few moments later Madam Scargill came back carrying a tray with two cups and a pot of steaming tea. She hesitated when she realized the horseman's absence, and Ian watched as she looked around the corner into the dining hall. She then set down the tray, opened the door, and peered out into the rain.

The wind had picked up a bit and it howled fiercely. In the distance Ian could hear the horse's hooves pounding away from the keep. And as Madam Scargill began to close the door again, something else sounded in the gloom of the night—something that made the hairs on Ian's neck stand on end.

The noise was unlike anything he'd ever heard before. It was as if a growl and a howl had combined into one long, horrible sound. Madam Scargill must have heard it too, because she yanked the door open and stepped out onto the front stair. She stood there for a long moment with her hand over her heart, and her head swiveling to and fro.

The sound did not come again, but as Madam Scargill turned to walk back inside, Ian saw that her face was rather pale. She shut the door tightly before throwing the bolt at the top—which was almost never used—and then tested the door to ensure that it was locked. Satisfied that all was secure, she turned to pick up the tray and head up the stairs.

Ian held very still again as she drew close, and squeezed himself into a tiny ball when she topped the landing and passed right by his hiding place. He waited until she had turned into the nursery to come out from under the table and take a step toward his room, but his curiosity about the newest member of Delphi Keep compelled him farther down the hallway.

As he approached the nursery, he could hear the head-mistresses talking in low tones, and he inched toward the open door, ready to dart into the linen closet to the left of the room if he heard the swish of skirts headed his way.

"I tell you, Maggie, I heard what I heard!" Madam Scargill was saying. "It was the beast. I know it."

"Gertrude, you know there is no such thing," Madam Dimbleby replied with a small chuckle. "That is a tale told to children to make sure they are home and in bed before dark."

Madam Scargill gasped. "Children's tale? You remember what happened on our family holiday to Brighton?"

Madam Dimbleby sighed. "I remember," she said wearily. "You've hardly let me forget it all these long years."

"I know what I saw." Madam Scargill sniffed. "It was *real*, Maggie. It was."

"You were six years old, Gertrude. How can you be sure your imagination wasn't playing tricks on you?"

"We shall need to be extra-vigilant with the children," Madam Scargill continued, ignoring her cousin's skepticism.

"We mustn't let the older ones out beyond the walls after dark. I'll tell Landis to keep a watch."

Madam Dimbleby chuckled. "All right, Gertie, if it will make you feel better, we'll keep an eye out for your beast. Now, here, hold the babe while I have a sip of that tea, will you?"

Ian crept a little closer to the door and peered through the crack by the hinge. He could see Madam Dimbleby handing the child, now dressed in a nightgown and wrapped in a blanket, to her cousin. "Well, would you look at that?" Madam Scargill said. "She's fast asleep. I'm always amazed at what the little ones can sleep through. It must have been frightful out there alone in this weather," she added, and Ian saw her severe features soften a bit. "How old do you think she is, Maggie?"

"I'd guess she's near two years," Madam Dimbleby said as she picked up the pot of tea and poured the steaming amber liquid into a cup.

"She's small for two," Madam Scargill replied.

"Yes, but her teeth are well formed, and those eyes were quick to follow my chatter until she fell asleep. I believe she's between twenty-one months and two years. She's also got an interesting birthmark on her left shoulder," said Madam Dimbleby. "It almost looks like an eye."

"You don't say?" said Madam Scargill, and Ian saw her pulling gently at the neckline of the toddler's nightgown. "Ah, I see it," she said. "Yes, that's quite unusual."

"The girl appears to be in good health," said Madam Dimbleby, sipping her tea. "She's well fed and seems to have been well taken care of."

"We'll have to name her," Madam Scargill remarked as she sat down with the child in the rocker.

Ian pushed closer to the crack, wanting to get a look at the new child.

"I think we should leave that up to Master Wigby," replied Madam Dimbleby calmly, setting her cup back on its saucer in her hand. "After all, he's been intent on watching every bit of her arrival."

Ian's eyes bulged in alarm and he jumped back flat against the wall, his heart racing as he thought about fleeing down the hallway back to his room.

Madam Dimbleby chuckled. "Won't you join us in the nursery, Master Wigby?"

Ian gulped and took a deep breath. There was no getting out of it now. With his head hanging low, he pushed the door of the room fully open. "Hello," he mumbled. "The man at the door woke me with all that pounding."

Madam Dimbleby sipped her tea again, a smile at the edges of her lips. "I suspect the storm had you up even before that," she quipped. "Now come in and say hello to our newest family member."

Ian walked forward with leaden feet, knowing that the headmistress might be kind to him at the moment but children caught breaking rules were seldom left unpunished. And the rules of the keep were strict. They had to be, with so many orphans running about.

One of the central rules was that children were not to be out of their rooms past bedtime. He'd probably lose his breakfast over this, which was awful, because Ian dearly loved his breakfast. "She's very pretty," he said as he stood before Madam Scargill, who did not seem nearly as amused by his presence as Madam Dimbleby.

"You are aware that children are not to be out of bed past their curfew?" Madam Scargill sniffed.

"He's aware, Gertrude," Madam Dimbleby said with a sigh. "But I expect you'll want him punished for his curiosity."

"Rules are rules, Maggie," her cousin said haughtily. "Without them, all we've got is anarchy."

"Oh, very well," Madam Dimbleby said. "But I shall be the one to administer the punishment." Setting down her teacup and saucer on a nearby table, she turned to Ian and said, "Your punishment shall have two parts: First, you must name this child, and think of a name that you like, Ian, because you'll be using it quite a bit from now on. And the reason you'll need to choose wisely is that the second part will be to entrust the care of this little girl to you. She will be yours to watch over as if she were your own flesh and blood, your own baby sister."

Ian gulped again. Older children were often entrusted with the care of the younger ones. It helped establish a sense of family for the lonely orphans, and it also helped the two headmistresses keep order in a large keep full of children.

But orphans as young as Ian were never given ward of other children. Usually the responsibility fell to those no younger than seven. Madam Scargill complained, "He's too young, Maggie."

But Madam Dimbleby was not to be dissuaded. "He's always been mature for his age, Gertrude. He'll be fine."

Ian looked at the toddler in Madam Scargill's arms. She was petite and seemed fragile. Her hair was blond, like his own, and though her eyes were closed, he suspected they'd also be light in color. Her face was oval, her cheeks were round, and her nose was a perfect little nub in the middle. As he looked at her, he realized there was something familiar about her that called to him. "All right, ma'am," he said. "I'll try to watch out for her."

"Of course you will, Ian," Madam Dimbleby said with a confident smile as she sat back in her chair and picked up her teacup again. "Now go along to bed and think on her name. We shall want to know it tomorrow at breakfast."

"Oh, but I already have it," Ian said.

Madam Scargill scoffed. "This should be interesting," she muttered.

"What name have you come up with, then?" Madam Dimbleby asked with a smile, ignoring her cousin.

"Theodosia," Ian said matter-of-factly. "Theo, for short, and for a last name . . ." He pondered for a moment before he said, "Fields, for where she was found before she was brought to us."

Both Madam Dimbleby and Madam Scargill looked surprised as they sat blinking at him for a beat or two. Finally, Madam Dimbleby said, "It's a perfect name, Ian. Perfect."

Ian beamed at her, then gave his goodnights and trotted off to bed, eager to get some sleep before taking charge of his new baby sister in the morning.

SORCERER OF FIRE

An Empty Flat Near London,
Earlier That Evening

Magus the Black stood before a stone hearth, staring blankly into the glowing embers of a flame that heated the room to an uncomfortable degree. Flanking him were two massive beasts, keeping diligent watch, their red eyes darting about the room as drool dripped from their long, vicious fangs. Outside, there was a loud clap of thunder as a storm began to rage.

In the corner of the small flat, lying prone on a dirty cot, was the prisoner, who was now barely recognizable after suffering so through her resistance. She was quiet after her long battle, but this hardly pleased Magus the Black.

Tendrils of inky smoke curled and twisted about the sorcerer's dark cloak like irritated cobras, reflecting his own frustrations. The flame in the hearth flickered and danced, casting an eerie glow over Magus's hollow cheeks, sunken eyes, and blister-scarred skin. Thin lips pulled pensively over a double row of small, sharply pointed teeth, and two narrow streams of light gray smoke trailed out of his angular nose.

He had thought that the woman was stronger and would withstand the suffering. He'd been quite disappointed to find that she was weaker than she appeared. He growled low in his throat and the beasts eyed him nervously. He paid them no heed while his mind sifted through all that the woman had told him . . . and all that she hadn't.

Suddenly, the beasts sniffed the air and growled like their master, their black greasy hackles rising as they both eyed the door. There was a knock and then the door to the flat opened. The beasts continued to growl and a quivering male voice said in his native German, "Master? You've sent for me?"

Magus turned and noted the slight flinch from the man in the doorway as their eyes met. The sorcerer's lips curled slightly. He liked invoking fear. Before speaking, Magus held up his hands in a command to settle the beasts, and they ceased their growling at once and lay down on the stone hearth but continued to watch the man in the doorway intently.

"The woman has revealed that she left the babe in an open field somewhere near the village of Dover," the sorcerer said, also speaking German, in a voice that was high-pitched and coarse like fine-grade sandpaper. "She believes a horseman she spied from the woods might have rescued the child. Take one of my pets, find the horseman, and bring the child to me—alive."

The man in the doorway glanced nervously at the tortured figure on the bed. "Dover is a large village, master, and there would be many residents who might own horses. Can she tell you anything more about the location of the field or the horseman?"

Magus turned back to the hearth and did not answer for a long moment. Finally, he said, "She can tell us nothing more, Dieter. Ever."

"I see," said his servant quietly. After a pause he added, "I shall leave for the village immediately and look for the boy."

Magus turned back to Dieter. "It is a girl child you search for, Van Schuft."

"A girl?"

"Yes."

"Are you sure . . . ?" Dieter began, but then caught himself. "What I mean, master," he said, quivering even more, "is that the prophecy states we should search for a boy child."

Magus rounded on his servant, flames licking the edges of his cape as a choking sulfur stench filled the flat. "You *dare* question me?" he spat.

"No!" said Dieter quickly. "Of course not! I only meant . . . It's just . . . I'm merely pointing out that . . ."

Magus glowered at the frightened man trembling in fear across the room. "I am aware that the prophecy names a boy," he rasped in his awful voice. "It would not be the first time the Oracle has sent us in the wrong direction. The woman was clear. The child she bore was a girl."

"Yes, master," said Dieter, bowing low as he attempted to back out of the room as quickly as possible.

"And, Dieter," said Magus.

"Yes, master?"

"Send your wife in to clean up this mess. The stench from that cot displeases me."

"As you wish, master," said Dieter, and he made a hasty retreat.

When Dieter had bowed his way out of sight, Magus eyed his she-beast. "Go," he said, and the hellhound jumped to his bidding. "Kill the horseman, Medea," he said to the four-footed fiend, "but bring me the child alive. I shall want to assess if she is the One before I kill her."

To that the she-beast gave an almost imperceptible nod, then trotted out the door.

THE BOX

The White Cliffs of Dover, Eight Years Later,
August 1938

"Which tunnel do you like, Theo?" Ian asked, pointing to the crude map he'd made of all the tunnels he and Theo had discovered since they'd started exploring the cliffs outside their orphanage.

"It's your birthday, Ian," Theo said loudly above the noise of the wind coming off the water. "You choose."

"Right," he said, hurrying down the small path leading toward the cliffs and the sea. He stopped at one rocky outcropping and climbed up a boulder to have a look at the landscape.

The White Cliffs of Dover soared majestically some three hundred and fifty feet above the turbulent waters of the Strait of Dover—the narrowest section of the English Channel separating England from continental Europe.

The terrain at the top of the cliffs was often battered by fierce winds that swept in off the sea, making the vegetation lean over on itself and the rocks and boulders look pockmarked. To the west, at the base of the cliffs, was the port of Dover, where ships from neighboring countries such as

France, Belgium, and the Netherlands docked. Ian and Theo would often watch the large ships come into port and unload their cargo of people and goods, and they would talk about the places they'd go when they were old enough to book passage and explore the world.

A kilometer behind Ian was the domineering facade of Castle Dover, a monstrous structure that stood sentry in its regal pose as it surveyed the surrounding countryside and offered the best views of the sea and the coastline of France.

And a kilometer behind Castle Dover was the much smaller structure of Delphi Keep, the residence of the Earl of Kent until Castle Dover had been built about five hundred years later. The keep had been turned into an orphanage by the current Earl of Kent, who held that an eight-hundred-year-old fortress that had withstood assault from foreign invaders for centuries could surely hold up against the thirty-odd children who ran, roughhoused, and played within its halls and called it home.

To the rest of the world, Dover was fairly small, but it was the only home Ian, Theo, and many of the other orphans had ever known.

Ian in particular loved this little patch of England because it offered him such opportunity for adventure. There were the keep and Castle Dover with their many nooks and crannies, the port at the base of the cliffs, the quaint village, and of course the rugged terrain where he now stood, which was host to an abundance of hidden tunnels and secret passageways carved out of the soft, chalky limestone that provided the white cliffs with their beauty and their name.

But at the moment Ian wasn't thinking about the majesty of the cliffs or the port below. His attention was focused on his map as he turned atop the boulder and considered the terrain against the markers he'd carefully documented. Theo was standing at the giant rock's base, looking up at him with mild curiosity. "Have you decided yet?" she asked him.

"I think we should check this area," he said, jumping down from his perch and indicating a rather blank section on his map. "You never know when we'll find that one tunnel that might contain a bit of treasure," he added enthusiastically.

Like most boys his age, Ian loved the idea of exploration and hidden treasure. He often fantasized about discovering some gem or historical relic within one of the many tunnels he and Theo explored. His dream was to find something of value so that he could sell it and use the proceeds to help secure his and Theo's futures once they left the orphanage. At the very least he considered these underground jaunts to be good training for the day when he became a *real* explorer, traveling the globe in search of lost civilizations and hidden treasure. This had been Ian's life's ambition since he was seven and read the book *Treasure Island*.

To that end, he and Theo had spent many happy hours belowground, tracing the steps of villagers and warriors from the Middle Ages who had first dug out and even lived in the chalky space under the earth.

Most of the tunnels wound their way through the top part of the cliffs. Some led to caves that opened up to the strait; others led all the way into Castle Dover, through the host of secret entrances in the mighty structure. Still others came to a dead end and offered little in the way of entertainment.

As Ian walked, he traced on his map some of the branches of tunnels he'd already explored. Theo caught up to him and looked over his elbow. "This tunnel," he said, pointing to one particularly broad vein. "We never did go down the south fork of that one. I bet there's a secret outlet, and I bet it's somewhere close to here."

"You've always had a knack for ferreting out secret entrances," she said. "So I'll go along with that."

The pair continued to walk, and Ian used a staff he'd crafted to poke holes in the soft earth. They were not far from the edge of the cliffs, and the wind swirled the grass around them. Luckily, it was a lovely, warm day, so the wind didn't bite as it usually did when they were this close to the sea.

While Ian paused again to get his bearings, Theo looked southeast across the strait and said, "Look, Ian. We can see clear to Calais."

Ian glanced up at the French city, which was just visible. "Yeah, no fog or mist to get in the way today."

"Someday I'd like to go to France," she said wistfully.

Ian laughed. "Good ol' Theo. Always wanting to be someplace other than where she is." But just as he turned to smile at his sister, Ian's staff pushed right through the scrub and slipped out of his hand, disappearing under the grass. He heard it clank a moment later. "Theo!" he said excitedly as he knelt down and began to pull at the scrub. "I think we've got something!"

Theo came to crouch beside him as he tore at the place where his staff had disappeared, and sure enough a hole barely half a meter wide opened up in the ground before them. "Here's the torch," Theo said, handing Ian the flashlight so that he could look inside.

Ian leaned down and pushed his arm and his head into the hole to shine the light about. Quickly, he pulled them out and with a brilliant smile announced, "We've hit the jackpot!"

"Another tunnel?"

"Yes!" he said. "And you wouldn't believe the size of it! There's plenty of room once we widen this hole. Come on, help me find a rock and we'll get to work."

The pair found some stones and began to pound out a larger hole. The rock underneath the scrub was made of white lime—chalk—and was extremely soft. In no time they'd managed to widen the hole enough for Ian to squirm through. "You'll have an easy time of it, at least," he said, looking at his much smaller companion.

Theo smiled brightly at him and moved to the entrance. "I'll go first," she said. "That way I can pull you in if you get stuck."

Before Ian could stop her, Theo had slipped easily down into the tunnel. He poked his head in after her, and as he handed over the torch, he said, "Next time let me go first to make sure it's safe, all right?"

She rolled her eyes. "It's perfectly safe. Now come on. We're wasting time."

Ian pulled his head out of the hole and had a moment of uncertainty about whether to go in headfirst or feetfirst, but he finally decided headfirst might be best. The hole wasn't quite as wide as he'd hoped, and Theo had to pull on his arms a few times before he made it through and landed inelegantly on the chalky floor.

"Here's your staff," Theo said after he'd dusted off his trousers.

"Thanks," he answered, then looked around the large cavern where he and Theo had landed. Unlike many of the other tunnels, where he'd had to duck his head to explore, this cavern held plenty of room for him to stand up to his full height. Theo bounced the beam of the torch off the walls, and the pair simply stood there for a few beats, amazed that such a large room existed just belowground.

"Do you think this could be a natural cavern?" Theo asked.

Ian reached forward and guided her hand upward so that the beam shone on the ceiling. There were distinct grooves above their heads. "No," he said. "See that? This was manmade."

The beam of the torch moved off the ceiling and onto one of the far walls, revealing what looked like large Greek lettering tattooed on the rock. "I'd say you were right," Theo answered.

Ian walked over and touched the black letters. "This is fantastic!" he said breathily. "Theo, come here and have a look."

But instead of coming over to him, she said, "Did you hear that?"

"Hear what?" he asked, turning to look at her.

Theo cocked her head, listening. "I don't know, exactly.

But I swear I heard something down there," she answered, pointing the beam to the tunnel leading out of the large cavern.

"Well, let's go have a look, then," Ian said, his enthusiasm building. Not much caused Ian fear or trepidation.

But Theo held his arm, stopping him. "I don't like it," she whispered, and Ian caught sight of goose pimples forming along her arm. "I've got an awful feeling about exploring this tunnel."

"Don't be silly," he said gently, giving her hand a pat. "We're probably the only living creatures to be in this tunnel for centuries. Come on, you can stay behind me if it will make you feel better." And with that he lifted the torch out of her hand and marched forward into the tunnel.

When he didn't hear her following him, Ian turned and added resolutely, "If you're that scared, then you can stay here or aboveground if you like, but I'm going to see where this tunnel leads."

Theo frowned uneasily, and her eyes drifted up to the hole they'd just come through. Ian waited patiently for her to make up her mind, and after a moment she walked stiffly over to him and said, "Very well."

"That's my girl." He grinned, ruffling her hair before leading the way out from the cavern. The tunnel they moved into was narrow and roughly carved out. It also curved and twisted, and Ian held his torch in one hand as they walked so that he could glance at his compass in the other. At some points the path veered sharply east, then straightened out and turned back west, which he found fascinating, as most of the other tunnels they'd explored in the

23

cliffs were fairly straightforward, with forks or branches where a new direction was chosen.

Theo broke the silence. "This isn't like the other tunnels. The walls of the others were much smoother and they always took us in a straight line," she said, as if reading his thoughts.

"Yeah," said Ian, still staring at his compass. "Which means this one must be older. We could really be in a lost tunnel!"

Just then, Theo stopped abruptly and gave a hard tug on Ian's shirt. "What's that smell?"

Ian stopped, but the narrowness of the tunnel prevented him from comfortably turning around to face her. "I don't smell anything," he said, taking several whiffs.

Theo hadn't let go of his shirt, and Ian noticed that her voice was shaky as she said, "I swear I caught the scent of something awful. Ian, I really don't like this place."

"Aw, Theo." Ian tugged himself forward out of her grasp. "You're just claustrophobic. Take some deep breaths and focus on putting one foot in front of the other. It'll pass in a bit."

Slowly, the pair moved ahead and came to a sharp corner. When they rounded it, they stopped short. "Whoa," Ian breathed. They had arrived in a second large cavern. On the far side of the space was another narrow tunnel, the counterpart to the one they'd just come through.

But Ian wasn't interested in the opposite tunnel just yet. For now, the cavern captured his full attention. "Gaw blimey!" he exclaimed as he moved the beam of the torch along the walls, which were covered with what looked like the same ancient Greek script they had seen in the first room. "Would you look at that, Theo?" he said, fascinated.

But when he glanced at her, she didn't appear to share his enthusiasm. Instead, Theo stood pensively in the cavern's entryway with a fearful look on her face. "I really don't like this place," she whispered, her eyes never leaving the tunnel on the far side of the room.

But Ian was too distracted by the cavern to worry about her. He continued to bob the beam of the torch all about the cavern when suddenly something on the ground reflected the light.

"What's *that?*" he exclaimed, racing across the large space to stand above a shiny metallic object. "Theo!" he called as he dropped to his knees. In front of him, half buried in the chalky floor of the cavern, lay a small silver box with ornate engravings. "It's real treasure!"

He heard Theo come over to him, but when he glanced up at her, he noticed that her eyes were still warily darting to the tunnel leading deeper into the cliffs. "Can you get it out?" she asked him.

Ian set his compass down and tried to get his fingers around the edges of the box, but it was firmly planted in the ground. Thinking fast, he dug into his pocket and pulled out his Swiss Army knife. He opened the largest blade. "This could be an ancient artifact," he said smartly as he chipped away at the chalk, careful to avoid scratching the silver box. "It's best not to disturb it too much. We don't want to damage it."

Just then there was a distinct noise from somewhere deep

within the tunnel opposite. It was lower and more menacing than a dog's growl but had the same animal cadence. The noise made Ian pause and catch his breath. "What was that?" he whispered, his senses immediately alert.

"That's what I heard earlier," Theo whispered back, her hand gripping his shoulder. "And there! Do you smell *that?*"

Ian did smell something. It was a foul scent, a mixture of sulfur and something worse, like rotting meat. "Some animal's died down here," he said, but a moment later the growl echoed through their cavern again.

"Or something killed the animal," Theo said, gripping Ian's shoulder even more tightly. "And that something's still here."

Ian glanced back at the box gleaming in the bright light of his torch. It looked like it was worth some money, and for a boy who had nothing, leaving behind a treasure box was out of the question. "Come on," he said quickly, scraping again at the chalk with his knife. "Help me get this out of the ground."

"Leave it!" Theo whispered. "Ian, we've got to get out of here!"

Ian looked up into her frightened green eyes and felt a pang in his heart. "You go," he said, handing her the torch. Then he dug into his pocket and pulled out a much smaller pocket torch. "Take the larger light and go. I'll be right behind you as soon as I free this box."

Suddenly, there was another growl, even more menacing and quickly followed by the sounds of furious digging and rocks tumbling. Theo took the larger torch but hesitated when Ian put the pocket torch in his mouth and began to jab his knife with great effort around the edges of the box. A moment later she had dropped down beside him and was helping him by pulling up on the treasure as he scratched at the chalk. "We've got to hurry!" she whispered, the smell of sulfur and decay filling their nostrils as they both heard the echo of more rocks tumbling from the second tunnel.

Slowly, inch by inch, the treasure came away from its earthen cradle, but it still wasn't completely free. Ian heard a sound like a small cave-in coming from the darkness of the western tunnel, and he felt Theo shiver with fear. "We've got to go!" she insisted. Letting go of the box, she got to her feet and tugged at Ian's shirt. "Leave it!"

But Ian wasn't about to give up. His brow wet with perspiration, he gripped the sides of the artifact and pulled up mightily, and it finally gave way as he fell over backward. A howl louder and more horrible than any he'd ever heard before tore along the walls of the cavern. Ian scrambled to his feet, leaving his pocket torch, compass, and Swiss Army knife behind as he shoved Theo toward the east tunnel. "Go!" he said as he pushed her along.

She needed no encouragement. The pair dashed across the cavern and into the narrow opening. Theo was holding the bigger torch in front of her as they ran, the beam bouncing along the walls, and Ian had to squint into the dimness to follow the narrow corridor. Behind them came another vicious howl, and he knew that whatever horrid creature they'd disturbed was on their trail. "Fly, Theo!" he yelled as his thoughts turned to panic. "Run as fast as you can!"

Behind them came the sound of four pounding paws, and it was closing in. Ian gulped for air and tried to temper the urge to run over Theo to get away. His heart felt like it was about to jump out of his chest, and a cold sweat trickled down his back. He noticed with a pang that Theo smacked one of the walls with her hand so hard he could hear the *whap* of it against the rock. He knew that by running so close behind her he was pushing her to her limits, but the pounding paws behind them were gaining and his own fear propelled him forward.

Finally, just ahead he could see a small sliver of daylight, and he knew that at last the way out was close at hand. But then he remembered the small hole he'd barely managed to fit through. And with a sudden dread he knew he'd never make it out in time, though Theo still had a chance.

Ian shouted, "Just get out, Theo! I'll help you through that hole but don't look back! Run to the keep as fast as you can!"

The thundering paws behind them grew nearer still, and even above the pounding of the blood in his ears, Ian could hear the pant of some great beast as it swept closer and closer to them. They were almost to the opening. *"Go, go, go!"* Ian yelled.

He knew that with his help Theo would make it, but as he eyed the exit, his own chances seemed slim. He and Theo ran the last meter together, and in one swift move he tossed the silver box up through the opening, then hooked his hands about Theo's waist and heaved her out too. He heard her land on the rough terrain with a thud, but he had no time to apologize. He leapt as he attempted to clamber out, but as he'd feared, he didn't make it through. He became lodged at the hips.

"Get out of here!" he shouted at Theo when he saw her sprawled on the grass nearby. "I've blocked it in for now! Go, Theo, go!"

But she didn't leave him. Instead, with trembling limbs she crawled quickly to the opening and bent forward, grabbing Ian by his shoulders. While Theo tugged, Ian scratched and clawed at the earth. He imagined that at any moment he would feel the bite of whatever was chasing them on his dangling legs below. That fear spurred him to make one final attempt to dislodge himself. Setting his hands firmly on the ground, he pushed up with all his strength, and with Theo's help, he pulled free of the hole, tumbling forward on top of her.

Just as his legs got clear, there came a great *snap!* from behind him and Ian whipped his head around to look. His breath caught in his throat as he saw an unnaturally massive snout shoot through the opening and miss his ankle by inches. He and Theo scooted away from the hole and sat petrified as the snout became a head, and—oh, what an awful thing to see! The massive head was as large as a lion's but shaped like a wolf's, with thick black fur and bright red eyes. Its snout was long and broad, and black lips peeled away in a snarl to reveal impossibly long fangs, heavy with drool.

Ian and Theo scuttled on their hands and feet, trying to move farther away from the beast, which seemed unable to get more than its head clear of the hole. After growling and snapping at them, it pulled its head back and began to dig at the opening with giant paws tipped with nails that were sharp and cruel.

"We've got to get out of here!" Ian panted, staggering to

his feet, then grabbing the silver box from where it had landed nearby and pulling Theo up from her stunned position on the grass. "Run!" he gasped, and he tugged her along the hilly terrain, trying to get as much distance between them and the creature as possible.

Ian became aware of Theo's ragged breathing while she tried to keep up with his much longer stride, but he was too concerned with getting her to safety to slow down. "Come on, Theo," he said urgently. "We've got to reach the keep!"

And so the pair ran for their lives, stumbling over rocks, working their way back to the keep as fast as they could.

Only when the keep was in sight and he felt that Theo might be on the brink of collapse did Ian finally slow down. He settled for a brisk jog, allowing his ward to catch her breath, but he continued to look over his shoulder every few steps to make sure the beast wasn't right behind, and to his increasing relief no sign of it emerged. In fact, the only proof that they'd seen the horrid creature came when they reached the main road leading to the keep and they heard that awful howl in the distance.

The noise prompted Ian to grab Theo's hand again and run, and he had to admire her for making no protest even though he knew she had to be exhausted. Finally, the pair reached the safety of the outer walls of the keep and with the last remnants of their energy they stumbled through the large metal gates and up the short drive, staying to the right of the main building until they reached the front lawn, where they tumbled to the ground to lie panting and spent. It was a long time before either of them attempted to talk, and Theo spoke first. "What was that horrible creature?" she asked him.

"I don't know, but I do know I don't ever want to see it again," Ian said as he sat up and wiped his sweat-soaked brow.

"We've got to tell Madam Dimbleby and Madam Scargill," Theo announced.

"No!" Ian snapped, and grabbed her arm. When she looked in shock at his firm grip, Ian immediately let go and softened a bit. "We'll have to tell them we were in the tunnels," he whispered, feeling dread at the prospect of having to confess that.

Ian's thoughts drifted back to the previous summer, when one of the older tunnels near the cliff's face had collapsed, the soft chalk finally giving way to erosion and time. Because the tunnel had crumbled during the night, no one had been injured, but news of it had reached the keep the following day and since then their headmistresses had expressly forbidden any of the children to explore the tunnels near the cliffs. Madam Scargill had given a particularly stern warning to Ian and Theo, as she knew that they were most likely to be caught underground.

And since Ian was already in trouble for staying up past lights-out to read one of the many adventure books he'd borrowed from the earl's massive library at Castle Dover, he didn't want to risk yet another evening without supper or chance what he really feared: feeling the bite of Madam Scargill's switch.

"But, Ian!" Theo exclaimed. "What if it comes after us?"

Ian considered that for a long moment. "We'll stick close to the keep for the next few days. Even if that beast is able to squeeze out of the hole, it would have to track us all the way back here. As long as we stay behind the walls and on keep grounds, I'm sure we'll be safe enough."

"Are you *mad?*" Theo said, her hands on her hips and her eyes very large as she looked scornfully at him. "What if it follows our scent here and comes after one of the other children?"

Ian frowned. She had a good point. "Fine," he grumbled, then added quickly, "but let me do the talking, all right? You just stand there and nod."

"If you plan on telling them that you saw the beast along the cliffs, you're going to have to change your clothes," Theo said, pointing to his tattered shirt and chalk-stained trousers. "One look at you and Madam Scargill will know you're lying."

When she pointed to him, Ian suddenly noticed a wicked-looking injury to Theo's hand. He circled her wrist gently with his fingers. "Theo," he whispered softly. "What have you done?"

She glanced down at the deep cut on the top of her hand, which was swollen and mean-looking. "Oh, right," she said, pulling it out of his grip and wincing. "It must have happened when I smacked into the wall of the tunnel. It didn't hurt until you mentioned it just now."

Ian frowned, worried about the nasty gash. "We'll need to get that tended to. Come on, then. Let's sneak into the keep and get you cleaned up and a bandage put on your hand before someone spots us. Then we can think up a good story to tell them about the beast."

Just then a voice to Ian's right said, "Lookit the two lazy gits, lying around all day while the rest of us work on our chores!"

Ian cringed. The voice belonged to the most hated boy at the orphanage, Searle Frost. He was a recent addition to Delphi, having been dropped off one afternoon by an elderly aunt who claimed not to be able to care for him any longer. It soon became apparent why. Searle was a difficult child and a bully through and through. He was also one of the few boys at the orphanage who were bigger than Ian.

"Theo," Ian whispered. "Go on to the back of the keep and see if you can't get in through the laundry room in the cellar."

"But what about you?" she whispered back.

"I'll be along as soon as I've dealt with Searle."

"Ian . . . ," Theo moaned. "Don't cause trouble. Just ignore him—*ow!*" Theo's hand flew to the top of her head, where a rock had just bounced off.

In an instant Ian had jumped to his feet and was hurtling toward Searle. "How *dare* you hit a girl!" he roared.

Searle, who'd been laughing and pointing at Theo, quickly became serious and focused on Ian, charging toward him. He pulled up his sleeves, bracing himself as Ian barreled into him.

Ian and Searle collided with a great whump and Ian tumbled to the ground, pulling Searle with him. He rolled on top of the larger boy and got in a solid punch to his chin, but a moment later the air left his lungs as Searle's fist connected with his stomach. Ian lurched forward and tried to get his knee up into Searle's belly, but he missed and sent it into Searle's elbow instead, which, judging from the boy's yelp, hurt fiercely.

Squirming around, Ian quickly wound his arm under Searle's chin, attempting a headlock, but his adversary's elbow found Ian's rib cage and he grunted again in pain. He heard the shouting of other children who had come over to watch the fight, and somewhere, mixed into the frenzy of noise, he heard Theo shouting, "Stop it! Both of you, *stop!*"

But Ian didn't stop. His anger was fueled by fear from being chased by a giant beast as well as the building fury from being fed up with Searle. As the two tumbled around on the ground trying to gain the commanding position, Ian shoved his elbow as hard as he could into Searle's stomach. By this time Ian had his face buried under Searle's arm, but he heard a satisfying "Uhn!" as he made contact. A moment later his satisfaction evaporated when Searle's fist connected with his cheek. He saw stars before he was lifted off the ground by his shirt collar, then dropped to the earth like a sack of potatoes.

Ian sat dumbly for a beat or two, his head still a bit dizzy when he blinked and saw the keep's groundskeeper, Landis, with a choke hold around Searle. And then, from behind Landis, a chilling voice demanded, "*What* is going on here?"

Ian looked up to see Madam Scargill marching toward them, wearing a frosty look of anger.

"I caught these two having a bit of a row, ma'am," said

Landis. "I think they was fighting over this." With his free hand he held up the box Ian had found in the tunnel.

"That's mine!" Ian said, jumping to his feet and attempting to snatch it out of Landis's hands. But the groundskeeper held it high out of his reach. "Landis, that's my box!"

"Is not!" Searle snarled from the crook of Landis's elbow. "It's mine and you stole it from me!"

Ian's jaw dropped. He genuinely disliked Searle, but he'd never expected his nemesis to be so deceitful. "That's a lie!" he roared, his hands balling into fists as he readied himself to go at it with Searle again.

Landis must have sensed Ian's intent, because he shook his head in warning and said in a low, measured voice, "Now, now, Ian. Just calm yourself until we figure this all out."

Theo came to Ian's defense. "But he's telling the truth!" she said. "Landis, that *is* Ian's box. We found it just today, in fact."

"Of course you did," said Searle with a sneer. "You found it right where I left it, under my bed."

"I'll have that, Landis," Madam Scargill said, and she stretched out her hand expectantly. Landis gave her the box and Ian's fists remained balled as his face became red with anger that the treasure he'd risked his life for was quickly being taken away.

"Ma'am," he said through gritted teeth, "that box belongs to *me*."

"No it doesn't!" choked out Searle, still in the groundskeeper's hold. "He stole it from me, he did!"

"Landis, if you would please release Searle . . . ," said Madam Scargill irritably.

Landis abruptly let go of Searle, who sank to his knees with his hands at his throat, as if he'd been choked to within an inch of his life.

Ian rolled his eyes at the theatrics. Meanwhile, Madam Scargill held the box up to inspect it before saying, "I shall determine who is the rightful owner of this box by asking the following question: Ian, how did you come to discover such an odd item as this?"

The question took Ian completely off guard. If he told her where he'd found it, she would surely never give it back to him, to teach him a lesson. If he didn't come up with something, Searle would win the box. "I . . . I . . . ," he stammered, trying to think quickly.

"You see?" Searle jeered. "He can't tell you where he got it because he pinched it from under my bed!"

"I found it out in the fields near the cliffs!" Ian yelled, his mind finally settling on a slight version of the truth. "It was buried under some scrub. That's why it's covered in dirt." Theo, much to his relief, pumped her head up and down.

Madam Scargill, however, regarded the pair skeptically. She looked back at the box, her thin lips pulling down in a frown that clearly indicated she didn't like to touch things that were dirty. Turning to Searle, she said, "Searle? Please tell me how this item ended up in your possession."

To Ian's fury, Searle's face took on a mournful look and he cried, "My dear old aunt gave it to me the day she left me in your care, ma'am. She said it once belonged to my mother."

"Liar!" Theo yelled, pointing an accusing finger at Searle. "Madam Scargill, Ian is telling the truth. He and I were out along the cliffs this afternoon, and he happened on the box in the dirt."

"They probably nicked it from under my bed and took it with them to bury and that's how it got dirty," said Searle, glaring at Ian and Theo. "Oh, ma'am," he added in a convincing wail, "won't you please return my dear, dead mother's box to me?"

Madam Scargill looked from Ian and Theo to Searle, and then to Landis as if to ask his opinion. "I don't know who it belonged to, ma'am," he said. "I just found it beside the boys while they was fighting."

"Very well," Madam Scargill sniffed. "Until one of you admits that this box is not his, I shall hold on to it."

Ian scowled, but he'd expected her to say something like that. Madam Scargill was always confiscating something. Out of the corner of his eye, he saw Theo open her mouth to protest, and he quickly reached to squeeze her shoulder while he whispered, "It's okay, Theo. I have a plan. Let it go for now."

Theo closed her mouth, but he noticed she couldn't resist sticking her tongue out at Searle.

"As for the two of you," Madam Scargill added, pointing to Ian and Searle, "you shall both go without supper. Now off to your rooms, where you will reflect on your misbehavior."

Ian groaned, but before he turned to go, he remembered the giant beast. "Ma'am, may I say something?"

"This conversation is over, Master Wigby. You have lost possession of the box for now," she said firmly.

"But, ma'am," he tried to explain. "It's not about that—"

"I said this discussion is *over!*" Madam Scargill snapped, and Ian knew he dared not say one more word.

With an irritated groan he marched past Madam Scargill, his chin down, and sneered in the direction of Searle, who was smiling gleefully back at him the moment Madam Scargill's head was turned. Theo came alongside Ian and the two entered the keep. Searle was right behind them, cackling with glee at the trouble he'd caused them.

Fortunately, Searle's dorm room was located in the wing opposite Ian's, near a second set of stairs just off the large parlor and above the kitchen. Once they went through the main entrance, Searle turned left and Ian and Theo went straight ahead and upstairs. Ian glared over the railing at Searle's departing form, but he felt thankful that at least he didn't have to sleep in the same room as the nasty git.

"He'll get his," Theo whispered, and Ian could only hope so.

The pair crested the landing and walked only partway down the hall, to the first door on the right, which was where Ian's bed was. He paused as he was about to enter and said to Theo, "You best clean and get some iodine on that hand. It's a nasty cut."

Theo nodded. "That's where I was headed," she said reassuringly.

"And, Theo," he said, thinking she might at least be able to warn someone about the creature that had nearly killed them, "after you tend to your hand, I think you should go to Madam Dimbleby and tell her about the beast. But don't let on that we saw it in the tunnel. Just tell her we were out near the cliffs and some wild, wolflike thing chased after us and maybe word should be sent for someone with a rifle to do something about it."

Theo nodded. "Of course," she said, and Ian knew she was relieved that he'd decided to let her tell someone. "I won't see you for supper, but perhaps I can sneak a snack up to you later?" she offered.

"That'd be smashing. Thanks, Theo," he said, and he was glad to have her on his side.

Theo smiled, gave him a gentle pat on the back, then continued down the hallway to the water closet to tend to her hand. Meanwhile, Ian turned into his room and shut the door behind him with a weary sigh. He hated missing supper, and he vowed to get even with Searle someday soon.

He pushed away from the door and trudged down the long row of beds, his stomach growling angrily now that it knew it would go without a good meal until morning. He shared the long room with six other boys ranging in age from four to thirteen, Ian's age. Many of them he'd known since they'd first arrived at the keep, which for a few, like Ian, was shortly after birth.

Over the years, a scant portion of the boys he'd shared this room with had been adopted. Of the very few would-be parents who came to Delphi Keep, most were looking for babies no older than a few months. So boys who arrived at the keep as mere babes had a small window of opportunity, and once they passed the age of two, their chances of finding homes with adoptive parents were slim to none.

Ian had long ago accepted this reality, and when he thought about his future, it didn't include a mother and a father. Instead, he dreamed of setting out at sixteen, when most orphans were required to leave the keep, and immediately heading off in search of hidden treasure. He was about three years older than Theo, so his aim was to secure enough money by the time he was nineteen and she was sixteen to supply her with a home of their very own and the opportunity for a higher education.

Beyond that he didn't overly consider. His one goal was to take care of his adopted sister for as long as she needed him. This was of course fueled by the seldom-discussed fact that many of the young men and women who left the keep fell into poverty and often languished out in the world. It was a difficult thing to survive in a land where you had no family, no access to higher education, and no one to support you while you attempted to learn a trade. And Ian knew that the young ladies who left the keep were even more challenged than their male counterparts, because being orphans of possibly questionable lineage made it difficult to find men willing to marry them and offer a bit of security.

Ian's sense of urgency about this was why he was so intent on honing his exploration skills while he was still young and why he read any book he could lay his hands on about treasure hunting, exploration, and lands far away that might hold a bit of fortune. The trouble he got into for disobeying rules to pursue this hobby was a price he was willing to pay if it eventually led him to the security he'd need for both himself and Theo.

Ian knew full well that for now the keep was a very good place for a boy like him to call home. He'd heard stories from children who'd been transferred there from other orphanages, many run by nuns with few nurturing skills and many in some of the poorest parts of England, where the youngsters were barely given enough food to eat and often slept three or four to a bed.

Yes, the orphans at Delphi Keep were quite fortunate as orphans went. Their patriarch, the Earl of Kent, was the one to thank. The earl often said that he wanted to provide the children with proper living conditions and a good primary education. After all, he reasoned, it wasn't their fault they were orphans. And the earl figured that if there was blame to lay on them, then he'd be just as guilty, because he'd been adopted by his own parents, the former Earl and Duchess of Kent. He recognized how lucky he'd been to find such a wonderful home, and everyone knew that the earl was still haunted by memories of the deplorable conditions of the orphanage he'd lived in.

That was why when he'd inherited Castle Dover and Delphi Keep, he'd had the old abandoned building turned into a well-run, clean, and completely furnished refuge for orphans. He kept the facility fully staffed—several servants from Castle Dover came each week to help the headmistresses with food preparation, laundry, cleaning, and other chores—so that he could make sure every bed was occupied with well-kept children and the keep was always running at full capacity.

Ian knew that the bed next to him, where Charlie Dalton had slept for seven years, until he'd turned sixteen and left the keep the week before, would soon be filled, and Ian wondered whom the earl would bring to them. He also knew that he wouldn't have to wait long to find out, because the earl never left a bed at the keep empty for more than a week

41

or two, seeing it as his duty to rescue those unfortunate children he found in deplorable conditions.

Ian had always held a genuine adoration for the earl, who was a very likeable fellow indeed, and he eagerly looked forward to each of the earl's visits. Castle Dover was the earl's summer residence, and the children were often treated to his presence during the warm months of June, July, and August, then again just before Christmas, when the earl would bring them each a special gift, and at Easter, when their patriarch would arrange a massive egg hunt out on the keep's lawn.

As Ian took a seat on his bed and thought fondly of the earl, he couldn't help wondering what the earl would have said that day if he'd come across Ian and Searle wrestling around in the dirt. He doubted that the earl would have been pleased, and this made Ian deeply regret his actions.

His melancholy was disrupted, however, when out in the hallway he heard the clomp of footsteps pass his room. He knew that those heavy shoes belonged to Madam Scargill, and a crooked smile formed on his lips as he jumped off his bed and hurried quietly to the door. Opening it just a fraction, he looked out and saw Madam Scargill walking toward her room with his box tucked under her arm. Ian knew from having several of his homemade slingshots confiscated that Madam would take the box to her room and lock it up tightly, never to be seen again. His plan was to wait for her to lock up his treasure box, then find a way to sneak into her bedroom and retrieve it while everyone was at dinner.

Madam's bedroom was located at the end of the long

hallway, next to the water closet, and Ian peered out at her as she clomped her way down the corridor and paused just outside her door, fiddling with a set of keys. At that moment, however, the door to the water closet opened, and out stepped Theo, her hand tightly wrapped in white gauze.

"Theo," Madam Scargill said, moving her attention away from the keys to focus on the girl. "What has happened to your hand?"

Ian held his breath as Theo replied, "Oh, it's nothing, ma'am." And she tucked her injured hand behind her back.

"It doesn't look like nothing to me," said Madam Scargill with a frown.

"I fell while Ian and I were out walking the cliffs, is all," Theo said casually. "Really, it's just a scratch."

"Let me see it," Madam Scargill demanded. Theo looked reluctant as she extended her hand. Madam Scargill tucked Ian's silver box under her arm and unwrapped Theo's hand. "That's a nasty gash, young lady," she said. "Did you put iodine on the wound?"

"Yes, ma'am," Theo said.

"Well then," Madam Scargill said, winding the bandage up, "I shall want to keep an eye on it for the next few days. We should soak it tonight in salt water to make sure an infection doesn't set in."

"Yes, ma'am," Theo repeated with a small curtsy as she moved around Madam Scargill to hurry down the hallway.

Madam Scargill turned away as if to carry on about the business of hiding the box in her room, but Ian saw her pause again. "Miss Fields?" she called over her shoulder.

Theo stopped short and turned to Madam Scargill. "Ma'am?"

"Did Ian truly find this box out along the cliffs?"

"Yes, ma'am. Ian found the box." Ian smiled at the way Theo ducked the question of where he'd found it. "Searle didn't even know about it until Landis gave it to you," she added. Behind the door Ian beamed Theo a smile of gratitude.

"Then what were the boys arguing about?" asked Madam Scargill.

"Searle threw a rock and it hit me on the head. Ian was just trying to protect me."

Madam Scargill scowled. "Come here," she said to Theo, who obediently walked back to her. "Where did the rock strike you?"

"Here," Theo said, and pointed to the right side of her head.

Madam Scargill parted Theo's hair and looked at her scalp. Another deep frown formed on her face. "You've got a good lump there," she murmured. "Go downstairs and chip some ice off the ice block to put on that. I shall go have a chat with Searle about why he will not only go without dinner this evening, but breakfast tomorrow morning and why he will be doing all of your chores for a week. And I'll make sure he apologizes to you as well for his abominable behavior—throwing rocks at a girl indeed!"

"So you'll give the box back to Ian?" Theo said hopefully, but even as she asked it, Ian was shaking his head behind the door. He'd been under Madam Scargill's care a little longer than Theo and knew what her answer—and her reasoning—would be.

"I'm afraid not," Madam Scargill said with a sigh. "Searle will have to admit his lie first."

"But you believe me that Ian found it, right, ma'am?" Theo insisted.

Madam Scargill opened the door to her room and paused in the doorway. "Yes, Theo, I believe you. But I gave the terms of returning this box to the rightful owner in front of all the other children out in the yard, and I must abide by that rule. Remember, without rules, all we have is anarchy."

Ian mouthed Madam Scargill's favorite saying. "And you know what happens when anarchy rules?" she asked.

"Chaos quickly follows," Theo said obediently. She was also all too familiar with Madam Scargill's favorite lecture on rules and their purpose in keeping the world free from chaos.

Ian sighed and very gently closed the door. He'd known all along that Madam Scargill would not give up the box so easily. He felt deeply that the headmistress had never taken much of a liking to him, but she'd always seemed to have a soft spot for Theo. And Theo had convinced her that the box wasn't Searle's. That was a small victory at least.

Ian went back to his bed and waited. Sure enough, a few minutes later the clomping in the hallway returned and passed by his room. He waited several more moments before taking off his shoes and tiptoeing to the door. Very carefully he pulled it open and peered out. No one was around.

Quickly he slipped into the corridor, his back pressed

firmly against the wall. From downstairs he faintly heard the chime of the dinner bell, followed by the pounding of many feet as children raced inside for supper.

He crossed to the water closet and pulled the door closed, putting the Occupied sign out on the door handle. If anyone came upstairs and saw him standing there, they would think he was waiting his turn for the lavatory. He watched the hallway anxiously for several seconds, his attention focused on the stairs.

Sometimes one or two of the children went up to the second story to use the loo before sitting down to eat, and if that happened, he wanted to make sure it appeared that there was a line, which might cause them to go back downstairs and use one of the other two water closets on the main floor.

But no one came up the stairs, and soon the sounds of pounding feet and excited chatter were replaced by the scrape of chairs being pulled out and the clank of cutlery on china. Ian let go of the breath he'd been holding and edged nearer to Madam Scargill's bedroom door. He tried the handle. It was locked tight. He smiled as he pulled the small strip of aluminum he'd gotten off the top of a sardine can, which he carried for just such an emergency, out of his pocket and wiggled it between the doorframe and the door. He heard a faint click and the door popped open.

Ian was about to step into the room when he heard a hissing that stopped him cold and made his heart race. Turning his head, he saw Theo, looking very displeased, at the top of the landing with a plate in her hand. Ian felt the tension leave him immediately and he raised a finger to his lips.

Theo glanced over her shoulder, then hurried down the hallway to him. "What do you think you're *doing*?" she demanded in a whisper.

"Retrieving the box," he said simply.

"Ian, you *can't* go in there!"

"What's that?" he asked, pointing to the plate of food in Theo's hand.

"It's your supper, and don't change the subject," she said, her brows crossed in anger.

"But I thought I wasn't having supper."

"Madam Dimbleby said that no one should go without supper on his birthday, so she prepared a plate for you behind Madam Scargill's back and sent me up here to give it to you. She advised that you hide the plate until morning, then sneak it back down before lessons."

Ian smiled. He'd always liked Madam Dimbleby. "Did you tell her about the beast?"

Theo's scowl turned to a worried look. "Yes, but she seems to think we came across a wild dog. She said she'd tell Landis to keep a lookout, but I don't think she was overly concerned."

Ian sighed. "At least you tried," he said. "Everyone's inside for the night, so there shouldn't be anything to worry about for the time being. I'll have a talk with her tomorrow morning and see if I can't get her to take the beast more seriously."

"Would you?" Theo said, and Ian could tell that she felt she'd failed in her mission.

"Of course," he said with a grin as he ruffled her blond hair. "Now, keep watch while I get the box. If anyone comes up the stairs, cough, and tell them you're waiting for the loo." And without another word he snuck into Madam Scargill's room and pulled the door closed behind him.

Ian paused just long enough to catch his breath. He had a reputation for nerves of steel, and truth be told, he did get a thrill from tempting fate. He rarely got caught, which was why he was encouraged to try ever more daring stunts. Entering Madam Scargill's room was definitely risky, but he knew that Searle would never admit that the box wasn't his; therefore, Ian would most likely never see it again unless he stole it back.

He gazed about the room, hoping the box wouldn't be out in the open. If it was, then Madam Scargill would surely notice it missing. He sighed with relief when his cursory look around uncovered no sign of it.

Madam Scargill delighted in confiscating things; many a slingshot, whistle, set of jacks, and popgun had ended up in her possession. Ian figured that she had some sort of hiding place for all these items. And he reasoned that since she'd been the headmistress here for the past twenty years, her hiding place would be chock-full of treasures. If he was successful in taking the box back, it would hardly be missed among all the other trinkets and toys.

He began to pull open the drawers of Madam Scargill's dresser, but only her clothing stared back at him. Next he walked over to her bed, got down on all fours, and lifted the bed skirt to look underneath. Nothing was stored there. He stood up and looked around the room, which was sparsely decorated, and wondered where on earth such a cache of confiscated things might be. His eye fell on her closet and he quickly tiptoed over to the door.

Pulling it open, he smiled happily. There on the floor was a large trunk, and Ian's gut told him the silver box was inside. Lifting the lid, he found it right away and was about to pull it free and head out of the room when he heard a loud series of coughs coming from the hallway.

Quickly he snatched the box and shoved it under his shirt, then closed the trunk lid and hurried toward the bedroom door. From the hallway he heard a voice ask, "Why, Theo, what are you doing upstairs again away from the table?"

Ian stopped in his tracks. It was Madam Scargill. He was a dead man. "I'm waiting for the loo, ma'am," he heard Theo reply.

"Oh?" Madam Scargill said. "Who's in there?"

"Ian," Theo said. "I believe he's feeling a bit under the weather."

"Really?" Madam said. Ian then heard knocking on the loo door. "Ian?" the headmistress called. "Are you all right in there?"

Ian looked about the bedroom in a state of panic. He couldn't answer Madam Scargill. She would know he wasn't in the lavatory and quickly realize he was in her locked bedroom. "He's fine," he heard Theo say. "He's just embarrassed by his bout of diarrhea."

Ian covered his face with his hands and willed Theo to stop talking. Madam Scargill knocked again. "I should like to know that he is well enough to answer," said Madam.

Theo's tone suddenly became urgent as she said loudly, "Madam! The earl! He's coming here, this evening!"

Theo had a knack for knowing when people would be arriving at the keep. She was never wrong and could often tell ahead of time who would arrive and how many people they would bring with them.

"The earl?" Madam Scargill said, her attention temporarily diverted from Ian in the loo. "Theo, are you sure?"

"Yes, ma'am," Theo said excitedly. "And he's bringing two men and a young boy with him!"

"How long have we got?"

"We'd be best to hurry!"

"Oh, my," said Madam. She gave one more knock on the door of the water closet and called, "Ian, if you need me, please tell Theo. I shall be back to check on you later."

And with that he heard her clomping feet retreat down the hallway. He waited another few moments; then, as he was about to open the door, Theo knocked.

"It's safe, Ian," she said. "You can come out now."

Ian opened the door, quickly scooted out into the hallway, and pulled it closed behind him. "That was bloody brilliant!" he said to her. "Telling her that the earl was on his way was a stroke of genius. Though I'll admit you had me a little nervous with that whole 'Ian's in the loo with the runners.'"

"The earl *is* on his way here," said Theo. "But maybe not quite as soon as I let on to Madam Scargill. You, however, had best get back to your room and do a good job of looking sick, because I won't cover for you again!"

"Oh, come off it, Theo," he said, swinging an arm about

her shoulders and giving her a gentle hug. "I got the box back, after all." And he pulled it out from under his shirt to show her.

"Madam Scargill will find it in your room," Theo said crossly. "She'll know you stole it back, and then you'll be in a load of trouble."

Ian smiled down at her, his confidence unwavering. "I'm not going to stash it in my room," he said. "I'm going to hide it up there." He pointed to a door directly opposite Madam Scargill's room.

"The tower?" Theo whispered.

Ian nodded. "No one ever goes up there, and we can be sure that it won't be found and that we can have a look at it whenever we want to."

"But it's *horrible* up there," Theo said with a shudder.

There were two towers at the keep: the east tower and the west. The west housed the children's playroom and was a comfortable place to retire after lessons and before bedtime. The east tower, however, was a dark and gloomy place that almost every child at the keep explored just once—then never again. Most of the orphans who ventured there felt as if they were being watched by unseen eyes, and a few had noticed dark shadows following them about the room in the moments before they raced back down the stairs.

"Yes, I know it's creepy," said Ian happily. "Which is what makes it such a brilliant hiding place. Now, you keep watch for me just another minute." And before she could answer, Ian dashed to the door and disappeared up the stairs to the tower.

*   *   *

51

Ian crested the top stair and looked about. The light was dim, but he knew exactly where he wanted to hide his silver box. There was a bench built into the wall at the top of the stairs, with wooden slats for a seat. He could hide it in the bench until it was safe to bring it out and inspect it. As he reached for the loose slat, however, he took just a moment to study the box. He turned it around in his hands, admiring its detail. It was beautifully crafted and rested on four balled silver feet. He shook it gently and he could feel the small vibrations of something rattling inside. Curious, he tried to open the lid, but as hard as he tugged on it, it wouldn't give way.

With a sigh he decided it was best to leave it for now and attempt to pry it open later. He then quickly pulled up the slat and placed the box at the bottom of the bench. A few seconds later he was dashing back down the stone steps and through the door to the hallway, where Theo was waiting impatiently.

"All done," he said to her. "Thanks for keeping watch."

"You're going to get yourself into big trouble one of these days," she admonished.

"Not with you to look after me," he replied with a grin as he gave her hair another tousle.

Her face softened and she pushed his hand away with a smile. "Someone's got to look after you," she said. "Otherwise you'd go without supper so often you'd starve to death."

Ian was instantly reminded of the dinner plate she'd snuck up to him, and he realized she was no longer holding it. "Speaking of eating, what did you do with my dinner?"

"I had to hide it in the loo when I heard Madam Scargill

on the stairway." Theo disappeared into the lavatory and Ian was horrified as he watched her come back out with his food.

"You hid it *in there?*"

"Would you rather Madam Scargill see me standing at the lavatory door with it?" Theo snapped.

"Good point," he agreed. "Now, go on and finish your own supper," he said, taking the plate from her. "And say hello to the earl for me."

Theo gave him a small smile. "I'll tell him it's your birthday and perhaps he'll come upstairs to visit with you."

"That'd be brilliant, thanks!"

The two parted and Ian headed back into his room, where he ate his birthday supper in peace and quiet and watched out the window for the Earl of Kent and his companions.

THE EARL

Hastings Arbuthnot, the Earl of Kent, arrived at Delphi Keep shortly after the last dish from supper had been washed and dried.

Ian had become bored as he'd sat in his room, so he'd crept to the edge of the stairway, hid under his favorite table with its small peephole, and watched as Madam Scargill and Madam Dimbleby worked themselves into a state of furious activity. They each gave orders to the older children to help clean up the dinner dishes and attempt some housekeeping.

Madam Dimbleby then separated the younger children into three categories: presentable (the smallest group), in need of a little soap and water (the largest group), and those in need of a miracle. Madam Dimbleby took control of the miracle group and trotted them to the west wing's boys' and girls' dormitories to change and wash up.

Madam Scargill took the largest group and hustled them one by one through one of the two small washrooms on the main floor, making sure every child's hands and face were clean and shiny and their clothes properly tucked in.

At half past six all the children save Searle and Ian were gathered downstairs in the main parlor, doing their best not to fidget while they watched Madam Dimbleby and Madam Scargill take turns peering out the window. From his vantage point behind the table, Ian could see all the way into the parlor and watched as Madam Dimbleby finally clapped and turned to the children. "The earl is approaching!" she announced.

Madam Scargill stood and straightened her dress. "Come, children! Outside onto the front stairs to welcome our benefactor."

Ian ducked out of his hiding place, hurried into his room, and dashed to the window, where he could have a clear view of the drive and the earl's approaching motorcar. His heart beat faster when he saw the shiny yellow automobile approaching.

He set his dinner plate into the small trunk he kept under his bed and pulled out some clean clothes, hoping that Theo would be able to talk the earl into coming upstairs for a visit.

As quickly as he could, he changed and shoved his dirty clothes under his bed, then turned his attention back to the window. Peeking out over the ledge, he could see the tops of the children's heads as they waited obediently for the earl to stop and greet them. The yellow automobile had already come to a halt in front of the door, and Ian watched as the Earl of Kent stepped out along with two other gentlemen and a skinny boy with white-blond hair—just as Theo had predicted.

The earl was a strappingly tall man, well over six feet,

with carrot red hair, a freckled complexion, and dazzlingly bright blue eyes. He was broad of shoulder and narrow of waist, and Ian imagined that wherever he went, his height and gregarious smile attracted attention. "Hello, my children!" he greeted them jovially.

"Hello, my lord!" they answered in giggly unison.

"It's good to see you," he said, then nodded his hellos individually to Madams Dimbleby and Scargill and to Landis before turning to his three younger companions. "I've brought you some very special guests," he announced. "This is Thatcher Goodwyn and his twin brother, Perry. They shall be your new schoolmasters."

Ian had a good view of the two men standing next to the earl. The man named Thatcher was a few inches shorter than their patron, with a good solid frame, long legs, and straight brown hair. He wore glasses and had a pencil-thin mustache. His twin brother was identical to him, save for the mustache and the glasses.

Ian noticed Madam Scargill's features tighten at the announcement of the new schoolmasters. She had always been in charge of teaching the children lessons, so this must have been a most unwelcome surprise to her. The earl might have sensed this, because he turned directly to her and said, "But I want to acknowledge the exemplary job Madam Scargill has done of instructing you all thus far. This change will allow my dear friend a much-deserved rest."

Ian watched Madam Scargill blush and bow her head to the earl. Her feelings might be bruised but at least all her hard work hadn't gone unnoticed. "Thank you, my lord," she said with a small curtsy.

"And this," he said, turning to the young lad fidgeting by his side, "is Carl Lawson. I've rescued him from an overly crowded orphanage in Plymouth to join us here at the keep. Please welcome Carl to his new home, children."

"Welcome, Carl!" all the children said obediently. Ian watched the boy drop his chin shyly, his complexion turning bright red.

The earl gave him an encouraging pat on the back, then said, "Now let's go inside so that we can all get to know your new schoolmasters, shall we?"

Ian dashed to his door and was out in the hallway just as he heard the front door open again. He bent double and crept back to his hiding place under the table to peer out. He allowed himself a wicked smile as he took up his post, when he thought about how Searle had no such vantage points from his side of the keep and would surely miss out on all the action unfolding below.

The earl was the first to sweep into the keep, followed by his two new schoolmasters, then the headmistresses, and lastly the children. The large group filed into the parlor, and Ian watched the new boy standing shyly in the front hallway right below him, waiting for the other children to settle into the parlor before joining them.

Ian smiled as he caught Theo noting the poor lad and— being the outgoing girl that she was—walking over to him.

"Hello," she said with a smile.

"Hello," said Carl, shuffling his feet.

"My name is Theo," she continued. "I've been here since I was two. My older brother, Ian, is upstairs. He's been here since he was just a few days old."

Carl gave her a shy nod.

"I believe you two might be about the same age," Theo added, and Ian had to agree. "Ian's just turned thirteen."

"I'm twelve," said Carl. "I'll turn thirteen in December."

Theo's smile widened and Ian knew what she was thinking. The only other boy close to Ian's age was Searle, so she was no doubt very happy to hear that Ian and Carl had something in common. "I expect you two will get along very nicely," she said with a knowing glance up to the top of the stairs, where Ian was crouched under the table. How she knew he was there he could never figure out, but he barely resisted the urge to laugh when she winked in his direction.

Meanwhile, Carl gave another small nod and shuffled his feet again. "Come along, then," said Theo, taking his hand. "You'll sit next to me."

Ian watched as Theo led Carl to a spot near the fireplace. After all the children had settled down on the floor, the earl took a moment to look around at their eager faces, smiling at a few individuals, including Theo. Then he began his introductions. "Masters Goodwyn come to us from Cambridge, from which they both recently graduated. Schoolmaster Thatcher will be teaching you the finer points of language, history, and the arts, while Schoolmaster Perry will be instructing you in the arenas of mathematics and science."

"I was also quite the fencer at Cambridge," said Perry proudly from his seat on the chaise longue beside the earl. "If any of the children are interested in starting a fencing club, I shall have a sign-up sheet the first day of class." Ian made a mental note to sign up, because learning to be good with a sword might come in handy in the profession of treasure hunter.

"Splendid idea," said the earl with a smile and a nod to Perry. "Now, I realize you've all been very good students, but I shall expect you to rise to a level higher than we've previously set." Ian's eyes shot to Madam Scargill, who had bristled again.

Meanwhile, the other children were all looking round at each other, worry lining their faces. It seemed that Thatcher noticed the shift and said, "The earl has high hopes for the children of Delphi Keep. It is his wish that you have all the advantages of regular children with families who attend private schools, and therefore he sought out my brother and me, who are well versed in all the general education classes that will give you the best possible chance to enter society as adults properly educated."

Still the children squirmed where they sat. Ian knew that none of them had any doubt that the fairly easy regimen they'd had under Madam Scargill was about to become far more challenging.

"Very well said, Thatcher," the earl commented happily. "Now, why don't we all get to know our new schoolmasters? Come, come, children," he said encouragingly. "Let's have all of you introduce yourselves to Masters Goodwyn."

One by one the introductions were made, and the earl asked every student to name his or her favorite subject as well. By the time the last child and newest addition, Carl, was making his introduction, the sun had long since set and Ian could see that some of the children were beginning to yawn. "My name is Carl and I come from Plymouth. I'm twelve years old and my favorite subject is . . ." He paused, searching his mind before saying, "history."

Ian's eyebrows rose. He loved history as well and he wondered if he might have more in common with the new boy than he'd first thought.

After Carl had taken his place again, the earl looked around the room at all the sleepy children and stood up with a clap of his hands. "I believe that's almost everyone," he said, still looking about. "But what of Master Wigby?" he asked, and Ian was thrilled that the earl had taken note of his absence.

"He's in his room," said Madam Scargill with a sniff. "He and Master Frost were sent to their rooms without supper after quarreling in the courtyard this afternoon."

Ian's heart sank. He'd hoped to somehow avoid having the earl learn about the incident. And when he looked at his patriarch and saw his shocked expression, Ian felt even worse.

"Quarreling?" the earl said. Then he surprised Ian by grinning and looking around the room. "Ah, yes, now I notice that Searle isn't among us either. Well, I've been in a few scraps myself, Gertrude. I'm sure the boys were just being boys."

"It's Ian's birthday today," said Theo bravely, and Ian smiled gratefully at her again. "I'm sure he'd love it, my lord, if you'd honor him with a visit tonight."

"His birthday?" asked the earl, looking at Madam Scargill with a hint of disappointment. "Of course I'll go up to see him, Theo. And I'll introduce him as well to his new schoolmasters and to Carl."

"There is a bed next to Ian's that is currently empty, my lord," said Madam Dimbleby with a smile. "I'm sure the lad will welcome having someone so close in age bunking next to him."

The earl beamed at her. "Thank you, Maggie," he said, and there was something in the way the earl looked at the headmistress that made Ian wonder if the earl had known all along exactly which bed was empty and had purposely chosen to bring to the keep a new boy who was close to him in age. "We'll go wish Ian a happy birthday, show Carl his new accommodations, and then have a quick visit with Searle in the other boys' dormitory before lights-out. And if you and Madam Scargill would like to go about the business of getting the children ready for bed, you may."

The earl had barely finished his sentence when Ian quickly scooted out from underneath the table and scuttled back down the hall to his dorm room.

Ian ducked through the door, eased it shut, then hurried through the darkness to his bed beside the window, where he clicked on a small light and grabbed the adventure book he'd gotten from the earl's library. There he waited with pounding heart for the earl and the others to come to him.

Ian's window offered a perfect view of the bright half-moon hanging in the night sky. As he eagerly waited for the footsteps outside his door, he saw a movement out the corner of his eye. Ian's attention diverted from the book he'd been pretending to read to the brightly lit window, where he squinted through the glass pane. The glare from the lamp hampered his vision, so he turned it off and stared at the lawn. His good mood vanished instantly, and the book he was holding slipped through his fingers and thumped to the floor.

Something large and dark was moving about outside. A creature with the body of a lion, the head of a wolf, and black fur was roaming the grounds right below his window. "Oh, no!" he whispered, trembling in fear just as his bedroom door swung open and the main light switch was flipped on.

"Good evening, Master Wigby!" the earl said jovially. "I understand congratulations on reaching your thirteenth birthday are in order."

Ian popped off his bed. "Hello, my lord," he said in a shaky voice. "Might I have a word with you?" He had to tell the earl of the terrible danger out on the lawn and why that danger had found its way to the keep. He knew he'd have to tell the truth now and he'd likely be in horrible trouble for it, but he also knew that because of him, all the children were now in great peril, and perhaps even a few of the adults.

Standing behind the earl, Theo was regarding Ian quizzically. Her face suggested she could tell that something was terribly wrong but she didn't know what. "Of course," said the earl, his good humor and enthusiasm still intact. He obviously wasn't as keenly aware as Theo of Ian's frightened appearance. "But first I should like to introduce you to your new schoolmasters and your new bunkmate—"

"If you please, my lord!" Ian interrupted, feeling an overwhelming panic build within him. "I'm terribly sorry, but I really must insist on having a word with you, *now*." His eyes moved back to Theo, who appeared just as shocked as the earl by Ian's rude behavior. None of the children had ever been so impolite as to interrupt their patriarch. "It's the beast," he said into the stunned silence as he locked eyes with her. "It's out on the lawn."

Theo turned starkly pale. "It's here?" she asked in a squeaky whisper.

"What's this about a beast?" Thatcher asked, stepping forward.

And then the silence outside was broken by the most horrible noise. That growling, snarling howl that had sent terror through Ian and Theo in the tunnel was back and echoing across the grounds. "What in the . . . ?" Perry said as he crossed to the window. *"Good Lord!"* he exclaimed as he looked out on the lawn. "It's some sort of giant black animal!"

Everyone but Theo rushed to the window. Ian turned as well and was just able to make out the loping gait of the great beast as it paced and sniffed at the grass where Ian and Searle had fought just a few hours before.

"It's massive!" gasped Carl, gazing down at the beast.

"What *is* that thing?" asked Perry. "Some sort of wild dog, perhaps?"

"That's no dog," said the earl evenly as he stared through the window. "I've heard tales of such a beast. Some call it a hellhound, and if you believe the local legend, it's a beast straight out of the depths of hell."

"You've heard of this thing before?" asked Perry, staring at the earl, who had also gone a little pale.

"Yes, but I never believed the stories," said the earl.

"Until now. . . ." Ian was shocked that the earl knew about the beast, and racked his memory for any mention in the past by him, but he came up with nothing. "My mother used to say that when she was a child, a terrible beast roamed the land in search of children caught out past their bedtimes. She admitted to me years later that the stories had so frightened her that even as an adult she was careful not to be out alone past a certain hour. She also claimed to have known of a servant whose grandson was snatched from his bed one night and the only evidence of what had happened to him was a giant wolflike footprint by his bed."

Ian's thoughts momentarily drifted back to the memory of Madam Scargill the night Theo had arrived and her insistence that she had seen a similar creature when she was a child.

"Did your mother really believe the servant's story?" asked Thatcher.

"She did," answered the earl, staring with hard eyes through the pane. "And now I know why."

All eyes returned back to the beast for a long silent moment, until the earl seemed to break out of the spell and stepped away from the window. In a most commanding voice, he said, "Come, gentlemen! We must get to Castle Dover! I have a collection of hunting rifles there. We must make sure that beast never puts another child in danger." And with that the earl and the new schoolmasters rushed out of the room.

Theo was still in the middle of Ian's bedroom, shaking from head to toe. Ian moved quickly over to her and wrapped a protective arm around her shoulders. "It's all right, Theo," he said. "The earl will shoot that beast dead."

"We didn't have things like that in Plymouth," said Carl, nervously looking about the room as if he were trying to decide where to hide.

"Carl, is that your name?" Ian asked the thin lad.

Carl glanced at the space under one of the beds before meeting Ian's eyes. "Yes," he said, and extended his hand awkwardly. "It's nice to meet you, Ian."

Ian shook it quickly, then with an air of authority said, "Why don't you go downstairs with the other children? We'll likely be safer if we stick together as a large group. Theo and I will be along in just a moment."

Carl nodded and hurried from the room.

"How did it find us?" Theo asked after he'd gone, her voice cracking in fear.

"It must have followed our scent," whispered Ian. "It tracked us here."

"What does it want with us?"

"Perhaps by escaping we've made it angry," Ian said.

Theo gave him a grave look. "I knew we shouldn't have gone down that tunnel. I wish you'd listened to me when I said I had a bad feeling."

Ian's cheeks flushed with shame at having endangered them all with his foolish explorations. "I'm really sorry, Theo," he said. "Next time I'll listen to you."

Theo's hard look softened. "Come on, then," she said gently, tugging on his sleeve as she turned toward the door. "The headmistresses might need our help with some of the younger ones."

Downstairs the mood was bordering on panic. The earl, who seemed to be the only calm voice in the room, was giving clipped instructions to the headmistresses. "This creature is nothing to be trifled with," he was saying. "Everyone must remain indoors until the beast has been killed or captured."

"I *told* you, Maggie!" snapped Madam Scargill as her cousin regarded her worriedly. "I told you I heard that beast eight years ago. I know I heard it out in the night! And now, here it is on our grounds. Oh, the children!" she wailed. "What are we to do about the children?"

"Shutter all the windows on the lower level," directed the earl. "Then take them to the highest point in the castle and keep guard until we come to tell you it's safe."

Just then Landis burst in through the front door carrying a gardening hoe. "There's a massive beast out on the lawn!" he gasped, his face tight with fear.

"Yes, Landis," said the earl. "Do you perhaps have a rifle in your cottage?" Landis's small home was tucked behind the keep near a grove of trees.

Landis ran a hand through his graying hair. "Aye," he said with a frown. "The problem is I haven't any shells to put in it. Been out of ammo for near three years now."

The earl's face looked grave. "Very well," he said. "Then you'd best come with us back to the castle to retrieve my hunting rifles. Are you with us?"

"Yes, my lord!" said Landis. "I'm with you."

"Excellent," said the earl; then he regarded the frightened faces of the children standing nearby. His eyes lingered on Ian for a brief moment before he said, "We'll need a scout by the front door to let us in when the beast has been killed. Who's up for that task?"

Before Ian could raise his hand, Carl surprised him by stepping bravely forward. "I'll do it, my lord," he said with a small gulp.

"Good man, Carl," said the earl. "You'll need to secure the bolt behind us when we leave and watch through the spy hole. Don't open the door for any reason unless we ask you to, all right?"

"Right," said Carl.

Turning to Landis, the earl asked, "Where did you last see the beast?"

"Back o' the keep, my lord, behind the shed."

"Good. Let's hurry out, then, before this creature has a chance to make its way to the front!" The earl opened the door and he, Landis, Thatcher, and Perry dashed to the earl's motorcar. As they jumped in, Carl quickly shut the front door and pulled the bolt across, locking it tightly.

Ian thought he might take up watch with Carl, but changed his plans when Madam Dimbleby said, "Ian, would you help me shutter the windows and make sure all the other doors are secure?"

"Yes, ma'am," he said, glad to be put to use.

"I can help with that too," Theo offered.

"Very well," said Madam Dimbleby; then, turning to her cousin, she said, "Gertrude, gather all the children and take them to the west tower. It's the highest point and you can lock the door from the inside." Ian thought that the stairway leading up to the west tower might also be too narrow for the beast to navigate. It was barely wide enough for the adults to walk up.

"It'll be a tight fit up there with all thirty-two of us,"

remarked Madam Scargill as she wrung her hands on the skirt of her dress. "The east tower has more room."

"Yes, but the children are frightened of that room. Best not to unsettle them any more than is necessary, Gertie. Do what you can to fit them all in, will you?"

Madam Scargill nodded, then caught her cousin by the arm. "You'll be right up, won't you, Maggie?"

Madam Dimbleby patted her cousin's hand and said, "Of course, of course. If things get sticky down here, we'll be right behind you." Turning to Carl, she instructed, "Master Lawson, should that beast look like it might get inside, do not hesitate to make your way through the parlor and over to that door on the right." She turned him slightly and pointed to the door. "It leads to the west tower, where the other children will be hiding."

Carl nodded smartly, then dragged a nearby chair to the door so that he could stand level with the spy hole and watch for the beast.

Madam Scargill then turned to the group of shivering and frightened orphans and began issuing orders. "All right then, children, we are to proceed to the west tower in an orderly fashion. You lot, Catherine, Lizzy, and Judith, take the little ones up first. And make sure Harry doesn't hide behind the curtains again. Robert, go fetch Searle from his dormitory. You tell him to come down here and help you to gather up the next group of children for the tower room. And make sure you tell him not to dawdle. He's to report down here immediately or have me to answer to!"

"Yes, ma'am," said Robert, and he dashed off in the direction of the west wing boys' dormitory.

Madam Scargill then turned to another group and barked, "Howard, Angela, you come with me. We're going to collect some pillows and blankets from the east wing dormitories and the linen closet so that the younger children can get some sleep. Oh, goodness, it's well past their bedtimes as it is!" Madam Scargill swept out of the room with Howard and Angela hot on her heels.

Madam Dimbleby turned back to Ian and Theo and said, "Let's get to bolting those shutters and securing the doors."

While all the other orphans hurried up to the west tower, Madam Dimbleby, Ian, and Theo ran about the keep, securing the shutters and latching all the windows, then checked the bolts on the two remaining doors, one at the kitchen and the other off the headmistresses' study to the right of the front stairs. They all met back in the sitting room just as Madam Scargill was disappearing up the west tower steps, her arms loaded with pillows and blankets. "Our turn," said Madam Dimbleby as she waved the children ahead toward the door. Ian heard her give another warning to Carl to scuttle upstairs at the first sign of trouble; then, as they reached the door to the tower, Theo suddenly stopped in her tracks and let out a loud gasp. "Oh, no!" she said.

"What is it?" Madam Dimbleby asked.

Theo turned to the headmistress, her eyes wide in alarm. "The laundry room! Madam, that door's always unlocked!"

Ian's heart felt like it skipped several beats. The laundry room was down in the cellar, and the door leading in from the outside was never bolted. But worse still was that although it was a sturdy door, it was easy for even the smallest of the children to push open. All the beast had to do to enter the keep was find the stairway at the back of the building, make its way down the steps, and push against the door.

Madam Dimbleby's face drained of color, but she tried to sound calm. "Right," she said, swallowing hard before attempting a rather forced smile when she realized that Ian and Theo were waiting for her to give them some direction. "You two hurry on upstairs. I'll go to the cellar, bolt the door, and be back up in a jiffy."

"I'll come with you," Ian said firmly. He could see the fear all over Madam Dimbleby's face, and he didn't want her to have to go down into the cellar alone.

"Thank you, Ian," she said with a faint smile, "but it's not safe. You should go up with the rest of the children."

"But, Madam," Ian persisted, "remember how tricky that latch can be? I really think you might need help with it." The latch was indeed difficult to secure, but more important, Ian had noticed how badly Madam's hands were shaking and his heart went out to her.

Madam seemed to catch Ian's subtle glance toward her trembling hands, and she quickly tried to cover them by smoothing out her skirt. "Very well, Master Wigby," she said after a pause to compose herself. "Theo, up you go. Ian, come along."

Ian gave Theo a pat on her shoulder as she stood in the doorway of the tower staircase. "I'll be right up," he said reassuringly, but her frightened eyes bothered him.

"Hurry!" she whispered, and he left her and trotted after the headmistress.

The pair walked quickly through the kitchen to the door leading to the cellar but Madam Dimbleby hesitated ever so slightly before opening it. "If there's any nasty business down there," she said in a deadly serious tone, "I want you to get out of the cellar as fast as you can, and throw the lock behind you whether I'm with you or not."

Ian's eyes widened and he was about to protest when she leaned her face close to his and said, "I'm not joking, Ian. You must promise me this or you'll not come down with me."

He frowned but finally nodded. "Yes, ma'am," he said to her, even though he had no intention of leaving her behind, promise or no promise.

Madam Dimbleby seemed satisfied and she took a deep breath before opening the door a crack, then put her ear close and listened. Ian also strained his ears, but no sound came from the cellar.

Madam Dimbleby took another big breath and pulled the door open wide before reaching for the light switch and turning it on. A dim glow illuminated the stairwell, casting the space into an eerie gloom. Cautiously, the headmistress stepped onto the first stair, then the second, and Ian followed closely behind. He noticed that the headmistress would walk down two or three stairs, stop, listen, then continue for another two or three steps.

In this manner they made their way to the bottom without incident and Ian let go of the breath he'd been holding for the last few steps. Madam Dimbleby then turned to the right and squinted into the poorly lit area of the large cellar.

The door leading in from the outside was at the other end of the chilly room. "Let's get to it, then," the headmistress whispered, and she quickly picked her way through the clutter littering the floor, working toward the door with

Ian again close behind her until he saw something out the corner of his eye. He abruptly stopped and rested a hand on Madam's arm while he slowly turned his face toward the window above the cellar sink, and the most awful feeling of dread chilled him to the bone.

He felt Madam Dimbleby's eyes land on him, then shift to where he was looking, and he heard her gasp when she too spotted four giant paws passing in front of the small window. The beast was just outside. "It's right there!" he whispered. "Which means it's likely heading to the stairwell!"

Madam Dimbleby audibly gulped. The window was just to the right of the outside stairwell leading down to the entrance of the cellar. The beast might already have made it down the staircase and could be pressing its way inside in the next second!

Ian and Madam Dimbleby were a meter or two away from the door. "Stay here," she whispered to him, and she bravely tiptoed forward, edging closer to her target.

But Ian saw her come up short as they both heard something like a snarl from just outside. The beast was close. Again Madam Dimbleby edged forward while Ian willed her to hurry. He was rooted to his spot with the terrible fear that she wouldn't get there in time. The door was closed, but one good nudge from the giant beast would surely open it.

Madam Dimbleby took one step, two steps, three steps . . . and another snarl reverberated from outside, only this one sounded like it was near the bottom of the staircase.

Ian could see Madam Dimbleby trembling as she picked her foot up to take a step but caught an old chair piled with broken toys. The chair and toys tipped over with a loud clatter. The headmistress froze, and Ian could feel his heart thumping so fiercely he thought it might be visible through his shirt. The snarl from outside became a growl as loud as a motor. Worse yet, the growl grew closer, and in an instant a large black snout appeared in the small opening at the bottom of the door and the beast took a good long sniff through the crack.

Ian looked at Madam Dimbleby, who stood as still as a statue. "Madam!" Ian whispered. "The latch! You need to throw the latch!"

But Madam remained unmoving. Ian couldn't see her face, but he knew it was likely frozen in terror. He tried again to call out to her. "Madam, you're so close! Just throw the latch!"

Another loud sniff moved the dust around the crack at the bottom of the door. Madam Dimbleby still hadn't moved. And then the nose sniffing about seemed to catch their scent. Through the crack Ian saw the black snout inch over to the right, near where they were standing, petrified. The beast took several short whiffs of air right before a deadly growl rumbled along the pavement, and Ian knew he had less than an instant to act.

Quick as a flash, he shot forward, past Madam Dimbleby, running at the door with single-minded determination. When he was one meter from it, the beast's snout disappeared from the crack and two thumps sounded on the wood frame. To add to the horror, the door began to open, exposing black greasy fur, a huge snout, and one red eye. Ian leapt into the air, throwing all his weight against the door, and managed to slam it. With shaking fingers he reached for the latch, but it was very old and rusty and wouldn't easily move.

73

Just beyond the door rose a howl that turned his blood to ice. It was a horrible sound and it rang in his ears like a terrible nightmare, and then two more thumps echoed through the paneling and sent Ian springing backward as the beast threw its weight against the door.

He fell into Madam Dimbleby just as she must have leapt forward to help him. Luckily, her momentum launched him back into the door. "Get the latch!" she yelled directly into his ear. "Ian! Throw the latch while I push the door closed!"

Ian fought the panic spreading along his limbs as he and Madam Dimbleby pushed the door with all their might, closing it bit by bit. He leaned every ounce of his weight into the hard wood while reaching up to grasp the latch. His sweating palms and shaking fingers made pulling on the metal plate nearly impossible as he frantically fought to secure it before he and the headmistress lost their edge over the beast. Outside, the creature snarled and growled and the door shook as the thing dug its great claws into the wood.

With another snarl the beast thumped the door again, and to Ian's horror, he and Madam Dimbleby began to slide backward along the cement floor. "I can't hold it!" Madam Dimbleby shouted. "Ian, you've got to run!"

"No!" he groaned, locking his knees and straining with every ounce of strength he had. "We can do it, ma'am! *Push!*" But the beast had other ideas, and it thumped against the wood yet again. Ian and Madam were pushed back even more. The door was now open several inches and Ian could no longer reach the latch.

Refusing to give up, he twisted his body around, trying

desperately to gain purchase on the slippery floor, and gritting his teeth, he pushed with everything he had against the great hulking weight of the creature on the other side. He tried to ignore the smell of sulfur and rotten meat filling his nostrils and making his stomach lurch, as well as the grumbling growl that made the hairs on his arms and the back of his neck stand up. Ian saw a giant paw with nails as thick and sharp as spikes curl around the lip of the entry, and he knew that both he and Madam were likely seconds away from death.

Just when his legs began to shake from the strain and his arms began to slip down the door, there was a rush of wind from behind him, followed by a whump right next to him. The door edged closer to the frame and a small grunt came from his side. Craning his neck to look over his shoulder, he saw Carl, his face turning red with his efforts to help close the door. Then something else crashed hard into Ian's back and he was propelled slightly forward. He felt little hands pushing on his shoulders and he knew without seeing that Theo was pressing her small frame into his as she joined their fight. With tremendous effort they struggled and pushed and groaned and gained ground. "Quickly!" yelled Carl, his voice tight with strain. "We've got to close it *now!*"

It was all the encouragement they needed. In one great effort the four gave a tremendous shove and the door banged shut. Ian grabbed the latch with both hands and heaved it closed. With a screech of rusted metal, it clanged home and everyone let go of the door, exhausted and shaking in fear.

The beast gave an angry howl and thumped its paws

against the wood, making the door shudder on its hinges. The four of them quickly backed away and scurried toward the stairs. "Hurry, children!" said Madam Dimbleby, gasping for breath. "We must get upstairs and lock the cellar door from the kitchen in case the beast is able to break through this one!"

The four scrambled up the stairs, Ian closely following Theo and Carl. He looked behind him as he dashed up the steps and saw Madam Dimbleby hurrying as best she could, her breathing labored and her face flushed bright red. As he cleared the last stair, Ian turned around, reached out his hand to her, and pulled her up the last few steps and into the kitchen before Carl slammed the door to the cellar and threw the latch. Next he hit the light switch, and the kitchen was enveloped in murky darkness. They all paused for a moment, taking great gulps of air and keeping away from the shuttered windows. Every muscle in Ian's body felt weak and rubbery. Madam Dimbleby looked ready to topple over, and Ian was relieved when a watchful Carl pulled a stool from the corner over to the headmistress so that she could sit down.

The children recovered more quickly than their head-mistress, and between pants she said to them, "You . . . must . . . get . . . to the . . . tower. . . ."

"Not without you," said Theo, who hurried to the sink and filled a cup with water. "Here, ma'am, drink this." She offered the older woman the glass.

Madam took a sip gratefully, then stood from the stool. "Come now," she said, wiping her brow. "It's not safe down here. Up the stairs with all of you!"

Ian pulled Theo protectively in front of him as the four trotted quickly out of the kitchen. He was both grateful and angry that she had risked her life to come to his aid in the cellar, but this clearly wasn't the time to discuss it. He felt a horrid foreboding now that he had an idea of the beast's brutal strength. His only remaining thought was of getting Theo and Madam Dimbleby to safety as quickly as possible.

The four hurried to the door of the west tower, which Ian reached past Theo to pull open. Looking up the staircase, he saw Searle sitting on one of the lower steps, wearing his usual scowl as loud chatter echoed from higher up the stairwell. "Why are you on the stairs?" Madam Dimbleby asked from over Ian's shoulder.

"There's not enough room," said Searle with an annoyed pout. "It's a madhouse up there."

"Right," said Madam Dimbleby, biting her lower lip. "Come then, children. If there isn't enough room, we shall go to the east tower. Searle, either come with us or move up these stairs as far as you can."

"The east tower? I'll not go up there, no, ma'am!" the boy said with a shudder. "I'd almost rather face that beast than go up there again." Searle had once gone up to the east tower by himself on a dare. The door had mysteriously slammed behind him, and he'd been unable to open it for several panicky minutes.

"It'll be all right," Ian whispered to Theo, who was again shivering with fear. "I was just up there and it wasn't so bad."

Madam Dimbleby gave a nod to Searle and said, "Very well, but lock this door behind you before you go up, and the one at the top of the stairs too."

"Ma'am," Searle protested, "I told you there wasn't enough room! We'd all be smashed in if I had to shut the top door."

"*You will do as I say!*" roared Madam Dimbleby. Ian had never, ever seen her so angry.

Searle turned pale, and all talking on the stairway stopped. From above they heard Madam Scargill call down, "Maggie? Is everything all right?"

"Gertrude," said Madam Dimbleby, still glaring at Searle, "the beast is strong enough to gain access to the keep. You must get everyone inside the tower room and lock both doors!"

There was a pause before Madam Scargill said, "You're coming up, aren't you?"

"There isn't enough room and there isn't enough time to argue over it. I'm taking Ian, Carl, and Theo up to the east tower. We should be safe enough there." Madam Dimbleby didn't wait for her cousin to respond. She simply slammed the door in Searle's face, and after hearing him obediently throw the latch, she ushered the children through the parlor and toward the staircase.

The foursome hurried along, but Carl paused at the front door and looked at the chair he'd left just under the spy hole. "What about watching out for the earl?" he asked.

Ian noticed the boy's large frightened eyes and knew that none of them wanted to stay on the main floor. Madam Dimbleby wiped her brow again and looked about. "It's too dangerous for any of you to stay here. Carl, go along with Ian and Theo. I'll stay at the door until the earl returns."

"Why don't we all go up to the tower?" suggested Ian,

knowing that it wasn't safe for Madam at the front door either. "We'll have a good view of the grounds from up there, ma'am, and we'll be able to see when the earl shoots the beast."

Madam Dimbleby hesitated, looking from Ian to the door. "Please, ma'am," Theo said. "I'd feel better in that tower room if you were with us."

"Right," said Madam Dimbleby, giving Theo a tiny smile. "Let me just check the bolt on the door one last time and we'll head upstairs."

Ian, Carl, and Theo waited at the foot of the steps while Madam Dimbleby walked over to the front door and checked the bolt. She was about to turn back when she hesitated at a shuffling noise from outside. Leaning in, she pulled the small hatch at the top that served as the spy hole. A large red eye as big as a saucer glared right back and a low guttural growl reverberated off the outside wall.

"*Ahhh!*" they all screamed, and Madam Dimbleby backed away from the entry. "Run, children, run!" she shouted. At that moment a tremendous thud shook the door on its hinges.

Ian grabbed Theo's hand and bolted up the steps, nearly lifting her off the ground. Carl raced past him and crested the landing first. The three then ran down the hallway and yanked the door to the east tower open. "Go!" Ian said to Carl and Theo, looking over his shoulder for his head-mistress, whom he refused to leave behind. "I'll wait for Madam!"

Below, Ian heard another tremendous thud rattling the door. It was followed by the sound of splintering wood. Just as Carl and Theo disappeared up the stone steps, Madam Dimbleby topped the landing, one hand on her heart and the other on the banister, her face flushed from fear and exertion. Ian rushed back down the hallway toward her, afraid she might collapse under the strain. He reached her as a third thud came from the door, and more wood splintered. They heard the groan of metal hinges coming out of the rock.

"Hurry, Madam!" he said as he tugged at her arm to get her down the hallway. "You're almost there!"

The two reached the entrance to the east tower as one final thud shook the walls of the keep. This was immediately followed by a tremendous crash, and Ian knew that the beast had gained access to their home. Impatient to get the headmistress to safety, he indelicately pushed Madam through the doorway and followed her, slamming the door from the hallway behind him. But unlike on the door to the west tower, there was no latch to lock them securely in. Years before, Landis had removed it when several children who wandered into this section of the keep kept reporting that the door had mysteriously locked on them and they'd been unable to unlock it. It opened outward into the hall, making it difficult for a four-legged beast to pull it open. But this offered Ian little comfort, as he knew that if the beast could blast its way in through the front door, the thin door leading to the east tower was no match for it, and there was no second door at the top of the staircase like the one in the west tower either.

"Up you go, Madam," Ian said as he trotted next to her, pulling her by the arm up the wide circular staircase. He thought of the other children in the west tower and knew they'd be safer with both of their locked doors and the long, narrow, circular staircase. The east tower had a shorter, much wider one.

Ian doubted that the giant beast would be able to squirm up those west tower steps to reach the other orphans, and he gulped as he thought about the limited challenges it would encounter if it tried to pursue his small band. In fact, he knew that if the beast breached the door at the bottom of the stairs, they'd all be trapped, and as sure as dead.

"Hurry!" he urged as they neared the landing. "We've got to reach the tower room and find a place to hide!"

Madam crested the landing, huffing and puffing. Ian eased his grip on her arm. He knew she couldn't go on much longer like this. Her face was bright red and glistening with sweat, and she looked as if she was going to faint at any moment. While she wheezed and leaned against the wooden bench where he'd hidden his treasure box, Ian looked about the circular room, spotting Carl and Theo crouched down on the opposite side of the room, near one of the many windows that lined the perimeter of the tower.

"The beast is inside," Ian announced.

Theo let out a sob, her face an oval of fear. Carl reached over and put his arm over her shoulders. "There, there, Theo," he said kindly. "We'll have to hide you someplace safe, is all."

Madam Dimbleby was still trying to catch her breath. The poor woman was bent double with her palms on the bench and sweat dripping from her forehead. Ian rubbed her back and surveyed the room, looking for anywhere they could all hide. He knew from being up here on a few occasions, including one just several hours before, that it lacked options. The room was a large circle with six arched leaded-glass windows letting moonlight in.

To his left was the bench and he eyed it critically, wondering if it might be large enough to house Theo and keep her out of sight, but he worried about how close it was to the staircase, and if the beast had smashed the front door to smithereens, it could surely reduce the bench to kindling.

He then focused on a small pile of broken old desks, cots, chairs, and such that Landis kept up here to use for spare parts when newer furniture was broken.

Getting an idea, Ian gave Madam Dimbleby one final pat and walked quickly over to the frightened pair across the room. "Carl," he said, "come help me make a barrier."

Carl hurried with Ian to the pile of wood while Theo ran to sit with Madam Dimbleby. Somewhere below them, they all heard the crashing of furniture breaking and the smashing of porcelain. From the sound of it, the beast was quickly and thoroughly destroying their home.

Ian and Carl worked several of the desks and chairs into a wooden fort of sorts. It wouldn't keep the beast out for long, but it was better than nothing. Ian motioned to Madam and Theo with a deep bow. "Come, my ladies," he said, trying to keep the panic out of his voice. "Your fortress awaits."

Just as Theo and Madam crossed the room, they heard a particularly loud crash that sounded too close to be on the first floor. "It's upstairs!" hissed Carl.

"Quickly, then!" Ian said as Madam Dimbleby and Theo

hurried into the little fort, crouching down and huddling behind the pile of desks and chairs that Ian and Carl had stacked haphazardly.

Next Ian motioned to Carl to duck in after Theo and Madam, then he carefully pulled the large desk on the right of the entrance and squeezed into the space behind it next to Carl, who helped him pull it back, enclosing the foursome. "Quiet now," he whispered, and the four of them listened to the *thump, thump, thump* of their pounding hearts and the crashing sounds coming from the hallway at the bottom of the stairs.

They tracked the beast's progress by following the awful noises of breaking furniture and glass, the tearing of cloth, and the scratching of claws dragging along the wooden floorboards. With small gasps they listened closely to the splintering of wood that indicated that the monster had pushed through the thinner doors inside the keep with ease.

With a heavy heart, Ian realized that the chaotic smashing of their belongings came closer one bedroom at a time. He knew that the beast had destroyed his room, then the linen closet, and was edging closer to the nursery and Madam Scargill's room.

As if to confirm Ian's thoughts, the awful sounds filling their ears now seemed right below them. "It's in the nursery," cried Madam Dimbleby, and she put a hand to her mouth, tears forming in her eyes. "Oh, Heavenly Father," she wept, "please, please spare us!"

Suddenly, there was another tremendous crash. This one seemed to come from someplace across the hall. "It's in Madam Scargill's room now," said Ian, and he gulped as he realized what was coming next. "He'll only have two more doors to break down after that."

Theo buried her face in Madam Dimbleby's skirt. "This is horrid!" she cried.

More crashing suggested that Madam Scargill's belongings were being torn to shreds. Then, quite abruptly, the world outside the tower room went deathly quiet. And the silence was more terrifying than all the other noises combined. Ian quickly looked about their small cramped space for a weapon. There was nothing within the small fort he and Carl had built that might be suitable to use for defense. With a grunt, he pushed the desk a little and poked his head through the opening to scan the room again. His eyes settled on something across the floor that he hadn't noticed before. There was a broken axe handle leaning against the far wall by the staircase.

Without a second thought he squirmed out of the fort and hurried over to the handle. "Ian!" Madam Dimbleby whispered. "Come back here at once!"

But Ian wasn't listening. He knew he was responsible for leading the beast to the keep, and if they all stayed behind the barrier, their little group would surely die. But maybe he could engage the beast and allow the others to escape. Maybe he was enough. At the very least, he could buy them a little time before the earl returned.

Just as Ian grabbed the broken handle, there was a tremendous crash that shook the walls of the tower and sent him backward several paces. A howl echoed up from the bottom of the stairwell and made him tremble in fear. The beast had found them.

Ian moved to the wall opposite the fort where the others hid. He could see Carl's wide eyes peering out at him through a crack between the benches. He gave his new friend a nod and turned to face the *thud . . . thud . . . thud* of paws hitting the stone staircase, making their way up toward the circular room.

Ian braced himself against the wall as far away from the wooden fort as the room would allow. He stood bravely, holding the axe handle like a cricket bat. The beast would surely kill him, but he was determined to get a few good licks in while he could. "I'm going to distract him!" he yelled at the group hiding in the fort. "You lot, run for your lives as soon as its back is turned!"

"Ian Wigby!" Madam Dimbleby shouted sternly. "You get yourself back behind this barricade immediately!" But a low and angry growl echoed up the staircase, overpowering Madam's voice and filling the circular room with an icy fear.

The hair on Ian's neck and arms stood straight and his heart felt like it was about to burst out of his chest. He saw the paw first as it came up the last step, then the snout, then the red eyes, then the whole giant horrible head. Ian quivered as the rest of the massive beast came into view and the weapon in his hands became slick with sweat. The creature was enormous; at the shoulder the thing was as tall as Ian. Its fur was as dark as coal, and its hackles were matted in greasy clumps. Drool dripped from its fangs while it regarded Ian and his axe handle, and something akin to an evil grin seemed to cross its wicked features.

"You may win," Ian yelled, puffing his chest out at the

horrible creature in a show of bravado he certainly didn't feel, "but I'll not go down without a fight!"

The beast snorted, then tilted its snout in the air and sniffed a few times. Ian wondered what it could be sniffing for. He was right there in front of it, after all. So he was surprised when the beast ignored him and turned its ugly head toward the stack of desks and chairs that Theo, Carl, and Madam were hiding behind.

"Oi!" Ian yelled, trying to call the beast's attention as he waved the axe handle above his head. "Over here, you smelly cur!"

But the creature continued to pay him no heed, turning away as if Ian were a pesky fly not worth bothering about, and taking a step toward the barricade.

Ian heard Theo gasp, and saw her blond hair through a crack in the pile of desks. The beast let out a howl that reverberated off the walls of the room and nearly made Ian drop his handle to cover his ears. The sound was terrifying. Theo screamed and the beast bent low, prepared to pounce directly onto the benches and desks.

"Oh, no you don't!" Ian cried, racing forward with his handle raised above his head, and bringing it down as hard as he could on the beast's left flank. There was a yelp before the beast whirled around with lightning speed, swiping at Ian, who was sent flying backward through the air and landed with a hard thud against the wall.

The air was knocked out of him, and he shook his head, trying to clear it from the smack he'd taken. He willed his eyes to focus as the beast turned its full attention on him, loping over, ready to finish him off. Ian's hands reflexively reached out to his sides, and amazingly, his left hand settled on the axe handle. He brought it up a second before the beast's jaws were about to close on his throat, and it bit the handle instead. Ian was jerked up as the beast snarled and shook the wood back and forth, but somehow he managed to hold on. He knew that if he lost hold of the handle, he was dead for sure.

His arms felt like they were about to come out of their sockets as the beast shook him to and fro, and his head snapped back and forth, and he realized he couldn't outlast the rabid creature. Just as his grip began to loosen, there was a loud *thwack* from behind the beast, and it instantly let go of Ian and the axe handle. He fell to the ground and rolled away from the mangy cur but managed to glimpse Carl holding the top of a small desk in his hands just before he brought it down again on the beast's rear.

Quick as a flash the beast whirled and dove at Carl, who barely managed to get the wood up to cover his face in time. The monster pinned Carl to the floor while the poor boy desperately tried to hold the desktop up to protect himself. The giant creature bit at the wood, trying to gobble up the young lad underneath.

For a moment Ian watched in stunned horror, but he quickly realized that his new friend was moments away from a dreadful end. Gripping the axe handle tightly and springing to his feet, he charged the beast with a mighty battle cry. Funneling all his anger and fear into his attack, he struck the beast on the head hard enough to rattle his own bones. He then ducked down and spun around, using all his momentum to hit the beast's rear legs, his handle connecting with a mighty whack.

"Off him!" Ian roared, and spun yet again for another hard blow. "Get off him, you insufferable cur!"

A yelp and a snarl followed and again Ian was sent sailing through the air. His shoulder struck the stone wall with a nasty crunch that sent a sharp bolt of lightning straight up his spine. The axe handle clanked to the floor beside him, and he was helpless to pick it up. He looked up to see the beast charging toward him, lethal fury in its ugly red eyes.

Ian put his good arm up to shield his face—he couldn't bear to look at the thing as it devoured him whole—but suddenly the room reverberated with the sound of an explosion, then another in rapid succession. There was a horrible squeal so loud and so high-pitched that it cracked one of the glass panes, and just as Ian lowered his arm, he caught sight of the beast flying through the air above him and crashing through the window.

He was showered with glass, and he winced as a few pieces nicked his head and face before he had the chance to duck his chin. In the next moment someone was crouching by his side, whispering his name. "Ian? Are you all right, lad?" Ian looked up to see Thatcher hovering above him, a hunting rifle in his hand, and the smell of gunpowder filled the room even more heavily than the foul scent of the beast.

"Yes, sir," he said gratefully. "And I'm awfully glad to see you."

"How's the boy?" asked the earl as he stepped to where Ian sat against the wall.

"Seems all right," said Thatcher, standing up to have a look out the broken window. "What the . . . ?" he said, leaning his head far out the broken pane to peer at the ground below.

The earl edged closer to the window. "What is it?" he asked.

"It's gone," said Thatcher, pulling his head back through to stare in disbelief at the faces in the room. "The beast is gone! By God, what devil's work *is* this?"

"How could it be gone?" the earl said as he also leaned his head out the window. "Impossible!" he exclaimed.

"But we hit him square!" insisted Thatcher. "I know it! And that's a three-story drop! No earthly creature could survive that!" But as Ian stared numbly up at their astonished faces, he knew better. That beast had been as unnatural a thing as ever he'd imagined, and he wasn't surprised that it had survived to run away.

"And yet," said Perry, crouching low in the center of the room, "our beast bleeds." The earl and Thatcher turned to him. "See that?" he asked, pointing to a spot near his feet where a big splotch of dark liquid glistened in the moonlight. "That's the beast's blood."

"If it bleeds, we can kill it," said the earl gravely. "Come, gentlemen. Let's check to make sure everyone is accounted for and safe, and then we'll track that damnation down and finish it off."

Ian was helped to his feet by Landis, but he yelped in

pain the moment the groundskeeper touched his shoulder. "It's out of its socket, I'm afraid," said Landis. "Ian, we're going to have to pop it back into place, and it's going to hurt something terrible."

Ian felt dizzy. His head was pounding; his shoulder screamed in pain; and his knees felt ready to give way at any moment. "It's all right, Landis," he said wearily. "If it will stop the pain once it's back in place, it's worth it."

As Ian was helped down the stairs by Landis, he heard Carl behind him say, "I'm fine, my lord, truly. Just a few scrapes is all."

Once they reached the second floor, Ian let out a gasp as he looked at the hallway littered with debris. It was as if a great cyclone had been let loose within the walls of the keep and had vented its rage in every corner. Nothing was left untouched.

He and Landis picked their way slowly through the rubble until the groundskeeper found him a chair that had been toppled but had survived the wreckage. Ian sat down carefully and the groundskeeper came around to squat down behind him. "Turn your head away," he said gently over Ian's shoulder. "It's better if you don't know it's coming."

Ian turned his head to the side, bracing himself as best he could while Landis gripped his arm and the top of his shoulder firmly. The next second Landis jerked his arm up and back with a terrific yank. Ian heard a loud snap an instant before a searing pain rippled along his arm, shoulder, and neck and he blacked out.

THE HUNT

Ian awoke to a flurry of noise and activity. He was lying flat on his back, nearly level with the floor, and when he turned his head, the first thing he saw was Theo hovering by his side, her face still pale and her eyes large and vivid green. "About time you woke up," she said softly, forcing a smile. "We were beginning to think you were faking it to get out of the business of cleaning up."

Ian sat up with a wince and looked around, blinking confusedly at the litter of wreckage surrounding him. It took him a moment to realize that he was on the main floor of the keep, in the parlor room, lying on a mattress with no bed frame underneath. His arm was tightly bound to his chest with a thick layer of gauze.

"Landis says you shouldn't use that arm for the next few days. He also said you'd be very sore."

Ian nodded dully and continued to look around. "This place is a mess," he said as he watched children scurry around him, picking up the debris as best they could. Alarmed, he asked Theo, "Is anyone else hurt?"

"Carl has a few scratches. Other than that, everyone is fine. The beast never made it to the door of the west tower."

Ian rubbed his forehead. He had a splitting headache to add to his other aches and pains. "Thank goodness," he said.

"The earl is out with the new schoolmasters," Theo continued. "They're hunting the beast. Madam Dimbleby and Madam Scargill are doing their best to salvage what they can, but almost everything's been destroyed."

"Where's Landis?"

"He's standing guard at the front door, and two of the earl's men have taken up posts with hunting rifles at the other two entrances. There was brief talk of evacuating the keep, but the adults agreed that until the beast is slain, it would be too dangerous to move us all in the dark. Most of the little ones have been safely tucked away upstairs, which only leaves a few of us down here. The earl feels quite confident that we'll all be safe in here until first light."

Just then, Carl appeared with a steaming cup of tea in his hands. "Here you go, mate," he said as he approached. "I managed to find the kettle, and this one teacup survived in the wreckage."

Ian smiled at the lad offering him the cup. He'd never had someone call him "mate" before, and found that he was suddenly very fond of Carl. "Thanks," he said warmly, taking the cup. After sipping the hot liquid carefully, he glanced at the other boy. "You all right?" he asked him.

"Yes," Carl said brightly. "A few bruises, but nothing like what's happened to you."

"You saved my life," Ian said, forming a new appraisal of

the wiry young lad and realizing he was very glad Carl had come to live at Delphi Keep when he had.

"And you saved ours," Carl replied simply. "If you hadn't distracted that thing when it first came up the stairs, we would have been trapped behind that barricade, and I wouldn't give a halfpence for our chances."

Ian's lips attempted a smile, but his head hurt too much to give it any life. He looked round again at the children scurrying about, picking up the mess. All except Searle, who was sullenly moving a broom back and forth across the floor without really sweeping anything up.

"I expect I can help some," Ian said, not wanting to have Searle accuse him of being lazy again. But when he set the cup down and tried to get to his feet, the world spun and he sat back abruptly.

"There'll be none of that," said Madam Dimbleby, coming across the parlor room toward him. "You're to rest, Master Wigby," she insisted. "There's a nasty bump on your head, and I suspect you might have a slight concussion."

"How are you, ma'am?" he asked her. Although her complexion was back to normal, her eyes still held a frightened cast that Ian had never seen in them before.

"I'm fine," she said with a smile that came nowhere near her eyes. "But I'll feel much better the moment we hear that dreadful beast is dead and gone. Now, Carl, come with me and see if we can line up some of these mattresses. I want to get some sort of sleeping arrangement in place before you older lot start collapsing on your feet. Searle," she called across the room, "you're not fooling anyone with that broom in your hands. Come here and help Carl and me arrange some mattresses." Before leaving them, she added, "Theo, dear, you keep an eye on Ian and make sure he doesn't do anything silly like try to get up."

Carl leapt to his feet and followed Madam Dimbleby while Theo and Ian sat together and shared the cup of tea. When Carl and Madam Dimbleby were out of earshot, Theo whispered, "Ian, the beast didn't track you and me back to the keep. It was after me and only me."

Ian's eyes widened. "What makes you say that?"

"I watched it when it came up the stairs," she said. "It could've gone right for you, but it didn't. It knew I was there behind the barrier and it only had eyes for me."

"Maybe it just decided there was easier prey behind the barrier," Ian suggested.

"No," said Theo firmly. "Ian, you haven't seen what the beast did to my bed and my clothes. All the other beds it just tore, or broke. My bed—or what's left of it—was shredded beyond recognition. My clothing was torn to bits. Even my extra pair of shoes were completely in tatters. There's nothing at all left of my belongings," she said, her eyes watering a bit.

"Aw, Theo," Ian said softly as he reached out and awkwardly patted her arm until she'd taken a few breaths and her teary moment had passed. "You'd best remember that the beast got a good whiff of your blood when we were in the cave." He pointed to her bandaged hand. "Perhaps it was just angry and wanted to hunt down the person who'd disturbed its lair."

Theo took a deep breath and gave a small nod. "Yes, I thought of that, but, Ian, you were in that cave too. And you

94

were the one the beast just missed killing when you got free of the hole. And yet, it turned away when it had you cornered. It was after me, Ian. I just know it."

Ian knew it too, but he had no idea why the beast would be so intent on killing Theo. He didn't want her to dwell on it, however, so he said, "Not to worry. The earl and the new schoolmasters will kill that terrible creature soon, and from then on we'll never have to think about such things again."

Theo looked into Ian's eyes, fear and worry making her appear much older than she was. "I wish I agreed with you" was all she said.

Inwardly, Ian was terribly troubled about what it might mean if their fears were correct and the deadly beast prowling the Dover countryside was indeed after Theo, but he dared not frighten her further by going on about it, so he simply sipped his tea and sat quietly with her, periodically nudging her good-naturedly with his healthy shoulder to ensure that her thoughts didn't become too dark.

All around them the activity continued as several mattresses were lined up and the children were laid down for the night, using up the few blankets and pillows to have survived the beast's attack. Ian eventually gave up his mattress to Theo and one of the younger girls. He found a quiet corner to prop himself up in and leaned his head back on the wall, finally dropping off to an uncomfortable but deep sleep.

Sometime in the middle of the night, he awoke from his shivery, cold sleep to the hushed tones of adult whispers. The earl, it seemed, had returned with Perry and Thatcher, and Ian could just make out what they were saying in the front hallway. ". . . followed the trail to the edge of the cliffs but we lost it in the thick grass there. At first light, after we've moved the children safely to Castle Dover, we should round up as many men as we can and give the entire area a proper search," the earl was saying.

"What if the creature comes back tonight?" asked Madam Scargill, her voice quivering ever so slightly, and Ian shivered, not just with cold, but with that terrifying prospect.

"We'll be ready for it," said the earl confidently. "We'll rotate the men guarding the doors. Landis, you, Freddy, and Charles continue your vigils at the doors for another few hours or so, then wake us no later than three a.m., and Thatcher, Perry, and I will relieve you. Masters Goodwyn, you two get some sleep near the men you'll be relieving, but have your rifles handy should the beast come back."

"Right," said several men in unison, and Ian heard the shuffle of feet as they moved off to their positions.

"How are the children?" asked the earl after another few moments.

"As well as can be expected," said Madam Dimbleby. "They've had a very frightful evening, and I'm sure there will be quite a few nightmares to deal with in the coming weeks. Thankfully, none of the children save Ian, Theo, and Carl actually saw the beast. The rest only heard it. We've tried to salvage as much as we can from the wreckage. There's very little left in working condition, I'm afraid, so we most appreciate you bringing these blankets and pillows over, my lord."

"The least I could do, Maggie," said the earl. "I've got my staff readying some rooms for the children at Castle Dover.

We'll move them there at first light, when it's safe, and they can stay until we return the keep to its proper order. And you two are not to worry about what cannot be salvaged. I will replace everything that was broken. You'll have to remember that it could have been much worse," he finished gravely.

"Yes, it certainly could," said Madam Dimbleby. "Come, Gertrude, let's make these brave men some tea for their watch and cover the children with the blankets, shall we?"

Ian listened as the two women moved off and quiet followed. He was quite troubled with the guilt he was feeling about leading the beast to the keep and he lay awake for a long time. He did, however, try to feign sleep when Madam Dimbleby came into the parlor to cover some of the children who hadn't been given a blanket earlier. He had to smirk when he felt her lay a blanket over him and whisper, "I know you're still awake, Master Wigby."

Ian opened his eyes. "It's not easy to sleep sitting up," he admitted.

"Here," she said, gently leaning him forward. "I've given all the other pillows away, but I did manage to find one of the sofa pillows in the wreckage. It's small but it might help."

"Thank you, ma'am," he said, attempting another smile.

"Ian," she said, and something about the way she was holding herself filled him with concern. "I want to apologize to you and Theo."

Ian was shocked right down to his socks. "Pardon me?" he said. "Madam Dimbleby, whatever could *you* be sorry for?"

"Theo came to me this afternoon and told me the two of

you had spotted some sort of wild dog out along the cliffs. I'll admit, I was attending to supper and I didn't pay her much heed. If only I'd alerted Landis and maybe someone from Castle Dover . . ."

"Madam," Ian said, his insides filling with guilt, "if anyone is sorry, it should be me." He was about to explain further but in the corner of the room one of the girls began to wail in her sleep.

"Oh, my," said Madam Dimbleby as she got gingerly to her feet. "Another nightmare. Get some sleep, Ian." She stood to leave. "We'll talk more in the morning." She softly swept his hair and regarded him with kind eyes before hurrying over to calm the crying girl.

Ian knew that eventually he'd have to set the record straight. He wondered with great remorse if, after he told everyone the truth about the beast and the tunnel, Madam Dimbleby would lose that look of motherly gentleness she always had whenever she glanced his way.

The next morning Ian blinked blearily as he awoke. His shoulder throbbed terribly and the rest of his body felt bruised and stiff. Theo was already up and helping with some of the younger children who were also awake. "How are you feeling?" she asked when she noticed that he'd opened his eyes.

"Awful," he said, rubbing his shoulder. "I feel like I've been hit by a train."

"The earl has gone to Castle Dover to get more motorcars. He's moving us all to the castle!" she said excitedly. "I've never stayed at Castle Dover before."

Ian nodded dully. He felt tired, achy, and out of sorts, and he wasn't quite sure if he was hungry. "I spent several nights there once," he said. Although he was a frequent visitor to the castle's library, overnight visits were rare. "The fourth year I was here, one of the pipes burst upstairs and we all spent Christmas there."

"What was it like?" Theo asked.

"Big," Ian said. "And you can't touch anything."

Theo gave him a quizzical look, but before she could ask him more questions, they heard the growing rumble of several engines charging toward the keep. The earl's personal fleet of motorcars came up the drive and pulled to a stop in front of the demolished door.

Most of the children had heard the approaching vehicles and were now rushing to the doorway, chattering with excitement. After a moment the earl waded through the mob of excited children into the front hallway, patting several small heads on his way to the foot of the stairwell.

"Good morning, ladies," he said to Madams Dimbleby and Scargill, who had emerged from the kitchen at his arrival.

The headmistresses each gave a small curtsy before turning their attention to the children. "Everyone please settle down," instructed Madam Scargill. "The earl has an announcement."

By this time, Ian and Theo had joined the rest of the crowd and stood anxiously by the banister of the stairway. Carl, who'd been near the door when the earl had entered, squeezed his way over to stand next to them.

When everyone had settled into silence, the earl began in his booming voice. "Children of Delphi Keep, we will be shuttling you to Castle Dover, where you will be served a warm breakfast this morning and have the opportunity to nap if you were unable to get a good night's rest last evening. Our plan is to house you at my estate until we can return the keep to an inhabitable state. You will be quite comfortable at Castle Dover, so not to worry.

"I am asking that in the next ten minutes you gather yourselves and whatever small personal articles you've managed to recover from this wreckage and proceed into the courtyard, where I'd like you to queue up according to height. We will be chauffeuring the smallest children to the estate first, the older ones next." The earl finished by smiling winningly. When no one moved, he said, "Off you go, then!"

Immediately, the group began to scurry about, grabbing the few possessions they could find. Ian was ready to bolt upstairs and look through the boys' dormitory for some article of clothing or other that might have survived when he caught the dejected faces of Carl and Theo. "There's nothing left of mine," Theo said sadly.

"I'm wearing the only belongings I have," said Carl, looking at the ground and shuffling his feet.

Ian's heart panged with guilt. "I'm sure there's nothing left in my room either," he said, thinking that he'd already lost his most valuable possessions—the knife, the compass, and the pocket torch—back in the beast's tunnel. "I suppose it's best not to look if I don't want to be disappointed."

Theo eyed him skeptically. "You sure?" she asked. "I mean, isn't there *anything* you might want to nab while you've got the chance?"

Ian realized that Theo was secretly referring to the box hidden in the east tower, but one look at Carl's sad face told him that if he returned with anything, it would only make the newest orphan feel worse. And what if one of the other children saw him with it? Madam Scargill would likely confiscate it again and he'd be even more hard-pressed the second time to try to retrieve it without her noticing.

He decided that the box was safe for now in its hiding place and he could collect it later, after they'd all returned to the keep. "I'm sure," he answered. "Come on, then. Let's go outside and queue up like the earl asked us."

Ian led the way outside, excited to see the beautiful shiny automobiles lining the front drive. At the front of the queue was the earl's personal favorite, a beautiful canary yellow Packard Speedster with a black cloth convertible top.

"Blimey," Carl said when he spotted it. "She's gorgeous!"

"The earl likes to ride around with the top down in the summer," said Theo.

"Someday I'll own one of those," Ian murmured dreamily.

"Oh yeah?" Carl said, turning to him with interest. "Where do you expect to get the money for something as grand as that, then?"

Ian blushed. He believed firmly that one day he'd be a wealthy explorer, able to afford the finer things in life, but no one except Theo was privy to his daydreams. Luckily, he was saved from further explanation by the appearance of a horde of children on the front steps. "Come now," said Madam Scargill, clapping her hands to gain their attention. "Queue up according to height so that we might expedite the trip to Castle Dover."

Ian left Theo in the middle of the quickly forming line of children and walked toward the back with Carl, who found his place two in front of Ian. Behind Ian were only two others: Rachel Albright, a girl who was impossibly tall for her eleven years, and Searle, who made sure to give Ian a poke in his sore shoulder as he passed by.

The earl came outside as the last of the children were taking their places, and gave a nod to the many chauffeurs and helpers standing beside his fleet. The men then began to open car doors.

Meanwhile, Madam Scargill and Madam Dimbleby shuffled up and down the line of children, bending low to whisper in their ears, "You must be on your best behavior at the castle. No roughhousing or carrying on, and remember not to touch anything!"

From the back of the queue, Ian noticed that Perry and Thatcher had also come to assist with the shuttling of children. "Good morning," Thatcher said warmly to him. "How's the shoulder?"

"Fine, sir," Ian lied. "It barely hurts at all."

Thatcher raised a skeptical eyebrow but flashed Ian a broad smile. "Right," he said. "Well, even though it feels fine, that sling should stay on for a day or two."

"Yes, sir," Ian answered, grateful for the excuse to favor his left side a bit longer.

The earl had walked the queue of children and came to stand with Perry and Thatcher. While the small children were being loaded into the first group of motorcars, the earl and the new schoolmasters spoke in low tones that Ian strained to hear. The men discussed how to go about hunting the beast.

"I've sent out the word," the earl was saying. "There is a

hunting party forming as we speak. Anyone able to carry and shoot a gun will be meeting us at the castle in an hour. From there we shall attempt to track the beast and kill it once and for all."

"What if we're unable to pick up the trail?" Perry asked worriedly. "Those cliffs are heavy with vegetation and caves. Even something as large as that creature could disappear into one of the outlying caves and not be seen again until it kills an unsuspecting passerby."

"Please, sir," said Ian, not able to keep his silence even though he knew that this was the moment he would likely get into terrible trouble. "I think I know where the beast may be hiding."

All adult eyes and a few of the surrounding children's shifted to Ian, who suddenly felt very self-conscious. "Did I hear you say that you know where the beast is hiding?" asked the earl, stepping close to him.

Ian gulped. "Yes, my lord," he said bravely. "I believe I know where its lair is. I believe the beast lives in a specific tunnel near the cliffs."

"And how do you know *that*, Master Wigby?" asked Madam Scargill from just down the row of children, her hands firmly planted on her hips. Ian jumped at her voice and mentally cursed her sharp hearing.

"Er . . . ," he said, struggling to come up with an explanation while Searle giggled wickedly behind him.

Madam Scargill marched down the row of remaining children. "Yes, please explain how you know this, Master Wigby, especially as it has been expressly explained to you that you are *forbidden* to go anywhere near those tunnels."

Ian gulped again. He knew now that there was no avoiding it—he was in trouble for sure—but as his mind raced, he realized that there was no help for it. Lives were at stake and he'd have to fess up. "Yesterday, Theo and I may have gotten a little closer to the edge of the cliffs than we realized, and we were about to turn back when we discovered a small hole in the ground that opened up to a large cavern and a series of tunnels."

Out the corner of his eye, he saw Theo glare at him, so he quickly added, "Theo, of course, begged me not to go into the cavern, but I wouldn't listen, and I dropped through to take a quick look."

Madam Scargill opened her mouth, obviously prepared to give Ian a thorough tongue-lashing, but the earl put his hand on her arm and said gently, "Let the boy speak, Gertrude. I'd rather find the creature's lair than worry about the explorations of the lad, just yet."

Ian cleared his throat, unsure if that meant he was in serious trouble or not. Still, he went on. "The cavern fed into a tunnel that led far underground, and I followed it for a while before I came to a second large cavern. That's where I got the box, Madam," he admitted to Madam Scargill. "It was set in the dirt there." Madam Scargill's eyes narrowed at him, but the earl's hand on her shoulder prevented her from telling Ian what she thought of him at that moment.

"What box?" asked Thatcher.

Ian turned to his new schoolmaster. "We found a small silver treasure box, sir."

"I confiscated the box," interrupted Madam Scargill.

"There was an argument over it on the lawn and I thought it better to hold on to it until the issue was resolved."

"And where is this treasure box now?" asked the earl.

Ian caught himself before answering. If he told them that he'd hidden it up in the east tower, everyone would know that he'd done the unforgivable and trespassed into Madam Scargill's room.

Madam Scargill said, "It was in my room. But I daresay the thing must be destroyed by now. The beast made a complete wreckage of everything up there." She gave a small sniff.

"I could go look for it," Ian said quickly. "It might still be intact, and I bet I could locate it if I had to."

The earl regarded him with a wry smile. He was a wise man and he seemed to have caught the way Ian had been quick to offer up hope that the box had survived the beast's wrath. "Very well, Ian. But first, tell us about this tunnel. How do you know that's where the beast is?"

Ian knew that he had no choice now but to tell the entire story, start to finish, so he explained. "While we . . . er, I mean, while *I* was pulling the box free, I heard a horrible noise behind me. It was like a howl and a growl combined. So I yanked up the box and ran for my life, and with Theo's help I barely escaped out the hole I'd come through before the beast got to me."

"But why didn't the beast just follow you out the hole?" asked Perry.

Ian resisted the urge to shudder as his memory took him back to the image of that giant snout sticking out of the hole he and Theo had barely made it through. "It was too small for the beast to fit through. But I suspect it either found a way to make the hole larger or it found another way out."

"So it's *your* fault?" yelled a voice right behind him. Ian turned to see Searle, who was furious, his hands curled into fists and his chubby cheeks flushed with anger. "*You* brought that horrible thing directly to us!" he yelled. "You and that wretched box!"

Ian's eyes grew wide as he glanced around at the faces of the children, who were all looking at him the same way Searle was. Even Madam Dimbleby looked angry with him. "I . . . I . . . I . . . ," Ian mumbled, not knowing how to explain his way out of it.

"We'll deal with whose fault this is later," said the earl firmly with a stern look at Searle. "For now we must get you children to safety and hunt down the beast."

Ian breathed a sigh of relief and looked gratefully at him. "Thank you, my lord," he said quietly. "I'm terribly sorry," he added, and the earl smiled kindly at him.

Searle made a vulgar sound behind him, and the earl's smile faded quickly. "That's enough out of you," he warned, and Searle flushed to the top of his ugly brow. Then, turning back to Ian, the earl said, "You shall ride in my personal motorcar. While we load the other children, why don't you go inside and see if you can locate your bit of treasure?"

Anxious to retrieve the box and get away from the accusing glares all around him, Ian dashed into the keep and up the stairs. He headed back up to the tower, taking the steps two at a time. Once at the bench he had to struggle with the plank, because he could use only one hand, but he managed to move it after just a few moments, then dashed back down the steps to the second-story hallway.

He was about to bolt down the main stairs again, but thought it might be too obvious if he showed up with the box so quickly, so he slipped into Madam Scargill's room and spent some time shuffling through the mess, kicking at the bits of broken furniture and clothing.

Just as he was turning to leave, his toe knocked away a piece of splintered wood, and something caught the light below his shoe. Curious, he bent low to see what it was. He set the silver box on the floor, then he moved one of Madam Scargill's tattered shawls aside, revealing a necklace of gold and crystal. It looked strangely familiar. He picked it up and held it to the light, examining it.

The gold chain was attached to a charm made of a beautiful frosty crystal with a hint of pink at its center, encased in a rim of gold. The crystal was luminous and didn't seem to reflect the light as much as it appeared to give off a light of its own.

Ian had a hard time taking his eyes off the charm, it was so lovely. He would have lingered over it longer, but in the hallway he heard approaching footsteps, and he quickly shoved the necklace deep into the pocket of his trousers. It was a good thing too, because just as he finished stuffing it away, Madam Scargill appeared in the doorway, a deep scowl on her face. "Have you located your box, then, Master Wigby?"

Ian fought the urge to flinch at the intensely irritated

look she was giving him. "Yes, Madam," he said, and he bent over to pick it up. "Lucky thing that it's not broken or damaged."

Madam Scargill's scowl deepened. "I'm not sure how lucky you'll feel once all this is over and we discuss your punishment for going places you know are expressly forbidden to you."

Ian's eyes fell to the floor and his heart sank. He'd been hoping that the earl's words might have gotten him out of that punishment bit. "Yes, Madam," he mumbled.

"Go on, then!" she snapped, clearly agitated that he'd disobeyed so many rules. "The earl is holding his motorcar for you and you'd best not keep him waiting any longer."

Ian bolted out of the room and rushed down the stairs. Once outside, he looked about. All the other children, including Carl and Theo, had apparently been dispatched to Castle Dover. He dashed down the steps to the earl's beautiful motorcar and got inside without a backward glance. "Did you find your box?" asked Thatcher from the front seat.

Ian smiled happily, holding up the silver treasure, realizing that the ownership of the box was no longer in question, so he would likely be allowed to keep it. "Yes, sir. You may have a look if you'd like."

Thatcher took the box and turned it over in his hands a few times as he tugged gently at the lid, which held firm, before he closely examined the carvings on the sides of the box. "Incredible," he murmured after a few moments.

"What's that?" asked the earl as he circled the drive and aimed the Packard out of the keep's gate.

"These engravings . . . ," muttered Thatcher. "I believe they're a form of ancient Greek."

"You don't say?" said the earl, glancing at the box in Thatcher's hands. "How did a Grecian artifact end up in a cavern within the White Cliffs of Dover?"

"That's what I'd like to know," said Thatcher. Turning to Ian, he asked, "Master Wigby, once we've dealt with this ghastly beast, might I borrow your box and ask an old professor friend of mine to have a look at it?"

"Certainly, sir," Ian said, although his heart sank a bit. It seemed that keeping the small treasure all to himself was proving harder than he'd expected. Still, he reasoned that perhaps this professor friend of Thatcher's might be able to tell him how valuable it was. Thoughts of newspaper headlines declaring a priceless artifact found by a young boy explorer floated briefly through his mind.

Thatcher handed the box back to him. "Very good," he said. "It's a fascinating relic to be so far from home."

Ian held on to it tightly as they drove the short distance to Castle Dover. Massive and situated on top of one of the highest hills in the surrounding countryside, the castle could be seen from either tower of the keep, and Ian was always eager to visit the old building. He was a frequent visitor, as he'd been allowed access to the earl's personal library and was often traipsing through the opulent and well-manicured gardens on his way to select a new book.

As the parade of motorcars entered the castle's gates and continued down the long driveway, the earl announced, "I've had the cooks arrange breakfast for the children while the rest of the staff prepares adequate sleeping quarters."

"How long do you think it will be before they can return to the keep?" asked Perry, next to Ian in the backseat.

"I've got my man Binsford on it. He's a very capable chap, and he'll have it repaired in no time," said the earl confidently. "Master Wigby," he called into the backseat.

"Yes, my lord?" said Ian, enjoying the thrill of riding along in the earl's fabulous motorcar.

"I've asked the cooks to prepare us a simple breakfast of toast and tea to allow us to get to that tunnel straightaway. When the other children are sent into the dining room, you stay with the schoolmasters."

"Yes, sir," Ian said with a vigorous nod. He didn't mind that he would be skipping the hot and probably lavish meal prepared by the cooks of Castle Dover. He doubted he'd be able to eat much, anyway. He remembered clearly how tight the corridor that linked the two caverns was, and he had a flash of fear as he thought about the beast devouring them one by one in that cramped space.

The earl parked his Packard at the head of the fleet of motorcars, and one by one the car doors were opened and all the children hurried out to queue up again in the driveway, waiting for the command to go inside. Many of them openly ogled the huge castle and the beautiful grounds. Ian walked over to join Carl, who was next to Theo, and Ian smiled at the look of amazement on his new friend's face. "It's even better on the inside," Ian said to him knowingly.

"I've never seen anything like it!" breathed Carl. "Blimey, you'd need a map just to find your way to the loo!"

Theo and Ian laughed. "Best we get in the queue," said Theo as more and more children gathered from the cars.

"You two go on," Ian said to them. "I've been asked by the earl to lead the men back to the beast's lair."

Theo looked worriedly at him. "Be careful, all right?" she said. He gave her what he hoped was a reassuring smile and she and Carl moved to their places in line.

Madam Scargill was once again encouraging the children as she moved about the group, saying, "Queue up by height, everyone, smallest children first."

Finally, when the last of the children had taken his place, the massive wood doors of the castle swung open and out stepped a man and a woman, both crisply dressed in dark gray. The woman, Ian noticed, eyed the group of children warily as she stepped down the stairs to greet the earl, and Ian thought he saw her sniff and wrinkle her nose as she took them all in.

"Everything is prepared, my lord," said the man with a low bow.

"Good man, Binsford," the earl answered. Then, glancing at the woman wrinkling her nose, he said, "Not to worry, Miss Carlyle. They'll be here only as long as necessary."

"Yes, of course, my lord," she answered with a deep curtsy. Ian couldn't help curling his lip a bit at her reaction. He remembered Miss Carlyle from his last stay at the castle. She'd been most curt with the children, insisting that they whisper and eat dinner silently. He remembered that even Madam Scargill had taken issue with her attitude back then.

As Miss Carlyle made her way back up the stairs, the earl turned to the group and with a clap of his hands said, "All right, my children, in you go, single file. Please follow Miss Carlyle and do not wander off. It's easy to get lost in the

111

castle, and we don't presently have the resources to spare searching for you should you wander off."

Many of the more well-behaved children nodded directly at the earl before hurrying forward single file to follow Miss Carlyle while Madams Dimbleby and Scargill brought up the rear. Ian noticed with a satisfied smirk that Searle quickened his pace as he passed the earl, obviously still stinging from the earlier rebuke.

As the last of the children disappeared through the doors, a group of servants came out and descended the steps. They were loaded with rifles, ammunition, and hunting supplies. "How many men could you secure for the hunt?" the earl asked Binsford.

"Ten, my lord," he said, and as if on cue, Ian heard the rumble of another parade of motorcars coming down the castle's long driveway.

Ian watched as the first automobile parked and out bounded a short portly man with a bushy mustache that curled into little loops at the tips. "Hastings!" the man called with enthusiasm as he waddled up to the earl. "I came as soon as I heard!"

"Thank you for joining us so quickly, Ciaran," said the earl, shaking the man's hand vigorously. Ian wondered how such a rotund man was going to manage through the narrow passage of the tunnel they were about to explore. And he was surprised when two additional men, much taller, leaner, and younger than Ciaran, appeared at his side and were introduced. "You remember my sons, Henry and Alfred?"

"Yes, of course," said the earl, and he shook their hands too.

"Father told us there's a wild beast roaming the area," said Alfred.

"Yes, I'm afraid so," answered the earl. "It attacked my orphanage last evening, and very nearly killed a few of the children."

"Dreadful!" said Ciaran, the little loops on his mustache bouncing as he spoke. "Your man Binsford said it's some sort of giant wild dog."

The earl's face became very grave. "I'm afraid it's much worse than that, old friend," he said. "When I was a lad, my mother told me stories about a wild beast straight from the gates of hell roaming Europe and snatching up children from their beds."

"Are you referring to that old wives' tale about the hell-hound?" asked Alfred. The earl stared him straight in the eye and nodded. "Surely, my lord, you must be joking!" Alfred said, laughing.

"I'm afraid this is no joke," said the earl solemnly. "The hellhound exists. I've seen it with my very eyes, and this boy, Ian Wigby, has personally been attacked by it." The earl nodded at Ian, who flushed as the attention was suddenly turned on him.

Under the astonished stare of so many eyes, Ian waved awkwardly and offered a meek hello.

The earl rested his hand on Ian's good shoulder and told the group, "It was a sheer miracle that this brave lad was in fact able to hold off the beast with only an axe handle until we could arrive to shoot it twice, and still it survived our gunfire and managed to leap through a third-story window and run off with barely a trace left behind."

Ian, embarrassed right down to his toes, attempted to smile at the men now openly gaping at him. "How do you do?" he mumbled as others from the parade of motorcars joined their group to hear the tale and offered to shake his hand.

"We'll need to set off straightaway," said the earl. "Master Wigby has agreed to lead us to the underground cavern where he first discovered the hellhound. We'll need a hunting party both aboveground and below. One group can flush out the beast and the other group can finish it off if necessary. And I must warn all of you, we got two rounds into the creature last evening and it barely flinched. When you shoot, don't think once will be enough. Keep firing until you're sure it's taken its last breath."

"Yes, of course," said Ciaran. "The boys and I would like to volunteer to be in the party going down into the cavern." Ian was surprised that the earl's friend was so quick to volunteer. He didn't really strike Ian as the sporting type.

But the earl nodded and gave Ciaran a pat on the back. Ian heard someone cough behind them and turned to see Binsford holding a thermos and a bit of toast wrapped in wax paper. "Your breakfast, my lord," he said with a small bow as other servants passed out thermoses and toast to the hunting party. Ian politely declined the toast and tea, feeling too anxious for breakfast.

The earl took his food and the thermos from his butler. "Very good, Binsford, thank you. Shall we be on our way, then?" he said, and headed off down the drive and around the side of the castle to a pathway that Ian sensed might lead directly to the cliffs.

Ciaran and his sons marched quickly after the earl,

leaving Ian, the new schoolmasters, and the rest of the small crowd to hurry along and attempt to keep up with the brisk pace the earl set.

As they rounded the high wall of the castle, Ian realized that he was the only member of the hunting party not equipped with a rifle. He looked about and saw that Thatcher was carrying a very large gun as he walked beside his brother. Ian decided that the best place to be was near someone carrying a weapon like that, so he nonchalantly inserted himself between the two brothers.

Perry gave him a warm smile when he noticed Ian squirming his way between them and he kindly offered him a bit of toast. Ian's stomach was still in no mood to accept food, so he politely shook his head while his insides gave another flop from nerves.

"Master Wigby," said Perry with a frown. "You really should eat something. After all, we could be out here a long while."

Ian shrugged. He knew that his stomach would refuse the food. "Thank you, sir, but I'm not hungry."

"Very well," said Perry, biting into the toast.

They arrived at the cliffs a short time later, and as they neared the entrance to the cavern, the terrain became rockier and more difficult to navigate. The wind had picked up and the sun from the morning had given way to dark gray clouds, which threatened more rain. Near the edge of the cliffs, Ian sped up a little and tugged on the earl's coat. "My lord," he said, feeling a small spurt of adrenaline, "the hole where we found the first cavern is over in that direction." And he pointed to his right.

"Lead the way, Master Wigby," directed the earl.

Ian turned right, scanning the ground for signs of the boulder he'd stood on the day before. It took him a little while, but he finally spotted it. "Over here!" he said, picking up his pace and hurrying to the landmark.

"Wait for us!" puffed Ciaran, lagging far behind the rest of the group.

Ian's eyes darted back and forth across the ground as he walked. He knew that the opening to the tunnel was close, but he and Theo had left so quickly that he was having trouble remembering its exact location. Finally, something out of place to his right caught his eye and he spotted the mammoth hole in the ground that had fresh dig marks and exposed dirt from torn-out vegetation. "Here!" cried Ian, running to the opening. "It's here!" he said excitedly, but immediately realized he was standing very close to the edge of a hole where the beast could right now be lurking, waiting for him to come near enough to snatch him from the ground. Ian quickly took two steps back and waited for the men to approach.

The earl, Thatcher, and Perry were first to reach him, their guns loaded and ready as Ian pointed eagerly at the ground. "My heavens!" said the earl as he approached. "Look at the size of those claw marks!"

Perry bent down and poked a stick at the exposed chalk, with its series of deep gouges. "The beast's paws are enormous," he said, his voice filled with awe, as he ran his finger along the nail marks in the soft lime. Ian shivered as he watched Perry trail the grooves. He knew all too well how large and deadly those paws with their giant nails were.

116

When the rest of the group had joined them, the earl gave his instructions. "Right, then," he began, his face grimly set as he eyed the tunnel entrance warily. "I'll take the boy, Thatcher, Perry, Ciaran, and his sons into the cavern. The rest of you lot spread out along this side of the cliffs and be on the alert. If this was originally too small for the beast to get out, there has to be a larger way in and it's likely not far away."

All the men in the hunting party nodded and Ian caught a shared look between Thatcher and Perry. He hadn't expected that the earl would want him down in the tunnel, and he tried not to gulp when his patriarch gave him a firm pat on the back. "Are you ready, Master Wigby?"

"Yes, my lord," Ian said, his voice barely above a whisper. He was trying to put on a brave front for the earl, but in the face of that giant gap in the earth and those claw marks, it was hard not to think about the vicious beast so close at hand.

"I'll go first," said Thatcher, readying himself at the mouth of the hole. "Perry, after I drop down, stick your gun through the opening, and if anything other than me moves, shoot it."

Perry nodded and pulled his rifle up to his shoulder. "Ready when you are," he said.

Thatcher swung his rifle round to his back and clicked on a torch Binsford had given him, then he braced himself and crouched low beside the hole. Inhaling deeply, he glanced at Ian with a grave expression before dropping into the hole. Perry immediately edged to the lip, aiming his rifle into the dark below. No one else moved or said a word while they waited to hear from Thatcher.

117

Ian held his breath and watched the light from Thatcher's torch dance and bob while the schoolmaster swung the beam to and fro. "It's clear!" he finally shouted. "No signs of the beast. The rest of you can come down."

Perry pulled his rifle out of the opening and, like his brother, swung it round to his back before dropping in. The earl motioned for Ian to go next. "Do you need help down?" the earl asked him, indicating Ian's bound shoulder and arm.

"I think I can manage, thank you, my lord," said Ian as he edged his way over to the lip and gauged the jump. He took a small leap and landed easily on the floor of the cavern, then moved quickly to the side and out of the way for the others to come through. The earl, Ciaran, Alfred, and Henry followed the others, although Ciaran needed considerable help getting through the hole.

The cavern was well lit now with all the torches being switched on and Ian noticed the men staring wide-eyed at the spacious opening to the tunnel. "I've never been in this particular vein," said the earl, and Ian turned to look at him, surprised by the admission.

"What's that, my lord? What do you mean by 'this particular vein'?" asked Perry.

The earl's eyes found Ian's and they shared a knowing smile. "Castle Dover was built atop a maze of tunnels all leading out to caves along the cliff's face as an escape for the inhabitants should the castle ever be taken by enemies," the earl explained. "As a child I explored just about all of these tunnels, but I don't ever remember having been in here." Ian felt an even greater welling of admiration for the earl and their shared youthful interests.

"Pardon me," interrupted Thatcher. "But I believe we should all have a look at this."

Ian turned to where Thatcher was, and noticed that he was standing in front of the big black lettering that Ian and Theo had seen the day before.

"What have you got there?" asked Ciaran, edging closer to the schoolmaster.

"This is written in Greek," answered Thatcher as his hand traced the outline of the writing. "I'm not an expert, but I believe I can sound it out." Thatcher's voice halted abruptly while his beam went back to the beginning of the lettering, then scanned slowly along the wall and stopped. He turned and stared at Ian.

"What?" Ian asked, feeling uncomfortable under his scrutiny.

"Did *you* write this?" Thatcher demanded, his tone sharp.

"No, sir!" Ian said quickly, astonished that his new schoolmaster could possibly think that. "That was there when I first came into the cavern."

"My good man," said the earl to Thatcher, "please tell us what it says."

Thatcher turned to his employer, his lips pressed tightly together as if he were weighing something. Finally, he said, "It literally translates, 'Young boy, Wigby, come this way.' "

Ian and several others in the cavern gasped. He was so stunned that he simply stared dumbly at Thatcher for a long moment.

The silence that followed was broken by the earl as he gave a snort of laughter. A moment later, Alfred, Henry, and

Ciaran followed with chuckles, and Ian grinned in relief as he felt the tension leave his shoulders. His schoolmaster was obviously joking.

"Now, come on, Master Goodwyn, what does it *really* say?" Ciaran asked after he'd had a good laugh.

"I'm not joking," Thatcher said, his words clipped and his face never breaking out of its serious expression. "It truly says, 'Young boy, Wigby, come this way.' "

The earl cocked his head, as if he were waiting for Thatcher to give up the joke, but the younger man's expression held. Slowly, the earl turned away from him and looked directly at Ian. "Master Wigby," he said sternly, "tell us the truth, lad. You wrote this on the wall, didn't you?"

Ian's heart was racing wildly. He couldn't take his eyes off the big black lettering. Something about it seemed oddly familiar, but he was sure he'd never seen such a message before, and he knew nothing of the Greek language. "My lord," he said in his most sincerely honest tone while he held up his good hand. "I swear to you on my honor, I had nothing to do with that. It was already here when I came into the cavern yesterday for the first time. And for that matter," he added, willing the earl to believe him, "I don't have the foggiest notion about how to read or write in Greek."

No one spoke for several long seconds and it seemed to Ian that every person in the cavern was taking a measure of him and the truth of his words. He especially hated the feeling that the earl might believe he would do such a thing. "I *swear* to you, my lord!" he insisted, hoping it was enough to convince the man he so admired.

Finally, the earl gave one curt nod and said, "All right then, Ian. I believe you."

Ian let go of the breath he'd been holding. "Thank you, my lord," he said.

The earl looked round at the others as if to let them know that they were not to hold Ian in judgment, and said, "Let's move forward, everyone, and look for the beast. Maybe we'll learn more about who it was that wanted Ian, in particular, to travel deeper into these tunnels."

Ian walked over to the tunnel leading out of the cavern, anxious to get the attention off him and back onto hunting the beast. He paused and glanced back at the earl, unsure if his patriarch wanted him to go first.

The earl waved his hand and said, "Yes, Ian, you lead us forward. Perry, stay right behind him and have that rifle ready."

"Yes, my lord," said Perry, pulling his hunting rifle off his back and readying it to follow Ian.

Ian gave one more look behind him and noticed anxiously that Thatcher was scrawling the message from the wall down in a small notebook he'd brought with him. Ian frowned, because he thought he might not have heard the last about his role in the writing on the wall. Still, as he turned toward the dark tunnel in front of him, he reasoned that Thatcher could at least double-check his translation and might even discover he'd gotten it wrong.

He almost felt better until he remembered with a quick twang of apprehension that the sides of the second cavern held far more writing. He wondered if Thatcher's translations there would point an additional finger of suspicion at him. He could only hope that his name wasn't among the scribbling on that wall, and he wondered what he might say in his defense if it was.

He waited until Thatcher had finished his copying, and with a hand motion from Perry, he entered the narrow tunnel. Over his shoulder Perry said, "Here, Ian, you'll need this to see."

Ian glanced back and saw that Perry was handing him a torch. "Thank you, sir," he said, feeling relieved that he wouldn't have to venture forward without any light. He clicked the switch on the heavy torch and bounced the beam all around in front of him. Nothing moved within the beam, so he took some slow, careful steps forward.

Ian could feel the schoolmaster nearly on top of him, and out of the corner of his eye, he noticed the long barrel of the rifle extending above his shoulder. Still, he was very nervous about going first, as he was terrified of the beast, especially since the hellhound seemed barely to flinch at being shot twice before.

The entire group walked stealthily without speaking, careful not to make much noise until they reached the next cavern, where Ian braced himself again as his torch lit upon the walls covered in large black Grecian letters. "My word!" said the earl as he entered the cavern and moved his own torch along the sides of the space. "Look at this place!"

Thatcher quickly took out his notebook again to write down the lettering. "Do you know what it says?" asked the earl as he watched Thatcher scribble.

Thatcher shook his head. "Some of the letters and

phrases I think I can make out, but I'd rather have this translated by my professor friend at Cambridge."

"Ian," said Perry, "is this the room where you discovered the box?"

"Yes, sir," said Ian, stepping forward to the far corner of the cavern and kneeling down. "It was here, sir. Right—" Ian stopped abruptly.

"What is it?" asked Perry, stepping close.

"The beast," whispered Ian, pointing to the ground, and his heart thumped hard as he took in the large dig marks surrounding the area where he and Theo had pulled the box free. Next to the clawed earth were the crumpled remains of his pocket torch, compass, and Swiss Army knife, which looked as if they'd been sent through some sort of grinder. "It's been digging here and chewing on my things."

The men gathered round where Ian knelt and all of them pointed their torches to illuminate the spot where giant claws had scarred the ground and bits of metal lay scattered about. Perry knelt by Ian and picked up the flattened compass. "He's an angry beasty, he is," he muttered.

The earl cleared his throat. "Shall we move on, then?"

"Just a moment," said Thatcher as his scribbling intensified. "I've almost finished. . . ." Ian and the men waited while Thatcher turned in a circle to jot down the last of the writing on the walls. Finally, looking satisfied, he closed his notebook and said, "Got it."

Ian held his breath again, waiting for Thatcher to declare him a fraud, but Thatcher merely smiled reassuringly and said, "After you, lad."

Ian turned toward the second tunnel, with Perry again

right behind him. He gulped at the entrance, knowing that they were nearing the beast's lair, and tried to summon some courage to move steadily forward.

"What's at the end of this vein?" whispered Perry as he leveled the gun over Ian's shoulder again.

"I'm afraid I don't know, sir," Ian said hoarsely, remembering the horrible digging sounds followed by pounding paws and terrible howls that had come from this tunnel. "Theo and I only got as far as that last cavern before we had to run for our lives."

"I thought you said Theo stayed aboveground," Perry said.

Ian nearly faltered as he walked. "Er . . . ," he said, knowing he was caught. "I may have fibbed that part a bit, sir. You see, I pushed Theo into coming down here, and I didn't want her to get in trouble with the headmistresses."

The sound of Perry's quiet laughter filled Ian's ear. "It's all right, lad," he said. "Your secret is safe with me." Then his schoolmaster changed the subject. "So, the beast came through here?"

Ian nodded gravely. "Yes, sir. We barely got out with our lives."

"How did you manage to escape it?"

"We heard it digging and scratching; then it made that awful howling noise, so we had a bit of a head start. We were lucky. That last tunnel is so narrow, I believe it might have slowed the beast down a little."

Perry grunted. "Yes, you were both very lucky indeed. We'll hope that if that creature is up ahead, it gives us one of those warning howls again."

Ian gulped as he realized that all the beast had to do was lie quietly in wait for them and he'd have little chance against it. It was certainly large enough to swipe at him before Perry was able to get off a shot. With trembling knees he continued forward, gripping the torch tightly in his hands.

After a time Ian heard a sound filtering down the tunnel toward them, and he also felt a slight breeze on his cheeks. "What's that noise?" he asked in alarm. "And that breeze?"

"We must be close to another opening," said Perry, sniffing the air. "I'd say we're close to the cliff's face above the strait. You can smell the sea on the breeze."

Ian sniffed too, and he could just smell the briny scent of open water. After making a slight turn, they came to a sizable pile of rocks in their path. Beyond the pile came a cold breeze and the strong smell of the sea.

Perry put his hand on Ian's shoulder, squeezed past, and picked his way along the many large rocks littering the ground. "It seems the beast's lair must be beyond this pile of rubble," he said as the others moved in close to have a look. "It must have made a home for itself in one of the caves along the face of the cliff and I'd guess that the creature either heard or smelled the children and dug its way through here to get at them in the cavern behind us," he said.

Ian's gaze never left the large pile of rocks strewn aside like toy blocks. The sheer strength of the hellhound continued to astonish him.

"That's odd," Perry said, pulling Ian's thoughts away from the floor. Perry was staring at the ceiling of the tunnel.

"What's odd?" asked the earl from just behind Ian.

"Well, I would have thought there had been a collapse of

some sort from the ceiling, and that's how these rocks became piled here, but it's smooth and even, consistent with the rest of the cave's ceiling. It looks undamaged."

"So these rocks were placed here on purpose?" the earl asked.

"By the amount of lichen on these rocks it appears they were placed here a long time ago to seal this side of the tunnel off, but why I can't fathom." Perry glanced at Ian, a bit of wonder in his eyes. "And a good thing too," he added, "because if this barricade hadn't been here, and if the beast hadn't had to dig through it to get at you, I'm very certain you would not have made it out alive."

"I wonder why someone would go to all that trouble to seal this section off?" Thatcher mused from behind the earl.

"It is strange," Perry agreed, and Ian had an odd sense that the rocks had been purposely placed there as a barrier to help him, but he immediately dismissed the thought, because it was foolish, of course. "My lord," said Perry, "to your knowledge, have any of the other tunnels had sections sealed off like this?"

The earl shook his head. "No," he said. "None of them."

"Strange," repeated Perry, but then he shrugged and poked his rifle over the pile of rubble to the tunnel beyond, using his other hand to point his torch and illuminate the dim space. After a few moments he waved everyone forward, and Ian and the others stepped carefully among the fallen stones and scrambled over the main pile to the other side of the barrier.

When they were clear, they discovered yet another cavern, this one the largest of all. Ian had explored many of the caves along the cliff's face, but he'd never been in this one. The ceiling was high above the earl's head and the cavern was enormous. As the group filed in and waved their torches about, their footfalls and hushed voices echoed off the walls. Ian bounced his own torch beam around, looking for more of the lettering, but none of the walls appeared to have any sort of writing at all. Slowly, the hunting party spread out, investigating the cavern's nooks.

"Look here!" exclaimed the earl, and Ian saw that he was kneeling beside a small pile of fur and bones. Ian hurried over to have a better look. "The beast has made a meal of something," he said, his face pulled down into a scowl.

"That's not all it's been up to," said Alfred from the far end of the cavern. "Or rather, *she's* been up to."

Henry, Ciaran, the earl, Ian, and the schoolmasters quickly gathered around Alfred, who was also kneeling by something on the ground. When Ian got close, he could see that the beast had hollowed out a space in the soft lime, lined it with fur from its own coat, and padded it with bits of grass and dried leaves. But that wasn't what was so shocking. Between the matted fur and leaves were other scratch marks carved into the chalk floor, only these were much smaller, though just as distinct. "Oh my," said the earl as he knelt beside Alfred and ran a hand along one of the smaller grooves. "Our hellhound's had pups."

THE PHOTO

Ian gasped. If the beast had given birth to pups, it meant that she had a mate that might also be loose about the countryside. And, he thought with a lead feeling in the pit of his stomach, if she had a mate nearby, was it even larger and more terrifying than she was? Ian shuddered at the thought of facing not one hellhound but two. And what if they didn't find the she-beast and her litter soon? What if it took months to track her, her mate, and their offspring? That could mean that a whole pack of wild beasts would soon be terrorizing the area.

Perry knelt beside the earl. "How many do you think she's had?"

"Four," said the earl, his face grim and hard. "And I'd say they were at least a few weeks old by the look of these marks. You can see here in the center of her nest where they began, rather small compared to the ones out at the edge over here." Ian leaned in to get a better look. Even the pups' claw marks looked large to him.

"And look there," said Ciaran as he pointed his torch

outward from the nest. "They've been digging in other parts of the cave as well."

"So, where are they?" asked Perry. "Where are the mother and her litter?"

The earl stood and looked toward where the wind was whistling in from an opening at the other end of the cavern. "I suspect she's moved them," he said. "And I think that her fury with Ian was instigated by her natural instinct to protect her litter. You entered her territory, and she might have considered you a threat that needed to be hunted down and eliminated."

"But we . . . er . . . I didn't come anywhere near this side of the tunnel," insisted Ian. "Plus there was that sealed wall to separate us," he added.

"Doesn't matter," said the earl, standing up and wiping the white dust from his trousers. "You must have come close enough for her to feel threatened. And in the wild there is nothing more dangerous or unpredictable than a mother predator protecting her young."

"There's dried blood over here," said Alfred, calling everyone's attention away from the nest.

Ian and the earl walked over to where Ciaran's son stood pointing his torch beam down on the cavern floor. "Yes," said the earl, kneeling again beside several drops of blood on the ground. "We managed to get a bullet or two into her last night. Although it doesn't seem to have slowed her down much."

"What do we do now?" asked Henry.

"We keep hunting," the earl said simply, standing. "We know that the she-beast has moved her litter somewhere else in the hours between yesterday afternoon and this morning. We also know that she's injured, so it's likely that she hasn't gone far. If we can find her new lair, we might be able to catch her by surprise and kill the whole despicable bunch. I tell you, I'll feel a great deal better when I've got that beast's ugly head mounted on my trophy wall."

"You're forgetting one thing, my lord," said Ian glumly.

"What's that, lad?" asked Ciaran.

"Her mate," he said. "If she had pups, she would have needed a mate."

The men stared in shock at Ian and around at each other for a long moment. It was quite evident that none of them had thought of that.

Finally, the earl said, "A very good point, Master Wigby. Let's start with the she-beast and that frightful litter, then work around to her mate after she's been dealt with, all agreed?"

"Agreed," said the group.

The earl gave Ian a pat on the back and looked down at him with a reassuring smile. But Ian hardly felt comforted. He noted that many of the other men looked even more determined and were gripping their rifles firmly, but Ian was terribly unsettled. He hated being in the beast's lair, even though it was clearly abandoned. It still held a nasty energy that made him shudder.

"Are you cold, Master Wigby?" Perry asked him.

"A little," he admitted. "Mostly I'd just like to get out of here."

"I agree," said Perry. "My lord, might we proceed?"

"Yes, of course," said the earl. "Come, gentlemen, this

way." The earl led everyone out of the cavern and into the last of the tunnels. This time Ian walked in the middle of the group, which made him feel more secure than being on point. The wind picked up considerably. It was a cold and bitter blast of air and it moaned forlornly along the walls as it whipped past the group.

As they marched, the tunnel widened into a low cave that faced the Strait of Dover directly. "We're on the face of the cliffs," said the earl, raising his voice above the wind while they all lined up beside him. Ian looked over the cave's edge to the swirling water far below. The horizon had turned a mean, dark gray and thick clouds covered the skyline.

"I can see why a beast like her would choose that cavern as a whelping ground," said Perry, raising his own voice above the sounds of wind and surf. "Back there, her litter was protected from the wind and she still had close access to the outside for hunting." He pointed to a narrow path along the edge of the cliff that seemed to lead straight up to the top bluff.

Ian gulped as he thought about how many trips he and Theo had taken near the edge of these cliffs in the past few weeks, and how on any one of those trips the beast could have easily snatched them without anyone ever finding a trace.

"It's amazing to me that we've had this enormous beast in our own village for so long, and no one has noticed it until now," said the earl. "Surely, some of the local farmers must have talked about a sheep or two missing?"

Ciaran perked up at that. "You know, Hastings," he said to the earl, "I have had a few complaints from my herders.

They said that they've noticed a few of the sheep missing from their morning head counts in the past fortnight without a trace—but my men thought for sure we had a problem with poachers, not some giant hellhound."

"How far away are your herds, sir?" Perry asked Ciaran.

"About five kilometers west of here," Ciaran replied.

"Then we know how long she's been in the area," said Perry. "At least a fortnight."

"But where did she come from?" asked Ian, puzzled. "And why hasn't anyone seen her or her mate until now? I mean, a giant dangerous animal like that is likely to draw some attention."

No one had answers for him, but the earl did say, "I've seen this sometimes in Africa, Ian. A lone female will get close to whelping her litter and set off to a place she thinks will be safe from her jealous mate. Male lions sometimes eat their own young. Perhaps it's the same with these ghastly creatures."

Ian could only hope that the earl was right and the mate to the she-beast was somewhere far, far away.

"Still, my lord, the lad has a point," said Alfred. "She had to come from somewhere, and surely she could not have traveled the countryside without at least someone taking note."

"If I didn't think it impossible, I would say that this isn't the she-beast's first visit to our village," said Ciaran.

"Excuse me, sir?" said Ian. He had no idea what Ciaran was referring to.

Ciaran and the earl exchanged looks that Ian couldn't read. "Remember that report about the missing rider and his horse?" the earl's friend said. "That was in our own backyard, Hastings."

"I'm sorry, but what report are you referring to, sir?" asked Perry, and Ian was grateful that someone else was just as confused as he was.

Ciaran explained. "Eight years ago a report was filed with the Dover inspector by old widow Thompson, who lives just outside the village. According to her, one morning after a terrible storm, she found a horse in her backyard, fully saddled but missing its rider. The horse appeared to have been through a terrible trauma and needed sedation merely to remove the saddle. As I recall there was a deep gash on its hindquarters that appeared to have been made by a large set of claws, and it was a nasty wound at that, according to my veterinarian, who tended the steed. He told me that if he didn't know it was impossible, he would have concluded that the horse had been attacked by a lion. To add to the mystery, no one ever claimed the horse, and its rider was never found."

The earl looked gravely at Ciaran. "That was a long time ago, my friend, and any number of things could have caused that gash and traumatized the horse. It's not likely that the beast was responsible after all this time."

A memory tore its way into Ian's mind and took him back to the night Theo had arrived with a strange man on horseback. Like Ciaran mentioned, there had been a terrific storm that evening, and Ian distinctly remembered the howl that both he and Madam Scargill had heard out in the hills beyond the keep.

Ian's heart began to race with the idea that maybe this

man's horse was the one discovered by old widow Thompson and perhaps its rider had fallen victim to the beast when he'd left the safety of the keep. An intense fear gripped his heart as he also considered that Theo might be right after all. Maybe the beast had been after her, not only the night before, but eight years earlier too. "I remember that evening," he said quietly.

"Eh?" said Ciaran, cupping his ear. "What did you say, lad?"

"Eight years ago, the night Theo arrived at the orphanage, sir. I was up because of the storm, you see, and I remember hearing an awful howl in the hills. The man who brought Theo to the keep, he left on horseback and we never saw him again."

Ciaran looked at the earl as if to say "Aha!" but the earl clearly wanted to move away from long-ago memories and get to the business of the present—hunting down the beast.

"Enough chatter," he said, waving his hand impatiently. "We'll need every bit of daylight left if we're going to locate the hellhound and her pups. I suggest we spread out in twos and threes to search the caves along this side of the cliffs. Hopefully she hasn't moved too far away and we can find her new lair without much trouble. Perry, Ian, you're with me on this central cliffside. Ciaran, Alfred, you take the southwestern slope. Thatcher and Henry, take the southeastern slope, and if anyone sees the other men up top, please advise them of all that we've found, and have them explore the northwestern side of the cliffs."

The men set off with renewed vigor, determined to end the threat to their homeland. As the morning hours passed, however, Ian's hopes were beginning to wane, and as morning turned to afternoon with no additional sign of the beast or her litter, he truly felt disheartened.

It was starting to look like the she-beast might have escaped them. As even more time passed, Ian began to shiver with cold from climbing up the face of the cliffs and searching the many caves while the frigid wind from the strait beat against him, leaving his face chapped and raw. Compared to the rest of the hunting party, he was miserably underdressed, with only his thin blazer to protect him from the chilly wind.

Eventually, Ian was shivering so intensely that his schoolmaster took pity on him. "My lord," Perry said to the earl, "I think I should take the boy to our cottage and give him some tea. He's not dressed as warmly as the rest of us, after all, and perhaps there's a coat in one of our trunks he can wear."

The earl, who had been acutely focused on the ground and finding any trace of the beast, seemed to notice Ian's misery for the first time. "Yes, of course, Perry. Take the boy. I'll join Ciaran's group."

The schoolmaster stepped over to Ian and took the silver box from his shivering fingers. Ian was so cold that he gave up the box gladly. He could barely feel his hands and he'd been worried about his little treasure slipping from his grasp and down the side of the cliffs.

"Come, lad," Perry said, putting the box into his coat pocket. "Our cottage is not far from here. I'll return this once you've warmed yourself up."

Ian walked dumbly behind Perry as they traveled up one of the paths leading from the caves to higher ground. He was so miserably cold that he felt foggy and out of sorts. They reached the main road that led to the village at the bottom of a set of hills that looked up to Castle Dover. It was a bit less chilly here away from the wind of the channel, but Ian still shivered. He truly felt like he might never warm up again.

Finally, they reached a modest cottage with a white picket fence and a small vegetable garden, and Perry led the way to the front door. "Now, come inside and I'll fix us some tea. I think Thatcher has an old coat that might fit you."

Ian walked into the home and immediately sat down at the table. He was tired and numb with cold and his shoulder ached in its sling. He felt as if his legs might be ready to give out and his eyelids were droopy with fatigue. Perry went out a back door and returned quickly with an armful of firewood. He placed this inside a black iron stove and lit a match, which ignited the fire. Soon the small kitchen was filling with heat, and Ian scooted his chair closer to the stove, hungry for the warmth it was giving off.

"There," said Perry as he set a kettle on the top of the stove. "We should have some tea in just a few minutes. Watch the kettle, Ian, while I go search out Thatcher's trunks."

"Yes, sir," said Ian, his teeth still chattering as he willed his tired eyes to focus on the kettle. Hovering by the stove, he pushed his hands close to the fire and felt the warmth slowly come back to his bones. The kettle began to whistle a short time later, so he picked it up and filled the teapot with hot, steamy liquid. He found two cups in the cupboard and put those beside the pot as he waited for the tea to steep.

While he waited, he wandered around the kitchen, noting that the furnishings looked decidedly frilly. He doubted that the brothers had decorated this cottage by themselves. They'd likely rented it from someone in town who'd furnished it.

Perry still hadn't returned, and Ian thought it might be rude to drink the tea without him, so to distract himself he headed out of the kitchen and into the sitting room. Again, he noted that the furnishings seemed to reflect a woman's taste rather than that of two bachelors—though he had to admit, the result was warm and inviting. A small framed photograph on the wall caught his attention. He walked over to it curiously, but as he got close his breath caught and his heart began to beat rapidly.

Just then Perry came down the stairs and round the corner. "I had to search through several trunks, but I've finally found it," he said as he held up a tweed coat. "It's a little out of style and will likely be too big for you, but it should keep you warm out there, at least."

"Sir," said Ian, pointing to the picture on the wall, "is this your photo?"

Perry gave him a quizzical look but came over to where he stood and gazed at the photo. "No," he said. "That was there when we got here. The landlady said that she'd inherited this cottage from her brother, who disappeared some time ago and was finally declared dead. They suspect he got drunk and fell off the cliffs one night. But as I understand it, this house has been empty for many years."

"I know who these two are," said Ian, putting his finger

up to trace the image of the beautiful lady with white-blond hair, who looked like a grown-up version of Theo, holding a small toddler in her arms. The toddler he'd first seen on a stormy night eight years before.

"Who?" asked Perry.

"It's Theo and her mother."

"The little girl who was with you when the beast attacked?"

"Yes," said Ian gravely. "Might I have this photograph?"

Perry seemed to hesitate for only a moment before agreeing to the request. "Yes, of course. If you're certain it's Theo and her mother, then she should have the memento."

"I'm certain," said Ian, feeling deeply that he wasn't mistaken. He carefully lifted the photo off the wall. "She'll be very grateful to you for letting her have it," he added.

Perry smiled. "Shall we have some tea, then?"

The pair shared the tea and some biscuits to abate their hunger. They kept to small talk, mostly about the weather and life at the keep, but Ian's mind kept drifting back to the photograph of Theo's mother and what might have driven the woman to abandon her baby on a violent stormy night.

Shortly after they'd sipped the last of their tea, Perry encouraged the boy to try on Thatcher's old coat. The schoolmaster helped him put on the woolen garment, and although it was rather large on Ian, he relished the warmth and protection from the cold. The pockets were also large enough to hold his box and the photograph.

Once they were bundled up again and had set their dishes in the sink, he and Perry left the cottage to rejoin the members of the hunting party. Ian felt much better now that he'd had a few biscuits and hot tea, and he kept pace with Perry as they walked briskly back to the cliffs.

They found the earl and Ciaran's group with little effort. Ian couldn't help noticing that the men in the hunting party were far less jubilant than when they'd started that morning. Finally, as dusk settled along the cliffs and the wind began to die down, the earl called all the groups together and announced, "I'm afraid we'll not find the beast today. Best to head back to the castle, have a proper supper, and begin our search again in the morning."

Ian gave one last long look to the terrain atop the cliffs, searching the shadows. He hated to think that the beast would be loose somewhere nearby for yet another evening, though he reasoned that at least they had the safety and shelter of Castle Dover, which was a far more secure environment than the keep. Still, he made a mental note to keep his eye on Theo until the hellhound was hunted down.

Ian heard his name called, and he turned and trotted after the ten men in the hunting party as they trudged up the path in the direction of Castle Dover. He walked behind the earl and Ciaran and listened while they talked about their fruitless search. "I don't think the beast is hiding in the caves," said Ciaran.

"What I can't understand is why there's no sign of her," said the earl. "We've looked all day for a drop of blood or a paw print or a scratch in the ground. . . . It's like she's vanished into thin air."

"Awfully hard to hunt a beast that leaves no trace of itself," replied Ciaran. "And we've searched almost every bit of the surrounding terrain. I suspect that after being wounded last night, she returned to gather her pups and got them to safer territory, someplace far away from here. By now she could be across the county." Ian's heart skipped a beat. After encountering the hellhound firsthand, he *knew* she would not give up that easily. He felt strongly she was still in the area.

"I think it best that we not give up just yet," said the earl, much to Ian's relief. He'd been worried that the earl would agree that the beast had left Dover, and not bother to continue the hunt. "In the morning I'll have Binsford call round to a few of the local villagers and see if some of the townsfolk won't join us in the hunt. At the very least perhaps one of them has seen the beast and can give us some direction."

Ian wondered if he'd be asked to go along again. It made sense that now that he'd served his purpose of showing the hunting party where her lair had been, he wouldn't be needed anymore. However, there were still several unanswered questions, not the least of which was why his name was scrawled across the cavern wall in Greek lettering.

He wondered if Searle had been up to his tricks again, though Ian knew that the boy was fairly daft, and the likelihood of the orphanage bully being able to write anything so sophisticated in a foreign language like Greek was surely next to nil.

The earl and Ciaran fell silent as the last threads of sunlight drifted beyond the horizon, and Ian was relieved to see the lights of Castle Dover just ahead. He was looking forward to a good meal and a warm bed after two exhausting days.

When the group finally reached the castle, they wasted no time getting out of the cold. Upon entering the front hall, the hunting party was immediately greeted by several servants who hurried forward to take their coats. Ian gave his up only after he'd emptied the pockets of his treasure box and the photograph. "Thank you," he said politely as a servant woman with a kind face helped him off with Thatcher's coat.

Binsford came into the room as the last servant was collecting Alfred's and Perry's coats, and he stepped up to the earl. "We've kept dinner for you, my lord."

"Good man, Binsford," said the earl. "How are the children adjusting?"

"They have all been fed and shown their rooms, my lord," said Binsford.

"And how is Miss Carlyle faring under the strain of so many little ones?" the earl asked with a grin.

"As well as can be expected, my lord," Binsford said with an exaggerated sigh and a slight smile.

"Very well, then," said the earl with a chuckle as he turned to address the hunting party. "Everyone, into the dining hall for a warm meal."

Ian hung back as the men eagerly filed out of the entryway. He wasn't sure if he should join the group or wait for instructions to rejoin the other children, so he fidgeted nervously as he watched them all leave for the meal. The earl took notice of him standing sheepishly in the front hall and asked, "Something the matter, Master Wigby?"

"No, my lord," Ian said quickly. "It's just . . ."

"Just what, lad?"

"I'm not sure where I should go," he admitted, feeling a blush hit his cheeks.

"To the table with the rest of us, of course," said the earl kindly. "It's been at least a day since you've eaten a solid meal, am I correct?"

Ian smiled broadly, feeling a rush of relief as he walked forward. "Yes, my lord, and thank you," he said.

As he was about to pass, the earl caught him gently by his good shoulder. "Ian," he said, turning the boy to face him, "after we hunt this beast down, we'll need to talk about the writing on that cavern wall."

"Yes, my lord," Ian said, vigorously nodding. "I'd like to find out why my name was there too." What he really meant was that he wanted to put an end to the prank that had so obviously been played on him.

The earl smiled down at the lad. "Very well, let's not waste any more time getting to the table, then."

The pair entered the dining hall together. Ian had been to the castle many times before but had never dined formally with the earl, so he was suitably awed by what he saw before him. An impressive room, long and narrow with mahogany paneling, intricately carved molding, and seating for twenty at the enormous rectangular dining table, presented itself. As he surveyed the spread of food, his mouth watered at the sight of so many delicious-looking dishes. He searched the group already seated, wondering where he should sit, when the earl gently nudged him in the direction of an empty chair next to Ciaran's son Alfred.

Once the earl was settled, the hunting party dug robustly

into roast duck, potatoes thick with gravy, steamed turnips, and warm fresh bread. Ian devoured his meal and to his delight was offered a second helping of everything. He polished that off too, along with a dessert of raspberry cobbler.

"Did you get enough to eat?" asked Alfred with a grin.

"Yes, sir," said Ian, leaning back in his chair and giving a pat to his wonderfully full stomach. "That was the most delicious meal I've ever eaten."

Then Alfred noticed the silver frame Ian had laid facedown on the table. "What's that you have there, Master Wigby?"

"Oh," Ian said quickly, reaching protectively for the photograph lest Alfred want to take it from him, "that's a family photograph of one of my friends, Theo. She's also an orphan at the keep. The photo is of her mother and her as a toddler."

"May I see it?" Alfred asked curiously, and Ian had no choice but to hand the photo over, as to do otherwise would have been impolite. Alfred took the frame and inspected it with great interest. Ian noticed with regret that the gentleman's face seemed to fall and his lips thinned out in a scowl of distaste. "I know this woman," he said softly.

"You do?" Ian asked with surprise.

"Yes. As I recall, her name is Jacinda Barthorpe. She attended St. Barnsworth School for Young Ladies and she went with my roommate for a time. She dropped out of St. Barnsworth and the social circles of London eleven years ago, about the time her parents were killed in a terrible motorcar accident. I haven't heard mention of her, in fact, in these past eleven years."

"Really?" said Ian, genuinely excited about being able to tell Theo a name and a bit of history about her mother, especially since he had no such tantalizing tidbits of personal information about his own parents.

"Yes," said Alfred as he laid the picture down and wiped his fingers as if they were dirty. "I'm afraid to say that Jacinda had a rather *sordid* reputation," he added, his mouth turning down even further.

"Sir?" said Ian, unsure of the gentleman's meaning.

"Never mind," said Alfred. "It's best that if your friend from the orphanage doesn't already know about her mother's reputation, you keep her blissfully in the dark."

"I see," said Ian. "Just one question, however, if I may?"

"What's that?" asked Alfred, turning back to his dessert.

"Do you by any chance know what happened to the lady's husband?"

Alfred gave Ian a mirthless grin. "Jacinda was never married, Ian," he said. "I'm afraid your friend's paternal lineage is somewhat in question."

"Oh," said Ian, finally understanding what Alfred was alluding to. "I see."

The orphanage was full of children born to unwed mothers too ashamed of the scandal it would cause to raise them, and although no one had ever told him for certain, he often wondered if this was the reason he had ended up at the keep too.

"As I said, you'd best not mention that part to your friend when you give her the photograph. She's better off not knowing."

But Ian wasn't sure that keeping Theo in the dark was a

good idea. In all the time he'd known her, Theo had mentioned her mother only once, and that was when she was six. Ian had overheard her asking Madam Dimbleby about a terrible dream she'd had of her mother getting lost in a storm and Theo being unable to find her. Theo had admitted that the dream had sparked the faintest memory of her mum and she had wanted to know if the headmistress knew whether the dream was real and what had actually happened to her mother.

Ian remembered Madam Dimbleby's gentle voice as she told the girl that her dream was part of a real memory, that her mother had been killed in that violent storm but a kindly man from the village had rescued Theo from a similar fate and brought her to Delphi Keep, where he knew she would be well cared for.

Ian remembered that night as well, and the stranger who had brought Theo to them had mentioned only that Theo's mother had abandoned the child out in one of the fields. Ian knew that the headmistress had been trying to be kind by telling Theo that her mother had died. It would have been far more difficult for a young girl to digest that her own mother had simply abandoned her, leaving her to the mercy of the elements.

But Ian wondered if Theo was better off knowing the truth: that her mother's fate was unknown. He knew that most of the children who had been brought to the keep as babes had never been told the circumstances of their arrival. The headmistresses believed that unless a child specifically asked about how he or she came to be orphaned, it was best to leave it unsaid.

Ian understood too that many of the children who hadn't asked held secretly to a hope that their parents were alive and would someday come to the orphanage in search of them. Ian knew this because he was one of those children. After thinking about what he should tell Theo, he found that he couldn't make up his mind, so he reasoned that he would sleep on it and decide what to tell her at breakfast.

While Ian sat lazily in his chair, his eyelids became droopy. He thought it might be improper to excuse himself from the table before the others had polished off their desserts, so he did his best to keep his eyes open and his head from bobbing forward, but it was a sincere struggle given how tired and content he felt. When he could barely hold his head up a moment longer, he heard his name being called from across the table.

This of course caused him to snap his eyes open and sit up straight as he searched for the speaker. He looked first at the earl and noticed that both he and Ciaran were looking at him expectantly. "I'm sorry?" he said, darting his gaze between them, unsure which one had called his name.

"I asked if I might have a look at your box," said Ciaran. "The earl tells me you discovered it in that second cavern."

"Oh!" Ian said as he fumbled clumsily with the artifact on the table beside him. "Yes, of course, sir. By all means have a look."

He handed the box to Perry, who was sitting closest to Ciaran, and watched as it made its way to the portly man. "My heavens," said Ciaran as he turned the box round and round. "What an odd item to turn up in an underground cavern." Ciaran then squinted as he looked closely at the seam between the lid and the box, then gently attempted to pull the lid open, but without success. He then shook it gently, and Ian knew that Ciaran could tell something moved inside, just as Ian had already observed.

"I believe it's Grecian," said Thatcher smartly. "There is some lettering in the engraving that appears to be ancient Greek."

"Just like the writing on the wall," suggested Alfred as he leaned against Ian to look at the box in his father's hands.

"Do you know how it opens?" Ciaran asked Thatcher, and when the schoolmaster held out his hands for the box, Ciaran handed it over.

Thatcher inspected it closely and he also attempted to pull up on the lid, but to no avail. Then, as Ian watched anxiously, the box was passed from person to person around the table to be inspected and shaken. Many attempts to open the lid were made—all of them unsuccessful.

While the box was making its rounds, Ciaran looked at the earl expectantly. "Don't you wonder, Hastings, about all of this?" he asked. "What I mean to say is that I find it a bit strange that this young lad found a lost tunnel, which it appears no one has been in for centuries, with *his* name scrawled on the walls in ancient Greek, a language he's clearly unfamiliar with. And further, while locating this treasure box, the lad unwittingly let loose a giant ferocious beast bent on killing him and anyone else who might step into its path."

"What's your point, Ciaran?" the earl asked curiously.

"Well," replied the man, "I suppose what keeps niggling at the back of my mind is that all of these extraordinary events might somehow be connected. Take for example that pile of rocks we found separating the beast's lair from the second cavern, where Ian found his box. Those stones were obviously placed there by human hands, which makes the barrier's placement rather curious, don't you think? Why would anyone construct a barricade that would prevent them from making a hasty exit if they needed to?"

Ian furrowed his brow. He was having a hard time following Ciaran. "What I mean to say," the earl's friend continued, "is that access from the cliff's face where we found the beast's lair to the two inner caverns was purposely blocked off, but what I can't think of is why. Why would someone wall themselves in like that? It makes no logical or strategic sense to cut off an escape route through the tunnels should an enemy come in after you from behind."

The earl squinted at Ciaran. "I hadn't considered that until you mentioned it, my friend," he admitted. "But perhaps the wall wasn't meant as a barricade against getting out of the caverns; perhaps it was meant as a barrier to prevent someone from entering the caverns from the cliff's face. Perhaps it was an attempt to keep the box safe from would-be looters exploring the caves along the cliffs."

"Yes," Ciaran said. "Or perhaps there was another reason."

"Like what, Father?" asked Alfred.

"Well," answered Ciaran, his pasty complexion flushing with excitement. "I'm wondering about the Greek writing on the wall of the first cavern we encountered—the one we entered into from aboveground. It clearly indicates that the author *knew* that Ian would come into that cavern first, not last. Whoever put that writing there seemed to be certain that Ian would not attempt to enter the caverns from the cliff's face as the natural path of the tunnels and caverns would suggest he would. How could this mysterious person be so certain that Ian would find a small hole in the ground covered by thick vegetation and work his way into that first cavern from aboveground?"

Ciaran looked round at the group at the table. They were all silent as they contemplated his question. When Ciaran's eyes settled on Ian, Ian shrugged. He had no idea.

Ciaran nodded solemnly, as if he'd proven his point. "Clearly whoever left the box for Ian to find had a rather acute prophetic sense and he might also have known that when Ian discovered the box, he would need time against an unseen danger to retrieve it. Perhaps the stone barricade was meant to keep out not only looters, but a terrible beast as well.

"So the question I have to ask is why?" Ciaran continued. "What is it about that box that is so important that one of your orphans needed to risk his life to discover it? And does the box have any kind of link to this beast? These two extraordinary things—the discovery of an ancient Greek artifact here in Dover and the emergence of a legendary creature—seem to have only your young orphan in common, and the timing of both of these events is quite remarkable, wouldn't you agree, Hastings?"

Ciaran's interpretation hit Ian like a thunderbolt. He moved his attention to the earl, anxious to hear his thoughts. Deep in his gut, Ian knew that the beast and the box were linked. What he didn't know was how or why.

The earl seemed to gather his thoughts, and by this time the box had been passed to him. Ian watched as he too turned it round and round and attempted to open the lid. "You know, Ciaran, you've got an interesting theory there," he said, holding the box up to his ear as he gave it a gentle shake. "Clearly there's something inside this box, but the lid appears airtight. Perhaps what's within will offer us a good explanation?"

"My professor friend from Cambridge should be able to tell us about the authenticity of the box," said Thatcher. "He's a professor of archaeology and spent much of his time in Greece. I believe he might also be able to suggest a way of opening it without causing the artifact undue damage."

Ian was quite relieved to hear that; he didn't want the box ruined in an effort to get inside. Whatever was in there could wait as far as he was concerned. He just wanted to be able to sell his treasure for as much as possible, and he realized that keeping it intact and in good condition was important to retaining the value. That was the only thing thus far that had prevented him from trying to wedge it open himself.

"Well," said the earl, handing the box back to Ian with a kind smile, "I had made up my mind that the beast was protecting its pups and that's what provoked the attack on Ian and the orphanage. And I must say that although I do find it a particularly odd coincidence that someone fluent in ancient Greek would write Ian's name upon the wall of a forgotten cavern, it still seems unlikely to me that this person would also know that the beast would be lurking within a nearby tunnel when Ian finally came along to remove the box.

"No, Ciaran, I believe that the simple explanation is the truth, that the stone barrier was put in place not because of some prophetic knowledge that Ian would face the danger of the beast, but for a more practical reason, which was to seal the cavern off from the corrosive elements of wind and sea, as well as to protect it from would-be looters. And so, I must conclude that it was nothing more than sheer luck that the barricade was in place when Ian found the artifact and a mere coincidence—albeit an extraordinary one—that Ian and the beast would both be there at the same time."

"So you're still of the mind that the beast was merely protecting her pups?" asked Perry.

"Yes," said the earl with a smile. "I cannot see a link between Ian's discovery of the box and the beast's attack other than the natural instincts of a wild animal defending her territory from a perceived threat."

But Ian wasn't so sure. His mind kept returning to how the beast had dug into the chalky floor ferociously after Ian had recovered the treasure. It also didn't explain why the beast was so intent on attacking Theo. He felt certain—as she did—that it had marked her as prey. He'd seen it in the beast's eyes up in the tower room when it had turned away from him to go after her. He wanted to bring that up for discussion, but the men were already off on another topic, so he let it drop.

Finally, when Ian's eyelids had again begun to droop, the earl suggested that the hunting party retire to the library for cigars and brandy, and the exhausted boy was excused to go to bed.

Binsford escorted him up two flights of stairs and down a long corridor to a door at the end of the hallway. "All the children are staying in this wing so that we can keep track of you," the earl's head butler said quietly. "We've separated everyone into the eight bedrooms on this floor. You will find an empty bed and some nightclothes in there," he added, halting in front of the last door on the left. "Breakfast will be served in rounds, beginning with the youngest at six-thirty a.m. Your group will be called to the table at eight. Should you need to use the lavatory in the middle of the night, it is the fifth door down from here. We've left the light on and the door cracked for your convenience."

"Thank you, sir," said Ian, noting the light from down the hall.

When he turned back, he noticed Binsford looking at him with a frown. "Will you need assistance getting into your nightclothes?" he asked, and Ian saw that the butler was looking at his arm still in its sling.

Ian felt his cheeks heat up. "Thank you, sir, but I believe I can manage. However, if you might help me off with this sling?"

The head butler gave a curt nod and carefully lifted the sling over the boy's head. Ian winced as it came free and he felt the dull throb of his shoulder thrum right down to his fingers, but getting his arm free of its restrictive bandage was still a welcome relief. "Thank you, sir," he said again.

"Rest well, Master Wigby," Binsford replied, and he turned abruptly and walked away.

Ian turned the knob on the door and entered his room as quietly as he could. After shutting the door, he leaned against it for a few moments, letting his eyes adjust to the darkness. He felt a tiny pang of homesickness for the keep as the details of the room slowly came into focus. This room was smaller than his dormitory back at the orphanage. When he could clearly make out shapes, he saw four beds with three sleeping boys. He was relieved to discover that his new friend Carl was one of them, and the twins Ethan and Benjamin were the other two. Ian crossed to the last bed, by the window, smiling as he thought about how the other boys had left that bed for him, as it was common knowledge that Ian liked the coolness of the night air on his face while he slept.

He made his way to the window and pulled back the curtain. The sky was no longer overcast and the moon lit the water of the Strait of Dover in the distance with a silvery glow. He yawned and cracked the window. Then he carefully took off his clothes, noting with relief that he was able to move his arm now without too much trouble. As he laid his trousers over the bed frame, he heard something clink to the ground. Bending over, he realized he'd forgotten about the crystal charm he'd found in Madam Scargill's room that morning.

He picked up the charm and held it to the window to better see it, but as the crystal shone in the light of the moon, something seemed to spark from within the heart of it. Ian caught his breath and he blinked a few times as he lowered the crystal and eyed it suspiciously. There were no more sparks, but there was something odd about the crystal. It felt hot.

He immediately reasoned that this was because it had been in his pocket all day and had probably been warmed by his body heat. But as he closed his fingers around it, he could tell that the charm was warmer than his own skin. There also seemed to be a pulsing sensation that he could just barely feel in his palm where the crystal rested.

"Odd," he whispered as he opened his hand again to study the thing. After a moment or two, he set the crystal on the windowsill and moved to hang his shirt and blazer on the side of the bed frame when something else caught his eye. The photograph and the silver box he'd brought with him upstairs were resting on the bed and Ian had the sudden urge to look again at the picture.

He reached for the frame and held it up to the moonlight, squinting at the black-and-white photo, studying it carefully, and he gasped when he suddenly noticed what he hadn't seen before. There, around Theo's mother's neck, tucked near the lace of her collar, was the very charm he'd just set on the windowsill. He now had proof that the necklace belonged to Theo and he resolved to get it to her as soon as possible.

He'd have to warn her, of course, about not letting Madam Scargill catch her with the charm, but even Madam Scargill couldn't deny the evidence in the photograph. The woman pictured happily with her baby looked so much like Theo that she could be her older sister. Ian set the photo and the box next to the charm on the windowsill. He hung his clothes up and put on the nightshirt that was left for him. It was a bit large but he wasn't about to complain. He was more tired than he'd ever been, and he couldn't be happier that he had something other than his dusty day clothes to wear to sleep.

Right before he turned to get into bed, a small movement called his attention back to the window. He blinked tiredly at the landscape of the large lawn and the rolling hills and his breath caught in his throat. He could swear he saw at the far end of the lawn a man draped in a long billowing cloak that seemed, to his amazement, to be fringed with glowing embers. The hairs on his arms and the back of his neck stood on end, and he watched as the figure seemed to glide along the lawn in his cloak, which danced and sparked with an unnatural quality. And then, at the bottom of the hill, the figure stopped.

Ian's heart hammered when he saw the stranger turn and his hooded head seemed to lift, looking along the wall of the castle to where Ian stood staring out the window. Ian gasped; then he quickly ducked behind the curtain, out of view. For a moment it had felt as if the creepy stranger's eyes had met his own and an icy terror had swept right through him.

He gulped and tried to steady himself; then, ever so slightly, he peeled the curtain back a fraction to peek out at the lawn. But the cloaked figure was gone. Ian stepped close again, using the curtain to shield himself, and he searched for any trace of the man he'd seen only a moment before— yet none remained.

He thought about going downstairs to tell the earl what he'd seen, but to what end? The stranger was gone, and all Ian could say about him was that he thought a man in an odd cloak had been walking along the lawn at the bottom of the hill. What if it turned out he was a member of the earl's staff and that his cloak had just been some sort of trick of the light? Ian would be a laughingstock. No, it was best to forget the whole thing and turn in. Still, even as exhausted as he was, sleep was a long time coming.

THE FURY

The next morning Ian awoke bleary-eyed and still very tired. Carl was awake and sitting up in bed, staring at him with an excited grin. "Did you kill the beast, then?" he asked when he saw Ian's eyes blink open.

Ian shook his head. " 'Fraid not," he said glumly. "What's worse is it looks as if there's more than one beast to worry about." He then went on to explain what the hunting party had found in the caves.

"Blimey!" moaned Carl. "That's blooming awful!"

"Yes, quite," said Ian. "And we looked all the rest of the day for any sign of the beast and her litter, but we couldn't find even so much as a paw print."

"I bet she's in one of the other caves," said Carl.

Ian rubbed his tired eyes while his heart weighed heavily with the fact that he'd had a direct hand in bringing the awful beast to them. "We've checked most of them. There's no trace of her. It's like she's vanished into thin air."

"So the earl's just giving up, then?" Carl asked, a hint of fear in his voice.

"No," said Ian with a yawn. "The hunting party is heading back out today to search again, and I believe the earl is calling for help from the village." He hoped silently that these additional men would be enough to chase the beast down once and for all.

"Will you join them again?" Carl asked.

"No," Ian answered, feeling grateful that he didn't have to go back out for another long, cold day of searching. "I don't think the earl has need of my services again, now that he knows that the beast's first lair has been abandoned."

"Well, that makes sense, doesn't it?" said Carl. "Anyway, you're going to love it here! There's loads to do. There's a game room and a bowling alley and a garden maze out back! Theo and I spent quite some time in that yesterday, trying to figure the way out. It's irritably confusing," he finished with a grin.

Ian stepped out of bed and shivered. "Sounds fantastic," he said over his shoulder as he turned to the window and shut it. He knew that Carl was excited about all that Castle Dover had to offer, but his own feelings were more subdued with the beast still on the loose. As he latched the window, he noticed the photograph and the necklace on the sill and was reminded about getting them to Theo. "Where is Theo, by the way? I need to speak to her," he said.

"I expect she's downstairs having her breakfast. They're going to call us next, so you best get ready. Ethan and Benjamin are waiting on the stairs; they wanted to be first in line when our group was called."

Ian smiled. "Sounds like them; they're like that at the keep too."

"Oh! Almost forgot to tell you," said Carl. "We've been instructed to give a list of things we'll need replaced at the keep to that man Binsford. And we're allowed to jot down a toy or two as well," Carl added with a huge grin. "I've asked for a new cricket bat, myself. You should ask for a new ball and wicket!"

Ian laughed at Carl's enthusiasm, then shimmied out of his nightclothes. Carl had to help him get his shirt on, as his shoulder still throbbed. "How's it feeling?" Carl asked as Ian worked to get his trousers on.

"It's sore today," Ian admitted while he faced the window and discreetly tucked Theo's necklace into the pocket of his trousers. "But I expect it'll be all right in a few days."

There was a knock on the door and a moment later Binsford came in and announced, "Breakfast is served, gentlemen."

Carl danced on the balls of his feet excitedly. "Thank you, sir!" he said jovially. "We'll be right down."

"I'd wager the food here is also to your liking," said Ian with a friendly wink at Carl.

"All food is to my liking. At my old orphanage we only got a baked potato and a crust of bread all day."

Ian's jaw dropped. He couldn't fathom anyone surviving on so little. *All day?* he asked.

Carl nodded. "Sometimes we'd get a bit more bread at supper, but usually we just got a bit of the stale stuff with watery broth and a cup of tea."

Ian looked at his friend anew and noticed for the first time how thin Carl's cheeks were and how his trousers were cinched tight by a rope belt around his bony waist.

Carl turned red under Ian's scrutiny and said, "Come on, then. Benjamin and Ethan have a head start on us, and you just know they're going to gobble up more than their fair share!"

Ian shoved his feet into his shoes, grabbed the frame off the windowsill, and turned to follow Carl.

Before the boys left the room, however, Carl glanced over at the silver frame Ian was holding and asked, "What've you got there?"

Ian held it up for Carl to see. "It's a photograph of Theo and her mother. I found it yesterday in our schoolmasters' cottage. Can you believe the luck?"

Carl examined the picture and nodded. "Blimey, Theo's really turned out to look like her mum, hasn't she?"

Ian had just been thinking the same thing. "It's the eyes and the nose," he said in agreement.

They reached the stairway and began to walk down when Carl asked, "What was a photo of Theo and her mum doing in our schoolmasters' house?"

"I've no idea," Ian admitted, "but I believe Theo's mum might have lived there for a time, and for some reason she ran off and left Theo in the middle of a field one stormy night. A passing stranger found her and brought her to the keep and she's lived with us ever since."

Carl's expression turned shocked as they reached the landing. "Her mum just *left* her out in the rain?"

Ian instantly regretted what he'd just said. He hadn't meant to reveal what he knew about Theo's past without first discussing it with her. "I don't know what the actual circumstances were," he said quickly. "No one does."

Carl nodded. "Well, me own mum would never have done that," he said. "She died of pneumonia, and the whole time she was sick, she still tried to fuss over me." As Carl said the last words, his voice cracked slightly, and Ian's heart softened for his new friend.

"Sorry about your mum," Ian said after a bit of silence passed.

Carl was staring at the ground as they walked into the dining hall. "S'all right," he mumbled. "Come on, let's find a place at the table and dig in."

The boys took their seats just as Castle Dover's kitchen crew were setting out scrambled eggs, ham, toast, and fruit. "Can you believe it?" said Carl as he watched the staff arrange platter after platter of food on the table. "It's like being on holiday here!"

Ian laughed. "You'd better eat as much as you can, Carl," he said. "You'll want to put on some weight before winter."

"Yeah," Carl said, dishing a huge portion of eggs onto his plate. "I'm a bit thin these days. Best to fatten up!"

While Carl ate as if his life depended on it, Ian barely managed to get down a few bites before his breakfast turned cold. All the children seated at the table wanted to know what had happened on the hunt. Ian decided it was best if he not panic the rest of the orphans by telling them that there were now at least five beasts to worry about. Instead, he said that the hunting party had determined that the beast was a female and had somehow managed to escape the area.

While Ian recited his story, however, he couldn't help noticing that Searle—seated at the other end of the table—sneered and rolled his eyes the whole time. "I bet if I'd been along with that hunting party, I'd have ferreted out that creature," he boasted, puffing his chest out. "Seems to me all you managed to do was bungle any chance of killing the brute by rooting around its lair," he added.

Ian ignored Searle and focused on reassuring the other worried children around the table. "There's no reason to be concerned," Ian said calmly to his fellow orphans. "The earl's a jolly good sportsman, and if anyone can hunt that beast down and kill it, it would be him." He made a mental note to say those exact words to Theo when he saw her. He knew how worried she'd be when she learned that the beast was still on the loose.

As Ian smiled confidently at the children, he noticed that some of them seemed to relax, but one or two still looked anxiously out the windows. Ian sighed as he thought that nothing short of the beast's pelt would reassure everyone. He decided to leave it at that and finish eating. While his food had indeed gone cold, it was still delicious.

When he had finished his first helping and Carl was just polishing off his third, Madam Dimbleby and Miss Carlyle came into the dining hall. "Children," Madam Dimbleby said, and Ian and the rest of the orphans looked up, "once you are finished with your breakfasts, please congregate out on the back lawn. We will be meeting there to discuss the plan to get you all back into your own beds at the keep, and the new schoolmaster will talk about the class schedules going forward."

Ian, who was a very good student, was happily surprised that they would be getting to their schoolwork so quickly after the attack, but Carl groaned. "That means we're not getting a holiday from school," he complained.

"It might not be so bad," said Ian. "I'm actually looking forward to our new subjects." Carl gave him a look that said he must be daft, but kept his mouth shut.

As the children gathered by the door to the lawn, Theo made her way through the crowd to Ian and Carl. "There you are!" she said as she neared. "Ian, I've been looking all over for you."

"Theo!" he said, bursting with excitement. "I've got something important to tell you and something even more important to give you."

"Is it a present?" she asked him happily.

"As a matter of fact, it is," he said with a smile, then looked around, feeling like they were being overheard. Carl was standing right next to him, giving him a winning smile, and then he noticed that many of the other children nearby were also looking at him expectantly.

"Er, sorry, but this is private, Theo. Might be best if we moved over there," Ian said, indicating a small nook away from prying eyes and ears.

Theo gave him a funny look but followed him to the nook, and when they were tucked discreetly away from the rest of the group, he dug around in his pants pocket and retrieved the crystal necklace.

"Oh, my," said Theo with a bit of awe as she took the necklace. "It's so beautiful, Ian. Wherever did you get it?"

Ian beamed, happy to give her such a treasure. "I found it in the rubble of Madam Scargill's room," he explained. He was going to tell her about the night she came to the keep and about how Madam Scargill had taken the necklace from the man who'd brought Theo to the orphanage, when she rudely pushed the necklace back into his hand.

"Ian!" she said crossly. "That's stolen property!"

Ian was startled by her reaction and whispered, "Shhh!"

"I can't believe you would want to give me something you pinched from Madam Scargill!" she spat, her voice barely hovering at a whisper. She then crossed her arms and began to move past him but he caught her arm.

"Theo!" he said, pushing the necklace firmly back into her hand. "You don't understand. I didn't lift this from Madam Scargill; she lifted it from *you*!"

Theo scrunched up her brows, obviously confused. "Now you're not making sense, and stop pushing that thing at me! I want nothing to do with it."

Ian sighed, trying to think of a way to explain it all to her. "The necklace belonged to your mum."

Theo frowned skeptically. "Really?" she said, her voice dripping with sarcasm. "And did she tell you that herself before you stole it from Madam Scargill?"

Ian was losing patience. "Will you please just listen to me?" he said, raising his voice a bit and feeling several eyes turn to stare at him. He sighed in exasperation and said, "Oh, forget it. Have a look at this and it'll sort things out better than I can." He reached into his blazer and handed her the small framed photograph of her mother.

Theo took one look at the picture and gasped. "I know her!"

"It's your mum," said Ian, feeling his shoulders relax now

that she wasn't making such a fuss. "And that little tot in her lap is you. It must have been taken right before you came to the orphanage, because you looked exactly like that the night you arrived at the keep. And this necklace," he said, holding it up, "was what Madam Scargill confiscated from the man who brought you. She was probably keeping it until she felt you were old enough to wear it."

"How do you know it belonged to my mother?" Theo asked, hugging the photo to her chest, her eyes glistening with moisture.

"Look again at the photo," he suggested. "There, you see? She's wearing the necklace."

Theo squinted at the spot Ian was pointing to in the photo. She nodded after a moment and held her hand out to receive the necklace. "Thank you," she said hoarsely, and Ian placed it into her palm. "Ian, I . . ." But before she could say another word, Madam Scargill appeared and clapped her hands.

"Children! Children!" she called. "Everyone please stop talking and gather out on the lawn for the meeting. Girls, queue up to the right, and, boys, do the same to the left."

Theo gave Ian a quick but fierce hug; then she hurried out the door to join the other girls on the lawn.

"Did you give the photograph to Theo?" Carl whispered as he sidled up to Ian.

"Yes," said Ian with a frown. "But I didn't have much of a chance to tell her about it."

"What's to tell other than you found the photo in the schoolmasters' cottage?"

Ian sighed. "It's a bit more complicated than that, I'm afraid," he said.

"Complicated?" Carl asked with a puzzled expression. "Like how, mate?"

Ian was about to answer him when Madam Scargill appeared at their side. "I said, *no* talking, gentlemen," she snapped.

"Yes, Madam," they both said, casting their eyes obediently to the ground.

Silently, the pair followed the line of children out onto the large lawn that surrounded Castle Dover. The boys stood in a line next to the girls and waited for further instruction.

When all the children had found their places, Thatcher stepped forward and addressed the group. "Good morning, children," he began with a warm smile.

"Good morning, Schoolmaster Goodwyn," Ian and the other children sang in unison.

"You've no doubt heard that we have as yet been unsuccessful in our attempts to kill the beast that attacked the keep. However, I want to assure you that the earl is doing everything in his power to ensure that the vile creature is driven from the land, never to return." Ian smiled smugly. That was exactly what he'd said to the group round the breakfast table. He hoped that hearing it from Schoolmaster Goodwyn would comfort the few who still looked worried.

"The earl has also advised me," Thatcher continued, "to inform you that when he can be assured of your safety, he will return all of you to the keep with new beds, furniture, clothing, and a new toy or two. Until then, you are all quite safe and secure here at Castle Dover, as we have many armed watchmen patrolling the castle grounds both day and night."

Ian's thoughts went back to the strange man he'd seen out on the lawn the night before and he wondered if perhaps it was one of the armed watchmen keeping them safe from another beastly attack.

Abruptly, Ian's thoughts were interrupted as he listened to the nervous murmurs around him. "I heard there's more than one beast out there!" said a girl named Alexandra.

"Bullets are no good against it! You'd need to get close enough to stab it in the heart to make sure it's dead," said Searle, doing his best to stir up the fear again.

"Is that true?" a girl named Rosemary asked as she tapped Ian on the shoulder. "Are there more than one of those awful beasts out there?"

Ian caught Theo staring at him wide-eyed nearby. "Yes," he said carefully, making sure his voice sounded calm, "but the others aren't more than four-week-old pups, barely bigger than cats."

Rosemary let out a breath and looked relieved, but Theo's expression never changed. Ian tried to reassure her with a smile, but Theo just nodded absently as her eyes held a faraway glimmer. She seemed incredibly troubled and Ian wished he could offer her something more than his reassurance.

All around him the children continued to chatter excitedly until Thatcher held up his hand for quiet. "That will do, children," he said patiently. He waited until they settled down again before he continued. "While the keep is being readied for your return, we shall be conducting lessons here at Castle Dover. As my brother, Perry, is off assisting with the hunt today, I shall be instructing those children whom we've assigned to secondary classes. We will begin with British history and later we'll have some instruction on French verbs and their conjugations. Meanwhile, Madam Scargill shall be taking the primary-studies children for lessons in reading and grammar."

Ian seemed to be the only student in his group who was excited about learning from Schoolmaster Goodwyn. Everyone else nearby was complaining about not being allowed a holiday while the keep was being repaired. "It's not fair," groaned Searle. "I can't think of anything more boring than history."

"I can," said Carl. "Latin. Now, there's a bugger of a subject if ever there was one."

Ian laughed and leaned out of line to poke Theo good-naturedly. She was a whiz at languages and had picked up Latin faster than anyone at the orphanage. But Theo didn't seem to be paying attention. Instead, she appeared lost in her own thoughts, and Ian noticed her hands wringing her skirt as if she was very nervous about something.

"It's all right," he said to her. "I expect the schoolmaster will grade on a curve if you're worried." Again, he got nothing more than an absent nod from her, so he decided to leave her be.

"Now, now," Thatcher was saying as the children continued to complain. "I realize you'd much rather be off exploring the castle grounds, but we can't ignore our schoolwork, after all." Pulling a list out of his pocket, he instructed, "If I call your name, please have a seat here on the lawn; otherwise you are to join Madam Scargill, who will take you into the drawing room for your reading lesson."

Ian was relieved when he, Carl, and Theo were among those called by their schoolmaster, and they quickly found a place to sit as several younger children stepped out of line and trooped over to Madam Scargill. "At least we're together," said Carl, giving Ian a nudge with his elbow.

"All right, then," said Thatcher. Reaching into a sack at his feet, he pulled out notebooks and pencils that he began to pass around. "I realize you do not have history books to read from," he said. "So this will be in lecture format and I will expect you to take diligent notes and follow along.

"Now, I was informed that you have been studying the period known as the Wars of the Roses. That time in our history is most fascinating, but I think I'd like to jump ahead, if I may, several hundred years to a different battle, one far more relevant to the turbulent times we find ourselves in today. I'd like to discuss the Great War. Who knows to what I am referring?" the schoolmaster asked, looking around the group. Ian knew the answer immediately and shot his hand quickly into the air. "Yes, Master Wigby?"

"The Great War of 1914, sir," Ian said confidently.

"Very good," answered Thatcher with a warm smile. "And whom did we fight against in this Great War?"

Again Ian shot his hand up eagerly and Thatcher gave him a nod to answer. "The Germans, sir," he said. He glanced sideways at Theo and noticed with relief that she seemed to have shaken her worried mood, as she was now

169

writing furiously in the notebook Schoolmaster Goodwyn had given her.

"Very good," said Thatcher with a smile. "Children, the Great War, as Master Wigby has correctly stated, began in 1914 and continued straight through to 1918. It was a massive conflict, involving all the powers of Europe and the United States, and one that, thankfully, we shall never have to see the likes of again—hence it is also known as the War to End All Wars."

Just then Theo jumped straight to her feet, her eyes large and round, and Ian noticed with alarm that her small frame was shaking. "That's not true," she said to the stunned audience.

"Is there something troubling you, Miss . . . Miss . . . ?" Thatcher said as he struggled to remember her last name.

"Fields," said Theo. "And yes, sir, I'm terribly sorry, but you're . . . well, you're just wrong."

Ian and several of the other children collectively gasped. All around him he could hear the furious whispering following Theo's rude statement.

Ian tugged gently on her skirt. "Theo," he whispered, attempting to gain her attention, "sit down and stop being rude."

But Theo pulled away and glared down hard at him. "You're wrong, sir," she repeated, turning back to Schoolmaster Thatcher, her voice wavering with emotion.

"I'm afraid I don't understand," said Thatcher, and Ian was relieved to see that he didn't seem cross, but genuinely curious about what Theo could be referring to.

"You're a fool to believe that there won't be another Great War," she said, and all the children gasped again.

Ian couldn't fathom what Theo might be thinking, so he stared up at her, and that was when he noticed with shock that her teeth were chattering and her lips looked blue, even though it was a gloriously warm morning. "There'll be another," she insisted, nodding vigorously as if to convince them all. "Only, the next one will be far worse than you could ever imagine!"

"I'm glad to see such passion in a student," said their schoolmaster calmly, although Ian could tell he was a bit rattled by Theo's sudden change in demeanor. "But as this is a lesson in *history*, and not a lesson in fortune-telling, I would ask that you please take your seat so that we can return to the lecture, won't you?"

But Theo refused to sit down. "They're coming!" she gasped, and to Ian's shock and embarrassment, she turned to him and shouted, "Ian, they're coming!" She then pointed down the hill toward the Strait of Dover. "You all think they won't come after us, but you're wrong! The man in the chamber, he must be warned!" Theo was shaking violently now as she stared wildly about like she'd gone absolutely mad. All around, the children were whispering to each other and moving away from her. Even Carl had edged back a bit.

Alarmed and frightened by Theo's outburst, Ian jumped to his feet. He put his arm around her, pulling her close, and whispered, "What's got into you?"

"Ian!" she gasped, gripping his blazer tightly. "The great wolf will rise up from the east and sweep down upon us, bearing his crooked black cross on a sea of blood! He'll call himself the Fury and he'll hang his banner from every hill and building, and where it hangs, all will know that a tyrant of death rules the land!"

Ian's heart filled with dread. He had no idea what was happening to Theo, but he could feel her terror radiating from her trembling form. He glanced helplessly at his schoolmaster, who looked back now with worried eyes. "Master Wigby, what's happening?" Thatcher asked him.

"I don't know," Ian admitted, hugging Theo protectively. "I think this could be some sort of aftereffect of the attack from the beast." But the truth was that he feared it was much more. He couldn't help thinking that Theo's mind might have snapped, and that she'd suddenly gone insane. "Sir, may I please be excused to take Theo to Madam Dimbleby?"

"Yes, of course," said Thatcher, his face filled with concern.

"Do you want some help?" asked Carl meekly. Clearly he felt ashamed of how quickly he'd scooted away from poor Theo.

Ian shook his head. Theo had been his responsibility since he was five years old; he'd take care of her. "No thanks, mate," he said. "I've got it."

"I'll take notes for you, then," Carl offered as Ian swiveled around and, still holding tightly to Theo, picked his way through the children. He had to half carry, half drag her along, because her legs were shaking so badly that she was struggling to walk, and all the while she sobbed inconsolably into his chest.

When they got inside, Theo's carrying-on bordered on

hysteria, which sent Ian into a state of panic himself. He'd never seen her behave like this, and he couldn't imagine why a simple history lesson would have sparked such a reaction from her. He looked desperately about the large sitting room, trying to decide what to do. Finally, he moved Theo to one of the couches and sat her down. Easing a throw over her lap, he gave her arm a squeeze. "I'm going to find Madam Dimbleby. You stay here and I'll be right back."

Theo didn't answer him, her hysteria rising. "The Fury is coming, Ian," she wailed. "He really is, and we're all doomed!"

Ian blinked hard against the moisture forming in his own eyes. He loved Theo more than anyone in the world, and to see her like this was almost more than he could bear. With one final squeeze of her arm, he bolted from the room and ran down the hallway, looking for anyone who might know where he could find Madam Dimbleby. As he was running toward the kitchen, he slammed headfirst into Binsford.

"Oomph!" said the castle's head butler.

Ian stepped back quickly. "I'm sorry, sir!"

"What on earth are you doing running through these hallways?" demanded Binsford, gripping his stomach.

"I need to find Madam Dimbleby!" Ian said. "It's Theo. Something's terribly wrong with her!"

Binsford straightened up from the slightly bent position he'd been holding. "Is she ill?"

"Yes, sir," Ian said with a nod. "At least I think so. She's been crying and saying things and shaking all over!"

"Bring me to her," directed Binsford.

Ian obediently led the way back to the sitting room, and to his immense relief he saw that Madam Dimbleby was already beside Theo, holding her close and rocking the child back and forth as she tried to calm her. When Madam saw Ian, she said, "I found her like this alone on the couch. Ian, what happened?"

"I don't know, ma'am," he answered, his eyes wide with alarm as he sat down on the other side of Theo. "We were having our history lesson and she just stood up and started going on about some furious man with an army and how he was going to bring his cross to hang on the hillside—"

"No!" Theo interrupted, pulling away from Madam Dimbleby's embrace. "You've got it wrong, Ian!" Turning to Madam Dimbleby, she pleaded, "Madam, you have to believe me! The Fury . . . he's coming! And no one will be safe! His army is going to bomb the shores and the towns and kill all the people! We've got to warn them! *We've got to warn everyone!*" Theo screamed the last part and Ian felt his heart beat with panic. His little Theo had indeed gone completely mad.

"Child!" said Madam Dimbleby, shaking her gently by the shoulders. "Listen to me! You're safe. You've been through a terrible fright and you're having a waking nightmare—"

"I'm not!" she insisted, yanking out of Madam Dimbleby's grasp. Theo jumped up from the couch, her body trembling in earnest. "It's true! What I've said is true! It *will* happen!"

Ian got up himself and tried to put a soothing hand on Theo's shoulder. She brushed it away but grabbed at his shirt desperately. "Ian, you've got to help me warn them! They're all doomed unless we tell them!"

"Who's doomed, Theo?" he asked her.

"Everyone! Here in Dover, in London, in Bristol, Liverpool . . . *everyone*! It's the Fury, he'll strike the lands to the east first and one by one they'll all crumble underneath him until he reaches our shores!" Theo was hysterical. Her sobs racked her body and made it difficult to understand her. Ian pried her hand from his shirt as he attempted to hold it, and he noticed how cold and clammy it was. He gazed into her panic-stricken eyes, and willed her to stop speaking such utter nonsense.

"Theo, dear," Madam Dimbleby said urgently, a look of intense worry on her face, "please try to calm yourself!"

But Theo would not be calmed. Instead, she took a ragged breath and shouted, "We're doomed unless we hurry! We must warn the man in the chamber! The Fury is coming! *The Fury is coming!*" And with that final desperate wail, she fainted.

Ian lurched forward awkwardly, barely managing to catch her before her head struck the floor. He grimaced when her full weight hit him, as his shoulder was still very sore. Ignoring the pain, he cradled her in his arms while he eased her gently to the floor, but for a long moment he wouldn't let her go. His mind kept rejecting the reality of her breakdown. How could she dissolve so quickly into madness?

Madam Dimbleby bent down next to him and pulled Ian from his troubled thoughts by gently lifting the girl from his arms. "Let me take over," she said, and with his help the pair got Theo's limp form onto the couch.

"Please help her, Madam," Ian whispered, choking on his own emotions.

The headmistress gave his hand a gentle pat. "Of course, Ian, of course," she assured him.

Binsford cleared his throat from nearby and said, "Shall I send for the doctor, Madam Dimbleby?"

"Yes, please, Mr. Binsford," she said, placing a pillow under Theo's head and brushing the hair away from her face. "And tell him to hurry," she added.

Ian watched Binsford turn and head quickly to the telephone in the front hallway. He noticed the worried lines on Madam Dimbleby's face. "She'll be all right, won't she, Madam?" he asked, hoping she'd tell him that this was nothing at all to worry about. That the doctor would have Theo back to normal in no time.

But Madam Dimbleby took several moments to answer, and when she did, she avoided his eyes. "I'm sure she will, Ian. Now, go back out to your lessons. There's nothing more you can do here. I'll look after her until the doctor arrives."

Ian hesitated. He didn't want to leave Theo.

"Go," said Madam Dimbleby sternly. "Do as I say, Ian, please."

Grudgingly, he obeyed. "Yes, ma'am," he replied, getting up and heading gloomily back out to his lessons.

He made his way carefully through the children sitting on the lawn to his place beside Carl, who gave him a look filled with distress. "Is Theo all right?" he whispered when Ian sat down.

"She fainted," Ian whispered back.

Carl gasped. "What happened?"

Ian shook his head. "I don't know, Carl. They've called for the doctor."

Carl seemed at a loss for words, and he simply stared straight ahead. Ian too was silent and the two boys sat quietly throughout the rest of the lecture, taking a few notes here and there, but Ian was so filled with fear and worry that he could hardly focus on anything the schoolmaster said.

Finally, the children were allowed to break for lunch and they filed inside. While Ian waited beside Carl to go in, Thatcher stepped up beside them. "How is she?" he asked.

"She fainted, sir," said Ian.

Thatcher's mouth pulled down in a frown. "She did? What could have brought that on?"

Ian shrugged. "I don't know, sir. She kept going on and on about how the fury was coming and he was going to strike to the east before coming here to hang his crooked cross on our hillside. She wouldn't stop talking about how everyone was in danger. I think she might believe the world is coming to an end or something. . . ."

The concerned expression on Thatcher's face deepened. Pulling Ian gently by the collar, he said, "Come with me," and he led the way down a path to the far end of Castle Dover.

After seeing the look of alarm in Thatcher's eyes, Ian trailed the schoolmaster nervously. Footsteps behind him caused Ian to look over his shoulder, and he was grateful to discover that Carl had decided to follow as well.

When they reached the west end of the castle, Thatcher paused outside a double set of French doors that Ian was very familiar with. The schoolmaster held one door open for the boys as they trooped inside to the small library that Ian was allowed full access to. The room was filled from floor to ceiling with books alphabetized by author.

Once they'd entered, Thatcher shut the door and motioned the boys over to two nearby chairs. "Tell me *exactly* what she said, Ian."

Ian ran a hand through his blond hair and blew out a sigh, trying to recall the exact wording. "She said that someone named the Fury was coming here. He's bringing an army, and something about having a banner or a flag that's a crooked cross, floating on a sea of blood. When this bloke, the Fury, arrives, many people will die and a tyrant will rule the land. She said that the army would strike somewhere in the east first, then make its way toward us, and bomb our shores and cities, including Dover, London, and Liverpool. She said we're all pretty much goners unless we can warn a man in a chamber. She was talking nonsense, sir, then she just fainted."

Thatcher did not immediately respond and Ian became even more nervous as a serious mood permeated the room. He noticed that Thatcher's face looked deeply troubled and the schoolmaster stared at Ian with intensity for a few moments before speaking again. "Ian," he said quietly, almost thoughtfully, "has Theo ever shown any signs of having the gift of sight?"

This question caught Ian completely off guard. "Sir?" he asked after blinking in confusion.

"He means, has she ever been able to predict the future?"

said Carl. "When me mum was still alive, we lived next door to this old widow woman named Mrs. Timpleton. Me mum was a bit afraid of her. She said the woman had the gift of sight and knew when things were going to happen. Sure enough, the night Mum lay dying in her bed, the widow came to our door and stayed with us until the end. I never knew how that old woman knew Mum was going to die, but she did. She also knew that I'd be sent to two orphanages, and she told me before I left for the first one in Plymouth that I'd only be at that miserable place for a short while before a man with a red beard brought me to another orphanage, where I'd be well cared for."

Ian felt a new pang of sadness for Carl. "I'm sorry you went through that," he said, not knowing what else to say.

"S'all right," said Carl, blushing and looking away. "Anyway, that's what you mean, Schoolmaster, you're talking about someone who can predict the future, right?"

Thatcher nodded. "That's exactly right, Carl. I'm interested in hearing if Theo has ever had the ability to suggest that things were going to happen before they actually occurred."

Ian thought back through his many years with Theo as his closest companion and all those times she'd had the uncanny sense of knowing about things before they took place. "Yes, sir, she definitely has," he said. "It's been little things, really, like she always knows when the earl is going to show up unexpectedly, or when there's a storm coming. And she knew when Alice had fallen out of that tree last summer and broken her finger. Theo and I were helping to clean up after dinner one night when Theo told Madam Dimbleby that Alice had hurt herself, even though Alice was on the other side of the keep, well out of Theo's view."

"I see," said Thatcher, and his worried look intensified.

"She also knows when someone's lying," Ian added. "You can't get away with anything when she's around."

"And how long has she had this gift?" asked Thatcher.

"As long as she's been able to talk," Ian said, remembering a time when Theo was three and she'd announced, "Rain!" from her crib when he'd finally gotten her to bed. He remembered laughing at her as he'd turned off the light and headed out of the nursery, only to realize half an hour later that an abrupt storm had rolled in from the sea and had begun pelting the keep with rain.

Thatcher got up from leaning against a table stacked with books and began to pace the room. Ian was now very unsettled about revealing Theo's secrets. "Sir?" Ian said after a long moment.

Thatcher stopped pacing and looked at Ian. "Tell me what you know about the current political situation in Germany," he said.

Ian and Carl shared a quick look that said, "Huh?" Then Ian turned back to his schoolmaster and answered, "I'm sorry, sir, I'm afraid I don't know much about Germany other than they were the enemy the last time England was at war. In lessons, we've mostly been studying the Wars of the Roses."

"Yes," said Thatcher as he tapped his chin thoughtfully. "Would Theo know anything about what's going on in modern-day Germany? Would she know what the Germans call their leader?"

"I'm not following you," said Ian, more confused than ever. "Theo prefers Latin and music lessons to current events."

"I see," said Thatcher. "Would she know who our current prime minister is?"

"You mean Lord Chamberlain?" asked Ian, still confused by this line of questioning.

"Yes," said Thatcher. "What does she know of him?"

"Very little, I'd guess," said Ian. "I mean, she could know his name and all, but I doubt she knows much more than that."

"This is most troubling," said Thatcher, pacing again.

"Please, sir," said Ian, his fear and worry getting the better of him. "Can you kindly tell us what this has to do with what made Theo so upset?"

Thatcher sat on the edge of the table and looked directly at Ian. "The leader of Germany is a man named Adolf Hitler," he began. "They call him the Führer. And Germany's flag has changed recently. It could definitely be described as a crooked black cross on a sea of deep red, the color of blood."

Ian gasped and heard Carl do the same. "The Fury," he murmured.

Thatcher nodded, then continued. "My brother and I spent a few months in Berlin two summers ago, watching the Summer Olympics. It's where we met the earl, in fact. During our stay there, we got to know many Berliners, and what we heard from them was alarming. Many of the Germans we shared conversations with felt a great resentment toward Western Europe. They feel the reparations—the money owed to us by Germany as a punishment for starting the

Great War—were an overly harsh and unfair amount. In fact, Thatcher and I left Berlin early; the loathing many people had shown us made the place rather inhospitable. And it is my unpopular belief that Germany is quickly becoming a dangerous and unpredictable adversary."

"Gaw blimey!" exclaimed Carl. "Theo knows they're going to attack us!"

Thatcher's mouth thinned to a very narrow line. "I sincerely hope not," he said in a voice barely above a whisper. "If Germany and its allies ever issued an assault against us, we'd be pressed into another world war."

Ian felt the blood drain from his face. He couldn't explain how, but he knew in his heart that Theo's ranting did indeed refer to the German führer. "This is terrible," he said, looking at Carl, who nodded.

Thatcher paced back and forth some more. "Yes," he said. "And the situation is further complicated by the fact that Poland, France, and England have formed an alliance to keep Germany in check. If Germany were to attack anywhere, it would likely be Poland first—which lies to our east. If Germany were to make such a move, then France and England would be obligated to come to her defense."

"So what do we do?" asked Ian meekly after a long stretch of tense silence. His brain hurt from all these distressing thoughts.

"I'd like to talk with Theo," said Thatcher. "But I realize in light of recent events she might be in too fragile a state of mind. That's why I'd like to prepare a list of questions for her and I'd like you, Ian, to ask them."

Ian scowled. "I don't know, sir," he said protectively.

"She was really out of sorts. I think it might make her sick again to ask her about what she was seeing and I'd rather not." There was no way Ian was going to risk sending Theo back into hysterics just to satisfy his schoolmaster's curiosity.

Thatcher sat down in a chair with a heavy sigh. "Right. We don't want to make the girl any more distressed than she already is. Let's give her some time, and if she returns to a state of relative calm, then I'd like you to ask her a question or two at a time, Ian. If she reacts adversely, then we'll drop the subject. If she's able to give you some insight, then we'll proceed cautiously."

"Very well, sir," said Ian, not at all happy that he'd been put into such a delicate situation.

"Now, I've kept you two long enough," announced Thatcher. "Hurry on to your midday meal and we'll talk more tomorrow."

As Ian and Carl left the room, Carl whispered, "I don't like this business of bombs and war."

"Neither do I," said Ian, a cold shiver running down his spine.

THE VAN SCHUFTS

Ian ate his lunch with little enthusiasm. Beside him even Carl seemed too distracted to eat.

After lunch Ian and his group of students were again called out onto the lawn, where they had their first lesson in French with Schoolmaster Goodwyn. Although Ian was still distracted by worried thoughts of Theo, he was at least grateful that they would finally be learning a language other than Latin.

The lesson was difficult as Thatcher explained the conjugation of various verbs, but eventually the children were allowed to put their pencils down and take a short break before they began their English lessons. "At least we'll understand what he's saying," said Carl moodily as they left the lawn.

Ian gave his new friend a chummy pat on the back, then excused himself to dash inside and search for Madam Dimbleby. He looked quickly about the sitting room and the parlor before heading up to the first floor, where he finally spotted her outside one of the bedrooms with her back to him as she spoke in low tones with Dr. Lineberry, the doctor from the village.

Thinking quickly, Ian ducked into one of the bedrooms close by before the two adults saw him, so that he could hear what the doctor had to say about Theo. "As far as I can tell," said the doctor, "her hand is not infected, but the hallucinations and hysteria are a definite sign of fever."

"But the child's cold as ice," insisted Madam Dimbleby.

"Yes," replied the doctor. "I agree. The only other diagnosis is acute mental breakdown, and given the excitement the young lass has been through of late, it's not out of the realm of possibility."

"Oh, no," said Madam Dimbleby, and Ian felt cold fear grip his heart like a vise. "Dr. Lineberry, what are we to do?" the headmistress asked.

"I've given her a sedative to calm her nerves. For the time being keep her in bed and keep her quiet. If her condition worsens, call me immediately."

"And what will we do if she doesn't recover?"

Ian held his breath, waiting for the doctor to answer. He could feel his heart hammering as Dr. Lineberry paused before he finally said, "Maggie, we may have to consider admitting her to a sanitarium."

"Oh, my," said Madam Dimbleby, and Ian closed his eyes and sank to the floor. It was the worst thing the doctor could have said. "Dr. Lineberry," Madam continued, "do you really think her condition would warrant that?"

The doctor sighed. "The symptoms are certainly there, and we'll know in time if this hysteria is a permanent condition or a passing moment of nerves from her recent experience.

I'll be back to check on her tomorrow. Again, you must keep her as calm and quiet as possible until I return."

Madam Dimbleby thanked the doctor and walked with him down the hallway, past where Ian was quietly hiding. When their footsteps had become faint, he stepped out of the room and moved down to Theo's door. He knocked very softly before easing himself inside.

Theo was lying in one of the two twin beds in the room. Her face was small and pale against the pillow it rested on and Ian felt his knees wobble at the sight of her looking so frail. As he quietly closed the door, she opened her eyes and gave him the faintest smile. "Ian," she said sleepily.

Ian forced a smile onto his face, crossed the room to her, and took a seat on the edge of her bed. "Don't try to talk, Theo," he said, working hard to sound calm and push down the panic and fear that threatened to give him away. "The doctor says you need your rest."

Theo shook her head and sat forward, her hand going to her neck as she pulled at the chain with her mother's crystal. "It's the necklace," she said hoarsely. "The moment I put it on, I began to feel odd."

Ian helped her take the necklace off and immediately the color seemed to return to her cheeks and the worry in her eyes relaxed. "That's better," she said with a sigh of relief.

Ian dangled the pink crystal in front of his eyes, stupefied that something like a small crystal necklace could be at the root of Theo's breakdown. "*This* is why you got so upset?" he asked her.

Theo nodded adamantly. "Yes," she said firmly. "The

moment it was around my neck, I felt an intense worry, and then these horrible images began to play in my head and words came out of my mouth that I couldn't stop."

Ian wrapped the crystal in his fist, angry that he'd been the one to give it to her. "I'll get rid of it this instant," he promised her. "You'll never have to see this necklace again!"

"No!" she said in alarm, putting a hand on his closed fist. "Don't throw it away! Just keep it for me until I feel better."

Ian was taken aback. "But if this is causing you harm, we can't possibly keep it!" he argued.

Theo gave him a pleading look. "Please," she said wearily. "I can't explain it, but I know I'm not supposed to let it go."

Ian struggled over what to do. If the crystal was the source of her hysteria, then he was all for sending it straight over the cliffs into the swirling water below to keep her safe. But as he looked at her, he knew he couldn't deny Theo the only heirloom her mother had left her, and the look in her eyes swayed him in the end. Pocketing the crystal, he said, "Fine. But if this ever happens again, I'm chucking it to the fishes."

Theo sank back into her pillow, relief on her face and a small smile on her lips as her eyelids drooped. A moment later she was asleep. Ian watched her for several minutes, still struggling with the promise he'd just made. He couldn't bear the thought of seeing her go through another episode like she'd had out on the lawn, but he couldn't go back on his word to her either.

Finally, he pulled the bedcovers up under her chin, gave

her a gentle peck on the top of her forehead, and eased out of the room.

"Lessons are beginning again, Master Wigby," Madam Dimbleby said quietly from behind him in the hallway, making him jump.

"Sorry, Madam," he said, turning quickly from the door he'd just closed. "I only wanted to check on her."

"Yes," said Madam Dimbleby. "I assumed after you heard what the doctor had to say that you'd want to see her."

Ian blushed and murmured, "Very sorry, Madam."

The headmistress chuckled and stroked his hair. "You never were one for rules where Theo was concerned, were you, Ian?"

Ian looked up and begged, "Please don't send her away, ma'am! Don't let the doctor put her in that sanitarium! I *promise* I'll keep her calm."

Madam Dimbleby's eyes suddenly filled with moisture and she reached out abruptly to pull him into a fierce embrace. After a long moment she let go, smoothed out his hair, and said, "Now, hurry along to your lessons. I'll sit with Theo for now."

Ian fought back his own emotions and hurried down the stairs. Through one of the windows that faced the lawn, he could see the children taking their seats and Schoolmaster Thatcher shuffling through his notes. Ian dashed outside. As he sat down Carl whispered, "How is she?"

Ian forced a small smile. "I think she's going to be all right," he said, and his hand moved to the lump in his pocket. *If I can keep this away from her, at least*, he thought.

*　*　*

That evening as the children, Madam Scargill, and Thatcher were gathered in one of the large sitting rooms on the second floor, the earl and his hunting party came back to the castle.

Ian, who'd been working through his French homework, nudged Carl. "Let's have a listen," he whispered, and the two boys discreetly scooted out the door and made their way to the banister, where they could look down on the returning men as they handed over their coats and rifles to the earl's staff.

"I tell you, it's the oddest thing I've ever seen!" Ciaran was saying. "I've never been on a hunt where there was absolutely no sign of the prey at all. Even the hounds we brought along today couldn't pick up the trail!"

"It's like the creature has vanished," added Alfred.

"Or dived into the channel," said Henry as a footman took his coat.

"At least we've been able to alert the village," said the earl. "Should that horror show its face again anywhere near here, we'll know about it and we'll be ready."

"That's not good," whispered Carl. "I thought for sure they were going to kill the beast today."

Ian nodded, deeply troubled by the fact that the hellhound and her pups were still on the loose.

The boys watched as Binsford stepped up to the earl and announced, "Dinner is awaiting you and your guests in the dining hall when you're ready, my lord."

"Excellent, Binsford," said the earl, his cheeks still pink

from the cold outside. "We're looking forward to something warm for dinner. Did you have any luck making arrangements for the repairs at the keep?"

"I've hired two carpenters and several laborers from the village, my lord," he said. "Also, the furniture and supplies have been ordered from London and, I have been assured, will arrive on the next train. The keep will be repaired and resupplied by the end of the week, as you requested," Binsford finished with a bow.

"Brilliant job, Mr. Binsford," said the earl with a kind smile. "And how are the children faring?"

Binsford hesitated and Ian had a sneaking suspicion that the butler was unsure how to broach the topic of Theo's breakdown. "Most are doing quite well," said Binsford. "Only one of them seems to be struggling with the intensity of these recent events."

The earl frowned. "Which child?" he asked.

"Miss Theo Fields, my lord," said Binsford. "The poor girl had a bit of a collapse this afternoon during lessons. Madam Dimbleby is attending to her upstairs, in fact."

The earl glanced upward and Ian and Carl ducked away from the banister and edged quickly around the corner. "Do you think he saw us?" whispered Carl as the pair hurried back to the sitting room.

"I'd bet on it," said Ian glumly, ashamed of having been caught eavesdropping.

They snuck back into the sitting room and took their seats, and Ian felt his cheeks turn red as Thatcher looked directly at them while arching one eyebrow. "Looks like someone noticed we'd ducked out," murmured Ian.

Carl glanced quickly at Thatcher, then back to his homework. "Bugger," he said with a sigh as he flipped open his notebook again.

As the large clock in the corner dinged seven times, the earl appeared in the doorway, beaming at everyone in the sitting room. "Good evening, children!" he said in his charismatic, booming voice. "I trust that you've been on your best behavior, and your lessons went well."

"They went well until certain people started making scenes," groused Searle from nearby. Ian glared furiously at him, and his nemesis merely sneered in return.

The earl either ignored Searle's comment or he did not hear it, because he continued. "Children, by the week's end you shall all be moving back to the keep. Your clothing and furniture is being replaced, and repairs will have been completed. For the next few days, you will remain here and attend to your studies, but be prepared to move back to your home by Friday afternoon."

"And how went the hunt, my lord?" Thatcher asked.

The earl's smile never wavered. "We did not kill the beast," he said, and all the children moaned. "However," the earl continued, "I am thoroughly convinced that the creature has moved her litter someplace well away from Dover. I am assured, as I have seen no sign of her nearby in two days."

Ian saw Madam Scargill pull nervously at the collar of her dress. "Are you certain we'll be safe to return to the keep, my lord?" she asked.

The earl smiled at her. "Yes, Gertrude, I'm sure. But I've taken the liberty of adding two men with rifles to your staff and I've also hired several men from the village to patrol the roads and the area along the cliffs day and night for the next several months. And I've sent word to the neighboring counties to be on the lookout for the creature. I expect that eventually news will spread and the beast and her pups will be hunted down and properly disposed of."

Madam Scargill seemed to relax. "That's wonderful, my lord. Thank you for seeing to our comfort and safety," she said, giving the children a look that suggested they too needed to thank their benefactor.

Ian and the rest of the group obediently cheered a round of thanks to their patriarch, who chuckled and waved his hands humbly. "Yes, yes," he said. "Now, back to your studies, children."

As the earl turned toward the hallway, Thatcher got up from his chair, walked carefully but quickly through the maze of students to him, and said in a low voice that Ian was just able to overhear, "My lord, if I might have a moment with you in private?"

The earl looked quizzically at the younger man and replied, "Yes, of course, Thatcher."

"Thank you. And might I ask that my brother join us?" But before Ian could hear the earl's answer, the two of them had moved into the hallway and out of earshot.

"What do you think that was about?" whispered Carl.

Ian looked at Carl in surprise. He hadn't realized that his friend had been working to overhear too. "Probably what happened out on the lawn today," he grumbled. He didn't like having Theo be the focus of so much attention and was deeply concerned that the earl might want to question her when what she really needed was rest.

He didn't like the knot of anxiety that settled into the pit of his stomach every time he thought about what Thatcher had told him. Theo's predictions were likely to be accurate given Thatcher's revelations about Germany's führer. Even that bit about Poland bothered him.

"Ah," said Carl with a nod. "That can't be good," he added before turning back to his French homework.

Ian tried to concentrate on his studies again as well but his mind kept wandering back to how weak and frail Theo was in her bed just down the hallway.

He was saved from his mental struggles when, a half hour after the earl and Thatcher had left them, the schoolmaster reappeared in their doorway. "Master Wigby?" he said in a quiet voice, so as not to disturb the other children. "Won't you please join the earl and me for a moment downstairs?"

Even though Thatcher had spoken quietly, all eyes in the large sitting room turned to look at him, and Ian stood up quickly, embarrassed by being singled out. Carl gave him an encouraging smile and Ian turned and shuffled after Thatcher.

Nervously, Ian followed his schoolmaster down the hallway and the immense staircase and through several more rooms before they reached a set of large mahogany double doors.

Thatcher opened a door and Ian walked through, coming to stand awkwardly in the middle of the room as he looked with amazement at the large heads of zebras, gazelles, antelope, rhinoceros, hyena, and various other wild animals that dotted every wall within. "These are my hunting trophies," said the earl, pulling Ian out of his thoughts. Ian had missed spotting the earl when he'd entered, as his patriarch sat behind a huge intricately carved wooden desk at the back of the study.

Ian coughed softly, trying to find his voice. "Very impressive, my lord," he said.

The earl gave him a friendly nod and got to the point. "Thatcher tells me that our Miss Fields has been having visions."

Ian shuffled his feet and dug his hands into his pockets, fingering her crystal necklace. "It's not especially unusual for her," he said, trying to play it down. "Theo's always had that gift."

"Gift?" asked Perry with a snort. Ian noticed the other schoolmaster leaning against the wall behind and to his left, wearing a humorless look. "Was that what my brother put into your head?"

Ian's eyes darted to Thatcher, and he was surprised when Perry's twin curled his lip in a snarl. "I've put nothing into his head, Perry! And I'll kindly ask you to keep your disdain for the topic at hand to yourself for now."

Perry smiled politely at Ian, but the skeptical look in his eyes never wavered. "My apologies," he said dramatically, adding a small bow. "As you were saying, Master Wigby?"

"Yes, sir," said Ian. Even more uncomfortable after having witnessed the testy exchange between his two schoolmasters, he turned his attention back to the earl. "She's been able to predict all sorts of things ever since she learned to speak." Ian wasn't sure if what he was revealing about Theo was hurting or helping her cause.

"I see," said the earl thoughtfully, and Ian was relieved

that the earl didn't appear to be nearly as judgmental as Perry. "What sorts of things has she been able to predict?"

"Well . . . ," Ian said, searching his memory. "All sorts, really. She can tell when it's going to storm, even when the weather reports say we're going to have a nice day. And she knows when a new orphan's going to arrive. She can also tell us if we're getting a boy or a girl. And she knows when someone's going to be adopted. Like when Stuart left last May. And of course she always knows when you're going to stop by unannounced," he finished.

The earl gave a thunderous laugh and slapped the desk with his palm. "I've wondered all these years how my attempts to surprise you have been foiled! And here I thought perhaps your headmistresses had spies here at the castle!"

Ian hoped he hadn't gotten anyone into trouble with that last bit, but the earl seemed so tickled by his revelation that he smiled. Thatcher, who had taken a seat in one of the wing chairs on the opposite side of the room, asked, "Did Theo predict the beast's appearance?"

Ian turned to look at Thatcher as he thought back to the days leading up to their visit into the tunnels. "Now that you ask," he said, "a few days before Theo and I went exploring near the beast's lair, Theo said that she had a terrible feeling some dreadful storm was going to strike the keep someday. She said she kept seeing broken furniture everywhere, and she couldn't imagine what else but a powerful storm could cause such destruction."

"And what did you think when she told you this?" asked Thatcher.

Ian shrugged. "I didn't worry much about it, sir," he

admitted. "I mean, I believed that she was getting one of her feelings again, but sometimes things turn out to be a lot less dramatic than Theo's visions predicted. Like, once she told me that I was going to fall down the stairs and break my leg. The next day I was late for dinner and as I was hurrying down the stairs I remembered Theo's warning, so I had a hand on the railing. Sure enough, I lost my footing and tripped on the stairs. But I didn't break my leg; I only twisted my ankle."

The earl looked curiously at him. "But, Ian," he said. "If you hadn't been warned by Theo, you might not have been holding on to the railing, and you would have had a much worse tumble down those stairs."

Ian thought about that for a moment, surprised. "Yes, my lord, you're probably right."

"Oh, this is poppycock!" growled Perry from the corner. "The very fact that Theo told him he was going to have a tumble probably made him more nervous on the stairs."

"It is not poppycock, Perry," chided his brother. "Didn't you hear me when I told you what she said about the Führer?"

Perry rolled his eyes and sighed loudly. "Seems to me she was going on about a *fury*, not the Führer! Besides, much of what she said can be found in any newspaper."

"Theo doesn't read the newspaper," Ian said defensively. He didn't like the way Perry was so easily dismissing Theo's abilities.

Perry scowled at him. "If Theo is able to predict the future, then don't you think she would have stopped you from going into that tunnel in the first place, Master Wigby?"

"I don't think the gift works exactly in that manner," said the earl.

"What do you mean?" asked Perry.

"I have some experience with this sort of thing," he said. "A member of my family, in fact, is quite gifted. Which brings me to my next suggestion: I believe we should have Miss Fields visit with my aunt, Lady Arbuthnot. She lives in London, and I believe she might be able to tell us what level of skill the girl possesses as well as help Theo control her abilities and lessen her fear of receiving these visions."

For the first time in several hours, Ian relaxed. The earl wasn't going to lock Theo up in some sanitarium; he understood her condition, and he was going to help her. "I'm sure she would appreciate any assistance you could offer her, my lord," he said gratefully.

"I must be off in the morning to attend a Parliament meeting, but I shall leave directions to my aunt's flat in London with you two," he said, indicating the schoolmasters. "Please take Theo there as soon as she's well enough to travel. I've spoken with Madam Dimbleby," he added, "and I hear that Theo is doing much better this evening." The earl gave a knowing look to Ian. "I'm sure she's going to make a full recovery and will be fit to make the venture in a week or two."

Ian smiled gratefully and opened his mouth to ask if he could go along on the adventure, but Thatcher spoke first. "Should we ring Lady Arbuthnot to make the arrangements for our visit?"

The earl smiled. "I'm sure you won't have to. In fact, I would ask that you not make any attempt to contact her prior to showing up in London on her doorstep. Aunt Aggie is well blessed with the gift," he said with a chuckle. Ian felt that this was something of an inside joke to the earl. "Take Ian and Carl along as well for moral support," the earl added. "I want Theo to have her friends nearby should the trip to the city cause any stress on the young lass."

"Thank you, my lord!" Ian said, letting go of the anxious breath he'd been holding. "I'm sure Theo will be quite pleased to meet your aunt."

The earl laughed heartily. "I'll not take that bet until after they've met, Ian. Now, go back to your studies. I've kept you long enough."

Ian hurried out of the room, grateful that Theo wasn't about to be shipped off to the sanitarium and bursting to tell Carl of the adventure they were going to have. He could hardly wait.

As it happened, they didn't have long to wait at all. By week's end Theo had regained all of her composure and upon the doctor's final visit he pronounced her well enough to leave her bed and rejoin the other children, much to Ian's relief, of course.

Madam Dimbleby still insisted that Theo sit apart from the flurry of activity in the castle as the children hurried to collect themselves and return to the keep, but Ian was beginning to relax his vigilant watch over her.

Soon he was completely distracted. When Ian arrived back at the orphanage, all he could do was marvel at the new furnishings and lavish décor. The earl had clearly spared no expense for their comfort, as much of their heavily used furniture had been replaced by beautiful new items. Rose curtains had replaced the sun-worn blue ones that used to hang heavily in the parlor. Large comfy couches with big soft cushions had replaced the rather lumpy ones from before. And rugs with plush fibers adorned the bare wood floors, giving the old keep a much needed sense of lightness.

In the dining room, their rather cramped table had been replaced with several smaller ones, so that instead of sitting in one long row, the children could gather round to eat in smaller, more intimate groups for meals.

The cupboards in the kitchen had been rebuilt and sparkling china lined the shelves. The classroom at the very back of the keep, behind the west wing, hadn't been touched by the beast, and yet all the old rickety desks had been replaced by sturdy, larger ones.

Upstairs the earl's generosity was even more apparent. Ian made his way up to his dormitory and discovered several sets of freshly purchased clothes placed on the crisp clean sheets covering his new bed. He was also surprised to discover that even though he had never turned in a list of the personal items he'd like replaced, the earl had seen to it that he was given a pocket torch, a Swiss Army knife, and a compass, with a personal note that read *For future explorations*.

Ian smiled and tucked the compass, the knife, and the pocket torch into his trousers, feeling the necklace that he was keeping safe for Theo there too.

Next he pulled out the storage trunk that had been placed under his bed and lifted the silver box from his mattress, where he'd set it while he looked over his things.

Before placing the treasure box inside the trunk, he inspected it closely for perhaps the hundredth time, trying to figure out how it opened, but he was still at a loss as to how to get the lid up.

With a sigh he finally placed the box into the trunk along with his clothes and pushed the trunk back under his bed. Sitting on his mattress for a moment, he stared out the window, which had a brand-new pane in it, lending a much clearer view of the grounds outside. He was surprised to see a motorcar traveling up the road leading to the keep. And more surprised when Theo burst into the room. "Ian!" she said with a touch of the panic he'd seen in her a few days before. "No matter what, when that couple arrives, you do *not* want to be adopted and you do *not* know me!"

Ian's heart sank. "Oh, no," he said as he put his hands on her shoulders. "Theo, are you having another attack?"

Theo shook her head hard. "No," she said in an urgent whisper. "Just listen to me and do as I say!"

Ian didn't know what to do. The expression Theo wore was so similar to the look she'd had out on the lawn at Castle Dover that he was worried she might be having a relapse. He knew that if she had another attack, the headmistresses would take the doctor's advice and ship her off to the sanitarium. "Theo, please try to calm down," he whispered, feeling the knot of fear forming in the pit of his stomach. "We can't let the headmistresses see you like this again."

But Theo was having none of it. "Ian, don't be daft!" she snapped. "There is a couple coming to our door asking to adopt two children, one boy and one girl. Whatever you do, whatever you say, you cannot allow them to adopt you. And you *cannot* mention that you and I get along, all right?"

Ian nodded dumbly, thoroughly confused, because although Theo looked distressed, her eyes didn't have that far-off cast that they'd had when she'd been speaking about the Fury and his army. "Yes, yes, Theo," he said, deciding it was best to trust that she wasn't having another attack. "Whatever you want, as long as you promise to be calm, all right?"

Theo's intense expression relaxed, but then she said, "Oh! And I have to tell Carl too!"

Ian smiled and nodded over her shoulder at Carl, who had come into the room a few moments earlier and was hovering anxiously on the edge of his bed, taking in every word.

"Sorry," Carl said with a blush. "Couldn't help overhearing you two."

"No, it's fine," said Theo, turning to him. "No matter what, Carl, don't agree to go away with the couple. And you hate girls, simply *hate* them. You don't want a sister and you don't want to be adopted by anyone who would want you to have a sister, all right?"

Carl looked sideways at Ian, clearly unsure how to respond. Behind Theo's back Ian nodded vigorously, urging his friend to agree. "Yes, of course, Theo," Carl said, to Ian's relief. "Whatever you say."

Just then there was a loud knock at the front door downstairs and all the boys in the dormitory went silent. The keep rarely received visitors. A moment later, Madam Scargill's heavy footsteps clomped across the floor of the front hallway and the newly built front door squeaked open. "May I help you?" they heard her ask.

There was a bit of mumbling; then Madam Scargill said, "Oh, my! This is a surprise. You're interested in adopting two of our children? Why, won't you please come in?"

Relief and surprise washed over Ian. Theo hadn't had another attack; her powers of sight were simply working as they used to. He gave her an admiring smile.

She returned his look with her mouth set in a firm line and her eyes narrowed. "Remember what I told you," she whispered. "You don't want to be adopted, and you never play with any of the girls here at the orphanage." Then she turned and darted out of their room.

"What do you make of that?" whispered Carl in awe.

"I don't know," admitted Ian. "But I suspect we're going to find out."

Two hours later all the older boys with blond hair had been corralled into the dorm room that Ian and Carl shared. "Now, remember what I told you about minding your manners," advised Madam Dimbleby, sitting on a bed. "This couple has been peculiarly specific about what type of child they're looking to adopt. One boy of at least ten and one girl of that same age, both with blond hair. They plan to interview each child who fits that description until they find the right pair."

"Do you know anything about the couple?" asked James, a boy slightly younger than Ian.

"Madam Scargill and I have interviewed them extensively. Their names are Herr and Frau Van Schuft. They are from Austria, but are living here in England now, in the North Country near Newcastle."

"That's a long way away," said Phillip, the boy sitting next to James. "If we go with them, we won't be able to come back and visit."

Ian understood the boy's reservation. This was the only home and family that so many of the orphans at Delphi Keep had ever known, and while a good portion of the children dreamt daily about being adopted by people they could finally call Mummy and Daddy, some, like Ian and Phillip, were quite happy where they were.

"Now, now," Madam Dimbleby said to Phillip. "You know that this opportunity doesn't come round to you older boys very often. You may miss us at first, Phillip, but after you've had time to adjust to your new family, you'll hardly think of we sorry lot at all. And besides that, you'll have a sister from Delphi to remind you how lucky you were to be adopted."

Phillip seemed to brighten and the other boys grew more excited too as they chattered on about the possibility of finally being taken in by a real family. All except Ian and Carl. The two of them sat in uncomfortable silence, wondering about what Theo had told them. Searle spoke up then. "I for one can't wait to meet my new parents. I shall convince the couple that I am the perfect boy for them."

Madam Dimbleby gave him a serious look that suggested she dearly hoped so too and Ian hid a smirk. "That's the attitude, Searle," she said encouragingly. "But you might want to appear a bit more humble during your interview."

There was a knock on the door, and Ian looked up to see Madam Scargill pop her head in. "Is it the boys' turn now?" asked Madam Dimbleby.

"Yes," said Madam Scargill, a look of deep concern on her face. "But before we send them down, might I have a word with you, Maggie?"

Madam Dimbleby got stiffly up off the bed and went out into the hallway with her cousin. The boys were very quiet as they strained to hear what was being said. James put his ear to the door to listen, and the other boys looked at him expectantly. "They're talking about Theo," he whispered, and Ian felt a nervous shiver run through him. "Madam Scargill says that during Theo's interview, she threw a temper tantrum and had to be carried out of the room!"

"Uh-oh," whispered Carl, and Ian swore under his breath. He'd been right the first time: Theo must be having another one of her episodes. She was *always* polite and well behaved in public.

"Madam Scargill says that the couple want nothing to do with her," James continued.

Just as James finished speaking, the door opened again and Madam Dimbleby asked, "Who's first, then?"

Searle shot his hand up into the air. "I'll go, Madam!" he said.

"Very well," she answered with a sigh. "I'll walk you downstairs; then I must visit the girls' dormitory."

As soon as she shut the door, there was much nervous chatter as all the boys raced around to check their appearances and smooth out their clothing, each of them wanting to make a good first impression. But Ian and Carl didn't pay any attention to how they looked. Instead, the two sulked on their beds, worried about Theo.

Faced with the prospect of an interview with the couple

downstairs, Ian wasn't sure how to behave. He decided that it was best to follow Theo's directions. Even if the thought of having a real mother and father to call his own was somewhat appealing, Ian had no interest in being taken away from Theo.

"Do you think she's gone over the edge again?" Carl asked Ian quietly, pulling him out of his troubled thoughts.

"No!" Ian said defensively, then softened his tone. "I just think that what happened with the beast has caused her to lose . . ." Ian's voice trailed off as he searched for the appropriate words.

"Yes?" asked Carl.

"Perspective," Ian finished. "I think she's having trouble with her perspective."

Carl gave him a look that suggested Ian might be the one having trouble with perspective. "So I'm supposed to go down there and try to avoid getting adopted, knowing that Theo's a little off her nutty?"

"She's not off her nutty!" snapped Ian with a hard glare at Carl. It was fine for Ian to think it, but for someone else to say it was unacceptable.

"Fine," grumbled Carl. "She's having perspective problems. Still, I really want a family, Ian. What if these people like me? I mean, I can be quite charming, you know." Carl bounced his eyebrows up and down for emphasis.

Ian rolled his eyes, not remotely amused, and turned away toward the window. "Do what you want, Carl," he grumbled. "I promised Theo that I'd follow her instructions, and I intend to keep my word."

Ian continued to stare out the window moodily as the

other boys were called down one by one for their interview. The afternoon sun had started its descent when he heard Carl's name called, and Ian—feeling bad now—turned to wish him luck, but his friend was already disappearing out the door.

Ian sighed and turned back to his window to wait for Carl's return, as he was the only boy left to interview with the couple. Just ten minutes later Carl came back to the room and said curtly, "You're next."

Ian looked at him, hoping to get a hint about what the couple was like, but Carl simply went to his bed, lay down, and stared at the ceiling.

Ian sighed again, got up, and walked with slumped shoulders out of the room and down the stairs where Madam Scargill was waiting for him. "They are in the drawing room, Master Wigby," she said.

"Yes, ma'am, but might I ask how Theo is? I heard there was some sort of incident with her."

Madam Scargill raised one eyebrow. "Theo is perfectly well," she said. "However, her behavior will not be tolerated. She's in her room, where she'll stay for the next week. You may visit with her after your interview, if you're concerned, but only for a few minutes."

Ian felt a rush of relief. "Thank you, ma'am," he said, turning toward the drawing room.

"And remember," Madam Scargill called after him, "we expect you to be on *your* best behavior."

Ian flashed a smile over his shoulder. "Of course," he assured her. After all, Theo never said he couldn't be polite, just that he should insist that he didn't like girls and didn't want to be adopted.

When he got to the door, he knocked softly and heard a woman answer, "Enter!" Ian pulled open the door and stepped through to the keep's drawing room, which was primarily used as a study for the two headmistresses. "*Guten tag!*" said a beautiful woman with platinum blond hair, pale skin, and ruby-painted lips.

"Hello," said Ian, nervous about meeting the strangers.

"I am Hylda Van Schuft, and zis is my husband, Dieter," The woman nodded to the man next to her. Herr Van Schuft was as handsome as his wife was beautiful.

"Hello," Ian said again as he stood stiffly by the door.

"And you are?" Frau Van Schuft asked with a hint of mirth.

"Er . . . Ian Wigby, ma'am," he said, shoving his hands into his pockets.

"Come sit vith us," Frau Van Schuft said sweetly in her thick accent as she gestured to a chair on the other side of the table where they were seated.

Herr Van Schuft was smiling broadly at him and turned to his wife and said, "He looks like us, doesn't he, *liebling*?"

Ian wasn't sure why, but his insides turned icy cold. He didn't like the couple, even though they seemed perfectly nice. He couldn't help feeling that their smiles were forced and their words rehearsed. "Ja," Frau Van Schuft said. "He could easily pass for von of us." Turning to Ian, she said, "Vee vould prefer to have children zat look like vee do. There are always fewer . . . qvestions, ja?"

Ian said, "Yes, but I don't sound like the two of you, do I?"

His tone was abrupt and rude and Frau Van Schuft gave him a sharp look. " 'Tis no matter," she said, pushing the edges of her lips up into an even more forceful smile. "Vee are living in England now, so of course our children vill speak like you."

Ian shrugged. He had already decided to trust Theo's instincts and play this exactly as she had instructed.

In the awkward silence that followed, Herr Van Schuft said, "Tell us about yourself."

Ian looked down at his hands, nervously picking at his trousers. "What would you like to know?" he asked.

"How old are you?" Frau Van Schuft asked.

The question seemed harmless. "I'm thirteen," he said.

"Vhat is your favorite subject in school?" asked Herr Van Schuft.

Ian smiled to himself. This was a good opportunity for him to appear difficult. "I don't have one. In fact, I'm a dreadfully poor student."

Herr and Frau Van Schuft shared a look before Frau Van Schuft turned back to him and asked, "Vhat do you like to do for fun?"

Ian sensed that the couple was digging for information but he couldn't figure out what they might be looking for, so he asked, "What do you mean?"

"Do you like to go exploring?" asked Herr Van Schuft.

Ian narrowed his eyes. There was something suspicious about that question. "Exploring?" he repeated while his mind raced to understand what the couple was getting at.

Frau Van Schuft cut in. "Yes, do you like to, say . . . go to za cliffs and play in za caves?"

The hair stood up on the back of Ian's neck. How could this couple know about his love of exploring? "No," he said carefully, hoping that they didn't know he was lying. "Mostly I like to sit in my room and play jacks. Besides, it's against the rules to go to the caves along the cliffs. You wouldn't catch me near them, what with Madam Scargill keeping a firm eye on anyone who might go there."

Again, the Van Schufts shared a look, and Herr Van Schuft scribbled some notes on a piece of paper in front of him. His wife smiled sweetly at Ian and said, "As you may know, vee vant to adopt a boy and a girl. If vee adopt you, vich of za girls vould you like to have for a sister?"

In his mind he heard Theo's cryptic words. "None of them," he answered with a scowl. "Girls are nothing but a headache, and in my opinion, not one of them is worth adopting."

Herr and Frau Van Schuft both sat back in their chairs, clearly surprised. "Surely you can't mean all of za girls. After all, vee have met some very nice *fräuleins* today," Herr Van Schuft said.

Ian made a production of sighing and rolling his eyes. He wanted to appear as disinterested in the idea as possible. "I don't want a sister," he insisted. "If you two want to adopt a boy and a girl, then I'd rather wait for another couple who want me all to themselves."

Frau Van Schuft was drumming her fingers on the desk thoughtfully. "Ah," she said coolly. Then, after a moment, she stood and extended her hand. "*Danke*. I believe zat is all vee need."

He shook her hand gruffly and got up from the table. "Have a good afternoon," he said over his shoulder, moving to the door. Then a wicked and impulsive thought occurred to him and he turned back to the couple. "You know who goes to the cliffs a lot?" he said with a helpful smile.

"Who?" the couple asked in unison.

"Searle," Ian said easily, letting his smile broaden. "He's always talking about how much he likes exploring the caves and tunnels there."

"Ja?" said Frau Van Schuft, her eyes flashing with renewed interest.

"Vhich von vas he?" asked Herr Van Schuft, searching through his notes.

"Za little chubby boy," said his wife. "Za von who said you reminded him of his fazer before he passed avay."

"Oh, ja," said Herr Van Schuft, and Ian couldn't help noticing the slight look of disappointment on his face. "He didn't object to our adopting a *fräulein*, did he?"

"Dieter," cautioned his wife, giving her husband a pointed nod toward Ian.

"That's okay," Ian said reassuringly, relieved that their focus was apparently off him as a candidate. "Searle would be *perfect* for you." Herr Van Schuft gave him a cautious look, and Ian assumed he'd been a little too eager to offer up Searle, so he added, "Of course, we'd all miss him very much. He's really well liked here at the keep." He had to struggle not to snicker as he said those words. "Good luck in your search," he added, and stepped out into the hall, closing the door behind him. As he passed Madam Scargill, she asked, "How did you do?"

"Very well," said Ian with a smile.

Behind him he heard the door to the drawing room open again and Frau Van Schuft call out, "Madam Scargill? May vee speak vith za boy named Searle once more?"

"I'll get him," said Ian, careful not to laugh.

"Thank you, Ian. I believe he's in the west tower with some of the other children."

Ian nodded and dashed toward the tower. Racing up the narrow staircase to the playroom, he spotted Searle holding James in a headlock, knuckling his head while James screeched to be let go.

"Searle!" Ian yelled furiously, and moved to help free James. "Stop it! You're wanted by the Van Schufts again."

Searle dropped James like a sack of potatoes and said, "Really?"

"Yeah," said Ian, happy for the chance to rid the keep of this bully. "I think they really liked you best."

"Well, of course they did!" he said. "I told you they'd want to adopt me!"

"Yeah, it looks like it's you," Ian murmured, doing his best to pretend to be disappointed. "And it's actually confusing," he continued. "They really seemed like the kind of people who would have preferred to take me over you."

"What do you mean?" Searle asked, eyeing him suspiciously.

"Well, I guess they fancy the area. They kept asking me if I'd been to the cliffs to explore the caves and tunnels there, but I didn't know if I should tell them the truth, so I lied and

211

told them I'd never been. They said that was too bad, because they were really looking forward to having someone who knew the area show them around."

Searle smiled wickedly. "I could show them around," he said. "I've been to a few of those caves."

"Please don't tell them or you'll ruin my chances," pleaded Ian.

But Searle was already brushing roughly past him to the stairs. "Sorry, chap, looks like it's just not your day!" he sang.

As Searle's heavy footsteps thumped down the staircase, Ian looked around the room at the other children gathered there. He wanted to make up with Carl, then go see Theo. "Have you seen Carl?" he asked, helping James to his feet.

"Last I saw him he was in the dorm room," James said. Then he asked, "Are you sure they wanted *Searle?*"

Ian laughed. "Yeah," he said. When James looked disappointed, Ian added, "Don't worry about it. I really think that Searle was the best fit for them."

James shrugged and went off to sit with some other children, and Ian headed back down the staircase. Since he was closer to the girls' dormitory—which was on the opposite side of the keep from his—he decided to look for Carl after he'd spoken with Theo.

When he entered the girls' dormitory in the west wing, he discovered Theo sitting quietly on her bed, gazing across the room out the window. "Hello," he said, relieved to find her so at ease.

"Have they gone yet?" she asked, without turning her head.

"No. They're interviewing Searle again," Ian said with delight.

Theo turned to him, worry in her eyes. "Did you do as I said? Did you tell them that you didn't want to be adopted?"

Ian smiled, crossing the room to her and taking a seat at the foot of her bed. "Yes," he said. When she still looked concerned, he added, "Don't worry, Theo. I made sure they wouldn't take me. In fact, I made sure the only one they'd want was Searle."

"There's something wrong with them," Theo whispered, turning back to the window. Ian felt a little dejected. He thought she'd be happy that he'd followed her instructions and had come up with a plan to rid the keep of its worst nuisance.

"Well, they're not taking either of us," he said. "So as soon as they leave, we won't have to worry about them again."

Theo turned back to him. "Maybe we should try to warn Searle."

"Have you gone daft?" Ian asked, and instantly regretted it. "Er . . . sorry. What I mean is we'll finally be rid of that awful git! So what if they're not nice people? It's exactly what Searle deserves."

Theo's face was still creased with worry and Ian had to work to tramp down his impatience with her. He couldn't understand why she wasn't delighted with the way things had gone. "We're going on a trip to London, you and I," she said after a moment.

That caught Ian completely by surprise. And again, he was a little awed by her gift of foresight, as he knew that no one had told her about the trip yet. "Yes, we're traveling to London with the schoolmasters as soon as you're up for it."

Theo nodded. "It will be a good trip," she said.

There was a knock on the door and they looked up to see Carl there. "Hello," he said, and shuffled his feet in the doorway.

Seeing Carl so sullen made Ian feel even worse about treating his friend so dismissively. "Hello, mate," he said, hoping Carl wouldn't hold it against him.

"Carl," Theo said urgently, "you followed my instructions about the couple, right?"

Carl nodded. "Yes," he said gloomily. "I followed your instructions, Theo. I told them that I'd had a sister once who I'd dearly loved, only she'd died and no one could ever replace her. If the Van Schufts wanted to adopt me, they'd have to agree not to try to replace my dead sister."

"Is that true?" Ian gasped, horrified that Carl might have gone through losing a sister and his parents.

"No," said Carl with a frown. "I made it all up."

"That was genius!" Theo said with a clap of happiness. "Very good thinking, Carl."

Carl only glared at her. "But I liked them, Theo!" he complained. "I mean, I went along with everything you said, but they were so nice and I could tell they were really fond of me until I said that last bit."

Theo got up and went over to rub his shoulder. "I know," she said. "But I have a feeling about these people, and I'm convinced that you wouldn't like living with them."

Carl gave a dramatic sigh, shrugged, and changed the subject. "So, what happened with your interview?"

Theo giggled wickedly, and Ian was relieved. It was the first time he'd seen her crack a real smile in a long while. "I went wild!" she said, laughing.

"Wild?" Carl asked.

"Yes, it was loads of fun," Theo gushed as she clapped her hands. "I began by telling them that I only eat sweets and simply refuse to eat anything that's good for me. Then I said that I never went to bed on time, and that if forced to retire before I was ready, I would find ways to sneak outside and play."

"And they bought your act?" Ian said skeptically. Theo was such a well-behaved girl that he found it difficult to believe she could convince anyone she was otherwise.

"I could tell they weren't sure what to think," she admitted. "But the best part was when Mr. Van Schuft told me that if I came to live with him, I would be expected to follow the rules of the household. I went raving mad and threw a terrible tantrum, lying on the floor and kicking my feet," she added as she lay on the floor to demonstrate. "They couldn't wait to see the back end of me!"

Ian burst into laughter and Carl joined in. Theo pretended to stomp her feet and pound the floor to give them a full taste of her theatrics and the boys howled even more loudly. Just then, however, Ian heard Madam Dimbleby clear her throat from the doorway. He stopped laughing immediately, and Theo jumped up from the floor. Carl was the last to stop giggling when he finally realized that the headmistress was present.

When silence had returned to the room, Madam Dimbleby said, "That'll be enough out of you, Theo," and Ian gulped guiltily as he read the look of deep disappointment on Madam's face. "Masters Wigby and Lawson, please follow me downstairs to say goodbye to the Van Schufts. Miss Fields here will not be having any visitors for the next several days."

"Yes, ma'am," Ian mumbled as he snuck Theo one last smile and followed Carl and Madam Dimbleby out the door.

As they entered the hallway, Theo poked her head out and asked, "Ma'am, just one question if I may?"

Madam Dimbleby paused. "Yes, Miss Fields?"

"Who've they decided on, then?"

"Searle and Isabella," said Madam Dimbleby.

Ian looked at Theo to gauge her reaction. She met his eyes and he knew she was thinking the same thing he was, and this sent a shiver down his spine.

Isabella was a new member of the orphanage, having arrived at Delphi Keep only the month prior, and the one remarkable thing about her was how much she looked like Theo. Save for the birthmark on Isabella's left cheek, she and Theo could easily be mistaken for each other.

And although they looked like sisters, the pair couldn't have been more different in personality. Isabella was incredibly shy and liked to sit alone with her nose buried in a book or drawing in her sketch pad. Theo was happiest when she was surrounded by other children or off exploring with Ian.

That the Van Schufts had chosen Isabella made him believe all the more that there was something suspicious about their sudden appearance at the keep. He knew in his bones that they had been hoping to identify the two children who liked to explore the tunnels along the cliffs. Though for the life of him, he couldn't fathom why. He resolved to keep a closer watch than ever over Theo and not question her gift of forecast again.

"Go on, then," Theo said sadly to him. "And be sure to tell Isabella goodbye from me."

Ian turned and followed the other two down the stairs, but thinking about Theo and her remarkable gifts, he asked, "If Theo's restricted to her room, when will she be allowed to go to London?"

"Ah, yes," said Madam Dimbleby over her shoulder. "The trip to see the earl's aunt. I'm afraid that Miss Fields must serve out her punishment before she's allowed any excursions. If she behaves herself, I'll permit her to travel next Saturday."

"But that's a full week away!" moaned Carl, and Ian had to agree. He'd also really been looking forward to taking the trip to London.

"Be thankful it's not closer to a fortnight," said Madam Dimbleby sternly, and the boys fell silent as they trooped along behind her.

DEMOGORGON'S COMMAND

Toulouse, France, That Same Day

Magus the Black stood stoically in front of a stone hearth, staring into the flames of a blazing fire in an old, abandoned farmhouse in the South of France. No wood was evident in the fireplace, yet the fire raged on. Behind him a low growl came from the corner, where his favorite pet lay with her newborn pups. Her mate, a monstrous beast even larger than she and marked by a white stripe across his hackles, paced just inside the door. A third beast hovered close to Magus.

Still in his youth, the third hellhound was not yet fully grown. He was the only one to have survived from his mother's previous litter of some four years earlier, and only because he'd managed to kill off his littermates. There was a long ragged scar running from just under the young beast's right eye down to his muzzle. It was a souvenir from the brother he'd murdered only a few months before.

The youth eyed his mother's new pups menacingly. She growled at him as if knowing he would like nothing better than to rip them to pieces, which of course he would.

Just then, a tearing echoed about the room. From the

center of the flames, a rush of foul air poured out from the grate, filling the space with a horrible odor as hot gasses flooded the small house. "Magus?" said a terrible voice, the sound gritty and deep, like huge boulders grating and grinding over one another.

"Yes, Sire," Magus replied. "I am here."

"What news have you to share?"

"I have isolated the location of the girl," said Magus.

"Is she in your possession?" asked the voice.

Magus shifted ever so slightly on his feet. "My servants are working to capture her now, Sire."

The voice from the grate rumbled its irritation. "This is unacceptable, Magus. You leave the work I assign you to mere *mortals?*"

"The child is well protected," Magus said, defending his decision. "Medea was nearly killed when she attempted to hunt the girl down. I thought in this instance that a more subtle approach would suit our purposes best."

Smoke curled out from the grate in a huge black fist that unfolded itself and settled heavily in the tiny room, covering the floor, the beasts, and Magus with soot and ash. "How are your servants to know if they have captured the One we seek?" challenged the voice.

"I've instructed them to interview all the girls who fit the description, Sire. They know what to look for and what questions to ask."

"And what of her Guardian?"

Magus explained, "My servants will bring him along as well. We will recover the One and her Guardian and destroy them both."

The flames in the hearth roared and a blaze of intense heat soared up the chimney, crackling and popping with energy. "I'm sensing that you are a long way from their location," said the voice. "Why aren't you with your servants to be certain that they bring back the right children?"

Magus shifted again and his she-beast growled low from the corner. "Our expedition has returned from the south . . . ," he began, then paused as he searched for his next words carefully.

"And?" snarled the voice, rumbling with impatience.

"They have failed to return with the Star," he said, and pulled out an enormous sapphire from the folds of his cloak. "This is what they brought back instead."

Another giant fist of smoke curled out of the hearth, wrapping the sapphire and Magus's hand in a gloomy dark cloud. "You have killed them for their stupidity?" it asked.

"Of course," Magus said easily. "But as you know, Sire, the finger of Zeus points now to Jupiter and Saturn. The time for the Star's discovery is near and I could not risk missing it. That is why I have traveled here on my way to locate the gemstone myself and destroy it before it can be used against us. And, if our understanding of the prophecy is correct, eliminating the gem before it can be broken will work just as well as disposing of the One and her Guardian."

Again the fire within the grate intensified and a small stub of a candle left on the windowsill across the room melted and dripped onto the floor. "Yes," said the voice after a time. "Removing the Star from the prophecy would serve me well, Magus. You have pleased me with this solution."

Magus bowed his head humbly while a small wicked

smile pulled at the corners of his mouth. "Thank you, Sire," he said. "I had thought it a good alternative."

"But your plan to find and identify the child does not impress me," chided the voice, and Magus's smile quickly faded.

"What would you have me do?" the sorcerer asked, but instantly regretted it, because he knew what his sire was likely to ask of him.

There was more grinding from the hearth as the flames turned yellow, then bright red, before simmering down into brilliant orange. "I think we must call upon one of your sisters," said the voice. "Caphiera would be closest and likely best to serve this purpose."

Magus's head snapped up. "I would prefer to work alone," he said carefully.

"*Do not irritate me with your petty squabbles, Magus!*" the voice roared, and a wave of embers flew out of the grate and about the room. The younger beast yelped and darted for the door after one large ember struck him hard in the haunches. Magus bowed his head again. "I meant no disrespect, Sire," he said. "It is just that time is of the essence, and as you know, Caphiera's fortress is at least a few days' journey from here."

"We will need her eventually," growled the voice. "We will need all your siblings, in fact, but she will do for now. Go to the sorceress, strike a truce, and have the girl your servants capture brought before her while you continue south in search of the Star. Caphiera will be able to determine if the child is the One we seek, and if it is the girl, tell the sorceress to dispose of her immediately."

"As you wish, Sire," said Magus, bowing his head again

221

to hide his irritation at being forced to deal with his hateful sister.

After a moment of silence, the voice asked, "What news of our other plans?"

"They go well. The suffering has already begun."

Steam poured from the flames and filled the room with a muggy heat. "I have felt it," said the voice. "It pleases me."

Magus curled his lips away from his jagged teeth again. "You honor me, Sire."

"You have recovered the she-beast?" asked the voice.

Magus glanced toward the corner, where his favorite pet lay with her pups. "Yes. With rest she will recover, and we only lost one of the pups. While I travel south, Medea will stay behind. Her wounds have weakened her and it is time for the young one to prove himself."

"I assume that while you are looking for the Star, you will also recover the final chess set as well?"

"That was part of my plan."

"Kill the craftsman once the pieces are in your hands, Magus. We have no further need of him."

"It shall be done."

"Do not disappoint me this time, Sorcerer," warned the voice as yet another shower of embers flooded the small room.

Magus knelt and bowed low to the fireplace as he said, "I seek only to serve you, Sire."

"See that you serve me well," cautioned the voice, and with another ragged tearing sound it was gone.

As the room settled into silence, a thin stream of smoke rose out of the wall near the window where the candle stub had been, followed quickly by a burst of flame that instantly ignited what was left of the threadbare curtains hanging there.

Magus rose calmly from his kneeling position, and as he did so, flames erupted from the wall, climbing along the wood and fabric all around the window as they raced up to engulf the ceiling. The great hellhound by the door snapped his massive jaws and exited the cottage quickly.

The she-beast got stiffly to her feet and, with her three remaining pups, limped after her mate while smoke and fire rolled across the ceiling and flames began to crawl up two of the other walls.

Magus walked without haste to the doorway, his thoughts as dark as the air around him. Fingers of flame licked at his cloak like winged red dragons, and thick smoke snaked about his feet like charcoal serpents when he finally exited the inferno within the cottage.

He paused on the lawn to stare with narrowed eyes at the mountains that dominated the view to the southwest. About him the fire had spread to the dried grass around the small abandoned home, and as the sorcerer moved forward again, flames from the disintegrating roof jumped to a nearby tree, then to the patch of woods just a few meters away.

By the time the sorcerer reached the first of the foothills to the Pyrenees Mountains, the fire had consumed several hundred acres of prime French countryside.

TEA FOR TOO MANY?

The following Saturday, Ian, Carl, Theo, and School-masters Perry and Thatcher exited the train carrying them from Dover to London. Ian was bursting with excitement as they crossed the platform at Victoria Station and hurried to the stairs that would take them to the streets. During the train ride, he'd eagerly watched out the window as the green British countryside, populated sparsely with homes, had slowly given way to more dense clusters of housing the nearer to the city they drew.

He'd watched the commuters on the platforms of every train station they'd stopped at with equal curiosity, noting that the closer they got to London, the more people he saw wearing fashionable attire.

When they finally made their way to the streets, Ian stared openmouthed at all the view had to offer. There were huge buildings taller than Castle Dover and small shops with large glass panes showcasing the merchandise inside and people seemingly everywhere walking quickly in the late-morning sunshine.

The small group stopped a block from the station, and Ian and Carl waited on bouncing, excited feet as Perry attempted to hail one of the many black taxicabs bustling down the streets. Theo, who by contrast remained calm and unfazed, regarded the pair with an amused smirk. "You lot having fun?" she asked them.

Ian beamed a huge smile at her and Carl said, "I've never been to London before. The largest city I've ever seen was dreary old Plymouth, where I was born."

"Do you ever miss it?" Ian asked.

"No," Carl said in a tone that held no doubt. "Not at all. Before me mum died, we lived in this leaky old flat that was always damp and drafty. After that I was put into the local orphanage and it was even worse than our old flat. There was never enough to eat, and we only had one bed to share for every five boys. It was so crowded I usually slept on the floor—that is, when the weather was warm enough to allow it, which wasn't often."

Ian gave Carl a pat on the shoulder. "Well, at least you're someplace better now," he said.

At that moment a shiny black hackney cab pulled up, and Ian held the door while Theo, Carl, and Thatcher got in and settled. Perry hopped into the front and gave the driver directions, and once Ian had taken his seat and closed the door, the black motorcar pulled away and they entered traffic.

Ian had been in very few motorcars, and he immediately turned his face to the window to eagerly ogle the passing city, but Thatcher interrupted his sightseeing by asking, "Did you bring your silver box?"

Ian turned away from the window and nodded, patting the breast pocket of his new tweed coat. "I've got it, sir," he said.

"Did you bring my crystal?" Theo asked him quietly.

Ian frowned. "No. I left it back in my trunk for safekeeping." He didn't tell Theo but he'd made a point of leaving it behind. He was worried that if Lady Arbuthnot learned of its ability to evoke such powerful images in Theo's mind, she might insist on a demonstration, and Ian didn't want to risk having Theo go through another frightening episode.

Theo looked extremely disappointed. "Oh," she said quietly before turning back to the window.

"Sorry," Ian mumbled as he also turned away but not before feeling a pang of guilt, though he sensed that leaving the crystal at the keep was the right thing to do.

No one else spoke as they continued on their way, and Ian was soon lost again in the sights and sounds of the city. He focused more on the pedestrians as their car whizzed past. He was fascinated by the sheer range of humanity the city offered. There seemed to be people of all shapes, sizes, cultures, and ages, bustling along on their way here and there. Some carried shopping bags, others newspapers, and still others held maps and pointed up at buildings or landmarks.

A few minutes into their journey, the hackney cab paused before entering a roundabout, allowing Ian a moment to take in a busy corner lined with small shops and eateries. His roving eyes fell on something that caused him to gasp.

"What is it?" asked Carl.

"I don't believe it!" Ian exclaimed, and squinted through

the window. "Isn't that the Van Schufts?" he added, pointing to one of the restaurants. Inside, eating their breakfasts and enjoying the view of the people walking by, were a man and a woman who looked remarkably like the couple that had recently been to the keep. Ian was convinced that his old nemesis, Searle, sat beside them, staring dejectedly at a plate of food in front of him.

"Yes," said Carl excitedly as he leaned over Thatcher to get a better look. "Ian, I think you're right! That's the Van Schufts and Searle."

As their motorcar began to move again, the boys waved their hands wildly, trying to get Searle's attention. Just as they entered the roundabout, Searle looked up and his face registered surprise, but before he could wave back, the taxicab had zipped past and out of view. "I wonder where Isabella was," remarked Carl.

"Odd that they're in London," Ian said, wondering why the couple had delayed taking their new family home to the North Country. "I thought they lived in Newcastle."

"Perhaps they're just in town on holiday," suggested Carl.

Ian glanced at Theo, who was staring straight ahead with a far-off look in her eyes. "No," she said. "They don't live in the North. They live in London."

Ian and Carl exchanged a look, and Ian was about to say that the headmistresses had clearly told them where the Van Schufts lived, when Theo cut him off by meeting his eyes and saying, "They lied to us, about that and about everything else."

"Who is this we're discussing?" interrupted Thatcher.

"Just some people who came to visit at the keep last week," said Ian. "Carl and I thought we spotted them in a café back there."

"Ah, yes," said Thatcher. "There's nothing like a visit to London to remind you you're living in a small world."

The trio gave him the same patient look all children give an adult who has just said something silly, and turned back to staring out the windows, although Ian found he could no longer focus on the passing sights. His thoughts kept drifting back to Theo's haunting words about the Van Schufts being liars and to Isabella's absence from the table with Searle and her new parents.

Only a few minutes later, the taxi turned left down a street sheltered by huge oak trees. There were large brownstone apartments set back among the trees, and as the car came to a stop at the end of a cul-de-sac, they had a lovely view of a well-tended park nestled neatly at the end of the road. "Here we are," said Perry from the front seat. "Children, out you go."

While Perry settled the tab with the driver, Thatcher and the children piled out of the car and waited on the curb, staring up at the building in front of them. Large stone carvings encircled the door, which was painted peacock blue and adorned with a bold brass knocker. Ian was anxious to get inside and meet the earl's aunt, so once Perry had rejoined them, he and Carl raced up the stairs. Thatcher followed and grabbed the knocker on the door, giving it three loud clacks.

Ian could hear squawks and peeps and whistles inside, and he noticed everyone on the stairs looking a bit nervously at one another as the strange chorus continued. Finally, a clicking of heels told them the door was about to be opened, and when it was pulled wide, a tiny woman with big brown eyes and a small puckered mouth stood there. She was dressed in a maid's uniform. "Good morning," she said pleasantly; then over her shoulder she called out, "They're here, me lady!"

"Well, show them in, Bessie," called a melodic voice from deep within the flat.

"This way, then," she said, holding the door open.

Perry and Thatcher pulled their hats off as they entered the foyer of the spacious flat. "We're here to see the Lady Arbuth—" Perry began.

"Yes, yes," Bessie interrupted with a wave of her hand. "We know."

"The earl has called ahead for us, then?" asked Thatcher, pivoting to look at the small maid.

Bessie laughed like he'd said the funniest thing. "Oh, no," she said, giggling. "The earl would never spoil the fun."

Thatcher opened his mouth as if to ask a question but Bessie was already closing the door behind them, saying, "Me lady is in the parlor. This way, if you please." And she hurried down a hallway. Thatcher followed the maid; Perry and Theo went next, with Ian and Carl, exchanging quizzical looks, bringing up the rear.

As they walked deeper into the interior, Ian soon learned the source of all the noise they'd heard when they'd knocked on the door. To his amazement and delight, the parlor they were led into was filled with feathers.

There were brilliantly colored parrots and parakeets and

cockatoos and lovebirds, all resting on perches or in cages surrounding a pleasantly plump woman with curly blue-white hair, brilliant cobalt eyes, half-moon glasses, and a playful smile on her creamy white face. In front of her was a table with a large tray piled with seven tea settings and several plates full of delicious-looking biscuits. "Good morning to you," she said as they all filed in.

Behind her a large gray parrot with red tail feathers mimicked, "Good morning! Good morning!" Ian shuffled as close as he dared to one beautiful white cockatoo with a brilliant yellow comb on top of its head. He barely resisted the urge to reach out and stroke it while Perry offered a low bow to the lady and said, "Good morning, my lady. Your nephew the Earl of Kent sends his regards."

Lady Arbuthnot chuckled softly. "I'll bet he does," she quipped. Ian forgot the cockatoo and focused on the earl's aunt. He liked her immediately.

Perry stood straight again and he must have noticed the seven settings on the table, because he said, "Oh, my, I'm so sorry to intrude! You obviously have company coming and we've barged in unannounced."

Lady Arbuthnot tilted her head back and laughed heartily. "Oh, my dear young man," she said as she gave him a wave, "the company I've been expecting is *you*. Now, won't you please have a seat?"

Ian observed six chairs set neatly around the table. He caught Thatcher and Perry exchanging a curious look, but Theo had moved forward to take a seat and was offering Lady Arbuthnot her hand. "It's lovely to meet you," she was saying.

Ian gave Carl a nudge, and the boys took Theo's cue and quickly sat at the table. Thatcher sat down next, and Perry took the last of the seats.

Thatcher then cleared his throat, obviously unsettled by the lady's announcement that they'd been expected, and said, "Yes, well the reason we've come, my lady—"

"I know why you've come," she interrupted, and looked intently around at the children, who all squirmed slightly under her gaze. "One of you is an oracle," she said lightly, "and has the gift of sight."

Theo's hand squeezed Ian's under the table while his mouth dropped open in surprise. "Er . . . yes," said Thatcher. "Are you sure the earl hasn't called ahead to explain our visit?"

Lady Arbuthnot rolled her eyes but the smile never left her face. "I have not heard from my nephew in over a month, and that wicked boy knows that the next time he rings me, he shall have no excuses left not to visit with his dear auntie, but that's another matter. You're curious as to how I knew you were coming and how I knew of your mission?"

Ian and the others nodded.

The lady smiled wisely while she reached for the teapot and poured them each a cup. Ian noticed that when Theo's cup had been filled, Lady Arbuthnot looked her square in the eyes and gave a little wink. "I know of these things because, of course, I also have the gift of sight."

No one spoke. What was there to say, really? Congratulations?

That was all that came to Ian's mind, and he struggled with the idea that the lady seemed a bit off her own nutty.

"I assure you, I'm perfectly sane," she said, and looked pointedly at him as if she'd just read his thoughts. Ian felt an immediate heat shoot to the top of his head, and dropped his eyes to the table. "Now, drink your tea," Lady Arbuthnot said pleasantly. "And I shall give a look into each of your futures."

Not wanting to appear any more troublesome, Ian immediately picked up his teacup and took a sip. As far as tea went, he thought the brew was exceptional, with a light orange scent and a slightly sweet flavor without that bitter aftertaste. While he and the others sipped their tea, Lady Arbuthnot passed around one of the plates of biscuits and Carl took a handful before Perry cleared his throat and gave him a pointed look.

Lady Arbuthnot laughed again, the sound infectious in its merriment. "Oh, let him have his treats," she admonished. "The boy's been half starved until recently, poor lad. Here," she added, handing him the entire plate. "You have these, and if you want more, simply speak up, all right?"

Carl gave her a delighted smile and set the plate down in front of him while he shoveled several cookies into his mouth. "Fank ew, my wady," he mumbled through a mouthful of sweets.

"And you," she said, pointing to Ian, "you I shall read first, as I believe you're the one that trouble is most attracted to, no?"

Ian regarded her nervously, feeling embarrassed to be singled out. He didn't know what to say, so he simply shrugged.

"Drink the rest of your tea, young man," she commanded. "And hand me the cup when you're through."

Ian had no choice but to down the rest of his tea quickly. Lady Arbuthnot nodded with approval and took the cup from him. She gazed into it before she closed her eyes, and a moment passed before she spoke. "Yes," she said. "It's as I thought."

Ian didn't like the deep frown that replaced the happy expression she'd worn since they'd entered the parlor. "You're the one they're after, Ian," the lady said smoothly, and Ian jumped a little, because they hadn't formally introduced themselves to her yet.

"Who's after me, exactly?" Ian asked, and noticed that his voice quivered slightly.

Lady Arbuthnot opened her eyes and looked at him intently. "A great evil has your scent, Ian. Be very careful where you tread. But wonderful travels are ahead of you, along with great peril. You hold the destiny of everyone you've brought along here today in the palm of your hand. You alone hold the key. It is a difficult burden for one so young to carry," she said with a sigh. "But it is your destiny to be of great importance in this world."

Ian gulped as all eyes around the table looked at him. He'd felt the hair rise on the back of his neck while Lady Arbuthnot had spoken, and he knew that her words were indeed true. He couldn't fathom how he knew that, though. And how would he become so important, and what great peril lay ahead for him? He wanted to ask her but he didn't have the chance, because abruptly, Lady Arbuthnot set his cup down and looked around the table at the group. "Who's next?" she asked happily. Everyone hurried to put their teacups on their saucers. No one wanted to go next. "Oh, come on, then," she said with a chuckle. "You're up." And she pointed to Thatcher.

"But I'm not finished," Thatcher said lamely as he lifted his cup and took the tiniest of sips.

"No excuses," Lady Arbuthnot said with a merry laugh. "Now, drink up." Thatcher was compelled to finish his tea quickly and hand her his cup. Ian felt himself tense as the earl's aunt looked into the bottom of the fine porcelain and again closed her eyes. He wondered if everything the lady predicted for her guests held such dire consequences. "I see a rooftop," she began, and Ian felt a tingle of disappointment. "It's made of thatch, and I am told this points to you."

"My name is Thatcher," the schoolmaster said with a slight gasp.

Lady Arbuthnot's eyes flashed open. "Yes, of course!" she said, and clapped her hands happily. "And who is this Elizabeth?" Ian saw Thatcher blush crimson as his brother let out a bark of laughter.

Thatcher cleared his throat and pulled at his collar. "She is a young lady I am an acquaintance of," he said meekly.

Lady Arbuthnot nodded wisely. "There is a choice before her, young man. And I know she will choose you, but events far out of your control will pull the two of you apart afterward. My advice is to save her this heartache and go forward alone."

Thatcher looked shocked. "What events?" he asked.

Lady Arbuthnot shook her head sadly but did not elaborate. "You will be asked to join a quest which centers around this young man," she said, again pointing to Ian, who felt his own cheeks flush with heat, and he began to wonder with irritation why the lady was picking on him of all people. "This request is not one you can ignore," she continued. "Although the way before you is fraught with dangers you can't even imagine, you must proceed through the fog."

Thatcher's expression turned puzzled as he glanced from Ian—who simply shrugged—back to the lady. "I'm afraid I don't quite understand," he said to her. "What sort of quest?"

Ian nodded. He wanted to know more about this quest too, but Lady Arbuthnot had already set down Thatcher's cup and was looking expectantly at Perry. "You're next!" she sang.

Perry handed her his cup and Ian noticed that his hand shook slightly. Lady Arbuthnot gazed into the bottom of the cup and again closed her eyes. "Ah, yes," she said. "P is for . . . Percy . . . no . . . no, it's more like . . . Perry, and G is for . . . Goodwill?"

Perry gasped. "Good*wyn*," he corrected. "Perry Good-wyn."

Lady Arbuthnot opened one eye. "That was good, wasn't it?" she asked with a knowing smile.

"Very good," he admitted, clearly impressed. Ian saw that his schoolmaster had gone rather pale.

"Yes, now, you," she said, opening both eyes and pointing to Perry, "are brother to him?" And she pointed to Thatcher.

"Yes, my lady," he said. "We're twins, in fact."

Lady Arbuthnot smiled. "You shall share much the same destiny. You too will be asked along on this quest. It will be fraught with the unknown and unexpected, but you are required to go as well. You must proceed even when you think there is no hope, for you see, Perry, there is always hope."

Perry's face reflected Ian's troubled thoughts. What quest was she talking about and why did she keep bringing up all of this danger business?

He opened his mouth to ask her, but the lady turned abruptly away from Perry and focused on Carl, who had also gone starkly pale when he realized it was his turn. "And now you, young man," she said.

Reluctantly, Carl passed his teacup forward, and the lady did the whole peering-into-the-cup-and-closing-her-eyes bit. Ian sat back in his chair and crossed his arms with a scowl. He was beginning to believe that maybe the lady was full of nonsense. He could hazard a guess that the next thing she mentioned would be that Carl was going on a quest filled with danger.

She surprised him, however, when she opened her eyes and a sad expression replaced the merry one she'd been wearing. "Oh, my . . . you poor, poor boy," she said softly. "You've been through some awful ordeals for someone so young."

Carl let out a small noise that sounded like a squeak.

"Your mother, Jillian, is very sorry she had to leave you, dear. She tells me that she held on as long as she could, as she very much wanted to stay with you, but her lungs were very weak and she couldn't battle her illness any longer in the end."

Carl's lower lip began to tremble and moisture welled in his eyes as he struggled to hold on to his composure. Again, he made a squeaking noise.

"Your mother also tells me you've been very brave and she was with you in that awful place by the water. You were in another orphanage before my nephew found you, am I right?" Carl nodded and dropped his eyes to the tabletop.

The lady continued. "Well, she's thrilled that you've come to live at the keep. But, she wonders if that was the right move, because she knows that now you will be asked to become a warrior as brave as any that have ever walked the earth. She says that it is your destiny to be a keeper of sorts for this young man." The lady glanced at Ian, who squirmed under her focus again. "He will need your protection and your fierce courage and you shall not fail him, even if it means putting your own life in danger."

Carl sniffed loudly, cleared his throat, and looked up at Ian, and in that moment something odd passed between the boys that felt to Ian like a silent understanding that from this date forward, the two would always be the best of chums.

"Your mother says she will be with you along this journey, and you must never doubt her love or the pride she has for what a fine young man you are," the lady finished as she handed Carl his teacup, and the boy looked at the bottom as if he were searching for the face of his mother among the bits of tea leaves.

"Thank you, my lady," he said in a croaky whisper.

Without delay, Lady Arbuthnot swiveled her attention to Theo. "Now it's time for me to talk with this young lady in private," she announced, and Ian blinked in surprise. He had expected Theo's future to be told to the lot of them, just like the others. "The rest of you may take a biscuit and wait out in the foyer," she instructed. "I will send your friend along shortly."

Theo gave Ian a panicked look as he got up from his chair, and Ian hesitated. "I'd like to stay, my lady," he said.

Lady Arbuthnot smiled patiently. "Ian," she said, "what I have to say is for Theodosia's ears only. She will be in the best of care with me, and you shouldn't worry. All right?"

Ian looked back at Theo, who gave a reluctant nod. "It's all right," she said. "I'll be fine."

"You sure?" he asked.

Theo nodded again, and after squeezing her shoulder, Ian walked out with the rest of the group to the foyer, where for a minute or two no one spoke or looked at each other. Finally, Carl broke the silence. "That was . . . odd."

Thatcher let out a short laugh and Ian broke into a grin as the tension in the room evaporated. "*Very* odd," Thatcher agreed. "I'm afraid I don't quite know what to make of it."

"It's all rubbish," scoffed Perry. "She could easily have gotten our names from the earl and played a parlor trick on us in there."

"But what about what she told Carl? She called his mother by name," protested Ian. It was strange that, like Perry, he'd been eager to believe the old woman a fraud until she'd talked about Carl's deceased mother. "And how she knew about your friend Elizabeth," he added, turning to Thatcher, who again turned a brilliant shade of red at the mention of the name.

"Lucky guesses," said Perry with a cough, but Ian caught a small shadow of doubt on his face. Perry added, "And did you see how the table was set for seven? There were only six of us gathered. If she is the gifted woman she claims to be, why the extra place setting?"

238

At that exact moment the knocker gave three loud clacks and Ian and the others jumped. Bessie hurried past them on her way to the door, and as she opened it, she said, "Ah, Miss Giles. So good of you to drop by."

Ian leaned out to see around Perry as a tall, slender, and impossibly beautiful woman with long chestnut hair and large brown eyes in a heart-shaped face stepped into the foyer. "Hello, Bessie," she said in a high, lilting voice. "I know I don't have an appointment, but I have a rather urgent matter and I was wondering if the lady was free."

"She's expecting you," said Bessie confidently. "Already got the tea laid out. She'll be with you shortly, as she's just finishing up with one last guest."

Turning to look at the four people huddled in the foyer, Miss Giles said, "Please excuse me if I'm intruding on your time with Lady Arbuthnot. I can come back later if you'd like."

Ian smiled shyly as her eyes passed over him, and Bessie, who had just shut the door, gave a wave of her hand and clucked. "Naw, naw. As I said, the lady is expecting one last visitor this morning. We didn't know it'd be you, but it's good that you're here now."

Just then Theo appeared in the foyer, a rather dreamy look on her face. "She's ready for you," she said without hesitation to Miss Giles. Ian was amazed at the transformation since only a few minutes earlier, when Theo had looked so afraid. He wondered what Lady Arbuthnot could have said that would have made Theo look so genuinely happy.

"You know the way to the parlor?" Bessie was asking the newest visitor.

"Yes, yes," said Miss Giles. Turning to the dumbfounded group in the foyer, she added, "So sorry again to have intruded."

"No, no," said Perry quickly, and Ian noticed a pink hue to his cheeks. "We were just leaving."

The woman gave them a nod and an enchanting smile before hurrying off, and Thatcher, Perry, Ian, and a mesmerized Carl watched her walk elegantly down the hallway and round the corner. Ian wished he could have talked with her a bit, because she'd been incredibly lovely to look at.

"We're ready to go, then," announced Theo, causing all four of them to jump again. Ian caught Bessie stifling a giggle.

"Yes," Perry said, coughing. "Of course, of course! Come along, everyone. It's time to be off. Bessie, would you please thank Lady Arbuthnot on our behalf for her generous hospitality?"

"Of course, sir," said Bessie with a warm smile as she held open the door for them.

Ian and Carl hurried out after Thatcher and Perry, and when Theo stepped onto the stairs, Ian heard her say, "Thank you, Bessie. I'll see you next Saturday."

Bessie replied, "Very good, young miss, very good. Next Saturday it is, then."

The group gathered at the bottom of the stairs and everyone seemed to be talking at once. Carl and Ian were going on about the sudden appearance of the beautiful woman, and Thatcher was slapping his brother on the arm, saying, "Explain *that*, Perry! The seventh setting at the table went to that lovely creature!"

"Coincidence," scoffed Perry, but he seemed rather shaky in his conviction.

"And what was all that business about quests and danger and fog?" Carl asked.

"Yeah, what *was* that about?" Ian said. "And what did she say to you?" he asked Theo, remembering belatedly her change in demeanor.

Theo began telling him but was immediately drowned out by the argument their two schoolmasters were having.

"You're joking!" Thatcher was saying loudly as he gave his brother a firm poke with his finger. "Perry, the lady's accuracy was uncanny! She couldn't have just *guessed* all of our names and the names of people we're connected to!"

"Rubbish," said Perry, pulling at his coat sleeves. "That was all rubbish."

"*Rubbish?*" Thatcher barked. "How can you say it was rubbish? If the earl didn't tell her about us, then she couldn't possibly have gained those intimate details through any other means! Besides, I'm quite certain the earl knows nothing about Eliza—er . . . my personal acquaintances."

"Let's not stand here arguing the point, Thatcher," his brother snapped. "After all, we've got an hour or two until our meeting with the professor, so let's get the children something to eat, shall we?"

"But—" Thatcher protested, not letting the point drop.

"I said enough!" Perry nearly yelled. Then he immediately softened his voice when he noticed the children all staring at him in shock. "I'm simply saying that I need more evidence before I am convinced of this fortune-telling business."

"Very well," said Thatcher stiffly. "Come along, children. I know of a fine pub a few blocks from here which serves the best bangers and mash in London."

They were soon comfortably seated at The Village Hog, a pub on the bottom floor of a large six-story building that reeked of stale beer and tobacco smoke.

Now that Theo wasn't skipping along ahead, Ian took the opportunity to ask her again what the earl's aunt had said. Theo furrowed her brow as she tried to explain it. "It was the oddest thing," she said. "Lady Arbuthnot didn't look into my teacup. She said there wasn't any need. She already knew what she needed to know about me."

"Which was?" asked Ian, and he was aware that everyone at the table was listening to their exchange.

"Well," Theo said, appearing to be working out the words, "she said that I was an oracle, someone able to predict the future, and that I am quite gifted. She asked me if I'd seen anything that had frightened me, and I told her about the visions that I'd had out on the lawn during lessons."

For all Perry's doubts, Ian noticed that his schoolmaster's posture suggested that he was very interested in Theo's experiences with Lady Arbuthnot. "What did she think of them?" Perry asked, leaning across the table to hear her over the din of the pub.

"She said she's had this most awful feeling for years that something terrible was going to overtake the land, but she hadn't known what it was. She said that the things that I saw in my visions were very detailed given that I've had no training, and that to help me she would be willing to tutor me in the development of my abilities so that I might better tolerate what I'm seeing."

"Did you mention the crystal?" asked Ian, wondering just how much Theo had told the lady.

"What crystal?" Thatcher asked.

Ian looked at Theo, who nodded. "The night Theo arrived at the keep, the man who delivered her had it. He tried to take it as payment for rescuing her, but Madam Scargill discovered his thievery and demanded the necklace be turned over to her. When the beast destroyed the inside of the keep, I found the necklace among the rubble, and I knew it belonged to Theo, especially after I saw her mother wearing it in that picture on the wall at your cottage," he said, looking at Perry.

Perry nodded but Thatcher looked at his brother and said, "What photo?"

"Do you remember the little photograph on the wall next to the desk?" Perry asked.

"The one with the woman and the child?"

"Yes," Perry answered. "That is apparently a photo of Theo and her mother."

"Odd coincidence," said Thatcher with a smug look and a wink at Ian, who understood that he was making fun of his brother.

"So what does this crystal necklace have to do with anything?" asked Carl.

"When I wore it, my visions became more . . ." Theo searched for the right words. "Clear. They were bigger and more intense."

Ian frowned. He didn't want to discuss the crystal and its

effect on Theo, because he was still worried that she'd want to try it on again and would have another frightful episode.

"Do you think that this crystal is acting as some sort of amplification?" asked Thatcher.

Theo gave him a puzzled look. "What do you mean?"

"It's possible that the necklace is enhancing your natural abilities," he explained. "It may be acting as a type of antenna."

Perry asked, "What type of crystal is it?"

"I'm not sure," said Ian, searching his memory to see if he'd ever come across something similar. "It looks very much like quartz. It's white and cloudy, except there's this bit of pink in the center."

"I should like to see this necklace," said Thatcher. "Theo, are you wearing it now?"

"No," she said, and her eyes met Ian's. "I took it off after that awful experience on the lawn and gave it to Ian for safekeeping."

Everyone looked expectantly at Ian, who squirmed under the sudden focus. "It's back at the keep," he admitted, and he would have elaborated but at that moment the barmaid arrived with a huge tray of food and began passing out everyone's lunch.

Conversation was limited while the hungry group dove in to their sausage and mashed potatoes. While they were eating, Carl asked Thatcher, "Schoolmaster, did I hear you say that we're not returning to the keep after lunch?"

Thatcher finished the mouthful of sausage he'd just taken before answering. "That's correct, Carl. I've made an appointment with an old professor of mine from Cambridge.

We'll be visiting with him after our meal here." Turning to Ian, he asked again, "You've still got your box?"

Ian reached into his coat and pulled out the small square silver treasure and laid it on the table. "I've been trying to open it for the past fortnight, but I still can't figure out how to get the lid up without prying it open."

Perry wiped his hands on his napkin and said, "You know, I didn't have a very good look when it got passed round the table at the castle. May I see it again?"

Ian handed the box over, hoping that maybe the schoolmaster could figure it out. Perry lifted the box to eye level and turned it about several times before pulling at the lid, which didn't budge. "I've tried that," Ian said, and Carl hid a smirk.

Perry gave him a weary look and turned the box about again, searching for a possible weak point. Finally, after a few more shakes and pulls on the lid, he handed it back to Ian. "I can't see how to get it open," he said. "But there is definitely something inside."

Ian nodded. "Yes, I've heard it too," he answered, "but I haven't a clue about what it could be."

"We'll leave it to the professor to have a look," said Thatcher. "He'll likely be able to decipher the lettering on the sides of your box, which might point to how to open it. He might also be able to give us some clues about the writing on the walls of the caverns."

"Perhaps he can also tell us why Ian's name appeared in the first cavern," Perry added, and Ian felt his cheeks flush when Theo and Carl each gave him a shocked look.

"Oh, yeah," he said to them sheepishly, remembering

that he hadn't shared that particular fact with his friends. "I forgot to tell you two, Schoolmaster Goodwyn was able to translate a section that had a message for me."

"What did it say?" asked Theo with large round eyes.

"Nothing to be alarmed about," he assured her, adding a laugh to show he found it all very amusing. "It just said for me to go that way—toward the box at the end of the tunnel."

Carl gulped. "That, or it was leading you toward the beast," he said.

All eyes pivoted to Carl, and Ian's good humor from just a moment before vanished instantly. "Oh, my," murmured Thatcher into the heavy silence that followed. "I never thought of that."

Theo's eyes shifted to Ian and she looked intensely worried. "It's more likely the writing was referring to the box," he said firmly, making up his mind that it must be that, because who could possibly want to cause him harm?

But Theo's concern seemed only to deepen. "When is the professor expecting us?" she asked Thatcher.

The schoolmaster glanced at his watch. "Shortly," he said. "Is everyone finished?" Four heads nodded, and after setting a few coins on the table, the group was off again.

THE SORCERESS OF ICE

Caphiera the Cold's fortress was nearly impossible to find. It was hidden in a mountain pass at one of the highest points of the Pyrenees Mountains. Few mortals had ever stumbled into it. None had ever managed to stumble back out.

But Magus the Black had been there before, so he remembered the way. He also knew that his sister would likely be aware of his presence within the pass long before he knew of hers. He worried a bit about how she might react to his visit. If it was anything like the last time they'd met, it was sure to leave a mark.

As the morning sun crested the great mountain range, Magus reached the pass and stood before it for a moment to catch his breath. His pets were not at his side. The she-beast, Medea, was too weak from her bullet wounds to travel beyond the small cave he'd found for her and her two pups—the third had taken a wrong turn into the jaws of his older brother—in the foothills of the Pyrenees. Her mate, Kerberos, remained at Medea's side while their master was away, and the young, still unnamed beast was ordered to hunt for food, to distract him from killing any more of his siblings.

Magus felt his pets' absence, but he knew that to have traveled through the pass with them would have meant certain death for the hellhounds. Caphiera would delight in that cruelty, so he hadn't risked it.

Now, as he stood alone at the mouth of the passage, he remembered that this harmless-looking entrance fed into a narrow corridor of rock, ice, and snow that twisted and turned back upon itself so often that those travelers unfortunate enough to attempt to navigate it became dizzy before they'd gone half a kilometer. Magus eyed the rocky alley sullenly, noting that the temperature within it dipped below this elevation's usual frigid degree.

He detested the cold and growled low in his throat as he prepared himself to enter the pass. Pulling the folds of his cloak more securely around himself, he pushed forward. He'd gone only a short way when he heard the faintest whistle from overhead. The sorcerer immediately spun to the right, ducking low underneath a rocky overhang just in time to hear three dull thuds behind him that shook the snow-covered ground. He glanced over his shoulder and eyed the place where he'd been standing just a moment before. Imbedded in the snowy surface were three enormous icicles.

Magus snarled and waved his hand at the deadly daggers. They immediately melted into small nubs barely big enough to poke out of the snow. "Caphiera!" he bellowed into the stillness of the pass. "Enough of this! I have come to talk about a truce."

All was quiet save for the echo of his voice. For long

seconds nothing answered his call; then suddenly the stillness was broken by a sound like the springtime cracking of ice over a frozen lake. The noise ran up and down the walls of the pass, reverberating until it rattled the ground. Magus braced himself under the overhang, gripping the icy ridge and grimacing against the unsettling noise as it bounced back and forth all along the corridor. Gradually, the rumbling grew louder and louder, until it was a roar that made the ground shake and small bits of rock from the high walls of the passage come loose, dropping to the ground like small grenades. Magus growled again before darting from under his outcropping and running as fast as he could.

Behind him a great wall of snow came tumbling down the mountainside and funneled its way into the pass. Churning white powder as powerful as any tidal wave chased him deeper and deeper into the narrow passage. Magus allowed himself one glance over his shoulder, and that was enough to encourage him to increase his speed.

Finally, running out of patience, he rounded a particularly sharp corner, twisted on his feet with unnatural agility, and held up both hands. The massive wall of snow followed, barely losing speed, and swelled up above him to a monstrous height, blocking out the sun as it prepared to devour him whole. But suddenly the snow was met with a heat so intense that it instantly turned the frozen wave to steam, which rose above Magus harmlessly before condensing into white clouds that covered the sky.

More waves followed the first, yet Magus used his powers against the crushing force again and again until finally the walls of snow stopped churning forward and settled into one great pile of white. Slowly the sorcerer lowered his hands. Though he was now safe from being crushed, he was firmly barricaded into the deepest section of the pass by a wall ten meters high of deeply packed snow.

He turned and surveyed the pass ahead, which angled down and away from where he now stood. The path was clear, if a bit icy, and Magus brushed off his white-dusted cloak, satisfied that he could move forward again.

For a good stretch he heard nothing, yet he kept careful watch lest his sister try to send another avalanche or shower of icicles after him. Finally, after he'd wound his way through a few more sections of the pass, he heard an eerie cackle that sounded much like two icebergs grating against each other. The sorcerer moved toward the noise and soon came to a stop in front of a bridge made of solid ice that spanned a great pit hemmed in by the mountain walls.

On the other side of the pit, perched almost demurely on a rocky ridge, was a glistening fortress made completely out of gleaming blocks of ice. Magus knew that inside the formidable structure his less-than-devoted sister lay in wait. The sorcerer understood she would not come out to greet him unless he found a way across the bridge.

Magus walked to the pit's edge and looked down. Dotting a rocky floor were thousands of menacingly arranged daggerlike icicles. Magus sighed and waved his hand over the pit and immediately the icicles melted. The sorcerer's lips peeled back in a satisfied smirk, but within seconds the icicles began to grow back, until Magus could swear they were twice as tall as before.

Again he waved his hand above the ravine, putting a bit more effort into it than before, and the icicles melted into nothingness, only to grow back even faster, until they were now three times as tall as they had originally been. Their tips came to just below the icy bridge.

"Clever," muttered Magus as he backed away from the edge. Another cracking of ice sounded from deep inside the fortress. Caphiera was having herself a good laugh. Magus scowled and walked over to inspect the bridge.

Planks of clear ice were suspended over the pit by frozen ropelike tresses. Tentatively, he placed one foot on the first plank. It held for a few seconds, then began to melt. In no time it cracked in half and fell away from the supports, striking one of the long icicle spikes and shattering into a thousand tiny shards.

Magus stepped back to the safety of the ledge and bent low while he studied the rest of the planks. He could tell from this angle that though they started out rather thick, the closer they got to the middle of the bridge, the thinner they became.

Anyone lured onto the bridge would soon find the planks melting away beneath his feet, and in the middle would reach wafer-thin sheets of ice that would easily break under the weight of even the smallest rodent.

Crossing the ravine by the bridge was out of the question. Frustrated, Magus looked about for anything handy he might use to get across the expanse. Nothing but ice, snow, and solid rock stared back at him. Adding to his irritation, yet another cackle sounded from inside the fortress. Magus spat into the snow, and when his spittle hit the white surface, it hissed, suddenly giving the master of fire an idea.

He turned his back on the bridge and the fortress and retraced his steps through the pass until he came to the wall of snow that barricaded him in. Here he found a narrow crevice within the rock wall and wedged himself into it while bracing for what was to come. Closing his eyes and concentrating all his power, he raised both hands and unleashed the heat he commanded in slow steady waves.

The temperature rose within that section of the passageway and the snow began to melt, first in small drips but very soon in earnest, until it was a stream of water trickling past his feet. Magus continued emanating the waves of heat until the stream became a river of cold water washing past him, carrying large blocks of snow with it. The sorcerer paused only to move his way up the crevice when the water became too deep, but that was the only break he allowed himself.

Finally, exhausted and soaking wet, he managed to climb along the face of the rock out of the now raging river and in one final command he called back all the heat he had expelled into the wall of snow. This warmed and dried him immediately while instantly turning the water into solid ice.

Magus stepped onto the slippery surface and walked calmly toward Caphiera's fortress. Just as he'd hoped, the river he'd created had gushed over the side of the ravine, filling much of the expanse, and was now frozen fast. The sorcerer had only to drop a short way and wind his way through the spikey forest before climbing up onto the other side.

When at last he pulled himself out of the pit and stood solidly on snowy ground, he came face to face with Caphiera the Cold, great Druid sorceress and master of the dark art of ice. She stood imposing and tall, resembling Magus only in stature and the shape of her sharply pointed tiny teeth. In all other ways she was like no one else on earth.

The sorceress was dressed in a long ivory fur-lined coat that trailed to the ground, pooling around sterling silver pointed-toe boots. Small clear crystals sewn into the hem of her coat glinted in the light and clinked and jangled together when she moved. Around her neck she wore an alabaster cashmere scarf fringed with white ermine tails tipped in black. But while Caphiera's garments were indeed refined and beautiful, they did nothing to enhance the appearance of their owner.

The sorceress's skin was a cool blue that shimmered with a dusting of sparkly white snowflakes. Her hands, which were a deeper hue than her face, were adorned with rings of topaz, aquamarine, and sapphire, and around her wrists were bracelets of blue diamonds set in polished platinum. And just like her clothing, as lovely as these baubles were, they could not detract from the sorceress's frightful bony fingers, which curled out like claws and ended in sharp daggerlike fingernails of ice.

Above the neck, things were even grimmer. Caphiera's nose extended several inches from her hideous face and ended in an icy point that nearly touched the top of her full azure lips when she smiled. Her hair was the color of snow, manelike, with small tufts sticking out wildly. But her eyes were perhaps her most disquieting feature. They were large, lined with long cobalt lashes, and completely white—irisless and void of any color save for two black pupils currently aimed menacingly at her visitor.

"Magus, my brother," she said in a low crackling voice, "what an unpleasant surprise."

Magus calmly wiped the snow and dirt from his hands as he stood up straight and firm. "Caphiera," he said, making sure to avoid her eyes. "I see you've gotten yourself a new cloak."

Caphiera cackled. "Shows off my eyes, wouldn't you say?"

Magus focused hard on Caphiera's hemline. "I'm sure it does, Sorceress."

Caphiera leaned back and let loose a great laugh that echoed the sound that had started the avalanche. "What, no kiss for your sister?" she taunted.

"Not this time," he answered, and got right to the point. "Demogorgon has sent me. He requires your assistance."

Caphiera's black pupils contracted as they roved her brother's face. "Bah!" she said. "Laodamia's riddle sending you on wild goose chases again?"

Magus bristled and smoke trailed out of his nose in two fine streams. "Our *sire* requires your involvement," he said sternly, reminding her of her obligations.

Caphiera spat into the snow herself, but where her spittle landed, a small icicle formed. "What have I to do with your riddles?"

"We have the child," Magus began.

Caphiera's white eyes widened. "You have discovered him?" she asked.

"We have discovered *her*," said Magus. "The child we seek is a girl."

"Why have you not destroyed her?" Caphiera demanded.

"She had eluded our efforts until last week and I have since been called to the south on more pressing business. In my absence, my servants have managed to capture a girl that fits the description of the One we seek, but as I am headed south, and my she-beast is too injured to travel back to England to compare her scent, I am unable to confirm if it is her. This is the reason Demogorgon requests your services. Only one of us can tell if she is the child we've been searching for."

Caphiera's eyes narrowed. "What is this more pressing business you have in the south?"

Magus hesitated and considered lying, but he suspected that his spiteful sister would smell the deception and then refuse to help. "I am in search of the Star," he said through gritted teeth. "The prophecy states that the time for its appearance has arrived, and it must not fall into the wrong hands when it is discovered."

Caphiera's expression turned to one of disdain and the wicked sorceress crossed her arms. "Magus," she said, tsking. "You and your beasts have failed to find that gem for centuries. What makes you believe you won't fail again?"

Magus's cloak began to smoke and all around him the air filled with the scent of sulfur. "Do not press me, Sister," he warned.

Caphiera's lips pulled back into a grizzly smile. She was enjoying herself immensely. "I told you what I required the last time we spoke," she said. "My demands for assisting you on your missions have not changed."

Magus's cloak smoked even more and small embers danced along its hem. "It is agreed," he said at last. "You will go to England and kill the child while I'm away in exchange for control of the lands of Prussia."

Caphiera's awful smile broadened and she rubbed her hands together greedily. "Now, tell me where to find this girl," she said.

"My servant and his wife have extracted her from the orphanage where she lived. It is an old keep near the grounds of Castle Dover," said Magus. "They are currently holding her in my flat outside London, in the cell downstairs, where her screams cannot be heard."

"And if your servants have bungled it again, and she is not the child we seek?"

Again, smoke wafted out of Magus's nose, and a small flame erupted along the edge of his cloak as his anger simmered. "My servants have also taken a boy from the keep. We thought him to be the Guardian, but he shows no sign of trying to protect the girl. Still, he may be able to tell us more about the children at the orphanage, and through him we might discover which child is the true Guardian. If the girl we hold is the One, the mark and her abilities should be in evidence."

"I am aware of what to look for, Brother," said Caphiera impatiently, and the temperature around her dipped another frosty degree. "Just make sure your servants do their part."

Magus paused before he said, "My she-beast has communicated to me that one of Laodamia's treasure boxes might have been discovered in a cave near the cliffs. My servants have confirmed this with the boy, who claims that the box was stolen from him by another boy at the orphanage. I would like to recover the artifact and I would like the true Oracle and her Guardian disposed of."

"Consider it done, my brother," said Caphiera coolly. "And consider them dead."

THE NUTLEY PROFESSOR

The group of five from Dover stopped outside Number 11 Cromwell Road. Thatcher reached the top step first and pressed the buzzer on the side of the door, and after a time they all heard a gruff "Coming! I'm coming."

The door was yanked open and a tiny man—no taller than Carl—with curly white tufts of hair sticking madly out the sides of his head and matching his overgrown mustache, stood there, squinting through round wire glasses up at the person on his doorstep. "Hello, Professor!" Thatcher said enthusiastically.

"Who's there?" asked the professor as he held his hand up to shield his eyes from the glare of the sun. "Ah, Master Goodwyn," he said. "Right on time."

Thatcher gestured to his side. "Good to see you again, Professer Nutley. You remember my brother, Perry?"

The professor looked at Perry and nodded. "Yes, yes," he said. "Good of you two to drop by."

"And we've got the young lad who found the artifact I told you about," continued Thatcher, turning to look behind him for Ian, who smiled and held up the box so that the professor could squint down at him.

Ian climbed the stairs and introduced himself. Carl and Theo followed suit, and after everyone's name had been passed around, the professor shuffled away from the door with a "Come in, won't you?"

Thatcher and Perry hurried through, but Ian and Carl exchanged a look as a rather foul smell coming from the interior of the flat met their nostrils. "Hurry up!" urged Theo, pushing from behind. "You don't want the professor to think you're being rude."

Ian grimaced at the scent of something old and musty, but hurried in, anxious to hear about his treasure box.

He noticed immediately that their host was living a life as unkempt as his hair. There were newspapers, books, and what looked like bits of tossed-away paper everywhere. Even the stairs leading to the next floor were covered in piles of clutter, making them look precarious to navigate. He suspected that if Madam Scargill were ever to see this place, she would faint dead away. His headmistress believed *strongly* that a virtuous life was a sparkling clean and uncluttered one.

"This way," directed the professor as Ian and the others lingered in the hallway, taking in the mess. Thatcher coughed uncomfortably and swung his head toward the professor's form disappearing around a corner. "After him, children," he said.

They all followed the professor, winding their way through the piles of clutter to turn a corner into what looked like a sitting room by design but was now a depository for more papers, books, newspapers, and odds and ends. "In here," called the old man, his voice drifting to them from the dining room beyond. Ian and the others continued with mild trepidation.

Finally, the group filed into a room at the back of the flat that appeared to be the professor's library. Ian looked around amazed. Bookshelves lined all four walls and were squeezed with so many books that the shelves themselves were barely distinguishable. Bits of paper were stuffed between the books, and here and there the odd clay pot or ancient relic managed to find a perch on top of piles of paper, books, and other junk. Among it all sat various cardboard and leather tubes. Ian could only wonder at what they might possibly contain. Only a small square in the center of the room was clear of debris.

The professor squeezed between a stack of books almost as tall as he was, around to his desk, and taking a seat, he peeked over the top of his overcrowded workspace at the group. "Let's have a look at what you've brought along to show me, shall we?" he said.

With little butterflies of excitement fluttering in his stomach, Ian handed over his box to the professor, who took it and set it on his desk. He then fumbled through several piles of paper and unearthed a bit of cloth. With this he wiped his wire-rimmed glasses before focusing on the artifact. "Hmmmm," he said as he focused on the relic, picking it up and turning it over several times before setting it down and opening a nearby drawer.

For what seemed like a frustratingly long time, the professor rummaged through the contents of the drawer, tossing bits of twine, paper, pencils, paper clips, and ink pens onto the desk as he searched for something. Finally, he gave a happy "Aha!" and pulled out a magnifying glass. This he placed over the top of the box, lowering it to focus as he whispered, "Fascinating."

Ian resisted the urge to fidget nervously while Thatcher asked, "You recognize the writing?"

"It's very old," said the professor. "The writing is Phoenician, from a period which saw some of the first lettering ever to come out of Greece, in fact. I'd put it at 1600 to 1200 BC," he concluded, looking back up at them. Blinking to focus his eyes again, he asked Ian, "Wherever did you find such a treasure?"

"In a cavern near the Cliffs of Dover, sir," Ian said. He wasn't sure how much detail he was supposed to give about the location of his discovery.

The professor turned to Thatcher quizzically. "You found this in a cavern near Dover, *England?*" he asked.

"Yes, Professor, about two kilometers southeast of Castle Dover, along with this bit of writing we found on the walls where the box was hidden," he said, passing forward the messages he'd copied from the cavern.

The professor pulled Thatcher's notebook close, and his bushy eyebrows rose in surprise. "Is this some sort of a trick, then?" he demanded, and Ian cringed as he thought about the earl's identical reaction back in the cavern.

But Thatcher seemed taken aback by the question. "No, sir," he insisted. "That's where we found the box and the writing."

The professor glanced back at Thatcher's notes and Ian

watched as his lips moved silently before he mumbled, "It isn't possible."

"What, Professor?" asked Perry.

"I'm afraid you two are the butt of a joke," the professor said, leaning back in his chair with a contemptuous smirk.

Ian and Theo exchanged looks, and Ian noticed she didn't at all seem pleased. "I'm afraid I don't understand," said Thatcher, pulling their attention back to the professor.

"This," said the professor, pointing to Thatcher's notes from the wall, "is written in Linear B script, or what is commonly recognized as ancient Greek and what the Phoenician alphabet—like the writing from this box—evolved into. I would date this writing from your notes as much younger than the lettering on the box, approximately 400 BC. As the Greeks weren't anywhere near the British Isles four hundred years before Christ, I believe someone's pulling a lark here, and I suspect it's these very clever children you've brought with you today."

Ian took a step back when both his schoolmasters turned as one to stare reproachfully at him. He vigorously shook his head. "I swear!" he said, holding up his hands in surrender. "I've played no prank!"

"He's telling the truth," said Theo, stepping up to Ian's defense. "He's not lying. We discovered the hidden tunnel with writing on the walls and the box in one of the chambers of the tunnel by accident. We had nothing to do with putting the script or the box there."

The professor gave them a doubtful look. "Then you are also the recipients of a rather sophisticated prank."

"But who would have done such a thing?" asked Thatcher, putting Ian's thoughts into words. "And who would have written this line?" he asked, pointing to the first page of his notes.

The professor held his magnifying glass up to the paper and translated out loud: " 'Young boy, Wigby, come this way.' " The professor furrowed his brow and he glanced back at Ian. "Your last name is Wigby?"

Ian felt that same haunting feeling he'd had when Thatcher had read that line in the cave. "Yes, sir," he said with a gulp.

The professor pushed the paper dismissively away while laughing merrily. "Which confirms that this is part of a prank, specifically on you, my young man. This box has obviously been stolen from someone's collection and was placed in a cave that they knew you would find. To cover their burglary, they wrote out this cryptic message pointing to you."

Again Perry and Thatcher looked at Ian expectantly but he thrust up his hands in surrender and shook his head. "But I swear," he insisted, "I don't know of anyone who would do that."

Everyone in the room glanced at one another as if hoping for an explanation. Theo broke the silence. "It's not a prank," she said softly. "There's something important in that box, Professor. I believe it is some sort of a message. One that we'll need your help deciphering."

Ian glanced at Theo and noticed that her eyes held that faraway cast she got when her gift of sight was acting up. He almost groaned when he noticed that the professor was regarding her with great skepticism. "What do you mean there's a message in the box?"

Theo's eyes suddenly focused, and she stepped up to his desk, picking up the silver box. "There's something inside here," she said, holding it up to him. "Something of great importance and I believe it's a message for Ian."

Ian gasped. What was she talking about? How could there possibly be a message for him inside that ancient relic? He caught Perry rolling his eyes and Ian glared hard at his schoolmaster, who quickly covered the look with a cough.

Meanwhile, the professor was blinking furiously at Theo as if he were trying to understand a foreign language. Finally, as if to humor her, he pulled the box closer and ran his magnifying glass slowly along the side of the metal container before he gasped and jumped to his feet. "Impossible!" he said, setting the box and the magnifying glass down before quickly shuffling past them to the far corner of the room. He searched among the many tubes nestled in the shelves, then quickly tugged one free and carried it back to his desk.

Pushing some of the clutter out of the way, the professor opened the top of the tube. Gently tipping it onto the desk, he tapped it until a very old-looking scroll slipped out. This he carefully unrolled, placing two paperweights at the top and bottom corners to hold it flat.

"What's happening?" Carl whispered into Ian's ear.

"I've no idea," said Ian, and he suddenly wished he'd never found that stupid box.

The professor ran his finger down the scroll to what

looked to Ian like a small drawing, and glanced back at the silver box.

"What is it?" Ian finally asked. "What have you found?"

The professor didn't answer him right away; instead he picked up the box and the magnifying glass, and after eyeing the artifact once more, he moved the glass to the drawing and peered at it with great interest. Ian leaned in and saw a stenciled drawing that even upside down closely resembled his silver box.

Finally, the professor sat back with an amazed expression and gently set the treasure on his desk. Looking up at Ian, he explained, "This is a scroll I discovered on an archaeological dig I was a part of some forty years ago just outside Delphi, Greece. The scroll was part of a collection found in a clay pot, remarkably left intact in the cellar of a prominent wine merchant. The merchant's daughter, Adria, was a disciple of Laodamia, the greatest Oracle the Greek world has ever known.

"Legend has it that Laodamia was able to foretell future events so accurately that her word was undisputed. Her powers were said to have been miraculous; she was credited with healing the sick, predicting the outcome of any Greek campaign, and moving objects without touching them, and her ability to predict incoming storms and yearly rainfall was uncanny."

"She sounds extraordinary," said Thatcher, and Ian had to agree.

"Yes," said the professor, sitting down in his chair again. "And that's quite the point. The Greeks were given to exaggeration. So much so that many historians consider her legend mostly that—exaggeration."

"What does this have to do with my treasure box?" Ian asked, feeling a burning excitement he couldn't explain building inside him.

The professor eyed him thoughtfully. "Laodamia was said to have commissioned several silver boxes to hide her most secret prophecies. Adria, who was quite the gifted sculptor, developed the design for the boxes, and this sketch is the one that was given to the silversmith."

"Were any of the boxes found in the dig that you excavated?" asked Perry.

"No," the professor said. "None of the boxes have ever been found, but many men have long searched for them. It is said that whoever finds one of Laodamia's treasure boxes will discover a great secret kept hidden from the world for thousands of years."

Ian was suddenly aware of the heavy silence that seemed to overtake the room. His heart was hammering and he felt a great compulsion to grab the box and run out of the room, but his feet seemed rooted to the floor.

"And you believe that *this* is one of those boxes?" Thatcher asked, his voice incredulous.

"There is only one way to find out," said the professor as his eyes darted back to the scroll that contained the sketch. Everyone waited with breathless anticipation while he read the ancient writing, mumbling to himself in a language Ian didn't understand.

Finally, the professor held up the box and studied the four balls that served as its feet. He gently attempted to turn the knobs one by one. On his fourth attempt, something extraordinary happened. The little foot began to unscrew.

"Blimey!" breathed Carl.

As the professor freed the ball from the box, everyone could clearly see that on the end of the little screw was a tiny key.

"Fascinating," the professor said. Glancing back at the sketch on the scroll, he turned the box right side up again in search of the keyhole. Ian let out a huge breath when the man finally exclaimed, "There you are!"

With shaking fingers, the professor wiggled the tiny key into the keyhole, and with great care, he slowly turned it. There was the faintest of popping sounds, and the box's lid separated from the case.

"Whoa," Ian said as he leaned way in over the professor's desk to have a look.

The professor gave him a nod before easing open the lid and peering inside. "My word," he said breathlessly, and he pulled out a small scroll and a tightly folded piece of paper that looked old enough to disintegrate on the spot.

Ian glanced at Theo and saw a satisfied smirk on her face. "Told you," she whispered, and he squeezed her arm with excitement.

"I'll need my gloves," said the professor, laying the two ancient-looking pieces of paper on his desktop before rummaging through another drawer.

He soon found a pair of white cloth gloves and pulled them on. First he focused on the folded piece of paper and very gently pried it open, but even with great care small flecks broke away from the body of the sheet and dotted his desk like tiny bits of confetti.

"Blasted," he said as he continued to unfold and more paper flaked off. "Fragile stuff, this," he muttered as the last of the folds was undone and the yellowish brown sheet was laid flat on his desk.

Theo gave a sharp intake of breath. "Oh, my!" she said.

Ian blinked and focused on the tabletop. Air rushed into his own lungs as he gasped in disbelief at what the professor had unfolded. "Impossible!" he said. "How can it be?"

"What?" Carl asked anxiously. "What is it?"

"It's your map," Theo said breathlessly. "Ian, it's *your* map!"

"What map?" asked Perry, looking from the ancient, weathered hand-drawn map in the center of the desk to Ian, who felt the blood drain from his face as a queasiness settled into his stomach.

Ian looked at his schoolmaster and it was a moment before he could speak. "I don't know how," he began, "but that's the map I drew of the tunnels and caves that run out from the castle."

"What do you mean it's the map *you* drew?" asked Thatcher sharply. "You mean you put this map inside the box?"

"No, sir!" he practically yelled. "I've never seen inside that box, I swear on my life!"

"All right, lad," said Thatcher, obviously a bit shocked by Ian's reaction. "Calm down. I believe you."

"But you don't understand!" Ian insisted. "Sir, that map there *is* the map I drew. See that? That bit of scribble there?

I'd drawn a tunnel there but it collapsed and so I scribbled over it to show that it wasn't passable."

They all looked at where Ian was pointing. The professor spoke next and his expression was again contemptuous. "How did you get the paper to weather so perfectly?" he asked, lifting a small corner of the map. "I know several forgery artists who would certainly like to get their hands on your techniques."

"But that's just it, sir," said Ian. "Other than being older and more fragile, this *is* the map that I have *at home*. It's in my room at the keep and I promise you that when I go back there, it will be in perfect condition. Not at all like this version. What I can't understand is how my map could be in both places at once."

"Did someone see your map and draw a replica?" asked Perry, searching for a plausible explanation.

Ian shook his head vehemently. "That map is always with me," he said firmly. "Well, except for today. I put it under my pillow this morning for safekeeping. And the only other person I've ever shown it to is Theo," he added, looking at Theo, who nodded.

"I'd recognize that map anywhere. I've seen it a hundred times or so," she said. "It's Ian's map."

Ian leaned in again over the professor's desk to look more closely at the paper that so resembled another. "Do you see that?" he asked, pointing to the tunnel where they'd found the silver box. "I only drew that this morning before breakfast! And see *this*?" he added, indicating the southeast end of the tunnel. "Where it says 'Beast's lair,' that's *my* handwriting!"

Everyone squinted at the parchment on the desk. "This doesn't make any sense," said Carl, rubbing his forehead. "How can this be *your* map if the one you drew is back at the keep and if you didn't know how to get inside the box?"

Ian was still transfixed by the map on the desk, and without answering Carl, he said, "That's odd. . . ."

"What could be more odd than your map appearing inside an ancient relic?" Perry asked, his voice dripping with sarcasm.

"I didn't draw that," Ian said, ignoring Perry's tone and holding his finger just above the fragile paper where an X marked the exact location of where the box had been. "That's been added along with that," he said, moving his finger to the other side of the paper, where a tunnel that was completely separate from all the others was drawn and labeled, again in his handwriting, with the word "Portal."

"So perhaps someone did come across your map, and they were able to make a very good copy of it and then they added these sections," said Perry.

"But, sir!" Ian protested. "How could someone have sketched in a tunnel that I only drew this morning before everyone else woke up? How could they have gotten the box and the map away from me without my knowing it, made these additions in my handwriting, aged the parchment, *and* known how to get inside the box? I mean, the professor didn't even know how to do that until he read it in his scroll!"

"Yes, how indeed?" said the professor sarcastically. "Come off it, lad," he snapped. "This is your clever hoax, is it not? I mean, you've had this box in your sole possession, correct? Perhaps you've managed to figure out how to open it on your own?"

"No!" Ian yelled as his hands balled into fists of frustration. "I swear to you, sir! You have to believe me: I had nothing to do with this!"

"But your friend here knew there was something inside the box," said the professor. "How did she know the box contained such an interesting artifact unless she saw you put this map and scroll in it?"

Theo glared at the professor. "I know many things, Professor Nutley. Not all of them are common knowledge."

The professor regarded her skeptically. "*Really?* Like what, young lady?"

"Like the fact that you," she said, pointing boldly at the professor, "have just been given the sack and you're no longer welcome at your post at Cambridge!"

Ian's heart skipped a beat. He knew that Theo was just sticking up for him, but even he thought she'd just gone too far. His fear was confirmed when he saw that Perry and Thatcher had both turned to stare at her in horror, then quickly faced the professor to stammer apologies. However, the professor was looking at Theo with such shock that the two men's voices trailed off. "How could you *know* that?" he finally asked her.

"It's true?" gasped Thatcher. "Professor, you've been sacked from Cambridge?"

Professor Nutley let out a sigh and removed his eyeglasses. "Yes, it's true. I was relieved of my post yesterday," he said sadly. "And to my knowledge it hasn't yet been announced," he added. "I expect the school paper will carry

271

the news on the front page but the vice chancellor promised me he wouldn't make the announcement until next week."

Theo blushed when she realized she'd embarrassed the old man. "S-sir," she stammered. "I'm terribly sorry. I didn't mean . . . It was just . . . Ian didn't put that map inside the box, sir, and I just wanted to get my point across."

The professor's face softened into the faintest of smiles. "Well, you've certainly done that, young lady," he said, then looked at her with something akin to respect. "And perhaps ancient Greece isn't the only place to find an oracle?"

Theo blushed and looked at her shoes as Thatcher said, "I'll write a letter of protest! And I'll contact all my former classmates. Don't you worry, Professor. We'll get you reinstated!"

The professor waved his hand dismissively. "Don't bother, Master Goodwyn," he said tiredly. "I'm an old man, who's been rather lax in attending to the business of teaching these days. The final straw was when I completely forgot to prepare a final examination for my students. I gave them all a passing grade, but several young men, the ones who enjoy being in the upper ranks, complained. I've been absentminded these past three years," he added. "And the thrill of teaching left me some time ago, I'm afraid."

"What will you do?" asked Perry.

The professor fluttered a hand at the mess surrounding his desk. "I'll sort through all this, I expect, and begin work on my memoirs."

"Please, sir," said Theo, "could you also translate that scroll for us? I believe that what is written on it will tell us a great deal about the mystery of the box and the circumstances surrounding it."

The professor glanced back at the scroll and the map on his desk. He picked up the magnifying glass again and unraveled the scroll a few inches, scanning the first few lines and frowning. After a few long moments, he scowled and set both objects down. "Gobbledygook," he announced. "Your scroll is nothing but nonsense."

"What do you mean?" asked Ian, his heart sinking at the professor's assessment. He'd been so hoping that Theo was right and that the answers to all these strange questions could be found in the scroll.

"I mean that there are some letters clearly from the Phoenician alphabet; however, the line of text makes no sense at all. Just some jumbled characters, some of which appear to be written backwards, not to mention a few others here that I've never seen before."

"Perhaps it's an ancient lost dialect?" offered Thatcher, and Ian turned his face hopefully back to the professor.

But Professor Nutley merely smiled patiently and said, "Thatcher, my good man, I know you mean well, but it would have to be a rare find indeed for us to come across some ancient parchment written in a dialect we hadn't yet heard of. Besides, even if some of these letters are from another source, I should still be able to make out a few words here and there. I'm afraid this is simply a jumble of letters clustered together that make no sense at all."

Ian felt his hopes plummet, but before he could dwell on it, he noticed that Carl had gone round the professor's desk to stand near the older man's elbow and was peering curiously at the scroll. "That looks like X, H, E," he said, pointing to the first group of letters. "You're right. It's gobbledygook."

The professor glanced at him impatiently. "That first letter is taw, not X," he snapped. "It's the ancient Phoenician letter for T."

"Oh!" said Carl brightly. "Well then, that first word is 'the'!"

The professor rolled his eyes and sighed, his patience clearly waning even more. "No, young man, it cannot be the word 'the.' "

"Why not?" Carl asked.

"Because the Phoenicians wrote their script right to left, not left to right as you're looking at it. And that cannot be an E," he said. "The Phoenician alphabet had no vowels. It wasn't until much later that the Linear B script came along and the concept of vowels was introduced into the Greek alphabet."

"Then what's that letter, right there?" Carl asked, pointing to the letter next to the H. Ian could see even from his angle that it looked very much like an E.

The professor's face grew red with impatience. "One that I've never seen before in this alphabet!" he roared. "And trust me, if anyone is an expert in reading ancient Greek, it would be me, young man, not *you*!"

Carl jumped back. "I'm sorry, sir," he said with downcast eyes. "I meant no disrespect."

The professor growled at him and rolled the scroll back up carefully, then placed it back into the box along with the map. Ian and the others waited in the uncomfortable silence as the old man put away his gloves and his magnifying glass. "I'm afraid I'm tired," he said at last.

"Yes, of course, Professor," said Thatcher. "We appreciate your time, and we're sorry we've been such a bother."

"Yes, well . . . ," the professor grumbled as he tried to hand the box back to Ian. But Ian shook his head.

"If you please, sir," he said, even though he hated to leave his precious treasure, "perhaps you might take another look at the scroll later. It seems it was a long scroll, and maybe there's a real message farther down the parchment?"

The professor scowled, his impatience brimming, but the look on Ian's face seemed to win him over. "Very well," he grumbled at last. "Now, you'll have to excuse me while I take my leave."

"Yes, sir," they all said, and waited while the professor squeezed from behind his desk and led them silently out of the library. When they got to the front door, Thatcher paused in the entryway and shook the old man's hand. "Thank you again, Professor, for seeing us today. And if there's anything I can do to get your post back at Cambridge, please let me know."

"I don't need help getting my post back, Thatcher. I need someone to help me sort through this mess," he said with a wave of his hand. And then an idea seemed to strike him and he turned to Ian. "You seem to be a bright boy," he said. "How would you like to assist an old man in cleaning up his clutter?"

"Sir?" asked Ian, feeling like he'd just been put on the spot.

"You come here next Saturday and help me make some

headway through all this mess. In exchange I'll pay you a few pence and have one more look at that scroll of yours."

"Oh, yes, sir!" said Ian. He never turned down the opportunity to earn a little money.

"May I come too?" asked Carl eagerly.

"Yes, yes," said the professor, softening his grumpiness with a dry laugh. "You may come too. But I'll expect you to work while you're here."

"Right," said Carl seriously. "Work it is, sir."

"We can all travel to London together," said Theo. "You two can drop me at Lady Arbuthnot's, then come here."

"We'll need to clear all this with Madam Dimbleby," said Perry seriously.

The faces of the children clouded over. "Oh, please tell her it's terribly important," said Theo. "Tell her it's *essential* that we come."

Ian pumped his head. "If *you* ask her and tell her it's important that Theo visit the Lady Arbuthnot and that Carl and I help the professor, she's likely to say yes," he added, crossing his fingers.

Perry smiled at the eager faces in front of him. "I'll do my best," he said. Then he clapped his hands and announced, "We'll be shoving off, then. Thank you again, Professor Nutley. It's been quite an adventurous afternoon."

The professor waved at them from the top step as the five set off, and the group made their way along the busy streets back toward the train station. The afternoon traffic had picked up and there were no hackney cabs available, so Ian, Theo, and Carl took the opportunity to lag behind their schoolmasters and discuss their day.

"No offense," Carl began, "but I think that old man should be called Professor Nutty. He didn't seem quite right up here. Know what I mean?" he said, tapping his head.

"He meant well," Theo chided, but Ian noticed the smile tugging at the corners of her mouth. "Besides, he's just been sacked. Don't you think that'd make anyone a bit irritable?"

"What I don't understand," Carl went on, "is how a map that Ian drew could be pulled out of a box from ancient Greece. I mean, how is that even possible?"

"Don't bring your map with you when you come next time, Ian," said Theo.

"What?" he asked, giving her a quizzical look. "Of course I'm going to bring it! I mean, how else is the professor, or anyone else for that matter, going to believe me?"

Theo shook her head vehemently. "You mustn't!" she insisted.

"Why not?" Ian asked, confused.

"Because something tells me that it would mean the destruction of one of those maps."

"What do you mean?" asked Carl.

Theo sighed heavily. "I mean that I believe that Ian's map at the keep is the same as the one that the professor pulled from the box. As no two things of identical nature can exist in the same place at the same time, I believe that one of them would have to dissolve into nothingness."

Ian scowled as he considered that, and before he could reply, Carl said, "She's got a point, you know."

"Well, thank you," Theo said drolly. "I'm *so* glad you believe me capable of making a good point."

"Oh, come off it," whined Carl. "I didn't mean it like that!"

Theo gave a small *humph* and quickened her pace, leaving Carl and Ian to stare at her back. "She's a bit sensitive, don't you think?" Carl whispered.

"She's all right," Ian said with a chuckle. "And she's been right about everything else so far, so I expect that I'll have to trust her on this as well."

The two boys walked silently for a bit before Carl asked, "What do you think the scroll's about?"

" 'Gobbledygook,' " quoted Ian in a voice that was a perfect imitation of the professor's.

Carl laughed. "Yeah, but the thing of it is, Ian, when I was looking at it, I swear it almost made sense. I mean, I really felt like some of those letters were in English along with those funny Greek symbols. I swear it's a mixture of the two. Plus I think he was reading it wrong. I mean, who reads from right to left, anyway?"

"Well, I'm sure we'll figure it out soon," said Theo over her shoulder. She'd obviously been listening to the boys.

"How can you be so sure?" Ian asked her.

"I just am, Ian," she said confidently. "I just am."

BONES IN THE WALL

Ian and the four others returning to the keep from London were greeted with bubbling excitement. All the orphans were eager to hear of their adventure, and Carl became the unofficial spokesman for the group as he stood in front of the children and retold what had happened at Lady Arbuthnot's home. Many in the group looked on in wonder, but Madam Scargill, like Perry, expressed some deeply held skepticism. "The earl most likely rang her up," she sniffed. "I'm sure he's getting quite a laugh out of pulling the wool over your eyes," she added.

Madam Dimbleby frowned. "I've never known the earl to go to such elaborate lengths to play a joke, Gertrude. Especially to involve his elder aunt. No, I think there might be a little something to the woman's keen abilities."

Perry let out a small cough and Ian caught Thatcher scowling at his brother. Carl continued with the story of Professor Nutley's messy house. "There was paper and books everywhere!" he said, using his hands to indicate the piles. "And Ian showed him the box he'd found in the tunnel, and the professor, well, he figured out how to open it and out came Ian's map!"

Ian started at the mention of his map. He hadn't thought Carl was going to bring up something he'd crafted in secret, so he quickly cleared his throat and gave Carl a warning glance. He didn't want it becoming common knowledge that he had a map of a place he'd been strictly forbidden to explore. And sure enough, as if ferreting out trouble, Madam Scargill asked, "And what map is this?"

"Er . . . ," said Carl as he caught Ian's eye. "It's the map of . . . of . . ."

"The map I was making of the coastline, Madam," Ian said, thinking quickly. "The map that fell out of the box slightly resembled my map."

Madam Scargill's nose twitched as if she were sniffing the air for a lie. "That's an interesting coincidence, Ian," she said.

"Very," said Ian, working hard to appear calm under her squinty-eyed scrutiny. "But I believe it's to be expected when someone puts a box from ancient Greece into an underground cavern. The map might be an indication that someone from a distant land brought it here."

"Someone from ancient Greece?" asked Winifred Simonds, a plump little girl a year younger than Ian.

"Highly unlikely," said Perry. "There is no evidence that the ancient Greeks visited our shores."

"But what of the writing on the wall?" asked Carl. "I thought the professor said that was written in ancient Greek."

Ian focused on his schoolmaster, very interested in

hearing his theory on who might have scrawled his name on the walls of the tunnel, but Perry shrugged and stuck with the professor's conclusion. "It is possible that the box was deposited in the cavern by a thief who stole it from either the Greek archives or a personal collection and the writing on the wall indicates that this is all some sort of elaborate hoax."

Theo scowled. "It isn't a hoax," she said quietly, but only Ian heard her.

"Is the box valuable?" asked Maxwell Kromby, a sickly little boy of about eight who had been at the orphanage since he was only a few days old. "If Ian found it, perhaps he can sell it and get some money for it."

Perry and Thatcher looked slightly uncomfortable with the question, and Ian felt his heart beat faster. Maxwell had unwittingly spoken Ian's secret plans for the box out loud, and as he saw the doubt form on his schoolmasters' faces, he knew he wasn't going to like their answer.

Thatcher said, "I expect that there should be an effort to find out the origin of the box first. If it was stolen, then it should be returned to its rightful owner, and only after an extensive search would I say it would be allowable for Ian to keep it and do with it what he wishes."

Ian's hopes sank, but Theo tried to cheer him by saying, "Not to worry, Ian. That box belongs with you, and I've a strong feeling you'll get it back before long."

This made Ian feel better, and he nudged Theo with his shoulder. "We'll split the profits, of course," he said to her, which made her beam.

The group chattered on for several more minutes before

Ian saw Madam Dimbleby glance at the clock and get to her feet. "All right, then," she said with a clap of her hands to get everyone's attention. "It's getting late and we have church services in the morning. Everyone to bed."

The children dispersed with only mild protest as they headed off to their rooms. Ian said good night to Theo and he and Carl walked up the stairs to their room.

As he entered his dormitory, he suddenly remembered that he'd wanted to check on his map, so he hurried to his bed and felt under his pillow. His map was exactly where he'd left it. But before taking it out, he glanced around at the boys in the room, who were busy getting into their night-clothes. No one seemed interested in what he was fiddling with under his pillow, so he pulled it out and unfolded the creases.

It was exactly as he'd last seen it. No additional mark-ings, and yet it seemed almost a mirror image of the one that had come out of the silver box, save for the age of the parch-ment. Ian studied the markings, baffled, when he heard Carl exclaim, "Blimey, *that's* the map from the box!" over his left shoulder.

Ian jumped and, turning quickly, hissed, "Shhh!"

"But, Ian," Carl said in a hushed tone, "that *is* the map from the box!"

"I know," said Ian as he folded the paper up quickly and looked behind him to see if any of the other boys had no-ticed. "I just don't understand how it could be in two places at once."

"This whole thing's a bit barmy!" Carl said moodily,

sitting down next to Ian. "I mean, we've got wild beasts and lost tunnels and ancient Phoenician boxes filled with scrolls that aren't written in Greek and your map in two places at once, not to mention your name in Greek on that wall. What's that about?"

Ian shook his head. "I don't know, Carl," he admitted, thinking that his friend was right to call all the recent events madness. "But I do know there is something you and I need to investigate tomorrow after church."

"What's that?" asked Carl, his interest suddenly piqued.

Ian unfolded a small section of the map. "Remember that tunnel that was added to the map from the box?"

"The one labeled 'Portal' or something?"

"Yes," said Ian. "That's the one. I think we need to try to find it."

Carl's eyebrows lowered skeptically. "Don't you usually go exploring with Theo?"

Ian smiled. He detected that Carl was just a bit jealous of his close friendship with Theo. "I do," he admitted. "But she's been through a lot in the last few weeks, and taking her on another exploration right now might rattle her. I figure it's a better job for you and me."

Carl slapped his kneecap. "That's brilliant!" he said just a little too loudly.

"What's brilliant?" called James from two cots over.

"Nothing!" both Ian and Carl said as Ian quickly put his map away before anyone became too curious. "We'll talk more in the morning," he whispered to Carl as the boys hurried to get into bed.

*　*　*

The next day, after they'd been released from morning services, Ian and Carl were easily able to slip away from the grounds. Ian had told Theo that he and Carl were running an errand for Madam Dimbleby, which wasn't exactly a lie. Madam *had* asked Ian if he would go to the bakery and pick up a few extra loaves of bread for supper. He in turn had asked her if Carl could come along to help carry the bread, and although she'd given him a look that said, "I know you're up to something, but I'm not sure what," she allowed Carl to go along.

Ian led the way as the boys sprinted out from the grounds of the keep and ran as fast as their legs would carry them toward the cliffs. He reasoned that no one would be too alarmed if they arrived back at the keep a little later than it would take to go to the bakery and back; however, if they took too long, they ran the risk of having the alarm sounded and a search party come looking for them—especially since the beast was still at large. As if to emphasize this, two men out on patrol along the roads, each with a hunting rifle over his shoulder, passed them. "Any sign of the beast?" Ian asked the second man.

The scrawny-looking man with several days' stubble on his chin scowled as if he was irritated with his assignment. "No sign a'tall," he said. "All's been quiet for weeks now."

Ian and Carl both smiled at him as they dashed past and cut off the road to run along the hilly terrain, dodging around rocks and traveling along well-worn paths, moving closer to Castle Dover's south end, until Ian finally held up his hand and stopped on a slope just beyond the castle's large back wall.

Ian wasted no time as he pulled his map out from his back pocket and unfolded it.

"How . . . are . . . we . . . going to . . . find the . . . tunnel?" Carl asked, wheezing, as he glanced up from his bent-over position.

Ian waited to catch his own breath before answering. "I've got to rely mostly on the memory of the map at Professor Nutley's. And I remember it being drawn somewhere near this tunnel," he said, pointing to the southwesternmost tunnel on his map.

"And where's that one located?" Carl asked, standing tall again.

"Right underneath our feet," said Ian with a smile.

Ian turned the map around in a circle, studying it closely as he periodically glanced at the horizon to gauge the direction and pinpoint his location. After thinking it through, he said, "Come on, I think it's this way."

Carl followed him as the boys crept up to some woods that bordered the outer wall of Castle Dover. Carl looked at them skeptically. "You want to go in *there?*" he asked, and Ian knew he was nervous about the beast.

"It's just a small patch of woods, mate," Ian said easily. "Besides, you heard the patrolman. There's been no sign of the beast for weeks. And the earl's had his hounds out patrolling the grounds daily. If there was any chance the beast was nearby, don't you think they would have sniffed her out by now?"

Carl still looked uncertain but shrugged and said, "I guess."

"Come on, then," Ian said, plunging forward into the dense scrub. "If we find anything at all that suggests the beast is about, we'll have just a short run up to the earl's garden path and through the gate."

"All right," said Carl grudgingly, and he followed Ian.

After a bit, Ian stopped and squinted at his map again. "It's got to be near here," he said, lowering the map to look at the terrain. "I remember the tunnel was marked by some steps."

"Really?" said Carl, glancing over Ian's shoulder at the paper in his hands. "I don't remember any stairs."

"Oh, trust me," said Ian, holding the map up for Carl to see. "They're there. See this symbol on this tunnel closer to the cliffs?"

Carl peered at the paper. "That zigzag?" he asked.

"Yes, that's my symbol for stairs. One end of the Portal tunnel was marked with that zigzag."

"You've got a better memory than me," said Carl as he looked around nervously at their surroundings. "Can't really see much of anything among these trees, though."

"Well, it's got to be here somewhere," said Ian, glancing around at the dense patch of woods.

Carl gulped but seemed to gather his courage as he asked, "Where shall we begin looking, then?"

"I think it's best if we split up. You go that way and I'll go this way. If you find the stairs, call out and I'll come to you."

Carl's expression clearly suggested he was less than thrilled with that idea but he kept his mouth shut and headed off in the direction Ian had pointed to. Ian walked in the opposite direction, pushing at plants and looking around stumps for any sign of the stairway indicated on the old map.

After a good ten minutes, he headed back to his starting place and found Carl coming through the brush at him from the opposite direction. "Any luck?" he asked.

Carl shook his head. "It's really thick back there," he said, pointing behind him. "You'd be lucky to find your feet, let alone a set of stairs."

"Well, if we don't find the stairs on this pass, we'll wait until after the next time we visit with the professor and get a better feel for exactly where they are."

Carl nodded and headed east. Ian turned west and searched again. Not even three minutes had passed when Ian heard Carl shout, "Oi, Ian! Come here quick!"

Ian whipped around and bolted as fast as he could toward the sound of Carl's voice, afraid he might have been wrong about the beast being nowhere about. To his immense relief he found his friend straightaway. Carl was jumping up and down with excitement.

"Look!" he said, pointing to a rather crude structure that was nearly completely hidden by ivy and brush. Ian moved closer and gasped when he realized that what he'd thought was just a clump of vegetation was actually four huge flat stones that formed three walls and a roof. These mammoth pieces of rock sheltered a set of stairs leading down to a metal grate door that stood slightly ajar.

"You've found it!" Ian exclaimed. "Good job, mate. Now, let's see what's down there!"

The stairs were narrow and the boys descended one at a

time, with Ian in the lead. When they reached the bottom, he paused at the gate, peering into the spooky darkness of the tunnel beyond the iron.

"Should we go in?" whispered Carl.

"Why are you whispering?" Ian whispered back.

"Why are *you* whispering?" asked Carl.

Ian rolled his eyes and gathered his courage. "Never mind," he said in his normal voice while digging into his pocket for the pocket torch the earl had replaced for him. Clicking it on, he attempted a joke. "We've got to be quick about it. Don't want anyone at the keep to think we've been eaten alive, or anything."

Carl went starkly pale. "You don't think the beast is in there, do you?" he asked in a shaky whisper.

Ian almost laughed at his friend's expression. But seeing that Carl really was frightened, he was quick to reassure him. "Of course not! I was only joking, mate."

Carl gulped. "Still, perhaps we should take a big stick with us, just in case we have to defend ourselves?"

Ian could have slapped himself for being so stupid as to make a crack about being eaten alive. "Sure, Carl, sure," he said. "I'll wait here while you get your stick."

Carl bolted back up the stairs and Ian could hear him tramping through the woods. He leaned against the frame of the door and shone the beam of the small torch into the tunnel opening. As he swirled the light around in small circles, something sparkled in the gloominess. Curious, Ian pointed his beam directly on the floor in front of him. Not far away something shiny glinted back.

"I found one!" Carl called from the top of the stairs.

"That's good," Ian said, still distracted by what his light was reflecting off. "Come on, then, or we'll run out of time."

Carl raced down the stairs and showed Ian his big stick, which was nearly as tall as he was. "Nice choice," Ian said to him, working hard to appear serious.

Carl flashed a winning smile; then he nodded and Ian turned back to the tunnel. He could hear Carl walking behind him with the *tap . . . tap . . . tap* of the stick striking the stone floor every other step. They went cautiously and slowly—Carl because he was clearly afraid of creepy dark tunnels, Ian because he wanted to examine the walls for indications of who had carved it out.

The stairs and the gate indicated that this tunnel was man-made. As they went in, Ian was surprised by how wide and spacious the interior was. Most of the other tunnels required anyone taller than he to duck, but this one had a great deal of extra headroom and was wide enough for three men to walk abreast. Ian bounced the beam of his pocket torch around the walls and ceiling but kept going back to the shiny object at the end of the tunnel. As he moved closer, he could see that the reflective surface was something about as large as a football, and almost as round.

"What *is* that?" Carl whispered as he too caught sight of the metallic object in the beam of Ian's torch.

"Don't know," said Ian, intensely curious now. "Come on. Let's have a closer look."

The boys picked up their pace, their focus now only on the shiny object. When they got close enough to touch it, they stopped and looked down. The thing was shaped much like an egg, with a bronze-coated surface that was lightly covered in dust and cobwebs. Ian had no idea what it was, so he kicked at it, and it rolled over, revealing a hollow center.

"It's a helmet," said Carl, poking it with his stick.

Ian squatted excitedly and picked it up, delighted to have found another bit of treasure. "It's heavy," he said, holding it at eye level and wiping the dust covering it on his trouser leg. Carl leaned in to get a better look and Ian smiled, thinking of a prank to play on his friend. "Here, why don't you try it on for size?" And he plopped the helmet on Carl's head.

"Hey!" Carl said as the heavy bronze headgear came down over his eyes and rested near his nose. "I can't see!"

Ian laughed and laughed while his friend stumbled around ridiculously, banging into something that gave an eerie clatter. "What was that?" Carl asked, laughing too while he reached up to tug up the lip of the helmet.

But all laughter died in Ian's throat as he saw the object now reflecting his torch beam.

As Carl continued to thrash about, Ian was frozen in place. He raised a shaking hand and pointed at the back wall, where the bony remains of the upper torso and skull of some poor soul were cemented firmly into the rock and protruded grotesquely out at him.

Carl, finally free of the helmet, blinked several times, trying to get his bearings. "What's the matter?" he asked when he finally noticed Ian standing there with wide, horrified eyes.

"That!" whispered Ian, pointing urgently.

Carl glanced to his right and let out a terrific scream as

he came face to face with the hollowed-out eyes of a human skull.

Carl flew forward, grabbed Ian's arm, and whipped him around. *"Run!"* he yelled.

Ian's feet finally agreed to move—and move fast. He raced past Carl as if his life depended on it. He'd suddenly found his voice too, letting out his own terrified scream, which, along with Carl's, reverberated off the stone walls. Ian raced up the stairs with Carl hot on his heels and neither boy slowed down as they crashed through the forest, back to the hilltop where they'd first paused to look at the map.

There, Ian finally collapsed on the grass, panting hard as he felt Carl thump to the ground next to him. Long seconds passed before Ian sat up and glanced at his friend. Carl was staring at the sky, his chest heaving and his right hand still gripping the helmet from the tunnel.

"Hey," said Ian, motioning to the helmet, "how did you manage to run so fast with that in your hands?"

Carl panted another beat or two before he glanced sideways at his hand, then sat up quickly and tossed the helmet away with an "Ahhhh!" For emphasis, Carl kicked it.

"Wait!" Ian said, reaching out to catch the helmet before Carl could do any real damage. "Don't ruin it!"

"It fell off that . . . that . . . *thing!*" Carl said, scrunching up his face and shuddering.

By now Ian had regained his composure and was genuinely curious about what he'd seen. "Yes," he agreed. "But who do you think he was?"

"Who cares?" screeched Carl. "Ian, did you see those bones? He was . . . he was . . ." Carl was at a loss for words.

"Cemented *into* the wall!" said Ian. He'd never seen anything like it and now that he was over his initial fright, he found it fascinating.

"Yes! Cemented, that's a good way to describe it," Carl agreed.

"How is that even possible?" Ian wondered.

Carl shivered and stood up. "I knew going into that tunnel was a bad idea," he grumbled. "Didn't I tell you it was a bad idea?"

"No," Ian said. "You didn't."

Carl glared at him while he dusted himself off. "Well, I *meant* to say it. We never should have gone in there!" he added with another shiver.

Ian got to his feet as well, lifting up the helmet. "We'll need to hide this for now," he said, thinking that they couldn't very well show up at the keep with another ancient artifact. Ian was quite certain that he'd get into a load of trouble if he admitted to exploring more tunnels.

"For *now?*" Carl asked, looking at Ian like he'd just grown an extra head. "Toss that thing off the side of the cliffs, I say!"

Ian gave him a level look. "Carl," he said reasonably, "this could be another ancient artifact. It could be worth loads of money! It could mean that you and I will have a bit of cash for the years after we leave Delphi Keep!"

Carl was still glaring at him, but Ian could see a small bit of cracking in his resolve, so he continued his argument. "Besides," Ian said, "this helmet is another clue linking us back to the box and the map and that scroll. Did you ever consider that the soldier who wore this helmet might be the same person who left the silver box in the tunnel? This could be the way for me to clear my name! If the schoolmasters see that skeleton with their own eyes, they'll know I had nothing to do with that writing on the wall or hiding the box in the tunnel. It could be the proof we need to remove any doubt about this being a hoax!"

Carl crossed his arms and his scowl deepened. "Lot of good it did that bloke back there to leave you that box," he muttered. "I expect if that *thing* embedded in the wall down there had to do it all over again, he'd have chosen tossing that box off the cliffs too! I say we go back and tell Madam Dimbleby. She'll tell the earl, who can seal off that tunnel and all the others for good!"

Ian sighed. Carl was more stubborn than he'd thought. "How about this . . . ," he said. "We'll tell the schoolmasters about it, but we'll do it *privately,* and we'll bring them down here so they can explore our discovery themselves."

"Look, mate," Carl said, puffing up his chest. He was a good two inches shorter than Ian, but that didn't stop him from trying to stand up to his new friend. "That unfortunate bloke down there *died* in that wall likely after he went exploring places. *You* almost died when you first found the box exploring that tunnel. Then *we* almost died when the beast came after us because you'd gone exploring near its lair. All that this exploring has brought us is a load of trouble and I, for one, have had quite enough of it!"

But Ian was undeterred. He would tell the schoolmasters about the helmet and bring them down to the tunnel to show them the soldier's remains with or without Carl. Maybe once they'd seen it with their own eyes, they'd believe that he had nothing to do with the writing on the wall or putting the map inside the silver box. "Come on," he said, ruffling Carl's hair good-naturedly. "Help me find a hiding place. I promise that once I get the schoolmasters alone, I'll tell them about what we've found."

Carl groused some more but eventually he helped Ian locate the perfect-sized nook between some large boulders where the helmet could be hidden. "Thanks, mate," Ian said after he'd covered the helmet with some grass and dried twigs to further conceal it.

"Don't mention it," said Carl with a frown before adding, "*ever* again!"

Ian laughed and motioned toward the road leading to the village. "Come on," he said. "We'll have to run to the village and hope there isn't a queue at the bakery."

Ian and Carl hurried to fetch the bread Madam Dimbleby had sent them for, and quickly made their way back to Delphi Keep. Puffing with effort, their arms loaded with bread, they returned to the kitchen, where Ian was surprised to find Schoolmaster Thatcher sitting at the small table by the pantry, sipping tea and chatting with Madam Dimbleby. "Hello, boys," he greeted them.

"Sir," Ian and Carl said together as they handed the loaves over to Madam Dimbleby.

"It's about time you two got back," she said to them. "I was about to send Master Goodwyn here out to look for you."

"There was a queue at the bakery," said Ian. He didn't elaborate about it being only two deep.

"I see," she said with a suspicious look. "Well, as long as you're here, you might as well help me carve the loaves for the table. Knives are in the drawer, and you'll want to make sure we have enough slices for all the children plus Schoolmaster Goodwyn, Madam Scargill, and me."

Ian let go a sigh of relief that she didn't question them further about taking so long and he nudged Carl in the direction of the hooks at the back of the kitchen, where the children put up their coats.

"And wash your hands first, boys," added Madam Dimbleby over her shoulder before the boys could begin their work.

As they hurried to the sink and got to it, they couldn't help overhearing their headmistress and Thatcher continue the conversation the boys had interrupted.

As he and Carl laid out the bread and fetched the knives, Ian listened in.

"This Professor Nutley has offered to pay the boys for their help cleaning up his flat?" she asked.

"Yes, Madam," Thatcher answered. "And I daresay it would be a wonderful opportunity for them. The professor was a favorite of mine at Cambridge. He was one of the best archaeologists of his time and would be nothing but a positive influence on the lads."

"I suppose it's all right," Madam Dimbleby said as she stirred the gravy. Ian smiled excitedly at Carl, who grinned back until Madam said, "I just worry about them running amuck in London."

"I will be happy to accompany them," Thatcher said. "It

would provide me with the chance to visit with the professor. Besides, there's still the matter of ferreting out the truth of where the scroll and the box came from." Carl glanced up, looking like he was about to let slip what they'd discovered that afternoon but Ian cleared his throat and gave Carl a warning look. Carl quickly focused back on the bread.

"Something wrong, Ian?" Madam asked, and Ian realized she was looking at him expectantly.

"Ma'am?" he asked.

"Your throat, is it bothering you?"

Ian felt himself blush. "Oh, no, ma'am. Just a bit cool today—and perhaps I'm not used to the weather yet."

Madam's eyes were suspicious again but she turned back to the sink and said, "It is unseasonably cold for September, isn't it?"

"The newspaper said it's even colder in London," Thatcher added. "Did you hear there was a frost there yesterday morning?"

"Really?" Madam Dimbleby said. "How strange!"

"Exactly," said Thatcher. "And some poor urchin girl apparently suffered for it."

Ian looked up from cutting the bread. He noticed the hairs on his arms had stood up, and he got the sense that something very bad had happened. "What girl?" asked Madam Dimbleby.

"A young homeless girl was found in an alleyway, frozen solid, if you can believe it."

"That's terrible!" Madam exclaimed with a shudder that Ian felt as well.

"Yes, quite tragic. I know the earl would hate to read that."

Madam tsked as she peeled the potatoes. "Poor lass," she said, and the kitchen was quiet for several long moments.

Madam Dimbleby was the first to break the silence. "Well, then I suppose it's fine if the boys want to earn a bit of extra money and help out the professor. It's Theo's request to visit with Lady Arbuthnot that I'm hesitant about."

"I assure you," said Thatcher, "the earl's aunt is harmless. And she seemed quite authentic too." Ian smiled as he worked. He was glad Thatcher was sticking up for the earl's aunt, as he knew that Theo was excited to go back and talk with her again.

"Your brother doesn't share your enthusiasm," remarked Madam Dimbleby.

"He's already talked to you about it, has he?"

"Yes. He stopped by early this morning before service. He knew you intended to talk to me about taking the boys to London, which he also approved of, but he wanted to caution me about sending Theo along to Lady Arbuthnot's. He said she was full of parlor tricks and it didn't bode well to have a young lady influenced by such things."

"Madam Dimbleby," said Thatcher, setting his teacup on the counter, "I must tell you that Perry is far more a man of science than he is a man of faith. I know that what happened at Lady Arbuthnot's was certainly no parlor trick. But I can't really explain why I believe that. I do consider Theo gifted in the same way as the earl's aunt. And I believe that her gifts frighten her to the point of becoming ill. If the lady can help her harness these gifts in such a way as not to cause the girl further upset, then I say it's worth considering letting her attend these Saturday visits."

Ian felt himself relax. He was starting to like his new schoolmaster very much and he exchanged a knowing look with Carl while the pair arranged the bread they'd sliced in the baskets for the table. Ian hoped Thatcher was right about Lady Arbuthnot's ability to help calm Theo. She had to learn how to make sense of her abilities before anyone else wanted to send her off to the sanitarium.

Madam Dimbleby turned to the boys. "Ian," she said, "what did you make of Lady Arbuthnot?"

"She seemed very nice," Ian answered carefully. "She served us tea and biskies and didn't mind if we had seconds." The truth was he wasn't quite sure what to make of the lady's abilities. His interaction with her had been a bit unsettling with all that doom-and-gloom stuff. But he didn't want to sway Madam Dimbleby with this, so he stuck to discussing the lady's hospitality.

Madam Dimbleby smiled. She knew he was dodging the question. "Carl?" she asked. "How did you find the earl's aunt?"

Carl's mouth opened wide with excitement as he answered, "She was brilliant, ma'am! She told me about me mum and she even knew her by name! The lady also said that she knew I'd had a rough go of it before the earl found me and brought me here, and she expected things should be a bit easier for me from now on."

"So you believe she has a gift?"

Carl nodded earnestly. "Oh, yes, ma'am," he said. "I

really, really do." Ian smiled at his friend, grateful that Carl could be such an enthusiastic voice.

And Carl's positive endorsement seemed to decide it for Madam Dimbleby. "All right, then," she said to Thatcher. "I shall allow Theo to go to her lessons on Saturday with Lady Arbuthnot, but I should like to accompany her for the first few visits, to see for myself that she's not being unduly influenced."

"Very good, Madam," said Thatcher happily. "That sounds like the perfect solution."

WATER ON THE HEARTH

The next Saturday, Madam Dimbleby, Thatcher, Ian, Carl, and Theo all stepped from the train, which deposited them again at Victoria Station in central London. Just like before, the streets were bustling with energy. Ian thought there were even more people about than on their last visit.

Thatcher attempted to hail a hackney cab but there were none available. Finally, Madam Dimbleby said, "Come, Master Goodwyn, the walk shall do us some good and warm our bones in this chilly weather."

The group kept a brisk pace as they marched through London's busy streets, and Ian decided that he preferred taking in the city as a pedestrian, because the ride in the motorcar had gone by too fast.

Theo trotted alongside Madam Dimbleby, who was just behind Thatcher, and Ian and Carl brought up the rear. When they could finally speak without being overheard, Carl leaned over to Ian and asked quietly, "Are you going to tell Schoolmaster Goodwyn about the helmet today?"

Ian flinched. He knew that he should have told the

schoolmaster earlier in the week, but there always seemed to be someone about, and he felt certain that revealing that he and Carl had been in another tunnel would not go over well with either of his headmistresses. "If I can get him alone," he said.

"We can tell him after we drop off Theo and Madam Dimbleby," said Carl reasonably. "Speaking of which, I hope we get a chance to see the lady. I'd like to ask her something."

Ian didn't ask his friend what he wanted of the earl's aunt, because his head was suddenly filled with troubled thoughts. He needed a reason to convince his schoolmaster not to tell the headmistresses of his most recent exploration. He knew that the earl was likely to hear of it at some point, but he was convinced that if Madam Scargill found out, she would insist on a severe punishment for him that was likely to include lost meals, a turn at the switch, and a restriction in his room for several weeks. He wondered if the earl might also be disappointed to learn that Ian was back to his old tricks again.

Ian walked along with these turbulent ideas and searched his mind for a plausible reason to offer his schoolmaster when suddenly he heard Theo exclaim, "Look! Up there! See who it is?" Ian's head snapped up and he realized with surprise that Professor Nutley was walking directly toward them.

"Professor!" said Thatcher, shortening the distance between them to greet his old friend. "We were just coming to see you."

Ian noticed that the professor looked a bit taken aback at

first but seemed to recover himself as Madam Dimbleby was introduced and the boys gave their hellos.

"I'm afraid I thought you were coming later in the morning," the professor explained. "I'm on an errand to Blythe House," he said. "It's part of the Victoria and Albert Museum. I've got some archival records there that I'll need for our discussion later on." Ian and Carl exchanged a look and shrugged. Neither boy knew what the professor was talking about.

"Ah," said Thatcher, and Ian could tell he didn't know how to respond. After a moment of uncomfortable silence, the schoolmaster said, "We were just on our way to drop off Madam Dimbleby and Miss Fields at Lady Arbuthnot's flat only a block away. Would you like for us to join you at the museum afterward?"

But before the professor had a chance to reply, Madam Dimbleby said, "Oh, my, Master Goodwyn, Theo and I can certainly make our way to Lady Arbuthnot's on our own. Why don't you and the boys run along with Professor Nutley and assist him in retrieving his records?"

The professor looked uncomfortable as he eyed Ian and Carl. "Thatcher, my good man, I really could use your assistance, but the archival records room is off-limits to children. Might the boys accompany you, Madam, and we can retrieve them on our way back?"

Ian's shoulders sagged. He'd been quite excited by the prospect of going to the museum.

"Of course, of course," answered Madam Dimbleby. "Ian, Carl," she said over her shoulder, "come along with us to Lady Arbuthnot's and your schoolmaster will fetch you after his errand."

"All right," groused Ian, and Theo gave him a sympathetic smile. She knew he'd prefer a museum over the lady's parlor. But Carl seemed very excited and he bounced along.

They gave their quick farewells to Thatcher and the professor and continued on to the earl's aunt's. Ian hoped she wouldn't be offended that Madam Dimbleby had insisted on attending Theo's lessons. As they climbed the stairs to her distinct blue door, he reasoned that if Lady Arbuthnot took issue with Madam Dimbleby's presence, she could always take it up with her nephew.

Ian arrived at the top of the stairs first and waited until Madam Dimbleby was beside him before he reached up to use the large brass knocker. Before he could even touch it, however, the door was pulled open by Lady Arbuthnot's maid, Bessie. "Hello, Ian, Carl, and of course, Theo," she said happily as she peered out at them. "Lady Arbuthnot's very excited about your visit today, young lady." She focused next on the headmistress. "And you must be Madam Dimbleby!"

"Er . . . ," said Madam Dimbleby, thrown by Bessie's warm greeting.

Bessie nodded as if Madam had formerly introduced herself. "Lady Arbuthnot's very happy you've decided to assist with the lessons," she said.

Ian covered his mouth to hide a giggle as he watched Madam Dimbleby's face register surprise. Finally, she asked, "How did she . . . I mean to say, when did the lady receive word of my interest in attending?"

Bessie laughed and winked at Madam Dimbleby. "The lady is good at knowing things before they happen, ma'am. Won't you please come in?"

The headmistress nodded mutely and stepped across the threshold with Theo at her side and Carl and Ian on their heels. Bessie showed them all into the parlor, where Lady Arbuthnot sat in a beautiful light peach dress with a diamond tiara on her head. "Good morning!" she said brightly as they entered.

"Hello, my lady," said Madam Dimbleby with a small curtsy. "It's lovely to meet you."

"Madam Dimbleby," said the earl's aunt warmly. "At last we make our acquaintance. So nice of you to accompany Theo here. I'm sure she'll be glad of your support."

Madam Dimbleby blushed deeply. "Thank you, my lady," she said.

Lady Arbuthnot next focused on the boys. "And Ian and Carl, good morning to you. Lovely of you to return, if only for a short visit this time? I expect you'll have a moment for some tea and a few tarts before you'll have to leave again."

Ian's mouth fell open. The lady's ability to know things was uncanny! "Yes, my lady," said Ian with a small bow.

"Me lady?" Carl asked, and Ian noticed that his cheeks had turned a bit pink.

"Yes, Carl?"

"If . . . I may ask you something?" he said shyly.

"Of course, child. What is it?"

Carl shuffled his feet nervously, hesitating before he said, "Could you please tell me mum . . . happy birthday from me?"

There was a collective gasp in the room. Madam Dimbleby immediately put her arm around Carl and squeezed him tightly. Theo was also moved and reached out and grasped Carl's hand, and Lady Arbuthnot's face held such a look of compassion that Ian found it difficult to swallow.

"Carl, my dear boy," the lady said to him with a shake of her head and a small chuckle. "You don't need me to be your interpreter. The dead can hear us loud and clear. It is the living who struggle to listen to those who have gone on. Your mummy knows whenever you're thinking of her, so I am quite positive that she is aware that today, she is in your thoughts and prayers and that you are wishing her a happy birthday."

Carl's pink cheeks turned a blaze of red and he lowered his eyes and shuffled his feet again. "Thank you, my lady," he said hoarsely.

"Now, come, sit down and take some tea," Lady Arbuthnot continued. "We've got a place for each of you, and Bessie has just returned from the market with some fresh tarts for our lessons."

Ian held a chair out for his headmistress under the approving eye of Lady Arbuthnot, and Carl seemed to realize that a certain politeness was required, so he hurried to pull Theo's chair out for her. Theo smiled shyly at him as she sat down, and then Ian and Carl took their seats.

Lady Arbuthnot looked at each of them warmly and began pouring them tea after motioning to the plate of delicious-looking tarts in the center of the table.

When everyone had been served, the lady began. "This lesson will be primarily for Theo, but you are all welcome to listen quietly, as I believe that even those without Theo's talent can benefit from the knowledge." This delighted Ian, because he was very curious about this fortune-telling business and how it all worked.

"Theo, dear," she said, turning her full attention to the girl. "We talked last week about some of the visions you've been experiencing and the terrible fright they'd given you. Have you had any such reoccurrences?"

"Yes, ma'am," Theo said. "I had a strange vision just last Sunday, but I don't know what to make of it."

"And what was this vision?" asked Lady Arbuthnot.

"Well," Theo said, frowning, "it was just after Ian and Carl ran off to the bakery for some bread. I had this very clear vision of the wall of a tunnel with a skeleton sticking straight out of it. I saw Carl in the vision, and somehow I knew he was with Ian, and both of them were terribly frightened, but I don't know why other than for the skeleton." Looking at Ian and Carl, she added, "I didn't tell you because I didn't know what to make of it and I didn't want to upset either of you."

Ian felt a cold sweat break out along his brow and Carl began choking on his tart, coughing and sputtering crumbs all about the table. Madam Dimbleby had to reach over and urgently pat his back while he attempted to recover himself.

Lady Arbuthnot looked pointedly at Ian, who dropped his eyes to the table and feigned a sudden interest in the pattern of the tablecloth. "That *is* an odd vision, Theo," said the lady with a slight chuckle. "And I suspect that someday soon it will make sense. In the meantime, may I ask if you've had any others?"

Theo hesitated before speaking, so Ian lifted his eyes off the table and noticed with alarm that she'd gone a bit pale again. "Just one," she said softly, "but it was too awful to describe."

Lady Arbuthnot looked thoughtfully at Theo. "You're probably wondering why most of your visions are so frightening," she said to her. When Theo nodded, Lady Arbuthnot picked up a tart, took a small bite, and chewed the treat before answering. "It's simple, really," she said. "Events that involve great sorrow or pain or shock or fear are much louder than most of the common occurrences of every day."

"My lady?" Theo asked, seeming not quite to understand.

"Think of it like this, dear," replied Lady Arbuthnot. "Let's pretend that one day I invited you over and while I was here in the parlor, you were in my library, looking at my collection of books. Now, say that you spot your favorite book way up on the top shelf. So, being a courageous lass, you get the ladder and set it against the shelf, climbing up to fetch the book, but what you don't realize is that my ladder has a weak spot, and that when you step on the sixth rung, it gives out and you tumble to the ground, where you let go a great howl of pain as you break your leg!"

Ian's eyes were large as he listened to the lady and wondered what this had to do with her point. "Now then," Lady Arbuthnot continued. "Let's imagine another scenario where you find the book you want on the bottom shelf and when you extract it from the bookshelf, you get a paper cut and let out a small hiss. Which of these two events am I likely to overhear, sitting here in the parlor?"

"The first one?" answered Theo, her brows knit in confusion.

"Yes!" said the lady proudly. "I'm far more likely to hear

the commotion of you falling off the ladder and breaking your leg than if you merely cut yourself on a bit of paper. The first event is louder, bolder, and holds much more pain. The second is soft, barely a whisper with only a bit of discomfort."

Theo's features lit up with sudden comprehension. "Oh!" she said. "I understand! The more frightful the event, the more likely I am to perceive it!"

"Exactly!" said Lady Arbuthnot with a smile. "It's not that you'll always see events that are frightening, just that right now, they are the *loudest* to your untrained senses and are overwhelming you. I expect that your awakening to such things has been causing you a bit of distress, likely making you believe that you're going a bit mad, and others, I should think, fear that too?" she added, looking expectantly at Madam Dimbleby, whose expression confirmed the truth.

Ian felt a powerful admiration for the earl's aunt and he realized suddenly that he was quite grateful that Madam Dimbleby had come along to witness this lesson, because she could see that the lady was someone who understood and could make sense of Theo's odd behavior. Clearly, Lady Arbuthnot didn't believe that Theo's rantings were a reason to send her off to a sanitarium.

Theo spoke next and her voice was haunted. "But how do I make them stop?"

Lady Arbuthnot frowned. "You don't, I'm afraid," she said. "From what I've seen of your abilities thus far, Theo, you're extremely gifted. Your sense is perhaps the greatest I've ever encountered and your natural abilities surpass even my own talents. That means, my dear, that you shall have to use temperance and caution around all of the visions that you receive. You must develop the ability to step back from the most frightening elements—those parts that are truly alarming—to gain perspective of the overall message of the vision. For, as you will discover, all visions are a mixed blessing of insight and caution."

"What kind of caution?" asked Madam Dimbleby.

Lady Arbuthnot turned her gaze back to the head-mistress. "Oh, that is for Theo to divine," she said. "I'm afraid only the seer can unlock the secrets to their own intuition."

Ian rubbed his forehead. All of this doubletalk was making his head hurt. He glanced at Carl, who was looking just as confused. "If I can't stop the visions," said Theo, "can I at least control them?"

"Not only will you be able to exert some control, my dear girl, but you'll soon learn how to master your gifts and help people with what you see. You are destined for greatness, Theo. Of that, *I* am certain."

Theo looked at Lady Arbuthnot in wonder and Ian's heart filled with pride. He'd always known that Theo was special, and now here was the earl's aunt confirming it. But his happy moment was cut short when the lady's attention turned abruptly to the doorway of the parlor, as if she'd heard something that alarmed her out in the hallway.

Theo too looked upset and she rubbed her shoulders as if she were cold, but Ian noticed that the small fire in the fire-place seemed to be filling the room with an unreasonable amount of heat. Lady Arbuthnot got up quickly from the table and hurried to the fireplace.

Ian watched in confusion as she took a large vase of fresh flowers off the mantel, and after pulling the blooms out, she doused the hearth with the water, extinguishing the flames. Smoke smoldered acridly about the room, and Lady Arbuthnot called out, "Bessie! Come here please . . . *quickly!*" With her elbow, she flipped off the light switch, throwing the room into a dim gloom.

A moment later Bessie appeared in the doorway. "Yes, me lady?" she asked, looking quizzically at the empty vase in Lady Arbuthnot's hand.

"The knocker is about to sound. You are not to answer the door under any condition."

Just then the front knocker clacked twice, causing everyone but Lady Arbuthnot to jump. "Shhh," she said quietly as she held a finger to her lips. There was a long pause; then two clacks sounded into the parlor again, this time more insistently, and they all held their breath and waited.

From his chair Ian had a glimpse through the sheer curtains and he could clearly see the form of a woman standing on the top step, looking expectantly at the door. He thought he recognized the woman, but couldn't quite place her until the stranger turned slightly and Ian had a good view of her face.

He gasped when he realized that it was Frau Van Schuft, the woman who had adopted Searle and Isabella. "I know her," whispered Madam Dimbleby, and Ian saw that she too was looking intently out the window. "She and her husband are from Austria. They came to adopt two children a fortnight ago."

Out the corner of his eye, Ian saw Lady Arbuthnot nod, but she held her finger to her lips again with a soft "Shhh." Ian looked back to the window and watched as Frau Van Schuft gave the brass knocker two more clacks, waited a few tense heartbeats, then walked down the steps and away from the flat.

Without looking, Lady Arbuthnot seemed to relax and flipped the light switch back on. "Bessie," she said calmly, handing over the flowers and the vase, "would you please refill this and get the fire started again for us?"

"Yes, me lady," said the maid as she turned to go.

"Oh, and Bessie," Lady Arbuthnot added, "from now on I shall want a pail of water by every fireplace with enough water to douse the flames."

"As you wish, me lady," said Bessie with a curtsy and a quizzical look before she hurried off.

Lady Arbuthnot went back to her guests at the table. "Shall we continue with our lesson, then?"

"She came to the keep, looking for me, you know," Theo murmured.

"Who?" asked Lady Arbuthnot as she took her seat and lifted the teapot to pour them all a little more tea, as if nothing odd had just happened.

"That woman at your door. She's been trying to find me," Theo said softly. "But she guessed wrong and took Isabella instead . . . and now Isabella is dead."

Another collective gasp circled the table. "What?" breathed Madam Dimbleby in surprise. "Theo, why would you *say* such a thing?" But before Theo could answer, Ian remembered the newspaper article about the urchin girl found frozen in the London alleyway, and knew, without knowing how, that it was about Isabella.

Across the table Theo looked into her teacup, her face very sad, and Carl tried to comfort her. Lifting the nearly empty plate of treats, he said, "There, there, Theo. Have another tart and you'll feel better."

But Theo wasn't so easily consoled. With eyes still downcast she shook her head and said, "Isabella's ghost came to me in a dream last night. That was the vision I was afraid to talk about earlier. She was blue with cold and shivering but she managed to tell me that she'd been killed by an evil woman with frightening eyes. She also said I was in terrible danger and that I needed to be very careful or I could end up frozen, just like her."

Madam Dimbleby's eyes were wide with horror and shock, and she opened her mouth to say something, but Lady Arbuthnot gave her a sharp look of caution and said, "I'm so sorry about your friend, Theo."

Theo gave a small shrug. "I didn't know her very well. I just knew that I couldn't go with that wretched couple. There was something about them that smelled of evil." Theo shuddered. "Do you think it's my fault Isabella is dead, my lady?" she asked, her voice laden with guilt.

The earl's aunt gave her hand a gentle pat. "No, my dear. I think blame lies solely with the woman who was just at my door. You should not worry, however. We shall keep those nasty people far away from you." Then, turning to the still rather shocked Madam Dimbleby, she said, "The couple that adopted Isabella, they shall return to your orphanage and tell you a lie about Isabella being lonely for a sister. You are to be polite, but tell them that you can't possibly give up another child to their care, as British law prohibits the adoption of any more than two children at a time to foreign nationals. You are not to let on that you know about Isabella, because to do so would put you all in grave danger. And if you're worried about the boy, don't be. We all make our choices in life, Madam Dimbleby. And we must all deal with the consequences."

"But . . . but . . . ," Madam Dimbleby stammered, appearing truly unnerved.

"No buts, Madam," said Lady Arbuthnot sternly. "You shall know the truth of what Theo has said soon enough and justice shall be served to those vile people. For now you must trust the advice I have given you. Do you understand?"

Slowly, Madam Dimbleby nodded. "Yes, my lady," she said.

"Very well," said Lady Arbuthnot with a friendly smile; then she turned to Ian and Carl. "Boys, it was a pleasure having you join us for tea today, but I'm afraid the other two in your party have returned to retrieve you." And as she finished speaking, there came another clack at the door, causing everyone but the lady to jump.

A moment later they heard Bessie's loud voice out in the hallway announce, "Hello again, Master Goodwyn! And you must be the professor. It's lovely to meet you, sir. If you'd like to wait here, I'll fetch the boys for you."

AS DARKNESS LOOMS
AND SHADOWS CAST

I an and Carl gave their goodbyes and hurried to the entryway. They met Thatcher and the grumpy Professor Nutley—who seemed very impatient to be off again—and gave their farewells to Bessie, who kindly handed them each a few tarts wrapped in a bit of wax paper. "For the road," she said with a wink at the boys.

The foursome arrived just a quarter of an hour later at the professor's cluttered and decaying doorstep and the old man waddled up the stone steps stiffly. He handed Thatcher his bundle of papers and folders while he fussed with his house keys, then opened the door and went right in. Thatcher glanced back at Ian and Carl, who were waiting at the bottom of the steps to be invited inside. "Come along, boys," he directed. "The morning is quickly slipping by."

The boys polished off the last of their tarts and trotted up the steps and into the flat. Ian was rather surprised that the mess from their last visit seemed even bigger and more disorderly this week.

"Blimey!" exclaimed Carl, reflecting Ian's thoughts exactly. "I didn't think it was possible for it to get worse."

"Shhh," cautioned Ian while he stifled a smile. "The professor might hear you."

Thatcher took off his coat and hat and hung them on the coat hook, then motioned for the boys to do the same.

Ian and Carl wiggled out of their coats, then followed Thatcher through the maze of clutter, on the lookout for the professor, who had disappeared. Their schoolmaster seemed to know he'd be in his library, and sure enough, as they entered that room, they found him squished behind his desk, sorting through his stack of papers and files from Blythe House.

Thatcher stepped into the room and waited for the professor to notice him, but after several long moments Ian finally cleared his throat and asked, "Excuse me, Professor, but would you like Carl and me to start tidying up for you?"

The professor's head snapped up and he blinked once or twice before saying, "No, my young man. I would like for you to take a seat and give me a moment to finish looking through this. Then you and I will have a discussion."

Ian couldn't imagine what the professor wanted to discuss, and his mind raced with possibilities. Perhaps he knew about the skeleton in the tunnel. Perhaps he suspected even more that Ian was part of a hoax that involved a duplicate map and the silver box. Perhaps there was some other awful thing Ian knew nothing about that he would be accused of being involved in.

The sound of a clock ticking faintly from beneath a pile

of clutter made Ian even more anxious and he began to sweat and fidget nervously. The professor looked back and forth between a very old piece of parchment nestled in one of the folders he'd brought back with him and something hidden behind a stack of papers. At one point he rooted around in his drawer again for his trusty magnifying glass, which he lowered to the parchment, then over to the item Ian couldn't see.

Finally, the old man set the magnifying glass down and removed his spectacles. Rubbing his eyes tiredly, he let out a long sigh. "Well?" asked Thatcher, and Ian noticed he seemed quite anxious about something.

"It is as I suspected, Master Goodwyn," said the professor. "The handwriting is unmistakable. It is Laodamia's."

Ian looked back to Thatcher, who appeared dumbstruck. "But . . . but . . . ," he said. "*How*, Professor?"

The professor shook his head slowly. "I haven't any idea, my good man." Then he turned his attention to Ian and regarded him for long seconds before speaking again. "Ian Wigby," he said softly.

Ian gulped and pulled at his collar, certain that he was in terrible trouble. "Y-y-yes, sir?" he stuttered.

"I cannot imagine how a woman who lived nearly three thousand four hundred years ago could have such a strong connection to a boy and a girl living today, but somehow, the powers of the greatest Oracle of Delphi far exceeded my initial observations."

Out the corner of his eye, Ian caught Carl turning and staring at him with a confused look.

"I'm sorry, sir," Ian said slowly, "but I'm afraid I don't understand."

The professor stood up and pushed his chair away from his desk, which allowed him the smallest space to pace back and forth. "Of course you don't understand, lad!" he said. "How *could* you possibly understand these things? And yet, here you sit at the center of the most remarkable archaeological discovery the world has ever seen!"

Carl began to giggle and soon he was laughing and rocking back and forth, pointing first at the professor, then at Ian, who couldn't help laughing too, and it all seemed very funny until the professor cleared his throat gruffly and snapped, "What is so amusing, young men?"

Ian stopped laughing immediately but Carl snickered some more and wiped his eyes. "Well, it's all a prank, isn't it?" he said.

The professor scratched his head and smoldered with irritation. "A prank?" he sniffed. "You're playing a prank with me here?"

Carl's smile faltered. "Er . . . no, sir," he said. "*You're* playing a prank on *us*, aren't you?"

The professor looked at Thatcher. "What is this confusing young man going on about?"

Thatcher pushed away from the wall he'd been leaning against. "I'm afraid he believes you were attempting a bit of humor, Professor."

The professor's eyes narrowed as he looked at Carl. "I assure you, young man, this is no prank!"

Carl's smile disappeared completely and he dropped his

eyes to the floor. "Oh," he said meekly. "I'm terribly sorry, sir. Please continue with your great discovery, then."

The professor snorted and turned back to Ian, who resisted the urge to flinch under that reproachful glare. "As I was saying, Master Wigby, before I was so *rudely* interrupted, I believe this scroll to be authentic and I believe the message inscribed in it to be as extraordinary a discovery as the Rosetta stone!"

Ian tugged again at his collar. He had no idea what the professor was talking about and felt conflicted about saying so after the crisp rebuff Carl had just received, so he simply nodded.

Fortunately, Thatcher stepped in to clarify things. "Professor," he said gently, "perhaps the lads could benefit from a bit of history here to help them understand the importance of what you've discovered."

The professor went back to his pacing and nodded. "Yes, yes," he said. "History is a good place to start." The old man then stopped pacing and looked at Ian and Carl thoughtfully before he began. "As I'm sure your schoolmaster has told you, I am a noted archaeologist and I've excavated many lost ruins throughout the world. One of the very first excavations I worked on was when I was about Master Goodwyn's age, and it was in my very own backyard, right here in merry old England. For my college thesis I chose to look at our Druids—an ancient and sophisticated civilization embroiled in myth and magic.

"Very little is known about the Druids, you see. We are witness to evidence of them all over the countryside in the form of some crumbling ruin or other, but these were not people who wrote anything down other than a few mysterious runes on a rock or two around the landscape. And yet we do know that these people had an incredibly advanced knowledge of astronomy and astrology, and they were quite proficient at making tools and weaponry from bronze. But there is something else that is truly extraordinary about the Druids: we still don't know how these relatively primitive peoples were able to accomplish such incredible feats of physics."

"Like what feats, Professor?" asked Carl, clearly confused.

"Have you boys ever heard of the Druid standing stones?" the professor asked.

Ian pumped his head up and down. "Yes, of course," he said. "Stonehenge has a whole circle of them, doesn't it?"

The professor winked at Ian. "Very good, lad," he said. "Yes, Stonehenge is perhaps the best-known example, but there are others that are even more impressive. You see, what makes these standing stones so extraordinary is their sheer size, weight, and often where they were quarried from. I know of one stone in a small village in Germany that is estimated to be at least sixty meters tall and weigh over twenty thousand kilos! And to give you an idea of how heavy that is, gentlemen, not even our most sophisticated cranes would be able to erect it. Yet, these rather primitive people carved it out of a distant quarry, got it across several kilometers of rough and hilly terrain, and then managed to set it upright, where it withstood the elements for centuries before cracking in half and falling to the ground."

Ian's eyes widened and his memory flashed back to the stones that covered the stairway to the hidden tunnel. He wondered suddenly where they had come from and who had placed them there. "What was it about these big rocks that made them so important to these people?" he asked.

"No one knows," said the professor. "But when I was a much younger man, I desperately wanted to find out. So I set about to excavate the ruins of Grimspound, in what is now Dartmoor in the southwest of England. And the discovery I made was extraordinary, but it has taken me these past fifty years to conclude that."

Ian and Carl exchanged another look and Carl shrugged. So both boys waited patiently for the professor to continue, and after taking a sip of water from a glass on his desk, he did. "You see, early in my excavations I discovered a very well-preserved hut, which contained three perfectly intact clay pots.

"The pottery depicted a fascinating story. The artisan was the daughter of a village elder, who, as a child, had been orphaned and was found wandering about near the village, clearly having suffered a terrible ordeal. The artisan said that her mother had remained mute afterward until her dying day, when she told her daughter the story of the four off-spring of Gorgon and how they had destroyed her village and killed her entire family."

"Who's Gorgon?" Carl asked.

"I'm getting to that," said the professor with an impatient wave. "The Druids believed, much as the ancient Greeks, in a series of gods who wielded their power both above and below the earth. Gorgon was the god of the underworld, and coincidentally, Demogorgon was the name of the same god in ancient Greece."

"I thought it was Hades," said Ian, remembering a book on mythology he'd read from the earl's library.

"Hades was the later version," said the professor. "The first was Demogorgon and he was a much nastier character indeed."

Ian shivered. For some reason he didn't like hearing the name out loud.

"Now, on these clay pots," the professor continued, "I discovered, the artisan said that before her mother had been found wandering in the fields near their home, she had belonged to a distant village and had a large family. On her maternal side, she had four beautiful aunts who were the prize of the village. Everyone knew they would marry well, and often suitors came to court them. But one sunny day, the four aunts wandered off and were lost for many moons. Searches were conducted far and wide, but no sign of them could be found, and the villagers decided the aunts had been kidnapped by raiders. But just as a war party was being formed to attack the raiders' camps, the four maidens appeared in the village again, each in terrible condition, with burns and cut marks and dirt covering their faces, and something else: all four women were now heavy with child.

"The aunts each told a similar tale of how they had been lured mysteriously into a cave by a voice which called them each by name. They had followed the voice and found themselves deep within the cave, lost and frightened. The farther they went, the hotter it became, but a light ahead pulled them forward.

"Finally, these sisters came to a beautiful chamber filled with pools of warm soothing water, and gold and diamonds sparkling from the walls. Being exhausted after their long journey, the maidens soon fell fast asleep. When next they woke, the four of them were with child and quite alarmed by that fact. Not knowing what terrible trick had been played on them, they hurried out of the chamber. For days they walked through the maze of caves and tunnels, and finally reappeared out of the rock and made their way back to their village. The very night the sisters returned, all four went into labor and each one died in childbirth."

"That's very sad," said Carl, and Ian knew that his friend was thinking about his own mother.

"Yes," said the professor, "but for the time, not that unusual. Now, many years later and while on her deathbed, the elder told her daughter that the children born to these maidens were the most hideous of creatures, barely passable as humans, in fact. But the village felt obligated to raise them, and so they did, but soon each child began to show signs of black magic. One child could start fires with the snap of his fingers, while another could turn a bucket of water into solid ice just by looking at it. Still another could tear up the crops by creating small wind-filled cyclones, and the fourth could open up the earth and make a grown man fall into the crevice just by thinking it."

Ian looked skeptically at the professor. This sounded like some sort of fairy tale. Still, he waited for the professor to continue.

"The village put up with these little devil children," the professor said, "until their antics became too much to bear, and the elders gathered and decided to banish them before they brought the village to ruin. The artisan's mother, it seems, was the only one who showed the departing four any bit of kindness, because as they were being tossed out, she gave each of them a bucket of milk and some cheese for their journey. And this, according to her, was why she was later spared their vengeful wrath.

"Within a season the children of the maidens were back and they reigned down the full power of their horrible abilities on the village. Huts were burned to the ground; whole families were swallowed up by the earth; other villagers were turned to solid ice; and anyone who remained was engulfed in a powerful cyclone and carried away, never to be seen again—except of course the artisan's mother, who was carried on a more gentle wind to a land far, far away, where she was laid down as if she'd been a leaf on a breeze. And this was where she was found wandering the fields, lost and afraid, and soon adopted by the new village."

"All that was on these pots?" asked Thatcher.

"Yes," said the professor with a chuckle. "I tell you, it was quite a story. And it was so rich with detail that I never forgot it. But, years later when I was on that expedition in Greece and excavating Adria's scrolls, a colleague of mine, Sir Donovan Barnaby, happened upon another bounty. He found a similar villa to excavate not far from where I was digging and he too discovered some scrolls. These appeared to be written by the Oracle Laodamia herself.

"Donovan was a right old chap, but a bit daft if I might say so, and he often put an importance on things that, quite frankly, weren't of great value, which is why his discovery of Laodamia's scrolls was largely ignored."

"If I might ask," said Ian, intensely curious, "what did the Oracle's scrolls say exactly?"

The professor took his seat, wiping his spectacles with his sweater sleeve as he answered. "They told of a great and impending danger," he said ominously. "Donovan and I used to share a bit of whiskey every night around dusk and discuss our separate excavations and I do remember at the time being startled to learn that Laodamia had such impressive examples of forecasting events far out into the future. According to Donovan, she had predicted the burning of the library at Alexandria in the third century BC, the Battle of Thermopylae in 480 BC, the birth of Christ, the rise and fall of the Roman Empire, and . . . well, many other events. And the astounding thing, again per my colleague, was that according to his translations, these events actually happened *exactly* as Laodamia predicted they would in her scrolls."

"Extraordinary!" said Thatcher. "Professor, did you have a look at Sir Barnaby's translations?"

"No," said the professor. "That is, not until this last week. Donovan and I got into an argument over whose discovery held more importance, and of course I believed at the time that much of his translations must have held errors, because I couldn't fathom a person able to foretell such events so accurately."

"So you rang him up to ask him?" Ian said.

The professor shook his head sadly. "No, my boy, I'm afraid Sir Barnaby was killed on a later expedition back to Phoenicia when the tent he was in caught fire. It was a tragic death, and later, when I learned he'd willed me all of the papers and notes he'd taken, plus a few of the scrolls, I was in a state of deep regret over our argument, as you can imagine, so I shipped them all off to Blythe House, where they've been collecting dust all these years."

"But now you've had a chance to review the papers?" asked Ian, hoping the professor would get to his point before sundown.

The professor chuckled. "Yes, yes, my dear boy. I have. And I've had a chance to go over Barnaby's translations and Laodamia's scrolls and found them to be accurate word for word. And now I have two bits of fact that through my own experience I can link together in a truly incredible way."

"What facts?" asked Thatcher.

"In reviewing Laodamia's scrolls I did indeed discover that the great Oracle of Delphi was extraordinarily gifted. Her writings talked in great detail of events that had not happened yet and they also discussed something rather profound. You see, Laodamia was haunted by dreams involving the god of the underworld."

"That Gorgony character?" Carl asked.

"Demogorgon," corrected the professor. "But you're close. As I was saying, Laodamia's dreams suggested a direct telepathic link with this nasty character, and in one of her writings, she recounted a most disturbing dream in which she had seen four maidens asleep in a chamber hidden deep underground.

"Within this chamber she beheld the horrible vision of Demogorgon himself laughing and plotting and suggesting to his underworld servants that he had finally developed a master plan to break out of his fiery prison. He said that each of the four maidens would soon bear him a child, one male

325

and three females who would grow up to become the greatest sorcerer and sorceresses the world had ever known. As Laodamia watched, the underworld god pointed to each woman's belly and called out four names—Magus, Caphiera, Atroposa, and Lachestia—and each unborn babe he gifted with command over one of the four earthly elements."

Ian scrunched his face up. "Excuse me, Professor," he said. "But aren't there lots more than just four elements?"

"Well, yes," said the professor, "but I'm not talking about the modern version of elements. I'm talking about the Greek version during Laodamia's time, which were only the four tangible elements of fire, earth, air, and water and one intangible element, which was thought, or ideas."

Ian gasped, finally understanding. "Oh!" he said. "It's just like those clay pots you found at Grimspound! The four maidens gave birth to those children that destroyed that village with fire, water, air, and earth!"

The professor smiled at him. "Yes, Ian, exactly. And how Laodamia could have dreamed such a tale and written it down in almost the exact detail as that Druid elder recalled half a world and probably several centuries away is profound indeed."

"So what do these children have to do with helping Demogorgon escape?" Ian asked.

"Ah, yes," he said. "The rest of Laodamia's dream told that once the children were born, they had one sole purpose, and that was to incite conflict.

"You see, in early Greek mythology, Demogorgon was one of the original offspring of the Titan King Cronus, along with his brothers, Zeus and Poseidon, and their three sisters.

But it was Demogorgon who took after his father in his truly evil ways.

"The mythology suggests that Zeus and the other gods discovered a plot crafted by Demogorgon to imprison them all deep within the earth. Their jealous brother had secretly forged out a place underground that no god could escape from. But in the end it was Demogorgon who was imprisoned as his brothers and sisters managed to ensnare him in his own trap within the fiery underworld.

"In her dream of the four maidens, Laodamia learned some important things: she learned that Demogorgon fed from human suffering. The more a mortal suffered before death, the more it fed and nurtured the underworld king.

"And this gave Demogorgon a truly hideous idea. He would have his halfling children, Magus, Caphiera, Atroposa, and Lachestia, serve him by inciting ever greater conflicts. The more people that populated the earth, the more sheep for his slaughter and his feast. And Demogorgon saw a time thousands of years later when the earth would be so densely populated that if enough mortals were swept up in a great conflict and suffered or died, he could gain enough power to allow him to break free of his prison and exert his revenge on the gods by destroying their precious planet.

"Laodamia foretold of a time when the earth would be generously populated and a great war, larger than any that had ever been waged, would be incited by and propelled by Demogorgon's children, and millions and millions would suffer and die. And because of this vision, she also knew that the future of mankind was in great peril."

Ian heard Carl gulp next to him. He turned and saw that

his friend's eyes were large with fear, and he knew that Carl must be thinking, like he was, of Theo's horrible prediction of the rise of the Fury and the devastation that would follow. "What would happen if he broke free?" Carl asked meekly.

The professor sighed heavily. "Armageddon," he said simply. "The god of the underworld would turn the world over to his children, who upon his release would be ten thousand times more powerful. He would give each child one quarter of the world to rule. Magus, the ruler of fire, would turn his quarter to a wasteland of lava and ash. Caphiera would bury her quarter in one hundred kilometers of ice. Lachestia would churn the earth in her quarter down to rubble and rock and not much else. And Atroposa would strip all the land bare in her quarter with wild cyclones and hurricanes. No mortal would be left alive and the earth would soon find itself as barren as the moon."

Silence fell on the room as everyone absorbed what that world would be like, and Ian felt a deep chill settle into his stomach. His logical mind told him that this was all a bit of myth that coincidentally matched up with another bit of myth a world away and just happened to slide nicely next to Theo's predictions of impending doom, but still, it all rattled him to the marrow.

Finally, Ian asked, "Did Laodamia say when these events were likely to occur?"

The professor lifted his hands into a steeple and rested his chin atop his fingertips. "That is where our story gets a bit murky," he said. When Ian cocked his head in confusion, the old man explained, "We believe that around the time Laodamia prophesized this gloomy portrait, things within her own city took a turn for the worse. The political climate shifted against her for some unknown reason, and she was forced to divine all other prophecies secretly. This was when the Oracle covertly commissioned the creation of the silver boxes to hold her most important prophecies. It was rumored that Laodamia knew of a power greater than Demogorgon and it became her mission to assist this beacon of hope by hiding her six most precious prophecies in the far corners of the earth. I know through the journals of Adria that Laodamia left these boxes with trusted friends, relatives, and disciples with explicit instruction that they were to hand them down from generation to generation until the offspring identified by Laodamia were to hide the boxes in specified locations.

"After authenticating the silver box that you discovered against Adria's blueprint—which has always rested in my sole possession and, to my knowledge, has never been reproduced—I believe that it, Master Wigby, is one of the boxes Laodamia had commissioned. I further believe that the great Oracle of Delphi knew that you and your friend Theo would play an integral role in some grand prophecy involving what she called the Rise of Demogorgon."

Ian felt the air leave his lungs, and the room took on a hot and stifling atmosphere. He struggled to breathe, panic overwhelming him. As if from the other end of a tunnel, he heard Carl exclaim, "Ian and Theo? But what've they got to do with it?"

"Professor Nutley has translated all of the writing on the cavern wall and the scroll found in the treasure box," Thatcher answered, snapping Ian back. "Professor, would you like to explain to the boys what you told me about the deciphering?"

"I took a cue from you, young lad," said the professor with a wry smile as he pointed a crooked finger at Carl. "It was how you looked at the writing on the scroll and saw the word 'the.' I told you then that it was impossible for the scroll to start out that way. For one, you were reading in the wrong direction, and for another, the ancient Phoenicians had no vowels in their vocabulary. Instead, the vowels were implied in the way the consonants were arranged. But when I took the scroll out and looked at it with fresh eyes, I realized that the characters that were unfamiliar to me actually *were* crude renditions of vowels that closely resemble ours in the English language.

"Further, I noticed that some of the consonants that were unfamiliar in Phoenician, because they were backward or completely invented, also resembled some of the consonant sounds in our own language. It took me the better part of the week to work out the alphabet, but once I worked that out, I also began looking at the wording from left to right, just as Carl had. That's when I made the remarkable discovery that the scroll was written in English using Phoenician traditional scripting and some of these crude letters for vowels and other missing consonants!"

Ian's heart was racing and he felt as if the unnatural events of the last several weeks might finally be catching up with him. "May we hear what it says, then?" he asked in a croaky whisper.

"Yes, yes," the professor said, and waved at Thatcher to come to his desk and take the small notebook he was lifting

330

toward him. "Master Goodwyn, if you will read first the translation from the walls in the cavern where the silver box was discovered by Master Wigby?"

Thatcher took the notebook and flipped it around to read.

" 'For the eyes and ears of Ian Wigby,' " Thatcher began. " 'Laodamia sends her heartfelt thanks and greetings. May this prophecy serve you and the Oracles well.' " Thatcher looked up again and the professor gave him an approving smile. "Now to the prophecy itself," the professor said. Ian was still trying to absorb that the great Oracle of Delphi had personally greeted and thanked him.

The professor flipped through his own notes and cleared his throat before reciting what sounded to Ian's ears very much like a dark poem.

> "The first of you shall be the last
> As darkness looms and shadows cast
> The god of Under strikes a blow
> As vile evil stirs below
> He calls upon his children four
> To find the orphans much before
> The fate of man can be ordained
> The death of many he must claim
> To break out of his fiery hell
> Hear this call to serve you well
> Gather courage and your wits
> Search for boxes—never quit
> Until the last of six is found
> And Delphi's mystics now are bound
> To face the Four and take a stand

Against the threat to all the land
But first you'll start with scroll and map
To lead you down a hidden trap
Into the cavern by the wood
Descend the stairs and hope you should
Have the Seer by your side
To ask the door to open wide
And save you from an icy death
Before her daggers steal your breath
Go beyond Caphiera's reach
The first such place upon the beach
A quest of six and no less few
To find the Seeker young and true
Seeker leads you to the Star
Vital to your journeys far
Seeker guides you deep in stone
Language now is not unknown
Serve you well upon your quest
Break the Star to serve you best
Tuck back through and do not tarry
Time is key to all you carry
Find the next, there's five to come
Each will give one part of sum
Will you win or will you lose?
It will lie in who you choose."

The professor set his notes down, and a long moment of silence followed while Ian blinked rapidly in confusion. He had no idea what most of the poem was saying, nor what he could possibly have to do with any of it.

Thatcher finally spoke. "What do you think, Ian?" he asked.

Ian looked up at his schoolmaster, his expression doubtful. "I'm afraid that I haven't the faintest idea, sir," he said. Then something occurred to him. "But maybe this Seer that Laodamia is referring to—could that be Theo?"

Thatcher beamed. "That's what I believe," he said, and he looked at the professor. "I've brought Professor Nutley up to date on all Theo's abilities and predictions."

"Remarkable girl," said the professor with a nod. "Much of the middle and end of this, however," he said with a wave of his hand over the translation, "doesn't make a great deal of sense to us either."

"That part about gathering Delphi's mystics . . . ," said Carl thoughtfully. "Do you think she was talking about her Delphi or ours? You know, how our home is called Delphi Keep?"

The professor shook his head. "I can't be sure," he said. "But I'll give you that it is a rather remarkable coincidence that both Laodamia and you lot should be gathered in a place named Delphi."

Ian agreed; the coincidence seemed too remarkable to shrug off and he wondered again what the Oracle could possibly want with him.

"Do you have a theory on what the Star could be?" asked Thatcher. "Perhaps this is a constellation that Laodamia referred to in other prophecies?"

The professor furrowed his brow. "There was no mention of any star or constellation in any of the scrolls Barnaby discovered on his dig in Delphi—but then, I must conclude that we likely have only uncovered a portion of the Oracle's writings."

"What's a Seeker?" asked Ian.

"Ah, well, that I may know a little bit about," said the professor. "One of Laodamia's many talents was her alleged power over crystals. She used them extensively in her healing practices and fostered a school for other gifted Oracles who gravitated toward harnessing the individual power of crystals."

"Crystals have *power?*" Carl asked, taking the question right out of Ian's mouth.

The professor looked thoughtful. "I have personally never given much credence to the idea, but it is based on a bit of real science. Crystals, you see, are formed from the condensation of gases and pressure deep within the earth. The result is a series of repeating lattices made up of molecules that form an overall unique structure. This latticework is what gives the crystal its shape, color, and clarity. Within every crystal there are molecules that get left out of the chain of latticework and become free-floating. When energy is introduced to the crystal in the form of, say, heat, it can excite these free-floating molecules and they begin to vibrate, bouncing back and forth within the walls of the latticework in a unique rhythm.

"People who subscribe to the idea of metaphysical attributes of crystals believe that there are certain individuals of powerful intuitive ability who can excite these molecules without using heat, that they can *will* them to vibrate, using their minds. The vibrations act as a sort of metronome. It is

believed that when this energized crystal is given to someone who has a physical malady, the crystal restores the body's
natural rhythms or creates some sort of medicinal effect.

"Laodamia called those intuitives who could create these
rhythms from crystals Seekers, because she noticed that
these Oracles were always seeking to bring out the power of
the crystal they encountered."

"So this Star isn't really a star, then," Ian observed, his
hand subconsciously smoothing over the lump in his trouser
pocket, where he carried Theo's crystal. He couldn't help
wondering if maybe she was both the Seer and the Seeker in
Laodamia's prophecy. "It must be some kind of a crystal?"

The professor looked down at his notes again and barked
a laugh. "I believe you're quite right, Ian. The trouble is that
the word 'star' is often used to describe many of the world's
most valuable diamonds and precious gemstones. I know of
several, in fact, that are within the collection of the crown
jewels, including the Great Star of Africa on the king's
scepter, which is also the second largest diamond in the
world."

"Do you think this Star that Laodamia wants us to find is
one of the crown jewels?" asked Thatcher, and his expression
suggested to Ian that he wasn't at all pleased with the
thought of nicking one of the crown jewels.

"I've no idea," answered the professor with a sigh. "The
prophecy states that we must look upon a beach, but I've
never heard of anyone finding such a precious mineral
there." Ian immediately discounted the idea that maybe the
crystal in his pocket was the Star. It had come to Theo from

her mother, not from the beach, and he thought that if her crystal was the Star, Laodamia wouldn't be talking about quests and seekers; she would just refer to the gemstone and be done with it. "Like I said," continued the professor, "much of this prophecy seems to make no sense."

The room fell back into silence as the foursome considered again the lines from the poem. Suddenly, Carl's face brightened. "Ian!" he said excitedly. "Do you think that part about the map and the trap and the cavern in the woods with the stairs could be that tunnel we found last Sunday? You know, because it doesn't lead anywhere but to a wall? And that soldier—he certainly got trapped, didn't he?"

Ian sucked in a breath and gave Carl a firm look, reminding the boy that the tunnel was a secret, but it was too late: the truth was out. Thatcher looked sharply at Carl and asked, "What tunnel and what soldier?"

"Er . . . ," said Carl.

"Um . . . ," said Ian, his mind racing to find a plausible response.

"Look here, lads," said Thatcher, his tone stern. "If you two know of something within this prophecy that makes sense, we'd best hear it and hear it now."

"Well," said Carl, fidgeting with his cuff and looking at Ian, who nodded reluctantly. Carl might as well tell them the rest. "It's just that we might have found the tunnel from the map that was pulled out of the box . . . you know, the tunnel that was left off Ian's original map at the keep?"

The professor reached into his desk drawer and carefully pulled out the silver box. He opened the lid, extracted the folded map, and unfolded it carefully; then, placing it in the center of his desk, he demanded, "Show me."

Carl hopped off his chair and walked over to the desk. "It's this one, right, Ian?" he asked over his shoulder.

Ian came to the desk and nodded. "That's the one," he mumbled. "We found it last Sunday, but I don't expect to go there ever again," he said quickly, thinking that he'd be in a load of trouble now unless he promised to quit his exploits.

Carl shivered. "I'll certainly never go there again!" he said. "Not after what we found."

"What did you find?" asked Thatcher. Ian could have thumped his friend on the head. Carl was making it worse before Ian had a chance to explain.

"It was horrible," Carl said dramatically, oblivious to Ian's discomfort. "We saw a skeleton sticking right out of the tunnel wall!"

"Skeleton?" gasped the professor, who looked to Ian for confirmation. "You found *human* remains?"

"Yes, sir," said Ian with a frown, and he tried to put the professor at ease. "Carl and I are certain the remains are very old. They might even be the bones of a soldier who hid Laodamia's treasure box in the cavern for me to find."

"Why do you think the skeleton is a soldier?" asked Thatcher.

"Because there was a helmet next to the bones in the rock and it looked very old and covered in dust."

The professor was eyeing them eagerly. "What kind of helmet?"

"Well," said Ian, "it looked a bit like an egg, and I believe it was made out of bronze."

The professor hurried to his bookcase and began running his fingers over the spines of the books jammed into the shelving. After a few moments he pulled out a volume and flipped it open. Bringing it back to the desk, he turned it around to show Ian and Carl.

Ian studied the black-and-white photograph of a helmet in the book but he shook his head. "That's close," he said, "but the one we found is a bit higher at the point, and the nose plate is thicker."

Carl nodded in agreement and the professor paused before taking the book and flipping a few pages forward. He lowered it so that the boys could see.

"That's it!" said Carl excitedly. "That's the helmet we saw in the tunnel!"

The professor sat down abruptly in his chair. "You're certain?" he asked.

"Yeah," said Carl with confidence. "We can show you where it is, if you'd like, and you can see for yourself."

Thatcher picked up the book and read the title aloud: " 'Armor of the Ancient Greeks.' "

"Yes," said the professor. "The one the boys have identified belonged to the era of Laodamia—roughly 1400 BC—and not to the era of the writing on the wall you discovered in the first tunnel, which I've already dated to be about a thousand years later—400 BC."

"How are both possible?" asked Thatcher, scratching his head.

"I've no idea," said the professor, "but I mean to find out." Turning to Ian and Carl, he said, "Boys, you will take me to this tunnel immediately! I must see this helmet for myself."

"Oh, it's no longer there," said Carl. "We hid it in some rocks just outside the woods."

The professor looked aghast. "You mean to tell me it's being *exposed* to the elements?"

"No," said Ian, hurrying to reassure him. "The rocks are protecting it and we added some grass and twigs to give it extra protection."

"Then we shouldn't wait for a good rainstorm to corrode it," said the professor, standing up and reaching for the thick sweater draped around his chair. "And I shall want to see this skeleton as well."

"Now?" Thatcher asked, glancing at his watch as the professor shrugged into his sweater and waddled stiffly toward the door.

"Yes, now!" said the professor. "Come, come, there's no time to waste!"

Ian hung back, his eyes darting to the scroll's translation, still on the professor's desk. "Sir!" he called to the older man before he could disappear down the hallway.

"Yes?" the professor said over his shoulder.

"Might I bring the translation along with us to study on the train?"

The professor waved his hand impatiently. "Yes, yes," he said, "just hurry along with it!"

Ian leaned over the professor's desk and grabbed the piece of paper before dashing out of the room to catch up with Carl and Thatcher, who was handing the boys their coats. "Quickly now," he said as his eye went to the door and the professor, who was already halfway down the steps.

"What about Theo and Madam Dimbleby?" asked Carl in alarm as they hurried out the door. Ian realized abruptly what they hadn't considered—that rushing back to the keep would mean leaving the pair behind.

His worry was short-lived, however, when they all heard a "Yoo-hoo!" echoing down the street. The four turned and saw the headmistress and Theo hurrying toward them. They paused in front of the group, and before anyone else could get in a word, the professor announced, "We're on our way back to Dover. The boys have discovered some remains within a new tunnel they explored last weekend and I'll want to take a look before it gets dark."

Madam Dimbleby's mouth fell open and her gaze turned to Ian. He gulped and began to offer some kind of an explanation but she cut him off with "Well, professor, let us not dally here. It's off to the train station, then!"

"Uh-oh," murmured Carl as she turned away. "I believe we're going to be in a load of trouble when we get back to the keep."

"Gee, mate, you *think?*" Ian said crossly as Theo joined them.

"What's the professor talking about?" asked Theo.

"I'll explain on the train," said Ian glumly. "Come on. They're waiting for us." And he set off after the adults, his thoughts dark and his mood grim. It seemed to Ian that only a short while before, his life had been rather uncomplicated. Now it felt quite out of control, especially with dark beasts,

340

cryptic prophecies, and evil people about. On the walk back to the station, Ian couldn't help feeling a bit sorry for himself, but then he realized as they boarded the train that he had only himself to blame. After all, he'd been the one to disobey rules and start this awful mess in the first place.

CAPHIERA'S CURSE

Ian was first on the train and he moved down away from the door in search of an empty berth. Finding one near the front, he sat down moodily. As he stared out the window, he soon became aware of someone hovering close by. He turned to see Carl standing in the aisle, looking shyly at the seat next to Ian. "Can I sit there?" he asked meekly.

Ian sighed tiredly and attempted a smile. "Sure, mate, have a seat."

Theo, who must have followed Carl, took a seat across from the boys and looked expectantly at Ian. "Out with it," she ordered as the train doors closed and the locomotive began to roll out of the station. "And don't leave *anything* out."

For the rest of the train ride back to Dover, Ian and Carl explained all that had happened in the newly discovered tunnel, and repeated what the professor had told them about the clay pots at Grimspound, Laodamia, the legend of Demogorgon, and the Oracle's prophecies. "Show me this prophecy from the box," Theo demanded, and Ian pulled it out of his coat pocket.

After studying it for a long, quiet moment, Theo mused, "Now I understand."

"What?" asked Carl. "If you mean you understand the prophecy, Theo, that's fantastic, because our lot didn't have a clue!"

"Not all of it," Theo admitted. "Just a few parts."

"Which ones?" asked Ian, leaning forward to peer upside down at the paper in her hands.

"Well, this part about a Star. When we were finishing up with Lady Arbuthnot, I kept hearing the words 'The Star of Licorice' running round my head."

"The Star of *Licorice?*" said Carl with a laugh. "You must be joking!"

"No," said Theo stiffly. "I'm actually not."

Ian scratched his head thoughtfully. He couldn't imagine a precious gemstone being given the name of a candy, but he had too much respect for Theo's abilities to dismiss it. "I expect we'll find out soon enough what it's all about."

Theo glared at Carl, her feelings clearly bruised by his scoffing remark. "Sorry," he said when he realized he'd offended her. "It's just a bit odd, you know?"

"And all of this other business of beasts, oracles, Druid sorcerers, prophecies, and hidden tunnels isn't?" she snapped.

Carl cleared his throat. "Good point," he said.

Ian saw that Theo was working herself into a good huff, and attempted to change the subject by asking, "What else made sense to you, Theo?"

She scowled one last time at Carl and said, "That bit about the Seeker . . . Yesterday I was helping Agatha look for her shoe—you know how that girl loses everything?" Ian nodded. "Well, while I was looking under her bed, I had a bit of déjà vu, you know where you think you've done what you're doing before?" Again, Ian nodded and Theo continued. "But I knew I wasn't remembering looking for Agatha's shoe. It was the oddest feeling, like I was remembering something that hadn't even happened yet, and it involved crawling around in the dark and there was this sensation that I was looking for something with a boy. . . ." Theo's voice trailed off as if she was thinking back on it, unable to put the event into words.

"What boy?" asked Ian.

"I don't know his name," she said, her face serious. "But I do know he had brown skin and there was a mark on his hand."

"What kind of a mark?" asked Carl, and Ian was relieved to see that he'd lost his mocking expression.

Theo closed her eyes. "It was very odd," she said softly, "like a birthmark on his right hand, but it was clearly shaped like a diamond."

"A diamond?" Ian repeated, thinking about what the professor had said about the crown jewels.

"Yes, a diamond," Theo said firmly. "That's all I remember, and it was really only the flash of an image in my mind's eye."

"Does anyone at the keep have brown skin and a mark on his hand?" Carl asked Ian.

Ian shook his head. "No one I know of," he said. "Jasper's skin is a little darker than ours. Do you suppose it's him, Theo?"

Theo frowned. "No, I don't believe it's anyone I've

met yet," she said. "But I do believe we might all discover him soon."

"How do you know that?" asked Carl.

"Because when I said it out loud just now, it felt right," Theo answered simply.

Carl scrunched up his face and looked at Ian. He obviously didn't know what to make of that. Ian shrugged and just then the conductor came down their row and said, "Dover Station in ten minutes!"

Ian folded the prophecy and tucked it back into his coat pocket, where it nestled against the cool steel of his pocket torch, knife, and compass, which went everywhere with him these days.

He then turned toward the window to gaze out at the passing terrain, and saw something so surprising that it made him gasp.

"What?" asked Theo.

Ian pointed to the window. "Snow!" he exclaimed.

"Blimey! Would you look at that?" cried Carl. "I've never seen snow this early before!"

Other passengers had started to notice the fluttering little flakes in the air and the train became abuzz with chatter.

"What do you make of it?" he heard Madam Dimbleby ask from somewhere behind them.

"Most unusual," replied Thatcher.

"I've never seen anything like it," added the professor. "Snow in September? Unheard of!"

"I'll need to get back to the keep quickly," Madam Dimbleby said, fretting. "Gertie will have her hands full when the children get wind that it's snowing outside."

The train rolled to a stop at Dover Station and everyone hurried off, anxious to feel the soft white flakes settle onto their faces. By the time Thatcher had ushered their group into the motorcar the earl had loaned him, there was a light coating of fine powder covering the ground.

"It's so pretty," said Theo as she gazed out the window.

"Yes, well, it's rather slippery to drive in," remarked Thatcher, and Ian noticed his knuckles were white around the steering wheel.

The group arrived back at the keep in short order and Thatcher dropped Madam Dimbleby off at the door. "Theo?" she asked over her shoulder. "Are you coming in?"

Theo gave her a pleading look. "Can I please go with Ian and Carl?" she asked.

"I'll look after her," said Thatcher. "And I'll stop by the cottage and fetch Perry as well. We've still got our hunting rifles and we'll keep watch over the children when we go looking for this tunnel."

"Oh, very well," said Madam Dimbleby, distracted by the commotion going on in the yard to the side of the keep. Ian could see all the orphans playing in the snow and Madam Scargill clapping her hands, working to get at least some of the children inside to put on their coats. Madam Dimbleby did pause just long enough, however, to turn back to the car and focus on Ian. "You and I shall have a chat after you get back, Ian."

Ian gulped. "Yes, ma'am," he mumbled.

"Can we please be off now?" asked the professor moodily. "We're wasting good daylight, after all."

Madam Dimbleby gave him a level look but stepped back from the car and waved them a weary goodbye. The group now had only to pick up Perry and be on their way.

"So, Ian, I hear you've discovered yet another tunnel," said Perry as he climbed into the car and sat beside his brother.

"Yes, sir." Ian pointed toward Castle Dover. "Carl and I found it round the far west side of the castle."

"And Thatcher also says that you've discovered some old bones as well?"

"Not just some bones, sir, we've found an entire skeleton!" said Carl dramatically. "And it was sticking right out of the wall!"

Perry shifted to get a better look at Carl squished next to the professor in the backseat. "You found a skeleton bricked up in one of the tunnels?"

Carl shook his head. "No, not bricked up," he said. "It was like he was part of the wall itself!"

Perry gave him a doubtful look. "*Part* of the wall?" he said with a smirk.

"Yeah, only his head and his right arm and half of one leg were sticking out. Like the wall ate him but couldn't quite swallow him down."

Perry and Thatcher exchanged amused looks. "I sincerely hope this isn't some wild-goose chase," said Perry.

Carl pouted in his corner of the car. "That's what it looked like, I swear!" he insisted.

"We'll see," said Perry. Ian couldn't wait for his schoolmaster to take a good look for himself and eat his words.

They arrived at the main road to Castle Dover and parked the car near the woods. "The helmet's up on that hill," said Ian. "Come this way, Professor, and I'll show you where we've hidden it."

Everyone followed Ian up the hill, with its dusting of snow, and watched as he and Carl gently pulled out the twigs and grass they'd used to cover the relic. Ian then moved aside one of the smaller rocks, and with two hands he pulled the helmet free. The professor stepped up to him and held out his hands, which Ian noticed were shaking slightly. He handed the helmet to the professor, who turned it over and looked inside. "Remarkable," he muttered.

Thatcher looked over the professor's shoulder and asked, "Is it authentic?"

The professor pumped his wobbly head excitedly. "Yes, I'd say so."

Ian smiled. He hoped the helmet might also be valuable and worth a few pounds to split between him and Carl. "Do you see this mark?" asked the professor, pointing to a small squiggle on the inside of the helmet. "That is the mark of the bronzesmith who made the helmet. The Phoenicians were remarkable craftsmen, and all the great smiths stamped each of their creations personally. This is the stamp of Icarius, who was one of the very best bronze workers of his time. He crafted for generals and men of power, but very few people alive today know about him, and certainly far fewer would be familiar with his stamp, as only a handful of his creations have survived."

Ian's heart beat with eagerness and he smiled broadly at Carl, who beamed back. Ian wasn't sorry any longer that

Carl had opened his big mouth and divulged their secret. Any bit of punishment was worth it if the helmet brought in a pretty penny.

Perry turned to the pair and said, "Show us where this came from, boys."

Carl scowled distastefully. "It's from the tunnel in the woods, over there," he said, pointing.

"Come on," said Ian, nudging his friend with his shoulder. "We'll take you there."

Ian led the way into the woods and found the odd stone structure and its hidden stairway with little trouble. "The staircase is just below these stones," he said, standing next to the opening.

The professor wobbled forward and Ian could see his face fill with awe. "Remarkable," he breathed as he brushed some of the ivy aside and inspected the massive stones carefully.

"Where did this come from?" asked Perry as he too moved to look at the stones more closely.

"It's Druid-made," said the professor and Ian's eyes widened. He'd been right after all to think about their similarities back in the professor's flat.

"Druid?" said Thatcher. "I didn't know they were this far west."

"Oh, they dominated this entire landscape for centuries," said the professor. "You'd be surprised where some of their structures turn up, but this is very curious indeed. These stones are granite, which excludes them from the limestone quarries surrounding Dover. I can't imagine where they came from or how they got here of all places, but it looks as if they were placed here to protect these stairs."

It seemed to Ian that everyone turned at once to peer down the staircase, then back up at him expectantly. He smiled uncomfortably and said, "The soldier's remains are in there. It's best if you have a torch if you go down. I have my pocket torch, but we'd be better off with more light."

"I'll be right back," said Thatcher, and he hurried off through the woods in the direction of the motorcar and returned with two large torches. He passed one to his brother and turned toward the professor and held out his arm. "Professor," he said, "why don't you stick close to me on these stairs?"

The professor took Thatcher's arm and they went down the staircase. Perry looked at the children. "Would the three of you like to stay here?"

"I would!" said Carl.

"I'll go down," said Ian.

"Me too," said Theo.

"Aww," complained Carl, "you're going to leave me alone, then?" he asked her.

Theo sighed impatiently. "What's wrong with staying here alone?"

"It's creepy," he said, eying the woods nervously. "Come on, Theo, stay with me, please?"

Theo rolled her eyes. "Fine," she groused. "Ian, you go on ahead and show them where you found the helmet. I'll stay here with Carl."

Ian nodded and pulled his pocket torch out of his trousers. Clicking it on, he followed the schoolmasters and the professor down the steps into the darkness of the tunnel. The group progressed slowly to make sure the professor didn't slip as he shuffled along. After a bit, Ian pointed ahead. "The skeleton's just up there," he said.

Thatcher's torch zipped from the ground to where Ian was pointing, and all the adults gasped at what the beam revealed: a gray piece of skull and bones sticking out of the rock. "What is that?" asked Perry, hurrying forward around his brother and the professor.

"My word!" exclaimed Thatcher, stopping near the bones. "Look at him!"

Perry was shining his beam directly onto the skeleton. "It's as if the wall formed around him!" he said excitedly. "How is that even possible?"

The professor placed his hands on the bones, gently feeling them. "It's a fake," he said, and his mouth turned down in distaste. "I knew it was a fake the moment I saw it." Ian looked at the ghastly figure projecting out of the wall. He wasn't sure how the professor could dismiss it so quickly.

"Are you sure, Professor?" asked Thatcher. "If it is a fake, how could someone have done such an impeccable job imbedding these bones into the rock? There are no cut marks or chiseled indentations to speak of."

"It is remarkable," whispered Perry, running his hands around the rock where it met with the bones. "I've never seen anything like it!"

"It's a forgery, gentlemen," insisted the professor. "There's no possible way for rock to form around a set of human bones like this. It's got to be a fake."

"What's that?" asked Ian, pointing to the ground where he saw something else just out of his torch's beam.

Thatcher's torch quickly shot from the wall to the floor,

351

and there, lying half buried in soot, was a long piece of metal. Thatcher bent down and carefully swept aside the dust, revealing a silver short sword with a bronze handle. "Oh, my," he murmured.

"Impossible," said the professor as he too bent low to inspect the artifact. "That is a fourteenth-century BC Phoenician short sword!" And he grabbed the handle and hauled it up from the dirt.

"It must go with the helmet," said Ian.

Professor Nutley gave Ian a sharp look. "Of course it goes with the helmet!" he snapped. "All we need is a shield and our ensemble is complete!"

"You mean like this one?" asked Perry, pointing his beam to the right, where a dusty shield rested against the wall. "And what's this?" he asked curiously, raising his beam to just above the shield. "That's odd," he said.

"What is it?" Thatcher asked.

"Something's been scratched into the surface of the rock here. . . . It says 'Rest in Peace.' "

"So we're not the first ones to come here and find this skeleton," said Thatcher. "Someone else must have come across this poor chap and written that on the wall."

Perry scratched his head. "Perhaps, but what's particularly odd is that the date here reads the sixth of June, 1943."

Thatcher stepped closer to his brother and Ian followed, curious about why someone would scratch such a specific date into the wall. "Why would someone put a date five years into the future on the wall?"

"Bah!" said the professor. "You see?" He wagged his finger at the brothers. "I told you this was poppycock! The whole thing is one great bundle of nonsense! It's got to be the work of one of my colleagues, thinking he can pull the wool over my eyes with his chicanery!"

But Ian wasn't so sure. There had been so many strange and unnatural things taking place recently that he wasn't about to make any snap judgments.

Just then they heard a scrambling sound at the far end of the tunnel. Thatcher and Perry immediately aimed their torches toward the noise and Ian saw that Perry leveled the shotgun he'd brought along toward the entrance.

It was Carl and Theo hurrying toward them.

"Let go!" Carl was saying to Theo as she pulled at his coat sleeve.

"Come on, you fool!" Theo whispered. "And lower your voice!"

"What's going on?" asked Thatcher as the pair struggled closer.

"Theo spotted Searle in the woods and she wanted me to follow her down here out of sight," Carl whined. "I don't understand what all the fuss is about. It's just Searle."

Ian's eyes swiveled to Theo, who was pulling Carl closer. He wondered what had gotten into her. But when he caught a glimpse of her terrified expression, he hurried to meet her. "What's wrong?" he asked immediately.

"I don't know," she whispered. "It's . . . I can't explain it, but something terrible is about to happen!"

"Like what?" Thatcher asked, his voice alarmed.

From the staircase they heard Searle's voice loud and clear. "I've found it!" he called. "They must have gone down these steps!"

Everyone held perfectly still and listened. After a moment of silence, the professor said, "Who is that?"

"Searle Frost," whispered Ian, feeling a bit of dread in his heart. If Searle was here, then the Van Schufts were too, and he remembered Theo's shaky telling of the fate of Isabella.

Theo had ducked behind him and pressed her face into his back, quivering in fear. "Something's wrong, Ian!" she whispered. "Can't you feel how cold it's just become?"

And sure enough, Ian realized that the temperature in the tunnel had dipped noticeably. He could even see his breath in the small amount of light their torches were giving off. And there was something else in the atmosphere that he couldn't put his finger on. Something terrifying that made him back up a pace or two and wait expectantly for whatever was about to descend those stairs.

Just a few moments later the tense stillness within the tunnel was broken by a loud click . . . and then another . . . and then another.

Out the corner of his eye, Ian could see Thatcher and Perry moving closer to the stairs. The light from outside illuminated the staircase as if the sun were shining directly down on it, and coming into view were two beautiful silver boots clicking loudly down the stone steps. A long cloak of white and silver appeared next, but then, as Ian squinted into the darkness, he thought his eyes must be playing tricks. Blue hands with horrible long bony fingers were tracing their way down the walls on either side of the staircase. Ian gasped as the figure descending the steps came slowly into view.

"Don't look at her!" Theo shouted, and she dashed out from behind Ian and slammed his and Perry's and Thatcher's torches to the ground.

"I say!" said Perry with irritated surprise. "What's gotten into you?"

"Turn your heads away!" commanded Theo. "Whatever you do, don't look into her eyes!"

"Blimey," said Carl next to Ian, and Ian noticed in the very faint light that Carl's gaze was caught on the descending figure. "She's got *blue skin!*"

Ian's heart was hammering. Something told him that the figure coming down into the tunnel was the vilest evil. In near panic he reached out and grabbed Carl's shirt collar and whipped him around. "Don't look at her!" he commanded, and the next sound they heard chilled him to the bone.

"Ahhh," said a voice, cold and cruel and so much like the grating of ice that it made Ian shiver. "Here you are at last!"

"I told you they were here," said Searle. "I told you!"

"Yes. You have pleased Caphiera," said the wicked creature at the bottom of the stairs, but Ian doubted there was any amount of warmth in the words.

To his right he heard Carl whisper, "Did she say *Caphiera?* Like Demogorgon's daughter Caphiera?"

"Oh, my," said the professor anxiously. "Oh, my, oh, my!"

There was a cackle that echoed down the walls at them. "You are familiar with my lineage, boy?" she called. "Ah, but I assumed my reputation had faded with my mother's people. Perhaps you mortals have learned a thing or two recently?"

"The boy is right!" whispered the professor. "If that is Demogorgon's daughter, whatever you do, don't look into her eyes!"

Theo had tucked herself back behind Ian and he could feel her shivering. The temperature in the tunnel was acutely uncomfortable and breathing in seemed to burn his lungs. His mind raced wildly as he thought about fleeing, but there was nowhere to go. Caphiera had them cornered . . . just like Laodamia said she would.

He next heard the wretched blue woman say, "Now, Searle, fetch me the girl."

Ian felt Theo stiffen behind him. He reached back with one arm and gave her a firm squeeze on her shoulder. He'd die before he'd let that beastly sorceress have her.

He could hear Searle approaching, and in the light cast by the torches onto the tunnel floor, he could make out the boy's feet clomping toward him.

Ian moved slowly to the left, pulling Theo with him. He then turned and nudged her close to the side wall. Then he turned toward Searle and walked forward to intercept him, being careful not to look too far down the tunnel at Caphiera.

"Out of my way, you lazy git," said Searle when they met in the middle, and the bigger boy moved to brush past Ian.

Ian, however, was far too angry to let the bully get by. He curled his hand into a fist and struck Searle hard in the cheek. "Stay away from her!" he yelled as Searle reeled backward, covering his face with his hand.

Behind him he heard Thatcher and Perry shouting, but

he was far too furious to care. Before Searle had a chance to recover, Ian had launched himself at his nemesis and the two boys tumbled to the ground, rolling over and over each other.

Searle had Ian by the hair and thumped his head against the rocky earth, sending a terrific bolt of pain through Ian's skull. He retaliated by hooking two of his fingers into Searle's nostrils and pulling up. Searle howled in pain and kicked furiously at Ian, but Ian wouldn't let go. Finally, Searle managed to get out from the hold Ian had on him, and he scrambled to his feet and dashed down the tunnel before Ian tackled him again and sent them both crashing back to the floor.

He became aware of the pounding of footfalls along the tunnel floor in the distance and he knew that Perry and Thatcher were going to put an end to their fight, but Ian wasn't about to stop on his own. He stood up and allowed Searle to get unsteadily to his feet. Panting heavily, Ian charged one last time. Searle put his arms up defensively but Ian lowered his shoulder right into the pudgy boy's gut, sending Searle toppling backward to land faceup right at the edge of those silver boots.

At that instant Ian was grabbed roughly from behind and he knew that one of his schoolmasters had finally caught up to him. But his eyes were pinned to Searle's face, because something terrible and truly frightening was happening to the brutish boy.

Ian saw that Searle's eyes had grown large and his face was piteously frozen into an awful look of terror. Slowly,

Searle's complexion was turning blue. Like an ink injected under his skin, the color was spreading along his cheeks, to his nose and lips, forehead and neck. An icy frost crawled along with the color until at last the boy looked like a stiff blue icicle.

"My heavens!" gasped Thatcher, and Ian realized that his schoolmaster was still gripping him tightly, peering over his shoulder.

"He's frozen solid!" said Perry, who was standing next to Thatcher and staring down at Searle in horror.

One of the silver boots kicked Searle's body. There was a clang when metal met ice. "That's ghastly!" exclaimed Thatcher.

"Oh, I believe it's an improvement," said the sorceress with a truly wicked cackle.

Ian found he had to fight not to look up at her. His heart was pounding and guilt like he'd never experienced raged through him. All he could think of was that last tackle that had sent Searle to sprawl faceup at Caphiera's feet. Numbly, he felt Thatcher pulling him again by the collar, backing away from the wretched scene. To his side he saw Perry moving in pace with them, the schoolmaster's eyes still pinned to Searle's cold body.

"Come away!" he heard Theo shout from the back of the tunnel. "All of you! Get away from her immediately!"

Her voice seemed to break the trance the three of them were under, and Perry, Ian, and Thatcher turned as one and ran.

Caphiera's vile laughter followed them the entire distance. "Never send a boy to do a woman's work." She clucked. Then, clearly turning her attention to Theo, she added, "You're obviously the girl we're after, and if you won't come to me, allow me to come to you."

Ian heard her silver heels clicking along the cold stone floor toward them, and the closer she got, the lower the temperature plummeted. "I'm so cold!" cried Theo.

"Schoolmaster!" Ian said to Perry. "Your rifle! Shoot a warning shot at her!"

Perry seemed startled to realize that he still held the weapon. He hesitated for the briefest moment before raising the gun at the approaching shadow of the sorceress. "I order you to stop!" he shouted. But the clicking of heels continued to come closer and closer. Perry fired a round into the wall near Caphiera's head. The sound was like a cannon blast that reverberated back and forth along the tunnel.

When the echo faded, Ian noticed that Caphiera's boot heels had stopped their clicking. "Very well," she said from midway down the tunnel. "Have it your way."

For a moment all was still; the only sound Ian heard was his own labored and panicked breathing. Suddenly, a bitter wind whipped by his cheek and then . . . the grinding began.

Ian couldn't resist the urge to look up and he heard the collective gasp of the others doing the same. Just ahead of them, a solid wall of ice that spanned from floor to ceiling, and wall to wall, blocked them completely in. Ian tentatively reached down and picked up his pocket torch, careful to keep it low lest Caphiera be in front of the wall. He still had no idea what her face looked like, but he guessed she was as horrible as Medusa—one look and you were frozen stiff.

Thatcher too had bent to retrieve his torch and he and Ian shined their beams along the wall of ice, gasping simultaneously when they realized their peril. The wall of ice was moving closer, growing sharp icicle daggers clearly aimed to impale them.

"This can't be happening!" said the professor from behind Ian.

"It isn't real!" added Perry. "It can't be."

"We're doomed!" cried Carl.

Ian watched as the icicles grew several more lethal inches.

Instinctively, he backed up until he pressed against solid rock. He waved his torchlight along the seams of the advancing wall of death, but no cracks or gaps appeared. As the icicles and the wall continued to advance, he had to agree with Carl. They were doomed.

THE STAR OF LICORICE

"It's getting closer!" Theo squealed as she darted out of the way of an approaching icicle only to stand next to the skeleton, mindless of its scary facade.

"I can't find even a crack!" called Perry, still scanning his side of the ice wall with his torch.

Ian saw Carl dart to the side, and realized that his friend had retrieved the soldier's short sword. With great bravery, Carl began trying to hack at the advancing ice. Ian, spurred to action, grabbed the heavy shield and lifted it to bang at the sharp icicles. But very quickly he and Carl both realized that when they lopped off the end of one of the spikes, it grew back within seconds—and to their horror it grew back longer, thicker, and with an even sharper point.

"Stop!" Ian shouted when he saw that they were only making things worse. Turning to Theo, he placed the heavy shield on the ground in front of her. "Hold this up," he ordered. "It might protect you."

He couldn't clearly see Theo's expression in the dim

light, but he sensed her gratitude when she said, "Squeeze in next to me!"

"There isn't room, Theo," he said softly.

"It's getting closer!" yelled Carl, and he ducked to the rock wall, his back pressed firmly against it.

"Professor!" shouted Thatcher. "Try squeezing yourself into that corner." And Ian looked to where he was pointing. On the opposite side of the cave from where he stood, Ian saw the smallest of niches.

"Let the children tuck in there!" said the professor, turning bravely to face the ice. "I'm an old man who's lived a good life. I'm not afraid to die."

Ian motioned to the crevice in the corner. "Carl," he said. "Go on with you!"

"Not without you, mate!" said Carl.

"There isn't room for both of us!" Ian yelled impatiently.

"Then there won't be room for one," Carl replied stubbornly. "Maybe Theo should try squeezing in there and holding the shield. I'll bet she could make it through this mess if she did that."

Ian felt a great welling of gratitude and kinship for his new friend, along with a sudden sorrow that their friendship might soon be cut short. He lifted the shield away from a terrified Theo and ushered her into the crevice. "No matter what," he ordered her shivering form as she squished into the tight corner, "you stay here and don't move this shield!"

"Ian!" Theo exclaimed, but he cut her off by placing the shield in front of her. Behind him the grinding of the ice wall became louder, and he noticed that the other four in the group were standing flat against the back wall, Carl still gripping his sword and Perry holding his rifle firmly.

Ian squeezed past the icicle spikes to join them, taking his place next to Carl as the wall approached them inch by terrible inch. "Perry!" yelled Thatcher above the loud noise of the advancing ice.

"What?" his brother yelled back, a note of panic in his voice.

"Blast it!"

"Blast *what?*"

"Blast the wall with your rifle! Maybe you can shoot a hole right through it!"

Ian watched anxiously as Perry yanked the gun up level with his chest. Gripping it with determination, he fired a round into the ice. A hole about the size of a fist appeared in the shiny surface. "Again!" shouted Thatcher, and Perry cocked the gun and fired a second time.

Ian's heart leapt with joy, as the hole was now large enough for a head to fit through. "You're doing it!" he shouted, squeezing himself as far back against the wall as he could. "Fire again before we're all dead!"

Perry cocked the gun and fired a third time, and the hole became large enough for Carl to fit through. "Can you make it?" shouted Ian.

Carl's eyes were wide with fear. "I think so!" he said.

"You'll have to duck around that big spike!" said Ian. "Go on, mate! Try to get out of here!"

Carl inhaled deeply and took one small tentative step toward the opening. But the moment he did, something terrible happened. Ice began to form rapidly over the hole; then—as if the wall were a living thing—a small nub formed and grew with increasing speed into a thick spike aimed directly at Perry's head.

The schoolmaster darted to his side, dropping his rifle just as the spike struck the back wall with such force that Ian could feel the vibration shake the rock behind him.

Ian's breath felt trapped in his lungs. He was unable to move, unable to breathe as he stared into the deadly spikes closing in on him. Besides his own fear, all he could feel was Carl's quivering form pressed up against his side.

The grinding noise filled his ears like a terrible curse and he saw grimly that he would be impaled by no less than three spikes. The only thing he had left to hope for was that it would be over quickly.

He closed his eyes but couldn't close his ears to the sound of Carl's agonized scream. Reaching over, Ian squeezed his arm, wanting Carl to know he wasn't alone in this terrible moment before death.

And then . . . as if in slow motion, Ian felt the solid flat firmness of the wall behind him evaporate. This unsettling feeling was immediately followed by the sensation of falling slowly through the air and landing with a hard *thunk*.

He hit the ground with such force that the back of his head bounced off the stone floor and he saw stars swim behind his eyelids as more pain ricocheted around the inside of his skull. And then someone was pulling at his arm and shirt collar and he realized that Theo was shouting at him. *"Get up! Ian, for God's sake! Get up!"* she cried.

Ian scrambled woozily to his feet as something sharp

pierced his left calf with an intense searing pain, causing him to lurch forward. "Carl!" he heard Thatcher shout. "Come on, lad! *Move!*" Ian shook his head to clear it as the stars continued to float about. "Perry!" Thatcher yelled to his brother. "Get the professor out of range!"

Ian tried to focus his vision while he felt Theo's small form duck under his arm and pull him forward. "Quickly!" she ordered, and with her help he staggered ahead several steps before collapsing back to the ground. With his head reeling, he looked over to see Thatcher half carrying, half dragging Carl's limp form. Ian could see that his friend still clung to his sword.

To his right he noticed Perry helping the professor away from the approaching spike wall. Ian's vision swam again and he closed his eyes and rubbed the back of his head, where an egg-sized lump was forming. When he opened his eyes again, Theo was at his left foot, lifting the cuff of his trouser to inspect his leg wound.

"It's not very deep," she said, her face relieved. "But I'll expect you'll want to clean it as quickly as possible."

Ian blinked hard. He was having trouble taking all this in. Behind him he became aware of the unmistakable sound of surf rolling in and out. He was also confused by the odd feeling of sand underneath him. He could feel its cool, yielding texture beneath his fingers. "What's happened?" he mumbled.

Theo looked at him with eyes that made her seem much older than she was. "I followed the prophecy," she said, and when Ian stared at her blankly, she added, "I asked and the wall opened."

Ian scrunched his face up in confusion. "You . . . *asked?*" he said.

Theo nodded but her attention was diverted by Thatcher, who was laying Carl down on the ground next to them. "He's fine," said the schoolmaster when he saw their concerned faces. "He just fainted."

But Ian could see a small red wound at the base of Carl's throat and knew that one of the spikes had barely missed killing him. A moment later, Perry and the professor dropped to the ground, safely out of the way of the advancing ice wall. "I can't believe this is happening," Perry panted, turning around to see the spikes still creeping forward. Ian gulped when he realized they were clearly long enough now to have impaled him if the rock wall hadn't given way.

His eyes roved the floor of the cavern, where the remains of the Phoenician soldier were now being pushed along the ground by the icy spikes.

"We've got a few minutes before we'll need to move again," said Thatcher, eyeing the advancing ice warily. "Can you walk?" he asked Ian.

Ian nodded. "Yes, sir, I can . . ." His voice trailed off when something else, too spectacular to be real, happened. The advancing ice was abruptly halted and the tips of all the spikes were completely sheared off with a loud crunching sound as the tunnel wall suddenly reappeared in front of them. Ian wouldn't have believed his eyes if it weren't for the dozens of pieces of ice that were now dropping to the cavern floor.

"*Extraordinary!*" the professor gasped.

Ian thought that summed it up nicely.

"Wha . . . ?" said Carl, coming out of his faint. "Am I dead?" he asked, his eyes fluttering as he tried to focus on Theo hovering above him. "Mummy?"

"You're fine," said Theo gently, and her face softened into a smile. "We're all safe."

Perry got to his feet and approached the rock wall with trepidation. His brother and the professor followed. Ian waited to make sure his friend was all right before wobbling to his feet and limping to the wall himself.

He stepped carefully among the many shards of ice resting in the sand and stopped in front of the wall, reaching up to touch it in disbelief. The rock felt cool and a bit wet. He looked at the ground and noticed with relief that his pocket torch had made it safely. He bent over to retrieve it and pointed the beam at the wall, then gasped when he realized that within the pores of the rock were icy crystals.

"Ian!" said Thatcher, next to him. "Look at that!" Ian turned to see the left leg of the skeleton and the heel bone of the right leg firmly ensconced within the rock.

"Unbelievable!" he gasped.

"My rifle!" exclaimed Perry, on the other side of Thatcher. He was bent low, running his fingers along the silhouette of the gun sticking oddly out of the rock, which seemed to have molded itself around the weapon like fresh cement that had already hardened.

"Extraordinary!" breathed the professor again. "I can hardly believe this is real!"

"Well, of course it's not real," said Perry, standing up and stepping back from the wall. "It's all a dream!"

Ian looked doubtfully at his schoolmaster. "Whose dream, exactly, sir?" he asked.

Perry blinked awkwardly at him. "Well . . . mine, of course!" he said firmly.

"Then how can I be having the same dream?" Ian asked rationally.

"And I?" said Thatcher.

"You might as well include me too," said the professor.

Perry looked round at them all and threw up his hands. "Poppycock!" he said. "I'm dreaming that you're asking me this." He turned to his brother. "Pinch me," he instructed. "I'll need to wake up immediately."

Thatcher raised his eyebrows skeptically but reached forward and gave his twin a good pinch. When Perry yelped, Thatcher asked, "Are you awake now?"

"Bah!" was Perry's answer as he stomped back toward Carl and Theo, then plopped to the ground and rested his chin on his fist, glaring at his brother.

Ian thought he resembled one of the orphan boys at the keep who was always pouting when he didn't get his way. Meanwhile, the professor had turned his attention to the sound of the surf behind them. "Time to explore our surroundings," he said.

Ian and Thatcher nodded, and as they turned, Ian realized abruptly that the sound of the waves crashing was coming from the wrong direction. He placed his hand on Thatcher's sleeve and said, "Sir, doesn't the strait hit the shore from the opposite direction?"

Thatcher stopped in his tracks and looked from Ian to the entrance of the tunnel, where the clear sound of the surf was reverberating along the walls. Ian noticed the worried frown on his face. "Yes," he said slowly. "You're quite right, Ian. The strait should be behind us."

Ian looked toward the entrance. "And have you noticed how unnaturally warm that breeze is?" he asked. A salty but decidedly humid breeze was swirling within their cavern.

Thatcher squinted into the light of the entrance. Not much could be seen besides sand and rocks. "Come along," he said. "Let's find out exactly *where* we are."

When Thatcher, the professor, and Ian stepped out into the brilliant sunshine, Ian blinked furiously, trying to get his eyes to adjust. Finally, the glare subsided, and with a hand over his brow, he was able to look around.

Ahead of him was a brilliant blue sea, which, he determined immediately, was not the Strait of Dover. This sea was a deeper blue than the murky gray waters of the channel. When he looked up, he saw with surprise that it was a cloudless day; gone were the storm clouds that had brought them snow earlier. He next focused on the horizon and he realized that no sign of France could be seen on the endless blue waves.

To his left was a huge wall of rock that cut the beach off and jutted into the water. The cavern they'd just come out of lay within this wall, which continued up a slope and a high cliff overhead.

To his right and down the beach was another outcropping of rock, but this one appeared not as steep or as formidable. "Where *are* we?" he asked the professor and Thatcher.

"Impossible!" exclaimed the professor, and Ian saw that the old man was staring at the distant outcropping.

"What isn't possible exactly?" asked Thatcher with exasperation. "That we're clearly not in Dover or that in all probability we're not even in *England?*"

"That outcropping," whispered the professor, pointing. "I know those rocks."

"You *know* them?" asked Ian. "You mean you've been here before?"

The professor scratched his chin and shook his head, staring at the outcropping with a faraway look. "Do you see that bridge-looking part there, where those rocks meet that flat section?"

Thatcher and Ian squinted toward the boulders. "Yes," said Ian.

"That's called the Mother's Cradle and I once spent an entire evening nestled there upon those very rocks."

Ian turned to the professor, amazed and relieved that the old man seemed to know where they were. "When?" he asked.

"Forty years ago," said the professor.

"The larger question is, *where?*" said Thatcher. "Professor, where are we?"

Professor Nutley's eyes seemed to linger fondly on the outcropping. "Larache," he murmured.

Ian frowned. He didn't recognize the name, but his schoolmaster did.

"*Morocco?*" Thatcher gasped.

"Indeed," said the professor.

"But . . . but . . . but . . . ," stammered Thatcher. "That's . . . that's . . . *impossible!*"

"Apparently not, my good man," the professor said.

"Would you look at that?" they heard behind them, and they all turned to see Carl in the entrance of the cavern. He held the bronze and silver short sword out in front of him while he gazed in wonder at the big blue sea.

A moment later Theo appeared, followed by Perry. The three joined them on the beach, Carl still transfixed by the beautiful water rolling in and out. "Where are we?" he asked.

"If you believe the professor," said Thatcher, "Morocco."

His brother's jaw dropped and Ian noticed that he seemed a bit peaked. "I'm hallucinating," said Perry, and he plopped into the sand again.

"Morocco?" asked Carl. "How'd we get here?"

"Through the portal, of course," said Theo, and all eyes swiveled to her. "Just like the prophecy suggested."

Ian dug into his coat pocket and pulled out the professor's translation. " 'Go beyond Caphiera's reach, the first such place upon the beach. A quest of six and no less few, to find the Seeker, young and true. Seeker leads you to the Star, vital to your journeys far.' "

Perry looked up at them, blinking in confusion. "What's all this business about Seekers and Stars?" he asked.

Again, Theo spoke as if she understood Laodamia's riddle perfectly. "We must find the young boy with the mark of a diamond on his right hand. He will lead us to the Star of Licorice."

Perry blinked twice more before breaking into hysterical laughter. "Oh, my!" said the schoolmaster, slapping the sand next to him. "I'm not hallucinating! I've gone *completely* mad!"

"Wait," said the professor, and Ian noticed he didn't

seem amused or skeptical, but genuinely interested. "What did you say about the Star, young lady?"

"The boy with the mark will help us find it," she said confidently.

"Yes, I heard that part," said the professor patiently. "But what did you call it, again?"

"The Star of Licorice," she said, and Ian scowled at Carl, who was covering his mouth to hide his own giggle.

"I don't believe it," whispered the professor as he again stared off in the direction of the Mother's Cradle.

"Well, that's the name I heard in my head," said Theo with a small stomp of her foot. "It might sound ridiculous to you lot, but that's what it's called!"

Ian reached around her shoulders and gave her a gentle squeeze. "I believe you, Theo," he said, and she smiled gratefully at him.

"Oh, make no mistake," said the professor. "I *do* believe you, Miss Fields. I'm just amazed that I didn't see it sooner."

"See what sooner, Professor?" Ian asked.

The old man had that faraway look in his eyes again. "Forty years ago I came here to the city of Larache, following an old Phoenician legend," he said. "There is an ancient city north of here on the banks of the Loukkos River. In its prime," the professor continued, "the city was a massive place, filled with culture and trade and completely controlled by the Phoenicians from about the seventh century BC until they were defeated by the Carthaginians and later the Romans. Around 400 BC, when the city was still in Phoenician hands, and defeat by Carthage looked imminent, the ruling general at that time, a man named Adrastus, hid a trove of priceless gemstones and gold coins somewhere in the city.

"Legend has it that amongst the gemstones was a very large five-pointed opal in the shape of a star. It was said that he who carried this priceless gem would be a stranger in no land; all would welcome him and a king in the making would become its rightful owner. This opal was named the Star of Lixus, after the city where it was discovered."

"That's *it*!" squealed Theo. "*That's* the name I heard, but it sounded like 'licorice!' "

The professor nodded. "I came here in 1897 to excavate the city, whose ruins had just been discovered. My real motivation, however, was to locate the treasure that Adrastus had hidden and to unearth the Star of Lixus."

"Did you find any of the treasure?" asked Ian, feeling a newfound respect for Professor Nutley, who he hadn't known was a real, live treasure hunter.

The professor turned back to the rocks at the far end of the beach, looking crestfallen. "No," he said softly, "though I did give it a bloody good go. I ran out of funding, and because we hadn't discovered anything of value on our dig, my financial backers pulled out and we were ordered back to England. The night before our ship departed, I spent a very lonely evening up on those rocks, contemplating my failure. The next day, when the sun rose, I endeavored to put it out of my mind for good. After all, we'd excavated a good portion of the lost city; I'd gotten enough material to finish my paper; and I'd learned much in the process. And so I did manage to put thoughts of finding the Star out of my mind for the next forty years—that is, until you mentioned it, lass."

Theo beamed up at the professor, and Ian was incredibly grateful to the man for what he'd said.

"Yes, well, I'm afraid that we have a much larger issue than locating some lost gemstone," said Thatcher, and he glanced back at the cavern. "How are we to get home?"

All heads turned toward the cavern and a heavy silence fell upon the group. "Maybe if we stay here for a bit, the wall will open back up," suggested Carl.

"And right behind it is Caphiera's wall of spikes," said Ian, shaking his head. "Even if we were able to get past *that*, there's no telling if she's still there or not."

"Quite right," said Thatcher with a shiver. "I'll be glad never to encounter the likes of her again."

"Poor Searle," Theo said sadly, and Ian again felt a pang of guilt slice through him.

But Carl quickly put things into perspective when he said, "I can't feel sorry for him. I mean, it's like Lady Arbuthnot said: Searle made his choice and met the consequences. He chose to do Caphiera's bidding, and we all know what would have happened to Theo if he'd gotten her away from us. I say, better him than her."

Ian felt Carl's words sink in and his guilt seemed to wash away like the tides rolling out from the beach.

"I quite agree," said the professor to Carl before turning his attention back to the cavern. "Gentlemen, and lady, we must face facts. The way behind us is clearly blocked, which means our only choice is to go forward on the quest that

Laodamia has set for us, and find the Star of Lixus." Ian couldn't help noticing how much the professor's eyes were sparkling at the idea.

"You can't be serious," said Thatcher, and he looked to his brother for support, but Perry didn't seem to be listening. Instead, Ian's second schoolmaster was staring at the sea with a humorous grin and a blank stare. Ian worried that he might indeed have gone a bit mad.

"Oh, I'm very serious," said the professor. "What other choice do we have, Thatcher? We can't go back and I believe the swim to Spain might be a bit challenging even for someone of your athletic nature."

Ian's schoolmaster scowled. "How far away is the city?" he asked.

"Just over that outcropping," said the professor, pointing to the Mother's Cradle.

"Am I correct in remembering that Larache is one of Morocco's larger points of port?" Thatcher asked.

"It is," said the professor.

"Then we'll be able to book passage on a boat to Spain at the very least!" he insisted.

"And your pockets are bursting with pound notes?" said the professor wisely. Ian watched as his schoolmaster blanched. "I didn't think so," said the old man with a triumphant smile. "My pockets, however," he added, "are filled with money." And to Ian's astonishment the professor pulled out a great wad of bills that made everyone gasp.

The professor eyed his billfold with a grin. "I never leave home without being fully prepared," he said. "But even this amount won't be enough to get all six of us back to England.

So this is what I propose . . ." Ian and the others listened intently as the professor suggested that they go to Larache and send word to England regarding their whereabouts so that money could be wired to get them back home. The professor figured that it would take no less than two weeks for word to reach the earl and for funds to be wired. While they waited, they might as well travel the short distance to Lixus and look about for the Star. If they found it, then they would have fulfilled Laodamia's prophecy, and this magical transport to Morocco would not go to waste.

Ian was brimming with excitement. He was finally going to get a crack at a real, live treasure hunt! Thatcher, however, didn't seem the least bit enthusiastic and his eye kept darting back to the cavern.

Finally, however, the schoolmaster relented and with a nod he said, "All right, Professor, we'll do as you say, as I suppose we've little choice in the matter."

"Good man," said the professor, slapping Thatcher on the arm. "Now, come along. I'll need some help making it up those rocks. I'm not as limber as I was the last time I was here." And with that the professor began to shuffle off through the sand, seeming fully to expect everyone else to follow.

Back in Dover, Caphiera the Cold clutched her arm and cursed the end of the tunnel angrily. She had thought the mortals' attempts to escape her icy trap quite comical, until that last gunshot had sliced into her arm.

Caphiera waited in the silence, squinting in the dimness to make sure her handiwork had finished off the despicable lot. From behind her she heard someone on the stairs call out.

"I am here, Dieter," she answered.

"We had no luck at the orphanage, mistress. I'm afraid they might be on to us."

"Oh, they are on to you," said Caphiera, her eyes still focused on the ice in front of her. She snapped her fingers, and above her head three icicles grew from the ceiling and cast a light along the expanse of the tunnel.

She heard Magus's servant come down the next few steps and gasp. "What happened to the boy?" he asked.

"He was overcome by my beauty," Caphiera replied drolly. "You and your wife will need to dispose of him the same way you did with the girl."

"Yes, mistress," said Dieter. Then the man noticed what the sorceress was looking at. "What's beyond that ice?" he asked.

"Let's find out, shall we?" she said, and with a wave of her hand, the wall evaporated. Caphiera shrieked. She had expected to find corpses, but to her astonishment, there were only the rock wall and some old bones jutting out. Gone was any sign of the mortals she'd cornered.

The sorceress cursed anew and charged down the tunnel, her silver boots making an awful racket. She stopped when she got to the end, and searched the corners of the cavern, but no trace of them remained.

With venomous fury she whirled around, studying the walls with suspicion. Dieter stood shivering by the stairs. Caphiera thought he might flee in terror, and she rather hoped he would, as she'd like nothing better than a good opportunity to vent her anger. Still, she thought that Magus might find the killing of his servant offensive, and as her brother was known to carry a grudge, she held herself in check . . . though just barely.

Instead, she stomped back down the tunnel, past Dieter and the frozen boy, and up the stairs to inspect the stones covering the entrance. She walked carefully around them, pulling at the weeds and vines. Finally, at the back of the primitive structure, she revealed a bit of writing in the rune script of her people. Her wretched blue lips pulled down in a deep frown as she read the words. "As I suspected," she said, and spat into the dirt. Her spittle, however, fell as liquid, never forming an icicle. "Bah!" she screeched, noticing that even now she was feeling weaker. "Come, Dieter!" she yelled, staggering away. "This place is a curse to me. I must leave it immediately!"

Caphiera stumbled quickly out of the woods, Dieter lumbering behind as he attempted to carry the frozen boy. The sorceress knew she must tell Magus about what she had discovered, but then a thought occurred to her, and with an evil grin she began to develop another, more sinister plan.

LARACHE

On the beach in Morocco, Thatcher was looking down at his brother with contempt. "Perry," he said firmly. "Get up."

"A fever!" Perry said. "That's it! I must have contracted a fever. It explains everything!" he insisted. "The hallucinations, the aches and pains, the fact that I'm sweating right now . . ."

Thatcher rolled his eyes. "You're perfectly well!" he snapped. "Now, come along. I'll need your help getting the professor over those rocks."

Perry got up from the ground, but Ian could tell he still fully believed that everything happening around him was a hallucination. He heard Theo giggle and he turned to see Carl playing near the surf with the short sword. As he slashed and parried the air, the metal glinted brightly in the sun.

"That one's a bit daffy," she said with another giggle.

"He should probably leave that here," Ian remarked, worried that the sword would call unwanted attention in the strange land.

But Theo turned to him with eyes that were intensely earnest and said, "No, he mustn't leave it behind, Ian."

"Why not?"

"Because . . . ," she said, searching for the reason. "Well, because I have a sense that he shouldn't."

"You have a sense?" he asked.

Theo nodded. "Yes, it's terribly important for some reason that he bring that sword with him."

Ian looked back at Carl still flailing away awkwardly at imaginary foes. "Well, he'd best learn to use that thing before he hurts himself."

Theo and Ian laughed again as Carl got a little too close to the edge of the water and a sudden wave came in to soak him clear up to his knees. "You help Carl," Theo said as the young boy slogged out of the water and began pulling off his soggy shoes and socks. "I'm going on ahead."

Ian trotted down to the water's edge and picked up Carl's sword to save it from yet another wave barreling into the beach. "Come on, mate," he said, motioning at the water. "Tide's rolling in and you're likely to get wet again."

Carl stuffed his socks into his shoes, then knotted his shoelaces together and looped them round his neck. Before Ian had a chance to comment, Carl smiled wickedly, yelled, "Race you to the rocks!" and took off at a full run.

Ian barely had a moment to process the challenge and he shot after Carl, pumping his legs for all he was worth. He never gained a centimeter—in fact, he lost ground.

Moments later he crashed hard into the rocks, where Carl had touched first. "Crikey!" Ian gasped for breath. "You're a fast one, aren't you?"

Carl's chest was also heaving, but he grinned with pride. "There were some older blokes at my orphanage in Plymouth who used to like to take turns giving me a few wallops—that is, till I learned to outrun them."

Ian laughed and held up the short sword. "Yeah, well, this might've weighed me down a bit."

There was a snort behind him and he turned to see Theo coming toward them. "Don't let him fool you, Carl," she said. "I saw the race and Ian would have lost even if the only thing he'd been carrying were his knickers!" The three broke into hysterical laughter, and Ian had to concede. "She's right," he admitted. "You're blazing fast, mate."

"Come on, then," said Theo as she looked up at the rocks. "Let's see what's on the other side, shall we?"

She began to climb and Ian and Carl followed, picking their way carefully along to the flat platform of the Mother's Cradle.

"Gaw, blimey!" said Carl as the three stood at the top of the rocks. "It's a whole city down there!"

Ian was too stunned to speak. On the other side of the outcropping was an enormous city of ramshackle huts topped with tin roofs, dozens of wooden stalls forming bustling markets, larger stone buildings with odd-looking cornices, winding streets that weaved aimlessly like a maze through the city in a zigzag fashion, and, at the water's edge, a large harbor with fishnets, wooden docks, and every color, shape, and variety of ship imaginable.

He could just make out several boats approaching the port to moor at the central dock. Along the coastline were enormous palm trees, which he'd only seen painted in some of the books he'd read, and he wondered how something so odd-looking could stand so stately against the bleakness of the grassless terrain.

Turning his attention back to the city proper, he had the sense that it teemed with the energy of a beehive, as thousands of people walked about.

Ian could see from his perch that Larache's male inhabitants had dark olive skin and were clad mostly in tunics of white linen that reached just past their knees and matched their trousers. Almost every adult male had facial hair and they wore funny white cloth hats or red felt hats topped with golden tassels.

The women were quite a surprise to him too, and far fewer of them hurried through the crowd. Most were covered from head to toe in dark cloth that obscured the entire body, and their faces were hidden behind veils of black or white. Small children clung to their parents' hands as they wound their way in family groups through the tangle of streets packed with people and a variety of animals, including donkeys, horses, cows, sheep, and, to Ian's immense delight, camels.

"Shall we go down?" asked Carl, bouncing on his feet, as anxious as Ian to explore the city.

"Let's wait for the professor and the schoolmasters," said Theo, glancing behind them.

Ian frowned as he also turned to look and saw that the professor was only midway up the rocks. He sighed and sat down on the flat rock, perching his chin on his hands as he stared in wonder at the weird and marvelous city below.

When he could hear the puffing sounds of the professor getting close to them, he noticed a small boy below on the beach near their perch. He was staring up at them, cupping his hand across his brow.

Theo must have noticed him too, because she leaned out and waved down, and after a slight hesitation, the boy waved back. "Seems friendly enough," said Carl.

"I . . . don't . . . remember . . . these rocks . . . being this . . . steep." The professor wheezed from just below Ian.

Ian got to his feet to make room for the old man as he finally crested the flat rock. "Would you like to rest here for a bit?" Ian asked, motioning to the nice piece of rock he'd just gotten up from.

"I believe . . . I would," panted the professor. Then he noticed the boy below. "Who's that?" he asked as he sat down gingerly.

"Dunno," said Ian. "Just a boy from the city, I guess."

"Marvelous!" said Thatcher, who had come up with the professor. Ian could see the amazement in his schoolmaster's eyes as he took in Larache. "Perry!" he called behind him. "Come up here and have a look!"

Perry climbed the last few sections of rock and stood dumbstruck next to his brother. "Oh," he said softly. "I hope I don't come out of this hallucination soon. I'd very much like to see this to the end."

Ian and Carl grinned at each other. "Wonder when it's going to hit him that he's really not gone off his nutty?" whispered Carl, and Ian snickered but quickly cleared his throat and hid his smile when Thatcher leveled a look at him.

"Look!" said Theo suddenly. "The boy's coming up to meet us!"

Sure enough, when Ian looked down, he could see the boy hiking up the rocks.

"*Bonjour!*" called the boy when he was just below them.

"*Bonjour!*" called the professor, and then he spoke rapidly in French. Ian frowned; he had no idea what the professor had said.

"He says hello and that we are pleased to make the young man's acquaintance," whispered Thatcher. "Now he's introducing himself to the lad." He waited for the boy's response before saying, "The boy's name is Jaaved of the Jstor."

"What's the Jstor?" asked Theo quietly.

"I believe it's some sort of clan or tribe," said Thatcher, his attention still focused on the professor and the boy. "Now the professor is asking the boy if he knows of any vessels for hire to travel up the river to Lixus."

Ian watched as the boy nodded eagerly and spoke. "What's he saying?" Ian whispered when Thatcher did not immediately interpret.

"He says that his master has a vessel for hire, but he doesn't think it's a good idea for us to go to Lixus."

"Why not?" asked Carl.

Thatcher frowned as he listened. "Jaaved says that it's dangerous for Europeans in the countryside right now. He says that there was some sort of incident with the Jichmach tribe and a group of Germans and that the clan is out for revenge. He says the Jichmach don't care if the people they take revenge against are actually German; they'd be satisfied with anyone who looks close enough."

"So we're not going to Lixus?" Ian asked, trying to hide his disappointment.

But the professor was speaking and Thatcher was too caught up in what the old man was saying to answer Ian. Instead, the schoolmaster began to argue with the professor. "I say, Professor," interrupted Thatcher. "The boy has just told us it isn't safe! We must immediately come up with an alternate plan and abandon this quest to Lixus. I think we should book passage to Spain. Surely the money you've brought along could see the six of us safely across the Strait of Gibraltar."

But the professor wasn't having any of it. "Poppycock!" he said. "Of course we must proceed to Lixus! The greatest Oracle in the world demanded it, Thatcher! Do you really believe Laodamia would send us all this way for us to give up so easily?"

"But think of the children!" argued the schoolmaster. "How can you insist on putting them in danger?"

The professor eyed Ian, Carl, and Theo thoughtfully. "I believe that in the past few weeks they've seen far worse," he replied. Again Ian had noticed the slight glint in the professor's eyes as he'd mentioned journeying to Lixus. He wondered if the old man had been overcome with that same longing that had brought him here forty years ago in search of the Star.

But Thatcher wouldn't let up. "It would be irresponsible," he said. "Really, Professor, I must insist that we book passage to Spain immediately!"

The professor growled and turned back to the boy on the rocks below. He spoke to him and Ian again asked his

385

schoolmaster to interpret. "Jaaved says that the next boat for Spain leaves in a fortnight," Thatcher explained, his face the picture of disappointment.

"You see?" sang the professor happily. "We can go to Lixus, search out our Star, and still make it back in time to board the boat to Spain!"

"No! If we can't get across the strait, back to Europe, then we should stay in Larache, where it's safe!" insisted Thatcher, looking to his brother for support, but Perry was still gazing off in a faraway haze.

The professor scratched his chin and gave Thatcher a patient look. "My good man," he said. "If you believe we'd be safer spending a fortnight in that city, then you really are naive."

"What do you mean?" Thatcher asked.

The professor turned back to Jaaved and spoke in French. The boy looked at Thatcher and nodded, saying something to him directly. "What did he say?" asked Theo.

Surprisingly, it was Perry who spoke up. "The lad agrees with the professor. The city is full of thieves, pickpockets, slave traders, and charlatans eager to take advantage of un-suspecting foreigners."

"Well then, where *does* the lad suggest we go?" exclaimed Thatcher in a bit of a huff.

"We're going to Lixus," said the professor firmly as he got to his feet again. When Thatcher opened his mouth to protest, the professor cut him off by saying, "Let's put it to a vote, Master Goodwyn, and allow everyone to choose for themselves." Thatcher scowled but the professor was already asking for votes. "All in favor of staying here in

Larache until our boat to Spain arrives, raise your right hand."

Thatcher shot his hand up into the air and kicked his brother's leg when he didn't immediately comply. "All right," groused Perry, and raised his right hand too.

Ian immediately crossed his arms and Theo followed suit. The professor grinned at the pair and also folded his arms across his chest. All eyes then turned to Carl, who stood unsure on the rock, his gaze darting from his schoolmasters to the professor, then to Theo and Ian, and down to the city and the boy on the rocks. "A tie means we stay here," said Thatcher smugly, and he gave a little nod to encourage Carl to raise his right hand.

Carl shuffled his feet and looked back at Ian, who shrugged and gave him a small smile. Finally, Carl tucked his sword into his belt and slowly crossed his arms over his chest, giving Ian a huge happy grin. "I say we go for it!" he said, and the professor gave a loud whoop and began hurrying to lower himself to the rock below.

"Come along, then, all of you," he said. "No sense fannying around here when there's good daylight ahead for us!"

As they followed Jaaved into the city, Ian couldn't help ogling people almost as much as they seemed to be ogling him. But he noticed after a bit that many of the men were frowning and shaking their heads at Theo.

He moved to her right protectively, keeping between her and the frowning men, and made sure to scowl back when he saw their disapproving looks. "Why do they seem so angry with me?" she said after a while.

"Who?" asked Carl, tearing his eyes reluctantly away from a man with a small monkey perched on his shoulder.

"These people," Theo said. "See?" she insisted as she caught two more men glaring openly at her and spitting into the dirt.

The professor looked back and said, "You're not dressed appropriately."

"What's wrong with the way I'm dressed?" she asked, looking down at her white blouse, plaid skirt, and knee-high stockings.

"It's your head," said the professor as he tapped Jaaved on the shoulder and signaled him over to a small stall.

"My *head?*" said Theo as Ian and the others followed the professor.

"Yes," said the professor, motioning to a woman on the other side of the stall before pointing to a white scarf folded on one of the shelves. "Your head is uncovered and here in Morocco that is unseemly." The professor then laid a few pence on the counter for the woman, who snatched the coins up eagerly and gave him a small bow.

The professor bowed back, then handed the scarf to Theo. "Cover your head and you'll be fine," he instructed, but Theo just stared at the cloth blankly.

Sensing more faces frowning at Theo, Ian gently took it from her and wound it around her head and across her shoulders like he saw some of the other women wearing it. "There you go," he said with an encouraging smile.

"Thanks," she answered, but her frown told him she wasn't at all pleased that she had to cover up.

"Come along, then," said the professor, and they continued on their walk to the smaller vessels at the far end of the harbor. In one of the very last berths, Jaaved stopped in front of the large figure of a man lying prone in a hammock strung up under a small awning of thatch. The man was snoring loudly and Jaaved tapped him on the shoulder.

He flicked at Jaaved's finger and snored even louder. Jaaved turned to the group and gave them all a sheepish grin, then he turned back to the man and tapped again. With a snort the man started and opened his eyes. When he realized that there were strangers standing expectantly nearby, he stood as quickly as his large girth would allow and spoke what Ian assumed were his apologies to their group.

The professor extended his hand and the two men began to converse. Ian looked behind him at Thatcher and said, "Would you mind translating for us?"

The schoolmaster's lips were pursed tightly in disapproval but he complied. Keeping his voice low and quiet, he said, "The man's name is Mohammad. He owns that berth and that ratty-looking sloop over there." Ian's eyes traveled down the pier to the one-masted sailboat that looked like it'd seen far better days. "The professor has asked to rent the vessel for a trip up the Loukkos River to Lixus for a few days," Thatcher continued, "and Mohammad is saying that he cannot possibly spare his precious boat for that long. He is suggesting a trip around the harbor instead."

Ian listened and turned to see the professor smile politely and reach discreetly into his pocket to pull out some pound notes. "The professor is telling Mohammad that he's quite

389

certain he would rather travel up the Loukkos and he'd be very happy if Mohammad would reconsider."

There was a pause in the conversation while Mohammad greedily eyed the money in the professor's hand. And then he spoke again.

"He has reconsidered," said Thatcher with a smirk. "And he is offering Jaaved to pilot us up the river."

"Can Jaaved sail that thing?" Ian asked, looking skeptically from the rickety sloop to the slight boy.

"Apparently," said Thatcher. "And Jaaved says his grandfather lives on the banks of the ancient city and would welcome us with a hot meal and a free tour of the ruins if we'd like to see them."

"Maybe he's the Seeker, then?" said Carl.

"Who?" asked Ian.

"That bloke's grandfather," said Carl.

"Can't be," said Theo. "In my vision I clearly saw a boy."

"Well, then how about that Jaaved character?" whispered Carl. "Do you suppose he's your Seeker?"

Theo's brows knit together. "No," she said, after considering him. "I mean, I didn't have a really clear vision of the boy, but the most distinctive thing I do remember about him from my vision was the diamond mark on his right hand, and Jaaved's right hand is free of any mark."

Ian squinted at Jaaved's hand. It was, as Theo said, free of any strange markings. When he saw that Jaaved was looking at him quizzically, he averted his eyes and looked back at the professor, who was shaking hands with Mohammad.

"Well, children," said Thatcher, "it seems we have ourselves a vessel."

Next the professor turned to Jaaved and asked him something in French.

When Jaaved nodded, Ian looked to his schoolmaster, who whispered, "He's asked Jaaved if he can arrange to get us some supplies for the journey."

Jaaved led the group to the very end of the harbor, where a rather steep set of stairs took them up to the top of a short cliff overlooking the harbor, and at the top of the stairs was a building. Jaaved pointed to the ragtag shop, its name written in some odd script, and said, *"Voilà!"*

The professor turned to Perry and Thatcher and said, "You two stay here while I take our young guide inside and have him help me select some supplies." He disappeared indoors before they could even answer.

Thatcher and Perry sat down wearily under the shade of a palm tree while Ian, Carl, and Theo occupied themselves by watching the boats coming into port. Ian found that he couldn't stop grinning as he gazed at the vessels and the people down on the dock. Looking off to his right, he could see the opening of the Loukkos River, where it emptied into the ocean. The river was wide and a deep rich blue.

Ian closed his eyes and inhaled deeply, feeling the hot sun on his eyelids and cheeks and smelling the salty air until he caught the smallest whiff of something foul.

Opening his eyes, Ian looked about and sniffed the breeze. What had that smell been and why did it seem so familiar? But he couldn't find it again, even though he was turning in a circle, sniffing the air. He heard Theo giggle and he looked over to see her laughing at him. "What on earth are you doing?" she asked.

Ian broke into a sheepish grin. "Nothing," he said quickly. "I thought I smelled something is all."

"You *smelled* something?" Carl asked. "I bet it was a camel," he said brightly. "I bet they're really nasty-smelling up close."

Ian nodded and joined them back at the edge of the cliff. "Yeah," he said, "you're probably right. I likely got a whiff of one of them on the breeze." But at the back of his mind, something nagged at him. The smell had been nasty, like Carl had suggested, but that he found it familiar troubled him.

His attention was stolen, however, by his schoolmasters. Thatcher, it seemed, had been patiently telling his brother about what had occurred at the professor's house, Laodamia and her prophecy, and how all the events that had recently occurred had been within the translated scroll from the silver box.

Perry turned to him and said, "Poppycock!" and Thatcher's face scrunched up in anger.

"How can you say it's poppycock!" he demanded. "I tell you, the translation is clear!" He motioned to Ian. "You've got the professor's notes, don't you, lad?"

"Yes, sir," he said, digging into his trouser pocket and pulling out the prophecy.

After he handed it to Thatcher, the schoolmaster read it to his twin.

"Rubbish!" announced Perry, waving his hand flippantly.

"You cannot call it rubbish!" shouted Thatcher.

Ian listened intently as Thatcher explained how it could all be possible, how there was obviously some sort of natural hole in the space-time continuum and that was how the

Portal could open up and dump them into another country. Perry was still convinced that he'd most likely gotten a thump on the head back in the tunnel and was right now having himself one jolly of a hallucination.

"You're not hallucinating," Thatcher insisted.

"If I were hallucinating, I would expect you to say that," Perry replied.

Thatcher rolled his eyes at his brother. "We cannot all be having the same hallucination, Perry!"

"Of course not," Perry said. "I'm the only one."

"If *you're* the only one, then how can I be here, experiencing the very same things you are?"

"Because *you* are a part of *my* hallucination!" snapped Perry.

Thatcher gave a terrific sigh and turned away from his brother toward Ian, who was trying to hide his smile when something seemed to waft right under his nose again, and he swore he'd just caught another whiff of that same nasty odor. "You all right, lad?" Thatcher asked, and Ian realized he had lifted his nose and was sniffing the air again intently.

Ian nodded. "Fine, sir," he said quietly. "It's just . . ."

"Just what, lad?" asked Thatcher.

Ian turned his head to look up and down the street before answering. "I think something's not right."

Thatcher pushed himself to his feet and came quickly over to Ian. "Really? What have you seen?"

"Nothing," Ian admitted. "It's just I keep smelling something foul on the air."

"I thought we decided you were smelling camels," Carl said.

Ian frowned. "Maybe," he said.

"It's this city," said Perry from under the tree. "No telling what muck is in these streets. I'm sure they don't have the same standards of sanitation that we have back in England."

But Ian wasn't so sure. His brain had finally placed the scent. It was that scent from the cavern where he'd found the box, and from the keep when the beast had attacked them in the east tower. He clearly remembered the distinct sulfuric smell.

He hoped that what he'd caught on the wind was just a combination of smelly odors that reminded him of the beast, because the alternative—having it lurking somewhere nearby—terrified him.

His troubled thoughts were distracted when the professor reappeared from the shop with Jaaved. "We'll need some of you to help us with the supplies I've purchased," said the professor. "And we should set sail immediately while we still have a bit of daylight left."

"What about getting word to the earl?" asked Thatcher.

The professor scratched his chin. "Right," he said. Then, looking down the street, he suddenly brightened. "There," he said, pointing to a small stone building with a swirling script above the door. "There's a post office. I shall send a letter immediately. You gentlemen load up and I'll be back in a jiffy."

Thatcher motioned to Carl and Theo. "You two, go with the professor while we pick up the supplies," he instructed. Carl and Theo waved to Ian and trotted obediently after the old man. Next Ian, Thatcher, Perry, and Jaaved went inside the supply shop to pick up the four newly purchased back-packs loaded down with camping supplies and equipment.

"Here you go," said Thatcher, helping Ian on with one of the packs. He pulled the straps tight, then gave Ian a pat on the shoulder as he stood back to appraise his handiwork. Ian found he couldn't stand up straight and was stooping forward uncomfortably. "Is it too heavy?" the schoolmaster asked.

"No, sir," Ian said with a grimace, working to appear stronger than he felt. "It's just that it's hitting the pocket torch in the back of my trousers."

"Here," said Thatcher, turning Ian around to pull up on the pack and fish out his light.

He tucked the small torch into the side compartment of his own backpack. "I'll hold on to your torch until we make camp," Thatcher said, then pulled out the folded translation of the prophecy and put that into the compartment, next to the pocket torch. "For safekeeping," he said.

Ian attempted to smile, but the strain of the pack made it difficult. Thatcher also took Ian's coat and eyed the top of Ian's pack skeptically. "I don't think we'll add any more weight," he said. "When Carl comes back, we'll have him carry all the coats."

"Can you just be careful of my compass and pocketknife in the pocket?" Ian asked, not wanting them to get tossed out when Carl was carrying the coats. Thatcher smiled and fished around inside Ian's coat, retrieving the compass and pocketknife. He tucked them into the compartment where he'd placed the light and the prophecy. "There," he said kindly. "Now all your treasures are together."

Ian smiled gratefully, though he was afraid it might have looked more like a grimace.

His brow had broken out in a sweat from the strain of the heavy pack, but he wanted to appear capable of carrying his own load, so he kept quiet and watched as Perry and Thatcher both hefted their own packs onto their backs with grunts.

Once outside, Ian's group joined the professor's, and Thatcher handed Carl all their coats. "If you would see these safely down to the sloop, Master Lawson?"

Carl took the bundle of coats eagerly. "Of course," he said.

"Word has been sent," said the professor. "I've informed the earl that we are safe, that circumstances beyond our control have landed us in Morocco, and that in a fortnight we will be booking passage to Spain, where we will need funds to see us back home to England."

"Very well," said Thatcher reluctantly. "Let's be off, then."

Ian and the others followed Jaaved to the top of the stairwell leading back down to the marina. The Moroccan boy paused while Perry, Thatcher, and Ian—who was huffing and puffing under the weight of his pack—worked to catch up.

"Do you want some help, mate?" asked Carl over the pile of coats he was carrying.

"No thanks," said Ian, anxious just to get down the stairs so that he could unload the pack. Before Ian had reached the others, Jaaved began down the steps, followed by the professor, Theo, Perry, Thatcher, and Carl, who waited at the top until Ian was close before heading down.

The straps of his pack bit painfully into his shoulders and the weight made his descent slightly hazardous. He could only imagine what would happen if he lost his footing.

By the time he was near the bottom, he could see that the rest of his group had already made it across the dock to the slip where the rickety sailboat waited to be boarded.

But Ian had to pause on the landing before the last steps to catch his wind and give his wobbly legs a rest. He watched as Jaaved hopped aboard the sloop and unloaded his knapsack. Scuttling around the various ropes and buoys, he went about preparing the boat to leave the dock. *"Par ici!"* Jaaved said, waving on the rest of the group.

Ian forced air into his lungs and saw Carl and Theo jump aboard first, then turn to help the professor, while Perry and Thatcher shrugged out of their backpacks before stepping gingerly onto the boat.

Ian realized he was holding them up, so he pushed off from the railing he'd been leaning against, when his foot caught on something and he almost fell down the last set of stairs. He noticed with a growl of frustration that his right shoelace had come undone. He made his way carefully down the last few steps, then stopped again to retie it, but he hadn't considered that bending over would throw him off balance, and the heavy backpack pulled him right over onto his side. His cheeks flushed red with embarrassment as he heard Theo and Carl break into hysterics and Thatcher call back, "You all right?"

Ian waved. "Fine, sir!" he said, and struggled under the bulky weight to right himself. Finally, he managed to get to his feet again and squatted carefully to finish tying his shoelace when a soft breeze carried the slightest hint of that foul odor to his nostrils. Ian lifted his head, sniffing the air in alarm.

Another breeze brought the smell again, but it competed with the briny scent of the sea and a hint of petrol. Ian hurried to lace up his shoe. He couldn't be certain the scent belonged to the beast, but he knew he didn't want to wait around to find out. Then he heard Theo's laughter abruptly stop, and an instant later she let out a bloodcurdling scream.

Ian's head snapped up and what he saw was both confusing and frightening. Everyone in the boat was yelling, but Theo looked out of her mind with fear and it was several seconds before he realized she and the others were all pointing and yelling *at him*.

He watched in a haze as Thatcher and Perry started climbing over each other in panic, trying to scramble back onto the dock, but the boat tipped precariously. Jaaved had already unwrapped one of the moorings, and his face was frozen in terror while his hands moved wildly to undo the other line. Ian squatted there for a few heartbeats, his mind slow to add things up, and then he heard the thundering of paws behind him.

He whipped his head around to look over his shoulder but the pack obscured his view. Turning his body carefully, he gasped when he saw the beast, its red eyes glowing and its lips pulled away from those deadly fangs in a frightening snarl, pounding down the staircase straight at him. For one horrible second Ian was frozen in place by his own terror as the beast raced at him with death in its eyes.

Theo's scream, *"Iiiiiaaaaaaan!"* finally broke the spell and urged him to bolt to his feet. He took two great leaps forward, but the heavy pack prevented him from gaining any speed. Ahead he could see Thatcher half in, half out of the boat as he held on to the pier with his fingertips while Jaaved pushed with an oar to send them out to sea. Perry was tangled in his brother's legs while everyone else on the boat was screaming for Ian to run faster.

Somehow, Ian did. He gritted his teeth, balled his fists, and dug for every step. He leaned forward and allowed the weight of the backpack to propel him. Still, on his heels he could hear the beast thundering closer, and closer . . . and closer.

His feet pounded down the dock, his brow slick with sweat and his heart hammering hard. He was almost there.

Just behind him came a growl that was deeper than he remembered and, if possible, more vicious. Ian's lungs begged for air while his mind screamed in terror. To add to his horror, Jaaved finally won out against Thatcher's efforts and the boat pushed away from the dock. The air all around was filled with nightmarish noises: Theo was screaming; Carl was pleading with him to run faster; Perry and Thatcher were yelling at Jaaved; and the professor was shouting incoherently at everyone while the beast's paws thundered ever closer.

He was steps away from the end of the pier when he felt the hot breath of the beast on the backs of his arms. The boat was slipping farther away from the dock and Ian realized he would never make it. In the last split second, he and

Theo locked eyes. He could see everything in them: her love for him, her terror at the beast charging him down, and her horror as she realized that Ian wasn't going to make it.

It was that look that gave him courage, and just as he felt the beast's paws hit his backpack, he lunged sideways, straight off the pier into the water.

The heavy weight of his pack immediately pulled him under, and as the contents became wet, he sank like a stone. Ian struggled and kicked with all his might to swim upward while his lungs—already deprived of oxygen—ached to inhale.

He clawed savagely at the water, making it up a bit with the effort of his strokes. The surface didn't look far away, but as hard as he tried, the pack kept pulling him down. It was hopeless. He'd never reach the surface and the straps were so tight that he couldn't manage to get out of them. If he stopped swimming to try to wiggle free, he'd descend too deeply to make it back to the surface at all.

His arms flailed and his feet kicked, but his efforts were growing weaker and weaker. He was sinking away from the air he so desperately needed and his vision filled with darkness and little bright stars. And then his mouth opened involuntarily and he inhaled, and the most pain he'd ever felt in his life racked his body as water poured into his lungs. He wretched and coughed and inhaled again, funneling more water into his airway. He shivered and shook in agony and the world around him became murkier and less bright until finally he lost the fight and let the darkness take him.

THE RIVER

"Ian!" he heard in the darkness of the tunnel he felt he'd fallen into. "Ian, *please!*" came the cry more clearly. He knew that voice. It was Theo's. He couldn't remember why she was pleading with him, and at the moment he couldn't worry about it, because he was in too much pain. Someone was hammering on his chest, and his mouth was opened and air was blown in. A second later, he convulsed and hacked up huge quantities of water while he coughed and sputtered and wheezed.

"Oh, thank heavens!" said Perry, who it seemed was leaning over him. "He's back."

Ian continued to cough while his body shivered from head to toe. "Here," said Carl. "Wrap up in this, mate."

Ian opened his eyes to see Carl holding a blanket out to him, but he was coughing too much to reach for it. Gratefully, Theo took the blanket from Carl and placed it around Ian's shoulders. "What happened?" he sputtered when he was finally able to speak.

"We thought you'd drowned," Theo said with a small hiccup. He realized she'd been crying.

"That beast almost had you!" exclaimed Carl. "He was right on top of you, and then you popped into the water."

"You went right under," added Thatcher, and Ian was surprised to discover that both he and Perry were soaking wet. "We came in after you. It was a miracle that Perry managed to bump into you down in that murky water and haul you up to the surface."

"That was far too close for comfort," said the professor, and Ian was touched by the look of deep concern on his face.

Ian coughed again; his cheeks felt hot with the effort. Everyone waited for him to finish before continuing with the story.

"The beast made like it was going to jump in after you when several fishermen on the dock came running after it with their oars and a net. It ran off back up the stairs, but not before it gave us a bloody good scare," said Carl, his eyes wide and frightened.

"Master Lawson," said Perry, "please watch your language."

The professor waved impatiently. "Let the boy be, Perry. We did have a bloody good scare."

Theo shuddered and looked back to the pier. "It's okay," Ian said gently. "There's no way that creature can track us now that we're on the boat." Theo glanced back at Ian, but her worried frown remained.

"Bad *chien*!" said Jaaved from his place at the stern of the boat, and Ian turned to look at him in surprise.

Thatcher asked, "Jaaved, do you speak English?"

402

Jaaved shook his head. "*Non,*" he said. "*Je comprends seulement un peu de ce que vous dites.*"

"He says he understands only a little bit of what we say," Thatcher translated.

"The locals here speak fluent French and Shamali, but enough British travel through this port that many of the natives can understand a few phrases and words," added the professor.

"What's Shamali?" asked Carl.

"A form of Arabic," explained the professor. "I speak a smattering of it, but my French is better."

"So how did the beast find us all the way in Morocco?" Perry asked, getting back to their terrible scare. "Did it come through the portal too?"

"Impossible," said Thatcher. "The stone wall was back in place when we left the cavern, not to mention that Caphiera's wall of ice would have needed days to melt and it certainly would have blocked that thing from following us through."

"Not if the beast somehow came through the portal first," reasoned Ian with a shiver.

"Maybe that's where it's been all this time, then?" said Carl. "All the while you lot were hunting it, that beasty was prowling around here in Morocco."

"It wasn't the same one," said Theo quietly.

She had spoken so softly that the professor, Thatcher, and Perry all leaned in and asked, "What's that?"

Theo looked back at the pier, which was becoming a distant dot on the landscape as they sailed farther into the mouth of the Loukkos. "Did you get a good look at it, Carl?"

she asked. "The beast that attacked us in the tower didn't have that white stripe along its hackles."

Carl turned his head, also glancing at the pier. "Yeah," he said thoughtfully. "Now that you mention it, Theo, I don't remember that white stripe from before either."

"The beast had a white stripe?" Ian asked. The only thing he'd gotten a good look at on his dash down the pier had been its cruel eyes and huge teeth.

Theo nodded. "And that beast," she said, pointing to the pier, "was male."

Ian curled the edges of the blanket about him tighter. "The mate," he said through chattering teeth. "It must be the she-beast's mate."

"Yes," said Carl, nodding. "But why do they always seem to be after *you*, Ian?"

"It must have to do with the prophecy and the Oracle," said Perry, to everyone's surprise.

"So now you believe this isn't some hallucination?" Thatcher asked.

Perry sighed and nodded. "If that jump into the water didn't shake me out of my delusions, then this must be real," he said soberly.

"He's got a solid point," said the professor. "That beast had the stink of the underworld on it. Did any of the rest of you catch the smell of sulfur?" Ian bobbed his head up and down; he'd certainly smelled it. "Yes," said the professor. "I'll bet that the beast is some sort of force controlled by one of Demogorgon's other offspring."

"Not Caphiera?" asked Carl with a shiver.

"No," said the professor. "From what very little I know of her from the clay pots at Grimspound, she's particularly cruel to animals. She likes to freeze them just for the sport of it."

"Then which of the other offspring do you think the beasts belong to?" asked Ian.

"Either the sorcerer, Magus, or his vile sister Lachestia. Magus is the sorcerer of fire and Lachestia is the sorceress of earth. Both would be good candidates to set those brutes loose upon the land."

Just then Theo gasped and Ian looked around them in alarm, thinking she'd spotted the beast again. When he didn't see anything, he asked, "What?"

She gripped his arm through the blanket, her face as white as a sheet, and said, "Do you remember my vision out on the lawn of Castle Dover?"

"Of course," he said, now even more worried. "Are you having another vision?"

Theo shook her head. "No," she said, looking up at Thatcher. "Schoolmaster Goodwyn, do you remember when I talked about the wolf rising from the east to launch his army on us and that a war far greater than the Great War would come to devastate our lands?"

Thatcher gasped, making the connection, and one by one the rest of them did too. "It makes sense!" said Ian. "Those gruesome creatures do look like overgrown wolves! And if this führer fellow from Germany wanted a powerful, scary brute by his side to invoke fear into his enemy, those nasty creatures would be the ones to have."

The professor inhaled deeply and met Ian's eyes. His

expression suggested that Ian's conclusion was likely the worst scenario possible. "Laodamia was right to be so concerned," he said quietly.

Ian thought about the extraordinary Oracle who seemed to be directing their every move. "Sir?" he said to the professor. "What more can you tell us about the Oracle?"

"What would you like to know?"

"Well, what happened to her? I mean, you mentioned that she fell out of favor politically, but what became of her?"

The professor's frown deepened and he said, "She was murdered, I'm afraid."

Ian gasped. He'd never considered that the greatest Oracle of all time could have met such a horrible end. "How?" he whispered.

The professor pulled at his chin and crinkled his nose. "I know of the Oracle's untimely death because of the scrolls I discovered," he began. "As I said before, there was a span of several years where Laodamia was the host of Phoenicia, but during her career as an Oracle, the young lady developed some powerful political enemies. She had a few potent allies, however, including her betrothed, Iyoclease, a Phoenician general with a long legacy of bravery. But Iyoclease was ambushed by Laodamia's enemies and killed before the couple could marry.

"That's when things got very grim for our Oracle. After she lost her most valuable ally, it wasn't long before her enemies were able to issue a decree of treason against her. An order was given to bring Laodamia before the Phoenician senate for judgment, but the Oracle fled Phoenicia and was soon discovered by an armed regiment in a cave on the outskirts of the city. When she tried to flee again, the soldiers inadvertently killed her."

"That's so sad," whispered Theo.

Ian felt as if a sharp dagger had hit his heart. He was unable to explain why he felt such a connection to the Oracle, but hearing that she'd been murdered upset him greatly.

"Blimey," said Carl in a breathy whisper, and Ian noticed he and Theo weren't the only ones with long faces.

"Blimey is right," said the professor. "Still, she was an extraordinary woman for all of the short years she lived. By my estimate she was only twenty-three or twenty-four when she died, and yet, she left us so much to consider and such detailed instructions to future generations, all in an effort to get a message to us."

"But how exactly do you think she was able to see so far into the future, Professor?" asked Thatcher.

The professor sat back against one of the packs, using it as a cushion as he considered Thatcher's question. "Well," he said, "I suppose that after reading her scrolls this week, I can conclude that, speaking of time as a vast ocean current, while other oracles were only able to look out from the sand at the horizon, Laodamia was actually able to follow the wave as it left shore, and ride it out to sea. In one of her scrolls, she specifically discusses seeing one hundred generations into the future, when a great war would be sparked in the lands west of Greece and bring on the end of the world."

"One hundred generations," said Thatcher thoughtfully. "That'd be roughly . . ." He paused while he sorted through the math. "Close to now," he said. Ian gulped. Laodamia's prophecy was too close to dismiss.

"But this is all just a myth," said Perry, and Ian noticed that he was looking round at them as if they were all having a great laugh at his expense. "I mean, it's not *real*," he insisted.

The professor regarded him soberly. "That is what I hoped, Perry, until earlier today when meeting Caphiera the Cold removed all doubt from the seriousness of the Oracle's predictions."

"So what do we do?" asked Theo, fear tingeing her voice.

"We find the Star of Lixus," said the professor. "And we find it quickly. Laodamia has told us of its importance and has ensured setting us on this course. Therefore, we must see it through to the end."

"But we don't even have the Seeker yet!" said Ian, feeling an overwhelming sense of gloom while he watched the fear and trepidation cast a shadow over the grown-up faces around him.

"All we need to do is follow the prophecy," said Theo confidently. "If Laodamia had clear enough vision to get us this far, Ian, then she certainly had the ability to see us through to the end."

The professor turned to Jaaved, who was busy navigating them through the traffic in the wide mouth of the river, and asked the boy something. Jaaved responded as he pumped his head enthusiastically, and the professor said, "I've asked Jaaved if he knows anyone who is good with crystals. He says as it happens, his grandfather is one of the best jewelry makers in all of Morocco. He works extensively with gemstones and crystals that he quarries out of the surrounding hillsides."

"If Theo's right and our Seeker is a boy, do you think he might know him?" Ian asked.

"It's worth asking him," said the professor. "Jaaved has assured me that his grandfather would welcome us as his personal guests. It's a good place to begin, I think."

"How long until we reach his grandfather's?" Ian asked, realizing they had only a fortnight before they must return to Larache.

The professor conferred with Jaaved. "He believes it will only take us until midday tomorrow to reach his grandfather's home."

"That's longer than I thought," said Ian, moody about spending so much time in the bottom of an uncomfortable boat.

"Geographically, Lixus isn't that far from Larache," said the professor. "But the Loukkos River winds through several deep curves and the current works against us going in this direction."

"Why didn't we choose to travel by land?" asked Perry, adjusting himself to a more comfortable sitting position.

The professor answered, "You'd need to travel by camel or horse. And the main road has never been safe for foreign travelers."

Turning to Jaaved, Thatcher asked the boy something in French. Jaaved pointed up to the sky and answered him. Thatcher said, "Jaaved suggests that we can sail as long as there's a good wind, but shortly after dusk the wind dies down and won't be strong enough to fight the current. We'll have to cast anchor and make camp."

"I was afraid of that," said the professor, looking uneasily at the shore. "And the one gun I purchased for the trip was lost in Ian's pack."

"My pack's gone?"

Perry nodded. "It was all I could do to get you to the surface," he explained. "I had to cut you out of the straps and the whole bundle sank to the bottom of the harbor rather quickly."

Ian's heart plummeted. "What else was in it?"

"Much of our food, I'm afraid," said the professor.

"Our food?" exclaimed Carl. "What will we eat?"

Jaaved must have understood some of what they were saying, because he pointed to the water and said, "*Poissons.*"

Carl gasped. "Did he just say the water is poison?"

Thatcher, Perry, and the professor laughed. "No, my good lad," chuckled the professor. "He said 'fish.' We'll have plenty of time to catch our dinner as we sail upriver."

The professor turned to Jaaved and spoke at length, then announced to the group, "I've just told him to please sail us as far as possible before it becomes too dark to navigate. I want to put some good distance between us and that horror back at the pier."

Ian couldn't agree more.

Several hours later, as the setting sun turned the western sky to rich shades of peach, purple, and orange, Jaaved navigated the little boat to a tiny island in the center of the river and they made camp and cooked the fish they'd managed to catch.

After everyone had finished eating, the professor suggested they turn in, as their group was exhausted from such a long day. "We should set a watch, however," advised Thatcher, and Perry agreed. "I'll take first watch," Thatcher said. "Perry, wake me in two hours for your turn."

"I'll go after Perry," said Ian.

"And I'll take the last watch after Ian," offered Carl.

Ian was asleep the moment his head hit his coat, which he'd wadded up to use as a pillow, and it felt like he'd been asleep only a few minutes when Perry was shaking him gently. "Your turn," his schoolmaster whispered.

With bleary eyes Ian followed Perry out of the tent and over to the small fire being kept up by the watchman on duty. "Give a shout if you hear or see anything alarming," Perry said with a yawn.

Ian nodded dully and slapped his cheeks to wake himself up, but soon his eyelids had grown heavy and he could feel his head bobbing forward. In the back of his mind he knew he should do something to fight the urge to sleep, but he was far too exhausted to care. Suddenly, however, he heard a sound that made him jump to his feet with his heart pounding.

He could swear he heard a horrible howl somewhere in the distance. Straining his ears, he waited and then faintly heard it again, but a second howl joined the first. Ian rushed to the tent where Perry, Thatcher, and the professor were sleeping. He shook his schoolmasters awake and motioned them outside. "I heard the beasts," he whispered.

"Where?" asked Perry.

"When?" added his brother.

"Just a moment ago," said Ian. "But both howls were faint and far down the river on the left side of the bank."

Thatcher tipped his head back and regarded the night sky. "There's about four hours before dawn," he said. "There'll be no wind to carry us further upstream until then."

Perry squinted into the darkness all around their island. "We're near the center of the river," he mused. "Even if the beasts caught up to our position from the shore, they'd still have to swim to this island to get at us, and with this river's current, that would be one mighty feat indeed."

His schoolmasters then looked at each other and turned back to Ian. "We should be safe enough here until morning," Thatcher concluded. "However, I'll join you on watch, Ian. Perry, you may take the last two hours before dawn with Carl."

For the rest of the night, Ian and the others strained their ears for any hint of the beasts, but nothing more came, which Ian thought was almost as troublesome.

Everyone was up and anxious to be on their way as the first rays of sunshine flickered across the sky. After the tents had been dismantled and the packs reloaded, Ian and the others piled back onto the ragtag vessel and got settled. Thatcher and Perry, it seemed, felt duty bound to watch the shore for any sign of the beasts, and as Jaaved hoisted the sail and lifted the anchor, the brothers took positions fore and aft, their heads swiveling from side to side as they watched the left bank for any hint of movement.

Because they were focused on the left bank, no one but Ian saw a movement on the right. In the distance he saw a figure moving in the faint light of dawn between the rocks and boulders that dotted the terrain. All Ian caught was a glimpse, but what he thought he saw was enough to make him shiver. It looked as if a cloaked figure walked purposefully just onshore. He remembered the cloaked figure that had walked the grounds at Castle Dover shortly after the beast had attacked them at the keep. He'd caught only a glimpse there too, but the eerie cadence in the movements of that figure and this one were strikingly similar.

He was just about to point it out to the others, but whatever had caught his eye disappeared behind a large rock, not to reappear. Ian watched the spot where the figure should have come out, but as their boat traveled farther upstream, the rock became small and any hope of spotting the form was lost.

"What are you looking at?" Carl asked, interrupting Ian's concentration.

"I thought I saw someone walking just onshore," he said, sitting up to squint into the bright sunlight.

"A man?" asked Perry, turning to give Ian his full attention.

Ian nodded. "Yes, sir, I think so. Just over there," he said, pointing to the rock in the distance.

Perry looked around at the terrain they were passing. Much of it was rocky and dry with bits of scrub lining the river. "It would be very odd for someone to walk along these shores," he said. "There's not even a path to make it easy for foot traffic." Turning to Jaaved, Perry said something in French. Jaaved replied, shaking his head.

"What'd you ask him?" Ian said.

"I asked if there was a road along the river. He said there

wasn't, that the terrain was too difficult to navigate by horse or camel."

"Probably just your eyes playing tricks on you," said Carl, patting Ian's shoulder.

Ian frowned. His insides still felt uneasy.

DEVIL'S STONE AND EYE OF ZEUS

The day dragged. There was almost no traffic on the river, and the shoreline became one long repetitive picture of scrub, rock, and bare earth. Ian tried to doze, knowing he'd need his wits about him when they landed.

Finally, toward late afternoon, Jaaved pointed ahead and announced, "Lixus!"

Everyone turned to look and Ian felt his heart sink. The ancient city was nothing more than a cluster of steep hills with a few crumbling ruins that were barely recognizable as anything man-made. The lost city was hardly worth all the fuss that the professor seemed to make of it.

But Ian's disappointment was in stark contrast with the professor's enthusiasm as the boat drew nearer and nearer. "Would you look at that?" he whispered next to Ian. "What a wonderful sight for these old, sore eyes!"

"Doesn't look like much to me," Carl said.

"Of course not," said the professor. "To your un-trained eye it hardly looks like anything is left after all this time, correct?"

"That's because there *is* hardly anything left," Carl insisted. "I mean, look at it, sir. Just a few crumbling rocks. What's there to get excited about?"

The professor smiled patiently. "Carl, what you don't see is what's under the surface. This was once a thriving city, with people from all over the known world coming here to trade and experience the wonder of Moroccan culture, textiles, and spices."

Carl glanced back at the site, his face registering doubt. "Still looks like a pile of rubble to me."

The professor chuckled softly, and then he said something that struck Ian as a very important thing to keep in mind. "What you must remember, lad, is that to find a bit of treasure, you must first locate the ruins."

Ian thought that was a rather genius perspective, and he studied what was left of Lixus with renewed interest before asking, "Whatever happened to it? The city, I mean. Why did people stop living there?"

The professor squinted into the distance of the hills. "Several reasons," he answered. "Lixus suffered some significant changes of power between the Phoenicians and the Carthaginians, then the Romans, who made it a military outpost. It saw a small revival under the Roman emperor Claudius the First, but sadly, as that particular empire faded from the landscape, so did this city. It became increasingly hard to defend and eventually its inhabitants abandoned it."

"What happened to all the people?" asked Theo, and Ian smiled, because it was just like her to worry about other people.

"Most of them relocated downriver to Larache. Others became nomadic shepherds who staked out territories near the river."

"And no one lives there now?" asked Carl.

"Not to my knowledge," said the professor; then he eyed Jaaved, who was bouncing with enthusiasm as they criss-crossed the river ever closer to the ruins. "Of course, according to our pilot here, there is one resident in the form of his grandfather."

"We should get ready to go ashore, then," said Thatcher, and he made his way from the stern to the middle of the boat and took a seat next to the mast, where he unpacked the two large backpacks and Jaaved's smaller knapsack. Placing their contents carefully onto the bottom of the boat, he began organizing them into three piles. Curious about what his schoolmaster was doing, Ian scooted next to Thatcher and asked, "Do you need some help?"

Thatcher glanced at him. "Yes, thank you, Ian," he said. "I think we should take to shore only those items we'll truly need for our excavations, like this shovel and one of the tents and perhaps one of those torches."

"Won't we need the rest of the supplies?" Ian asked, looking at the other tent, a few canned goods, and the fishing poles.

"We can come back to the boat as we need things," Thatcher said reasonably. "And if for some reason we have to make a hasty retreat, we won't need to worry that we've left all of our supplies in one location. We can rely on what we've got in the boat to see us safely back to Larache."

"That's good thinking, sir," Ian said admiringly.

Thatcher gave him a sardonic smile. "Thank you," he said. "Now, tuck this pack under the mainsail, would you? Oh, and here are your personal items," he added, handing Ian his light, his pocketknife, his compass, and the prophecy.

"Thank you, sir," said Ian, taking the items.

As he was stuffing his pockets with his things, Ian heard a shout from the shore and looked up to see a tall bearded man with a sizable belly. He was wearing a long white linen tunic and waving to them.

Jaaved shouted, *"Bonjour, Grand-père!"* and waved back with vigor.

Ian and Carl scooted to the bow of the boat, anxious to help tie it up when they finally docked. As their sloop cruised the last few meters, Jaaved's grandfather limped his way down the dock and stood at one of the pilings, ready to assist them. Jaaved navigated the sailboat closer and pulled up on one of the ropes, which dropped the small sail. Ian was impressed with the Moroccan boy's handling of the vessel as it sidled up easily to the dock and was stopped with little effort when Jaaved's grandfather put one foot on the bow and took the lead line that Ian handed to him. *"Bonjour!"* said the older man with a wide toothy grin as he quickly wound the rope around the piling.

The professor rose and greeted the man in French, and the two had a little chat while Perry and Thatcher quickly jumped to the dock and secured all the other lines. Jaaved wrapped a cord around the rudder before leaping out of the boat to fiercely embrace his grandfather. Ian was touched by the exchange and realized that he had developed a fondness for Jaaved and his patient, gentle nature. He could tell that Jaaved's grandfather had that same quality. He knew he was going to like the old man.

Ian turned away then to see about getting everyone on-shore, and he noticed that the professor was already working his way slowly out of the boat. He jumped to help him, sensing that Professor Nutley might not be as spry as he used to be. After the professor had made it safely onto the dock and continued conversing in French with Jaaved's grandfather, Ian held his hand out to Theo and she joined the group. Carl was busy getting his sword through his belt loop, and the moment it was bonded to his side, he leapt ashore with ease. While Ian was still in the boat, he handed Thatcher and Perry the two backpacks that would accompany them to shore, and finally made his way onto the dock, only then realizing he was the last person waiting to be introduced to Jaaved's grandfather. *"Bonjour,"* Ian said to him, working to pronounce the word correctly and extending his hand.

"Hello, young man," said Jaaved's grandfather as he took Ian's hand into his own.

Ian was startled. "Oh! I didn't know you spoke English," he said. "I'm Ian Wigby, sir. It's a pleasure to meet you."

"And it's a pleasure to meet you, my good young man. You may call me Jifaar. I am Jaaved's grandfather. Professor Nutley told me you were from England. I assumed it would be easier to converse in your native tongue."

"Yes, thank you, sir," Ian said, then looked down at his shoes as he struggled for something else to say. He hadn't expected Jifaar to be so civilized.

He was saved from having to make further small talk when Jifaar said, "Come along, everyone. I was just about to break bread. Won't you join me for a meal?"

Carl nodded eagerly. "We'd love to!" he said, and hurried to the old man's side. Ian allowed Theo and Jaaved to go ahead of him, then followed while Jifaar led them to the front of his house, where a large rug was laid out on the dirt under a tree. Jifaar told them all to make themselves comfortable on the rug; then he motioned to his grandson and they disappeared inside the house.

While they waited for their host to return, Ian had a chance to take in their surroundings. He was surprised that what he had first thought was a rather shabby-looking shack was actually a neat and tidy small wooden home, complete with a porch strung with two hammocks and a yard outlined with stones.

There was also a well-tended garden to the side of the house, and a weathered wheelbarrow and a rusty watering can showed definite signs of use.

The enormous tree they were under was close enough to the small house to give it plenty of shade and protect the garden from the long, hot rays of the afternoon sun.

In the distance, three hills rolled up from the flat plain, and the skeletal remains of a teeming city lay in crumbling ruin in clumps along them.

"Rather gloomy-looking up there, isn't it?" Theo whispered to him.

"I was thinking the same thing," he said. "I wonder where the professor intends for us to start looking for the Star."

"It's an awful lot of territory to cover," whispered Carl, on his other side.

"I wish we knew where to find our Seeker," said Ian. "It seems like he should have shown himself by now, don't you think?"

"It does," said Theo. She looked like she was about to say something more but Jifaar and Jaaved came out again. The older man's expression appeared concerned. His arms were laden with a huge tray of fruit and fish while his grandson carried another tray, loaded with a pitcher and several glasses. Ian jumped to his feet and hurried over to help Jifaar. "Allow me, sir," he said.

"Thank you, Ian," their host said, handing him the tray. "Come sit and let's chat about your journey."

When everyone had a portion of fish, fruit, and drink, Jifaar said, "My grandson tells me you are being pursued by some kind of wild beast."

The professor nodded. "Yes, I'm afraid so."

Over the course of their meal, he explained the troubles they'd had since coming to Morocco, but Ian noticed that he was careful not to elaborate on how exactly the six of them had gotten there.

"And you are here looking for the Star?" asked Jifaar. Ian was surprised that he'd made that leap so quickly, but then he reasoned that Jifaar had probably seen the shovel sticking out of one of the backpacks.

The professor smiled, and Ian realized that the old man wasn't likely to get much past Jaaved's grandfather. "It had crossed our minds," he said.

Jifaar leaned his back against the trunk of the tree and

placed his hands across his large belly. "If you believe the rumors," he said, with a playful twinkle in his eye, "then you will have heard that the Star has already been discovered. A group of Germans came upon it and smuggled it back to their country."

Ian gasped and looked round at all the other shocked faces—except for Theo's. "No," she said slowly, as if feeling her way along the truth. "That's not true. They haven't found it. They found something similar. The real Star of Lixus is still out there."

Jifaar appeared surprised. He looked sharply at Theo and asked, "How do you know this, sweet lady?"

Theo gave him a level look. "The same way you do, sir."

The old man threw his head back and laughed, slapping his knee and pointing to her.

"What's so funny?" asked Carl.

Jifaar winked at Theo. "The young lady knows without being told, am I correct? She sees the future of things before they happen?"

"She does," said the professor, and Ian wiggled protectively closer to Theo. He wasn't sure if Jifaar would scoff at her, and was ready to defend her if he needed to.

But Jifaar surprised him when he gave her an admiring smile. "My grandson's mother was also blessed," he said, nodding toward Jaaved. "Such a lovely woman, and a shame that she passed so young." Ian looked at Jaaved, who was happily eating a pomegranate, seemingly oblivious to their conversation.

Perry spoke up next. "So am I to understand that Theo is correct? That the Star has not been found?"

Jifaar nodded. "Oh, yes, the young miss is correct, but everyone across these lands believes the Star has been stolen." Jifaar's eyes were still filled with mirth, and Ian was having a hard time following their host's train of thought.

Carl must have shared his perspective, because he said, "I don't understand. Why does that make you smile?"

Jifaar's grin widened while he explained. "Several weeks ago a German patrol came up the river and stopped at my door. They showed me papers and said they were under special orders from their leader to find the Star of Lixus. They were so arrogant," he said, and spat into the dirt. "So, I told them I knew exactly where they should look for their precious gem."

"Where?" asked Perry, and Ian realized he was holding his breath. Perhaps Jifaar was their Seeker after all.

But Jifaar smiled wickedly, as if he were the holder of a particularly hilarious joke, and said, "I sent them to the Jichmach."

"The Jichmach?" Perry repeated.

Jifaar nodded. "They are a rival tribe to us. My son, Jaaved's uncle Raajhi, leads the Jstor. We are keepers of this ancient land. The Jichmach would like nothing better than to take this fertile soil near the river for their own. It was good that they encountered the Germans. It taught them a lesson."

"I still don't understand," said Ian, feeling like he might not be the only one who was having a hard time following this story.

"Something was stolen," said Theo, and Ian noticed that faraway look in her eyes. "Something of value."

Jifaar smiled approvingly at her. "Yes, the Star of Lixus was stolen right out from under the Jichmach's noses!" he said with a hearty laugh that shook his middle and echoed into the night.

"But I thought the Star hadn't been found," said Carl with a frown.

Jifaar took the last bite of his fish before replying. "The Jichmach are known liars," he said when he'd swallowed. "Many years ago they began a rumor that they had found the Star of Lixus hidden in some cave on the border between our two lands. Their hope was that it would make the Jstor jealous, that we would no longer think that Lixus was such a magical place without its valuable treasure. Their plan was that our people would give up this land, and the Jichmach could take it from us. But everyone knew that the Jichmach were lying—everyone, that is, but the Germans."

"So what did the Germans steal?" asked the professor.

"It is true that the Jichmach did find something of value. And it is also true that long ago a large sapphire was found by one of their tribesmen in a cave near the Atlas foothills. The Jichmach named it the Star of Lixus, and when the Germans came to my home demanding that I tell them where to find it, I sent them directly to the Jichmach!

"Later, I learned that the Germans found the Jichmach with little trouble and asked about the Star. The foolish leader of the Jichmach couldn't wait to parade the sapphire out in front of the foreigners, but of course he refused to sell it, no matter how much gold the Germans offered. That's when the Germans drew their guns, stole the Jichmach's horses, and made off with the sapphire!" Jifaar laughed

424

deeply again. His laugh was so infectious that Ian laughed too.

"Those Jichmach must really be peeved!" said Carl with a chuckle.

Jifaar nodded, suddenly sobering. "Yes, that would be an understatement, my boy. Raajhi has had to step up his patrol along the border between our two lands, as the Jichmach are feeling their foolishness and are looking for a fight."

Perry scowled. "We should have stayed in Larache," he grumbled. "This land is unsafe for us!"

Jifaar gave him a level look, then glanced up to the hills above where the old city lay. "Your worry is at an end, my friend," he said, catching a slight movement in the fading light. "My son, Raajhi, is here."

Ian and the others stood and looked up the hill. Down one of the trails came a fierce-looking warrior dressed completely in black linen, riding a tall black horse. He led several others dressed just like him. When he was within shouting distance, he raised his hand and called out something. Jaaved and Jifaar raised their own hands, calling back.

A few minutes later, the lead warrior dismounted and came over to greet the older Moroccan. Jifaar hugged him warmly and waved to the others; then, speaking to his son in Arabic, he sat down and motioned everyone else to do the same.

"I am Raajhi," the warrior said to them with an accent much thicker than his father's. "Welcome to the lands of the Jstor," he offered with a small bow.

Ian was relieved to hear the man speak English. The professor bowed his head too and introduced himself, then

425

pointed to each of the others and introduced them. Raajhi gave a slight nod before fiddling with his belt loop and unbuckling the huge curved sword by his side.

Ian sucked in a breath as the sword's handle reflected the late afternoon sun. The hilt was one of the most beautiful things he'd ever seen. It was intricately carved and imbedded with dozens of sparkling gemstones, and at the very end was a silver etching in the shape of a diamond. Ian thought it must be worth a fortune.

Raajhi barked out an order to his nephew before gruffly handing him the sword, and Ian realized that there'd been no greeting shared between Raajhi and Jaaved. Raajhi looked at his nephew with a pronounced scowl of disapproval, but Jaaved took the sword with great care and laid it gently on the corner of the rug before dashing back inside and returning with a cloth and a small jar of ointment. He then squatted down near Thatcher and began rubbing out the tarnish with focused determination.

Ian's eyes traveled back to Raajhi, and he couldn't help feeling an intense pang of sadness for Jaaved. The young boy surely didn't deserve such gruff treatment from his uncle. Jifaar had mentioned that Jaaved's mother had died. Ian wondered where the boy's father was.

Thatcher leaned over, pointed at the sword, and spoke in quiet tones to Jaaved, and after he had answered him, Ian leaned around Carl and asked about the sword.

Thatcher eyed Raajhi before responding, making sure they weren't overheard. "The sword was Jaaved's father's before he died in a battle with the Jichmach. It passed to his uncle, who is now head of the tribe."

426

Ian nodded, still wondering why Jaaved's uncle was so cold to him.

Dusk came and the grown-ups talked on. Luckily for Ian, Carl, and Theo, they mostly spoke in English. When the professor told Raajhi about their encounter with the beast in Larache and about Ian's hearing two separate howls the night before, Raajhi expressed his concern that he now had not only the Jichmach to worry about, but some giant dangerous beasts as well. "I must go to the camps and get more men for the patrol," he said. "You should come with us, my father. I would prefer to know you are safe in our camp rather than so far away from my sight."

The old man smiled patiently at his son. "I cannot, Raajhi. I am nearly done with my commission, and the man will be here before long to collect it."

Raajhi scowled. "Bah!" he said. "Father, you could bring your crystals and your tools back to the camp and work there. Your patron will find his way to you, and if he doesn't, then so be it. At least there I know you will be safe."

"I am safe here, Raajhi," Jifaar said calmly. "Leave me a gun or two and I will be fine."

Raajhi sighed heavily. "Stubborn old goat," he said, but Ian noticed that there was the smallest bit of a smile at the edges of his lips. "As you wish, then. I will leave you three of my men and a rifle for your personal use. As for the rest of you," he said, turning to look at the six of them, "what the likes of you are doing here so far away from your homeland is of no concern to me. But be warned, this land is not safe for Europeans right now, and it is even less safe for children. While you are on my land, you will

427

be protected, but once you wander off, I cannot be held responsible."

Ian felt a chill go up his spine. Would they ever be free of danger?

"Thank you for your protection, Raajhi," the professor answered, "but we have no need to venture far from the lost city. We will make sure to stay close to the ruins, and should anything troubling occur, we shall not hesitate to make our way back downriver."

Raajhi seemed satisfied. He stood and motioned to a few of his warriors, who came to him and listened while he spoke quietly. Then he took a rifle from the holster on his horse's saddle and gave it to his father. "My men will guard your home until I can return. Keep safe, my father."

"You as well, my son," said Jifaar. With that, Raajhi climbed back onto his great black steed and rode off with his many warriors into the night.

Ian and the others watched them go in silence. As the men crested the third hill and disappeared, Theo reached out and grabbed Ian's hand. He squeezed it and looked down at her. "You all right?" he asked when he noticed her eyes seemed pinched with worry.

Theo opened her mouth as if to say something, but closed it again as the pounding of horses' hooves faded into the night. She simply nodded.

Then Ian's eyes fell on Jaaved, still holding the cloth he'd used to shine his uncle's sword. Ian hadn't been able to help noticing the dejected look on Jaaved's face when his uncle had taken the sword and turned away from the boy without a word. He hadn't even said goodbye.

Ian leaned over to Jifaar and asked quietly, "Sir?"

"Yes, lad?"

"Why was Raajhi so unkind to Jaaved?"

Jifaar's eyes sparkled as he looked into Ian's. "You're a very observant young man, aren't you?" he said.

Ian didn't know how to respond, so he simply shrugged. Jifaar sighed sadly and his eyes moved over to his grandson. "It was Jaaved's mother," he said. "Both my sons were in love with her, and who could blame them? She was a beautiful woman with so many gifts. But she chose my eldest son for her husband, and when she died giving birth to Jaaved, well, Raajhi seemed to turn all of his jealousy and anger toward my grandson. And when he took over the tribe, Raajhi sent Jaaved away to Larache to be the servant of that drunken fool at the docks. I believe he did this so as not to be re-minded of his broken heart over the loss of his brother and the woman he secretly loved."

"Forgive me for saying this," said Ian, "but if Raajhi didn't want Jaaved near him at the tribe's camp, why didn't you tell your son to leave your grandson in your care here?"

Jifaar's eyes moved over to his house and Ian thought he caught a look of trepidation. The older man's answer was rather cryptic. "My home is not safe for my grandson right now, Ian. It is better, at least for a little while longer, for Jaaved to be far away from me and my work."

Ian was about to ask him what he meant, but Jifaar turned away and abruptly changed the subject. "Professor," he said, "I have a spare hammock in my house that would be better for your back than this cold ground. Children, come inside and take up a blanket for yourselves and the men. The nights can get cold here with the wind from the foothills."

Ian realized that their conversation was finished, and, sighing, he motioned with his head to Carl and Theo, who followed him, Jifaar, and the professor into the wooden shack. Once the professor settled himself in the hammock, they followed Jifaar through a small doorway and into what looked like a workroom. While they waited to be handed blankets, Ian had a chance to gaze around the room. A very long table dominated the space and butted up against the one small window letting in the last rays of the sun, illuminating the house in a lovely orange glow. The rays sparkled off something on the table, which, Ian saw upon further inspection, were dozens and dozens of crystals and colored rocks. Intrigued, he wandered over to the display to have a closer look.

He walked the length of the table, gazing intently at the many rough crystals at one end and the polished stones, pendants, bracelets, and even some chess pieces at the other. "Do you like what you see?" Jifaar asked.

Ian jumped. "I'm sorry, sir," he said quickly. "I was just curious."

Jifaar gave him a reassuring pat on the back and handed him a blanket. "It's all right, Ian. There is no harm in that."

"They're very nice," Ian said appreciatively. "Especially these," he added, moving all the way down to the end of the table, where there was an ornately beautiful chess set.

Ian was surprised to see that all the pieces were black instead of the traditional black and white, but he noticed that Jifaar had cleverly distinguished the opposing sides in other ways. He'd used gold and rubies on one set of pieces and silver and emeralds on the other. As Ian inspected them, Carl joined him to take a look.

"You like those, eh?" asked Jifaar.

"Oh, yes," said Ian, but he cocked his head slightly when he noticed Theo standing far away from him, at the other end of the table, with a mighty frown on her face. "Come have a look, Theo," he offered, thinking she was feeling left out.

But Theo shook her head and her eyes drifted to Jifaar, as if he would understand why she didn't want to move closer to look at the chess set. To Ian's surprise, Jifaar smiled broadly at her and said, "You can feel their energy, correct?"

Theo nodded. "I'm sorry," she said, "but there's something about those pieces that's . . . that's . . . wicked."

Carl and Ian shared a look, and Ian could tell that his friend thought Theo was off her nutty again. Carl reached out and gently lifted one of the pieces. "Wicked?" he said, inspecting a rook. "Aw, Theo, they're harmless. See?" And he held it up and wiggled it back and forth as if to prove to her that the piece was benign.

Ian was surprised again when Jifaar said, "No, no, lad, the lady is correct. That piece you're holding is deadly wicked."

Carl smiled, as if Jifaar had just said something funny, but the longer Ian stood next to the chess set, the more he felt something tugging at him. His mind was slowly filling with dark thoughts until, strangely, he was suddenly very angry at

Carl. "Put it down!" he snapped, and he tried to grab the piece away from his friend.

Carl looked at Ian in surprise but he held fast to the chess piece. "What's come over you?" he asked, but in an instant his brows crossed angrily and his lip curled up into a sneer.

"It's not yours," Ian said sternly, still trying to pull the rook out of Carl's hand. "You shouldn't touch things that don't belong to you! Or didn't you learn that from your dear *dead* mum?" Ian heard Theo gasp, and somewhere in the back of his mind he knew he'd just said something unforgivable, but he couldn't seem to control himself.

Carl tugged back on the rook, his fingers firmly gripping it while his other hand curled into a fist. "You take that back!" he yelled, his face contorted in rage.

"Will not!" said Ian stubbornly, and he felt his own hand curl into a fist. He was aware that he and Carl were on the verge of physical violence as anger seemed to be welling within him and he knew he'd lost all ability to see reason.

But before the boys could exchange blows, Jifaar's bulk was in the middle of them, pushing them apart. When they were separated, the older man carefully lifted the rook out of Carl's hand and set it gingerly back onto the table. He then scooted both boys down the length of the long table to the other end, near Theo.

After just a few steps, Ian noticed that the intense feelings of anger seemed to evaporate from him, and when he came to a stop next to Theo, he looked at Carl in astonishment. "I'm sorry!" he gasped. "I didn't mean that about your mum!"

Carl too looked surprised. "No," he said. "You're right. I shouldn't have touched it without permission."

Jifaar sighed as he regarded both of them; then he reached out and pulled a stool close to sit down. Ian waited tensely for the reprimand he was sure would follow, but instead, Jifaar shocked him by saying, "You two are not to blame for your outburst."

"It's the chess pieces," interrupted Theo, and her eyes were pinned on the beautiful set across the room. "They're evil."

Jifaar nodded somberly. "To most observers, that chess set is like any other, save for the artistic beauty, of course." Ian couldn't tell if Jifaar had just made a joke, so he kept his face neutral and let the man explain. "But the pieces are not just polished crystal. No, they are something much more than that."

"What are they made of?" Ian asked. He had guessed they might be carved out of ebony.

"They are made of one of the rarest crystals on earth, something known as Gorgonite—often called the Devil's Stone."

Ian shivered and he noticed Carl's eyes growing wide before Carl gasped, "Did you say *Gorgonite?*"

"Yes," said Jifaar, clearly not understanding why that might mean so much to the three of them. "And its more common name, Devil's Stone, is an apt name indeed, as you and your friend Ian here just experienced."

Ian's eyes moved back to the chess pieces. His heart was thumping. The coincidence between the name of the crystal and that of the underworld god could not be dismissed, but he waited to hear more.

"Gorgonite," said Jifaar, "is a crystal born of the most violent of volcanic eruptions, and it is usually found in the bottom of the crater of a dead volcano. Not more than a few ounces are ever discovered in one crater. Those pieces, in fact, were mined from no fewer than seven different extinct volcanoes, and I've had to be very careful in polishing their shapes to make sure no excess went to waste."

"But what happened when we touched them?" asked Ian. "I mean, why did Carl and I become so angry?"

"All crystals have certain powers associated with them," Jifaar explained, just as the professor had back in London. "Your friend Theo here is acutely sensitive to their powers, which does not surprise me, as she has the gift of sight and is probably more receptive to their energy."

Ian thought about the crystal necklace he was keeping for her, and subconsciously put his hand into his pocket to touch the gem. It was warm and he was surprised to discover that he felt a calmness settle in him. It was a stark contrast to what he'd felt by the chess set.

"Some crystals are subtle," Jifaar was saying, "like this blue fluorite over here." He picked up a blue heart-shaped pendant and handed it to Theo. "If you hold that long enough," he said to her, "you might feel calm and relaxed and there will be an orderliness to the way you think things through. But this piece over here," he said, removing the fluorite and handing her a ring with a fiery red crystal on top, "this is vanadinite and it will cause your mind to go blank, as if you're in a nice fluffy dream. Concentration will be difficult, and you may even lose track of time."

As Ian watched, Theo did seem to develop a blank look on her face and she blinked at Jifaar a few times as if she were having trouble understanding him. He laughed and lifted the ring out of her hand.

"Blimey," said Carl, who'd been watching Theo intently. "What else can you put in her hand?"

Ian reacted without thinking. He lifted the crystal necklace out of his pocket and offered it to Jifaar. "This makes her see things she doesn't want to see," he said, hoping the old man could explain why.

Jifaar's eyes lit up as he gazed at the crystal in Ian's hand. "You brought it along?" asked Theo, and Ian realized she was shocked to see he'd had it in his pocket all this time.

"Yes," he said. "I've had it with me every day save the first time we went to London."

"By Allah!" said Jifaar as he lifted the white gem out of Ian's palm and held it up to the window. "Wherever did you come across *this*?"

"It was my mum's," said Theo. "She left it for me before she died, only, like Ian said, I have trouble with my visions when I'm wearing it."

Jifaar dangled the crystal in the rays of the setting sun and Ian could see that pink essence in the middle of the white stone warm and brighten before their eyes. "Is it turning pink?" asked Carl, squinting up at the stone.

"It is," said Jifaar, and he placed the crystal in Theo's palm. "What you have there, young lady, is also one of the rarest gems on earth. It is called Zeusite, or the Eye of Zeus. It is found only at the top of the tallest mountains, and I know of but a handful of very wealthy people who could afford a piece as large as the one you have here."

"Crikey!" said Ian and Carl together, and they looked at each other and smiled.

Theo held the crystal in her palm nervously, and Ian knew she was afraid she'd start having visions again. "It makes her see terrible things," he said, holding out his hand so that she could give it to him again for safekeeping.

But before Theo could hand it back to him, Jifaar reached over to the table to retrieve a beautiful bracelet of blue and white stones. "Here," he said gently as he wrapped her wrist with the bracelet. "This will help temper the Zeusite until you can gain more control over your visions."

Theo gazed at her new bracelet with awe. "Thank you, sir, but we haven't any money to pay you," she said.

"Then it is my gift to you," said Jifaar with a kind smile.

"Why does the Zeusite make her visions so intense?" Ian asked, still curious about its effect on her.

"The Eye of Zeus is a powerful crystal indeed. It can bring out the true goodness and talent of the individual. It is most useful to those like you, Theo, who are gifted with sight. It can enhance the range of your abilities and make you all-seeing, but the images will be difficult to control until you've mastered the temperament of the stone. I imagine that you won't like the idea of wearing the stone, but the more you do, the more you'll familiarize yourself with it, and soon, you and the crystal will become like one. The longer you wear it, the more it will take on a pinkish hue." Jifaar pointed to the Zeusite's pink center. "It is also something that repels evil, so it is useful to wear as a good-luck charm."

"Whoa," said Carl.

Jifaar nodded and his eyes moved down to the end of the table, where the chess pieces were. "How interesting that within my humble house we have the two most powerful gemstones in all the world," he said.

"You were going to tell us about those chess pieces?" Ian reminded him.

Jifaar crossed his arms over his wide belly and got back to his story. "Just like the Eye of Zeus can bring out the best in someone, the Devil's Stone can bring out the very worst," he said. "It can reach into your soul and pull out the darkest part of you. It will enhance your anger and make you do and say things you'd never think of without its influence."

"It sounds awful," said Theo, fingering her new bracelet.

"Oh, it is," Jifaar assured her. "Devil's Stone radiates conflict and impurity. It was created through violence, the birth of a volcanic eruption, and it thus craves a constant return to that violence." Ian turned to look pensively at the chess set. He wished he'd never gone near it.

He turned back as Jifaar continued. "Like the Zeusite you've got there, Theo, Gorgonite seeks to bring out the true essence of a person. If the individual who owns it is inherently evil, the stone will quickly enhance that evil, making that poor soul's blackest thoughts even darker. Most people have some good in them, so many of us are soon repulsed by the stone and will resist handling it. I myself cannot work with it without wearing my protective gloves." Jifaar pointed to some thick woolen gloves on the bench. "And even wearing those and all of my best calming crystals, I must be careful to work only for short periods with the stone so that my thoughts do not become too dark."

"Why would you be making a chess set out of it, then?" Ian demanded, shocked that Jifaar would be so irresponsible as to make something he could sell to some poor unsuspecting person that would turn them evil.

Jifaar sighed heavily, as if he carried a great burden. "A long time ago, when I was a poor youth and my older brother still ruled the Jstor, I was trying to find my place in the world. I loved searching for valuable treasure in the hills near here and turning the gems I found into pendants, bracelets, rings, and such. It was my mother who suggested I find a way to make my living at it, and so, I traveled the world in search of teachers to apprentice under.

"As an apprentice, I was given the smallest of stipends, and I eventually ran out of money while I was in London, learning from a master craftsman there." Ian now knew how Jifaar had come to speak such perfect English.

"I'd made some pretty rings and pendants out of the small amount of gold I had left to sell in one of the London markets," Jifaar continued, "and one day a man came to my stall and offered me a great deal of money to craft him two chess sets out of a strange black stone I'd never seen before. I gladly accepted his offer, but shortly after I began to work with his pieces, I started having dark thoughts, which soon led to terrible violent outbursts. I got into fights and yelled at patrons, and the master craftsman who had taken me on as his apprentice quickly told me to leave his shop and never return."

"When did you realize that all of that was because of the crystals the man had given you?" Ian asked.

"Not long afterward," said Jifaar. "I had rented a room and stored the Gorgonite under a floorboard there for safe-keeping while I was out looking for more work, and I began to realize that all of these dark thoughts seemed to occur only when I was working on the chess pieces."

"Then what happened?" asked Carl.

"I started avoiding my commission," Jifaar said. "I simply couldn't bring myself to work with the Devil's Stone again. Eventually, the man who had paid for their creation found me and discovered that I had foolishly spent most of his money, and that I was only finished with half of the chess pieces."

"So what did you do?" Ian asked, gripped by the story.

"What could I do?" said Jifaar, raising both hands in surrender. "He was a very frightening man. I sensed that he could cause me great harm if he wanted to and I was terrified that he would kill me or report me to the authorities, so I begged him to show mercy. He did but he forced me into an agreement, one that I regret to this day."

"Whatever did you agree to?" Theo asked.

"He made me promise to finish his pieces within the week, and at some point in the future he would find me again and commission one more chess set from me."

"What could he be doing with three identical chess sets made of that awful rock?" Ian wondered.

Jifaar sighed. "Nothing good, I'm afraid," he said, then attempted to smile. "I have never had the courage to ask him who they were intended for, and I doubt very much he would tell me if I did. My instructions from him were to craft them in such a way that they would be too beautiful to resist. And he wanted them fit for a king, so he supplied me with extra gold, silver, rubies, and emeralds."

Ian glanced again at the ornate pieces on the table. "They certainly are beautiful," he said.

"Thank you," said Jifaar with a bow of his head. "Still, I will be glad when they are gone and my obligation to the man is at an end."

"When will you be finished?" Theo asked.

"I was going to polish those last few tonight," he said with a smile as he reached for the blankets he'd set on the floor and handed them to Ian, Carl, and Theo, "which means that you lot will need to leave me and get some rest."

Ian turned to go, then, remembering his manners, stopped and said, "Thank you, sir, for the blankets and for allowing us to stay with you."

"You are most welcome, lad," said Jifaar kindly as he walked them to the door.

Ian had several nightmares that night. It was the same dream over and over, in which two beasts thundered down from the surrounding hills of Lixus while Theo stood directly in their path. Each time, Ian dreamt that he was unable to save her. He'd awaken, hot and sweaty, and look to make sure she was still there next to him, and each time, he had to reassure himself that it was only a nightmare. That is, until his last horrible dream became all too real.

The sound of the beasts vibrated under him, the thunder of their paws making the ground shake. Shouts rang out in the night and Ian looked over to see that Theo was missing. He surged out of the tent, but Carl grabbed his shirt and began shouting at him. "Open your eyes, mate!" Carl yelled. But Ian was too frantic about finding Theo. He spotted her then, up the hill, and charging down upon her weren't just two beasts, but fifty.

"Theo!" Ian shouted. "Theo! Come back!"

But she only turned to look at him, innocent and pretty. Her bandaged hand was wrapped around her pendant, and she was saying something to him that he couldn't hear. Carl still held him by his shirt and was demanding that Ian listen to him. "*Theo!*" Ian screamed, his heart racing as he willed her to come to him. "Run, Theo! *Run!*"

But she wasn't listening. Instead, she kept gazing at her crystal, and in a moment the first of the beasts had tackled her small form. "*Nooooooo!*" Ian shouted. "No, Theo!" Carl still held him as he tried to run to her and Ian angrily shoved his friend, accidentally hitting him.

Carl fell back and shouted, "Owwww!" and that was when Ian opened his eyes wide, his chest heaving in panic as a chaos of noise surrounded him. "You hit me!" Carl cried, and Ian saw that his friend was lying on his back at the edge of the tent, rubbing his cheek.

"What's happening?" Ian asked. "Where's Theo?" he demanded just as a shot rang out.

Ian started and felt someone grab his arm. He turned and Theo was right next to him, her eyes wide and frightened. "There are men on horseback coming for us!" she said.

"Raajhi?" Ian asked, his thoughts muddled from his nightmare.

As if in answer, the flap of their tent was yanked open. "Children!" Thatcher said, sticking his head through the opening. "Come quickly! We've got to run for our lives!"

The three of them scrambled out of the tent. Perry was gathering up the backpacks and trying desperately to hurry along the professor, who looked rumpled and confused. "We're being attacked!" Thatcher yelled, motioning up the hill.

Ian tried to focus on the area Thatcher had pointed to. He could just make out in the shadows of the night the three Jstor guards firing rounds from their guns as a horde of charging men on horseback pounded down the hill. High-pitched war cries filled the air and flashes of light burst from their guns. "Get down!" cried Perry, pulling the professor to the ground.

"We've got to run for it!" yelled Thatcher, helping his brother with the backpacks. "Ian! Get Carl and Theo to the boat!"

Ian grabbed Theo's hand and Carl's arm and tugged both of them down the short hill where their tent had been pitched. As the three ran, they heard a tremendous boom. Ian looked back over his shoulder to where Jifaar stood proud and tall on his porch, holding a large shotgun level with his shoulder. Ian smelled the acrid scent of gunpowder as the light gray smoke curled around the barrel. "Get to your boat!" their host shouted at them. "*Hurry!*"

Ian hardly needed the encouragement. He half carried, half dragged Theo along as he and Carl raced for the boat, Ian's bare feet pounding on the ground.

Carl passed him as they got to the short dock, and leapt with agility into the belly of the bow. He turned and held his arms up as Ian and Theo reached the boat's edge. "Give her to me!" Carl said, and Ian swooped Theo in the air, hearing her gasp in his ear before shoving her into Carl's arms.

"Get her down under the mast!" Ian yelled before racing to the stern and hopping aboard. He lurched to the line tied to the buoy as more gunfire ricocheted across the hills. As he worked desperately at the knot holding their vessel to the dock, he took a short glance over his shoulder and saw Thatcher and Perry jogging awkwardly to the boat with the professor slung between them.

Carl, meanwhile, was standing as still as a statue, suddenly frozen in terror by what was happening on the hills. "Carl!" Ian barked, shaking his friend out of his frightened trance. "Untie the other lead line! It's at the stern!"

Carl jumped at the order, picking his way to the other end of the craft to untie it. "It's knotted!" he called back after a moment, his voice panicked. "Ian, I can't get it!"

"Keep trying!" Ian yelled, realizing he was having just as much trouble. Whoever had knotted these had secured the boat a little too tightly.

While he worked at the rope, he saw Thatcher and Perry make it to the side of the boat. Huffing and puffing, they attempted to lower in the professor, who was fighting them every step of the way. "Be careful!" he yelled. "Look out! You're going to drop me!"

Ian tugged at the lead line, working the knot in the dark with an increasing panic. To make matters worse, the pounding of galloping horses was growing ever closer, making his fingers shake and his palms sweat. "Bloody knot!" he yelled in frustration.

His eyes darted helplessly to one of his schoolmasters, thinking they might be able to get the knot undone, but the brothers were in no position to help him. The professor was dangling precariously between Thatcher, who was in the boat, and Perry, who was on the dock, as the sloop wobbled and threatened to tip.

Suddenly, a bullet hit a board of the dock and sent splinters flying by his shoulder. And then another bullet hit the wood right next to Carl, who dove for cover, abandoning the lead line as he joined Theo under the mast.

In that instant Ian remembered his pocketknife, and with shaking fingers he jammed his hand into his pocket and tugged it out. Another bullet smashed into the side of the boat, and Ian ducked low, finally getting the blade free. Reaching with one hand above his head, he began to saw the line as hard and fast as he could, but it was a thick rope and his blade was not as sharp as it could have been.

"Quickly!" Perry cried from right behind him, and Ian realized that both schoolmasters were in the boat. "We've got the other line to cut as well!"

Ian's brow was slick with sweat as bullets continued to pelt the dock and the boat. Then, finally, to his immense relief, he felt the line give way and the vessel turned about in the water.

"Give me the knife!" urged Perry. "I'll cut the other end!" But before Ian could hand over his pocketknife, the sound of hooves thundered onto the wooden dock, and above them a giant man on a great white horse appeared. *"Arrêtez!"* the warrior shouted at them. *"Sortez du bateau!"*

"He's telling us to stop and get out of the boat," whispered Thatcher, but no one moved. Ian looked from the warrior, towering above them, to the adults in the boat, waiting to follow their lead. It soon became clear, however, what to do. Breaking the silence, a knife struck the wood right next to Thatcher's foot and the schoolmaster yelped. "I believe we should comply."

THE JICHMACH'S REVENGE

The six of them climbed hurriedly out of the boat, and even the professor, Ian noticed, seemed to make a special effort to get out quickly and quietly. With arms raised above their heads in surrender, Ian and the others were herded back to their campsite, where they were greeted by a group of warriors, many of them holding both guns and long curved swords.

Of the three Jstor who had been guarding them, two lay dead on the hillside, and one was getting the stuffing beaten out of him by a group of the invading tribesmen.

To add to Ian's horror, a bloody Jifaar was being held roughly by two other men while the largest and fiercest of the warriors towered above him on his white stallion and shouted at the old man in Arabic, his words lost on Ian. The professor, who was standing next to Ian, translated quietly. "The man on horseback is their leader," he said. "He calls himself Najib of the Jichmach. He claims that Jifaar is responsible for the loss of the Jichmach's Star of Lixus."

Ian's gaze shifted to Jifaar, his heart filled with fear that the old man would be murdered before their eyes. But Jifaar hardly seemed worried. The older Moroccan merely smiled at his enemy and spoke in a mocking tone.

The professor continued, "Jifaar has called Najib a liar and a thief."

Ian barely managed to stifle a groan when Jifaar was rewarded for his insolence with a swift kick in the gut from the man on the horse. Theo gasped and hid her face in Ian's chest.

Najib then pointed to the six of them and shouted at Jifaar, as if he was accusing him of something else. The professor murmured, "Oh, dear."

"What?" asked Ian. As afraid as he was of the answer, he still wanted to know what was being said.

"Najib thinks we are more Germans recruited by Jifaar to steal from him."

"But we're not German!" said Carl, who was listening in on the other side of the professor.

"I think it matters little at this point, my young man," said the professor. "Najib is telling Jifaar that he is taking us as payment for the Star. If Jifaar is wise, he will consider the score even."

Najib spit at Jifaar's feet; then he used the butt of his vicious sword to thump the man on the head so hard that Jifaar collapsed into the dirt, unconscious. Ian lurched forward without thinking, wanting to help Jifaar or hurt Najib—he wasn't sure which—but his shoulder was grabbed tightly by the professor, who startled him with his strength. "Do *nothing* to anger them further," the old man whispered fiercely in his ear, and Ian immediately checked his temper.

With a sneer, the terrifying warrior turned to the men still beating the last guard, and made a slicing motion across his throat. Ian's jaw dropped as he realized what was about to happen. Swiftly, he turned his back and pulled Theo into his chest, shielding her from the scene, but Ian's ears caught the horrible thump and the gurgling of the man as he fell to the ground and breathed his last.

When Ian turned to look up again at Najib, he felt his insides go cold. There was murder in Najib's eyes. He stepped his horse forward to stand tall and imposing above them, and addressed them all in French. The professor responded first. Najib looked at the professor skeptically while the professor talked quickly and pointed to the rest of their group. Ian had the feeling he was begging Najib to spare their lives.

There was a long tense moment before Najib waved to one of his warriors and spoke to him in Arabic. The warrior nodded and got down from his horse, carrying with him several lengths of rope. One by one he tied each of their hands behind their backs, then tethered them all together with a longer piece of rope wrapped firmly about their middles, and set them roughly into a line.

Despite his discomfort, Ian tried to be grateful that it looked like their lives would be spared. But a moment later his heart nearly ripped in two. Theo, he noticed, hadn't been tied to the group. Instead, she was snatched from the ground by one of the riders and hauled up onto the front of his saddle.

Ian all but forgot the professor's warning. He screamed and struggled to break free of his ropes, but the warrior who had tied them up slapped him so hard he dropped to the ground. Through fading stars he heard Theo's voice call out to him, "Ian, please don't!" He blinked as he was yanked roughly to his feet again, and he managed to meet her eyes. "I'll be all right," she insisted.

Ian's only solace was to hope that she would be.

With nothing left for them to do, Ian and the others waited dejectedly while the invaders tore through Jifaar's wooden house, stealing the many beautiful crystals, before moving on to their campsite and tearing through the contents of the boat. Then Carl whispered, "Have you seen Jaaved?"

And Ian suddenly realized that he hadn't seen any sign of their young guide since spotting him asleep on his grandfather's porch hours before. "No," he whispered back.

"Maybe he got away," said Carl.

Ian nodded. He hoped for Jaaved's sake that he had either found a good hiding place or managed to escape, as Ian had little doubt that these invading tribesmen would kill Jaaved without hesitation.

He was distracted from these thoughts, however, when the warrior who'd tied them all began to search the group. Ian's pockets were roughly turned out and the warrior took his pocket torch and compass away. He was so upset that he barely felt better when the man shoved the prophecy back down into Ian's pocket as if it were trash.

When the man moved on to search Thatcher, Ian's eyes roved to the others making a mess of Jifaar's house. Surprisingly, they'd left all the chess pieces on the ground, as if they were junk. Ian figured that surely if they didn't want the chess pieces themselves, they would want the gold, silver, emeralds, and rubies adorning them. But it appeared that they tried to avoid them altogether—as if they knew that the pieces were cursed.

When the warriors had finally grown tired of ransacking Jifaar's house, one of them took a piece of kindling from the fire near their tent and tossed it through the window of the small wooden structure. Ian heard the *whoosh* of the flames as Jifaar's workroom caught fire, and his heart burned as hot as the fire with a loathing for the hateful men and their ridiculous war.

While the flames were still licking at the wood of Jifaar's house, Ian was roughly pushed forward by a warrior who pointed up the hill. "Come on, mate," urged Carl nervously. "Let's do as he says."

Curling his bound hands into fists, Ian walked grudgingly forward when the rope around his middle was pulled taught by Thatcher, going along behind his brother and the professor, and together they trudged up the hill after the Jichmach.

They marched for several hours, and as the sun rose and beat down on them, the ropes bit into Ian's hands and the hilly terrain made his legs ache. Before midmorning, the professor sank to his knees, gasping for breath. "I can't go on," he moaned. "I just can't."

Najib angrily reined in his horse. *"Levez-vous!"* he demanded, and Ian watched helplessly as Perry bent next to the old man, desperately trying to coax the professor to his feet.

The professor stood shakily but sank once again, and Carl shouted angrily at Najib, "He can't do it! He's an old man! Can't you see he can't walk for hours like this?"

Najib moved his horse over to Carl and slowly extracted his sword, then raised it above Carl's head as if to strike him down. Theo screamed and Ian grabbed the line he and Carl were tethered to and yanked on it hard, pulling his friend out of the way just as Najib swung his sword. Ian then jumped in front of Carl, his face contorted in rage. "Leave him be, you despicable brute!" he shouted at Najib.

Najib's eyes widened with surprise as he looked down at Ian. In the background Ian heard Theo becoming hysterical, and he let his eyes dart over to her as she slapped the man who held her captive before she boldly launched herself off the horse and came running as fast as she could to Ian and Carl.

Ian's temper sobered quickly as he watched her get down on her knees in front of Najib and beg for his mercy. For a moment Ian was convinced that both he and Carl were about to be hacked to pieces, but as his heart hammered, he saw something remarkable reflected in the warrior's eyes.

After a moment, Najib scowled, spat into the dirt, then turned his head to regard the nervous-looking rider who had let Theo get away. He shouted something in Arabic and the warrior dismounted quickly and came over to them. He pulled a knife out of his belt and sliced the rope tethering the professor to the rest of them and the rope tying the old man's hands, and then Najib's man pointed to the riderless horse. The professor nodded and managed, after one more failed attempt, to get to his feet again and hobble over to the horse, where he waited for the warrior to push him roughly up into the saddle before he got up behind him.

Najib turned his attention back to Ian and—pointing his sword at both him and Carl—said something guttural. Then, with a wave of his hand, he shouted to his troop and they began to move again.

They marched on wearily, and the pain in Ian's legs and feet soon became almost too uncomfortable to bear. He was the only one who hadn't had a chance to put his shoes on when they'd run for the boat, so his bare feet were crisscrossed with cuts and scratches from the scrub they'd hiked across. His hands had grown numb, and the rope around his middle wouldn't stop tearing at his skin. Looking down, he noticed spots of blood seeping through his shirt where the rope had rubbed his skin raw. Theo, untied from the rest of the group, had been walking close to him, and she began speaking to him. Ian realized quickly that she was trying her hardest to keep his mind off his discomfort.

"I wonder what happened to Jaaved," she said.

"Maybe he's gone for help?" Carl said wistfully.

"Yeah, for his grandfather, but not for the likes of us," said Ian, his aching body making him grouse.

He heard Carl sigh. "You're probably right. The Jstor won't care about coming after us, especially once we're off their land."

"I wonder how long it will take us to make it out of Jstor territory," said Theo.

"Who knows?" said Ian. "We could have already crossed the border and not known it."

Theo looked ahead at Najib. "I don't think so, Ian. Do you see how he keeps looking over his shoulder? I'll bet we're still in Jstor territory. It's when he stops looking behind us that we'll need to worry."

"What do you think they'll do with us?" asked Carl, but Ian closed his mind to the question. He knew that whatever the Jichmach decided to do with them, it wouldn't be good.

Toward midday the exhausted group was allowed to rest and have a small sip of water. The professor's face was flushed with heat and lined with worry. "They mean to sell us," he announced.

As hot as Ian was, his veins turned icy cold with fear.

"*Sell* us?" gasped Perry. "What do you mean, exactly?"

"There are still parts of the world where slavery is a common practice," said the professor. "And Morocco has a rather sordid reputation as being a center where one can acquire slave labor."

"But we're subjects of His Majesty the King of England!" Perry protested, then quickly lowered his voice. "We're protected by that sovereignty in these lands!" he said, and Ian prayed he was right.

But when he looked at the professor, he was disappointed. The old man sighed heavily and said, "I'm afraid that's of little consequence, Master Goodwyn. The Crown has very little proof of what happens to its subjects over here in Morocco. People disappear all the time and are never heard from again. There are no ransom notes, no letters to family. . . . It's as if they're simply swallowed whole by the desert. Without a trace of them, the British authorities have little recourse with the Moroccan government."

"I don't want to be a slave!" wailed Carl. "I want to go home!"

Theo moved over to Carl and wrapped her arm about his shoulders. "There, there, Carl," she said. "We'll find a way out of this." But the look Ian saw the professor exchange with Perry told him there was little chance of that.

After only a short rest, Ian and the others were forced to their feet again, and once the professor was loaded back onto the horse, they were ordered to march. Theo took her place beside Ian and he caught her watching him worriedly as he grimaced with every step. She turned to look at his hands behind his back and she gasped. "Ian!" she said. "Your wrists are bleeding!"

Before Ian could respond, Theo hurried away, up the line to Najib. Ian stretched to look and could see her ahead, trotting along beside the warrior, speaking to him and pointing to her wrists. Najib ignored her for the longest time, but she kept it up until finally he growled at her, then swiveled in his saddle and barked an order at one of his men. When the procession came to a stop, the warrior hopped off his horse, pulled out a sharp knife, and sliced through their ropes one by one.

As the warrior worked, Ian saw Najib look darkly at the professor before saying something to him in French, then noticed Thatcher blanch. "What'd he say?" Ian asked, suddenly much more nervous than he was before.

But Thatcher didn't answer, so Ian asked again. "Schoolmaster? Please tell us."

Thatcher met Ian's eyes and he leaned in close to whisper into his ear so that Theo couldn't overhear. "He's just told Professor Nutley that if any of us tries to escape, he'll kill the children first, starting with the girl."

Ian nearly sank to his knees. He was absolutely certain the fierce warrior meant what he said.

"Children," the professor was saying in a forced, calm voice, "our host has requested that we not try to escape. Please obey his orders as a personal favor to me, all right?"

"We understand, Professor," said Ian solemnly, pulling his aching arms in front of him. "We'll be good."

Once his group was free of their bonds, they made better headway, keeping up with the men on horseback, but Najib pushed them to the brink of exhaustion, and they walked at a brisk pace for the rest of the day and well after dusk. Theo's legs began to give out as the sun started to set, and Ian tried to carry her piggyback for a time until he began to stumble. Finally, one of the warriors came over and held out his hand to Theo, barking an order at Ian.

Ian gripped Theo more tightly and shook his head, but she whispered tiredly in his ear, "It's all right, Ian. Let me ride on the horse." Reluctantly, he gave her to the warrior and was just the smallest bit grateful that the man placed Theo rather gently in the saddle in front of him.

Finally, when the moon began to make its ascent, and it was too dangerous to push the horses over the rocky terrain, Najib held up his hand, halting the march. Ian slumped to the ground with relief and Carl collapsed right next to him. "I never want to move again!" Carl said, wheezing.

Thatcher and Perry came over and plopped down beside

them, and they were soon joined by the professor and Theo. "Ian, your feet!" she gasped as she sat next to him.

Ian looked down; his feet were two large swollen lumps with toes that were raw and bleeding. "They went numb a while ago," he said. "I haven't felt them in hours."

Thatcher scooted over to take a closer look. "They look bad, lad," he said gravely.

"There's not much for it, though, is there?" said Ian, knowing that the warriors behind them would have little sympathy.

Thatcher quickly unlaced his shoes and pulled off his socks. Handing them to Ian, he said, "Put these on. They might not be much, but it's better than nothing."

Perry also began yanking off his shoes. "Good idea, Thatcher," he said, shedding his own socks. "Here you go, lad."

And very soon thereafter, Ian had everyone's socks save Theo's, which were far too small to fit his feet. Ian's heart filled with gratitude, especially when he noticed that Carl's own feet were raw with blisters. "No thanks, mate," Ian said to him as he tried to hand Ian his socks. "I expect I have enough here to get me through."

"You sure?" Carl asked, and Ian felt his heart swell even more.

"I'm sure," he said, and nudged Carl with his shoulder.

To take his mind off his miserably sore feet, he watched the Jichmach warriors set up camp. A portable village emerged like magic out of the bleak terrain. A dozen large white tents were opened up with relative ease, and in the center was the largest tent of all: Najib's. The Jichmach leader did little of the manual labor; he just barked orders at his men and slapped a few who weren't moving as quickly as he liked.

Soon several fires were lit, and Ian was relieved to see that one was even lit for them. The tribesmen cooked tea and ate smoked meat with some bread. The prisoners were given cups of water and some moldy cheese along with blankets—exactly like the ones they'd been given by Jifaar. Ian was struck by the resemblance and his heart sank. "I hope he's all right," he whispered.

"Who?" Theo asked.

"Jaaved's grandfather," he said as he wrapped himself in the blanket. "I really liked him."

Theo looked at him seriously and reached up to touch the crystal at her neck, hidden under her blouse. The Jichmach had taken everything else from them—their backpacks, Carl's sword, Ian's compass and pocket torch, and the rest of the professor's money—but somehow they'd avoided searching or taking anything from Theo and she still held on to her crystal and the blue bracelet Jifaar had given her. "I hope so too, Ian," she said, but there was a sad look in her eyes.

Ian dropped the subject and lay back on the cold ground. Wordlessly, he and Theo huddled under their blankets and fell quickly asleep.

The fate of Jifaar was about to be determined by Magus the Black. The sorcerer had come upon the beaten old man just a few hours after the Jichmach had kidnapped the troop from Britain. "Tell me where they've been taken, Jifaar," growled Magus, smoke curling from his nostrils.

Jifaar struggled for breath, clearly in intense pain. "The . . . Jichmach . . . have . . . taken . . . them south!" He wheezed. "Please . . . I beg you. . . ."

But Magus was not in the mood for mercy. He turned away and picked up a chess piece lying in the dirt. Holding it up to inspect it in the moonlight, he said, "These are your finest effort so far, craftsman."

"Master Magus," gasped Jifaar, clutching his chest, "please . . . it burns!"

But Magus ignored him. "When I learned that the children were on their way here, I had hoped to find everyone together, but I suppose I can kill two birds with one stone when I reach the Jichmach."

"The . . . pain!" Jifaar moaned, rolling on the ground, writhing in agony.

Magus eyed him and sighed. The sorcerer seemed almost bored. "Well," he said at last, "I suppose your good work should not go without some sort of acknowledgment." He waved his hand at the Moroccan. Jifaar died before the echo of his scream had reached the third hill.

Magus then calmly bent and picked up the rest of the chess set, finding all the pieces in perfect condition, if a bit dirty. His beasts, Kerberos and his son, waited patiently by the burned-out wreckage of Jifaar's hut, but as Magus was dusting off the final pawn, the older male gave a low growl, causing Magus to look up and listen.

In the distance he heard a great many hoofbeats, and he scowled in irritation. "Come!" he ordered the beasts, and they fell into step behind their master as he headed south, away from the ruined home. "There are too many armed men about in these lands. You will keep to the shadows and out of sight until I command otherwise," he directed. But overall, the sorcerer was feeling rather satisfied. He had recovered the chess set, and he finally had the children cornered.

They had eluded him until now, and their presence in Morocco meant they had also eluded his incompetent sister. He would make sure to tell Demogorgon of Caphiera's failures. Perhaps his sire would reconsider using her the next time he needed something done, Magus thought bitterly. He was still angry that he'd been forced to compromise with the ice queen. But as he walked, an evil thought occurred to him. And as his idea expanded, Magus began to feel very good.

Soon the children would be dealt with, and the threat to their plans would be eliminated. After that, there was no reason he couldn't rise above his siblings to the top of his sire's favor . . . no reason at all.

A CRY IN THE NIGHT

For Ian and his companions, the next day was worse than the one before. The tribe woke at the first whisper of dawn, and they hurried about taking down the tents and tending to their horses to be under way as quickly as possible. Ian noticed that Najib was still looking back the way they'd come, and sensed that perhaps Theo was right, that they were still on Jstor land. He said a silent prayer then, that Raajhi would be so angry at what they'd done to his father that he'd waste no time setting out to exact his revenge.

He had little time to reflect, however, as after being given another small bit of moldy cheese and a cup of water, they were forced to march again. On this day, Ian felt the sun more than he had before. He could tell from the tightness of the skin on his cheeks that his face was horribly sunburned.

When they stopped near midmorning, he was surprised to discover they were near a watering hole, and the tribesmen allowed their horses to drink long and deep while they filled up their canteens and waterskins.

The prisoners were the last to be permitted to drink, and they hurried to the water's edge. Ian sank to his knees and drank and drank and drank. He'd never been so thirsty in his life. No one spoke until they had all drunk their fill, and finally, when Ian no longer felt the burning at the back of his throat, he gazed at their surroundings. Nearby he saw a fig tree and he managed to pick several handfuls of the fruits and pass them around to his companions before they were ordered to march again.

To pass the time, Ian focused on the details of their path, because although Najib's threats chilled him to the core, Ian's fighting spirit would not allow him to give up the hope of somehow making an attempt to escape.

By the angle of the sun and the cast of his shadow, Ian could tell that they'd been marching due south for the past two days. Much of that time had been spent walking along a worn dirt path that cut through thick scrub and scraggly-looking trees. The farther they trekked, the more the path began sloping upward, and in those moments when he looked up to check on Theo, Ian could clearly see why: they were slowly but surely inching their way closer to the Atlas Mountains.

Late in the afternoon, when the slope of the terrain leveled off slightly, their procession came to a stop. Ian lifted his tired head and looked around.

He was startled to discover that ahead of them was a huge valley, beautiful and green and dotted with large outcroppings. At the end of that valley was another slope, which led to the foothills of the Atlas Mountains. Najib pointed to those foothills and said, "Jichmach."

"Oh, my, Thatcher," Perry said to his brother. "We *are* still on Jstor land! Those foothills are the land of the Jichmach."

"You don't think he means to march us across this valley tonight, do you?" Thatcher asked.

As if in answer, Najib waved and the procession started again. Dusk came and went, and with it the warmth of the sun.

Not long after, the moon began to rise, offering fairly good lighting. Najib led them on a path that wound around boulders and outcroppings ever deeper into the valley. The Jichmach warrior did not stop, even though the horses were blowing in protest and pawing at the ground. It was clear that Najib wanted to get across the valley as quickly as possible.

They marched on, and much to Ian's relief, Thatcher glanced back and saw poor Carl stumbling behind while Ian tried to support him. His schoolmaster called to one of the warriors, pointing to Carl and speaking in French. The warrior ignored him for a while, but Thatcher was persistent and eventually the man steered his horse over to Carl, lifted him roughly up, and placed him in the saddle. Ian watched his friend with concern, but Carl's head bobbed twice and he was fast asleep in his seat.

For the next few hours, Ian and his schoolmasters simply focused on putting one foot in front of the other, and Ian knew he too was reaching his limit. Finally, near midnight, and just as Ian was sure he would not be able to go on, they crested the hill on the other side of the valley and Najib lifted his arm and the procession stopped.

Ian sank to his knees along with Thatcher and Perry. "Thank heavens," gasped Perry. "I couldn't take another step."

Again their group watched as the tribesmen hoisted their tents, Najib's going up first and the others around it. The warrior unbuckled the holster for his huge bejeweled sword before sliding it into his tent. "That is one frightful weapon," said Ian.

"It's called a scimitar," said the professor. "It's sharp enough to slice a man in half."

"Wish I had my sword," Carl moaned. "Those buggers pinched it off me back at Jifaar's."

Theo rubbed the crystal at her neck, a far-off look in her eyes. Suddenly, she turned to Carl and said, "I have a feeling you're going to get your sword back, Carl."

"Really?" he asked, brightening.

Theo nodded. "And when you do, it's really, really important that you not let it go again, all right?"

"Okay," he said with a smile.

But she didn't seem convinced. "Promise me," she insisted. "Promise me that no matter what, you'll not let go of it again."

Carl cocked his head quizzically at her. "Gaw blimey, Theo, I promise, all right?"

Looking satisfied, Theo let go of her pendant and sighed. "We should all get some sleep," she said.

Ian wanted to ask Theo why she'd been so insistent with Carl, but his eyelids closed before he could speak, as exhaustion claimed his body and sent him into a deep sleep.

* * *

It felt as if he'd been asleep only a few moments when a great commotion woke him with a start. He sat straight up and looked at Perry, Thatcher, the professor, and Carl, who each appeared every bit as alarmed as he was. The tribesmen of the camp were racing for their horses, while others surrounded the prisoners and drew their scimitars menacingly, their backs to the group.

"What's going on?" Perry asked as he attempted to get up, only to be pushed roughly back down by one of the tribesmen.

"There's someone out there," said Carl, pointing to the edge of the valley. "Someone's coming up the hill!"

A lone figure moved straight up the hillside toward them. In the moonlight he appeared tall, dressed in a long hooded cloak, his features indiscernible. Theo gasped and gripped Ian's arm in fear. "He's evil," she whispered.

The hairs on the back of Ian's neck prickled as the puzzle pieces fell into place in his mind. The cloaked stranger he'd seen on the lawn at Castle Dover, the figure he'd spied on their way up the river, and the vile being approaching them were all the same. As if to confirm his suspicions, in the distance came a howl that Ian and the others knew all too well.

The warriors stood alert, their hands firmly on the swords by their sides, and eyed the hills suspiciously. The beast hadn't sounded that close, but Ian knew that the animal had no trouble covering great distances quickly. As he looked around, trying to search the shadows, he noticed that Najib had come out of his tent and was moving to the front of the men. Once there, he stood tall and fierce between the cloaked stranger and the prisoners and shouted. There was no mistaking his tone.

"He's told the stranger to stop and turn back," whispered the professor, sitting next to Carl.

But the cloaked figure continued to climb the hill, as if he hadn't even heard Najib's command.

Najib motioned to one of the men on horseback, who pulled his scimitar from its scabbard and raced down the hill toward the stranger.

The tribesman closed in on the invader, his mount charging ahead. But as the horse got nearer, it suddenly halted and violently pitched the rider forward. The tribesman was barely able to hold on, but he managed to right himself and he kicked the horse cruelly in an effort to continue his charge.

The horse, however, was having none of it, and it reared up in the air. Again the tribesman had great difficulty keeping his seat, and the scimitar flew out of his hand. Cursing the horse, the tribesman kicked hard again, but his mount simply bucked, unseating its rider, then ran off at breakneck speed toward the south and the safety of the foothills.

Behind Ian, Najib roared in anger. The Jichmach leader pointed to another of his men and then down the hill to the stranger. The second warrior clucked his tongue and gave a high-pitched war cry as he spurred his horse forward and drew his scimitar, preparing to slice the cloaked stranger in half.

To Ian's astonishment, his horse reacted the same way, unseating its rider and running off to the hills. Najib's anger was palpable. He whistled to his white stallion and, yanking one of his warriors' scimitars right out of his hand, mounted his horse bareback in one smooth motion and charged down the hill himself, yelling what Ian thought was a particularly intimidating war cry, and waving the borrowed sword over his head.

No one was prepared for what happened next. Najib's mount suddenly planted its front feet and skidded to a halt.

A battle of sorts took place between rider and stallion as Najib drove his heels into the horse's sides. The horse screamed and reared up, and Najib was nearly unseated. When the stallion landed, the tribal leader used the flat side of his sword to swat the horse on the rump, but that only added to the animal's hysteria, and it reared again. This time when the steed landed, it fell to the ground and rolled onto its back. Najib jumped clear at the last moment, very nearly missing being crushed.

Ian watched in fascination as the horse got to its feet and rounded on Najib, pulling its lips back to bite its master. Najib turned and scurried up the hill before whirling around to watch his prized stallion follow the other two horses. He shook his fists at the horse's back and cursed it at the top of his lungs.

Ian nearly laughed out loud at the scene—until both he and Najib realized that the cloaked stranger had come closer.

Najib collected himself quickly and raised his scimitar in front of him while he yelled at the stranger, "*Arrêtez! Je vous commande de vous arrêtez!*"

"What did he say?" Carl asked.

"He's commanded him to stop," answered the professor. "But the bloody fool keeps coming!"

The cloaked figure continued to climb slowly and methodically up the hill until he was standing in front of Najib, who had raised his scimitar to a level where he could easily bring it down on the stranger.

For a long tense moment, no one moved—not the stranger, not the tribesmen, and not the children or their elders. The animals, however, were a completely different story. The remaining horses stomped their feet nervously and whinnied in fear.

Finally, the cloaked figure reached up and calmly eased his hood back from his head. Ian winced at the sight of him. Even in the moonlight he could tell that the stranger was a hideous man. The pale glow of the moon reflected off the stranger's bony, scarred face; long curved nose; recessed eyes; and bald head.

"Good evening," he said in English, and Ian felt an icy shiver of fear travel up his spine at the man's voice. "I am Magus the Black, Druid master of fire, and I have come to trade for the children."

Ian put a protective arm around Theo while he saw Thatcher place a hand on Carl's shoulder. "Don't worry," the schoolmaster said in a slightly shaky voice. "We won't let any of you go without a fight."

Ian's eyes darted back to Najib as he prayed that the warrior would bring down his sword and save them from the sorcerer. He knew that whatever fate lay in store for them at the hands of the Jichmach was nothing compared to the doom Magus the Black was about to unveil.

Slowly, Najib lowered his scimitar and spoke to the Druid in French. And even though Ian couldn't understand the words, he soon guessed what the warrior had asked when Magus nodded and reached slowly into his cloak to pull out two pouches. One of the pouches jingled, and Magus tugged open the string with his long bony fingers and shook out a few gold coins.

If Najib was impressed, he didn't show it; instead, he waited for the sorcerer to unveil what was in the second pouch. And Magus didn't waste any time. Quickly, he swapped the small bags and pulled loose the other's string. Then he carefully spread the folds of it open and unveiled the largest blue stone Ian had ever seen.

"Oh, my," gasped the professor. "It seems that Magus is returning the Jichmach's treasure."

Ian was startled when Najib raised his sword again and pointed it directly at the sorcerer, shouting at him in French in a way that was less than polite.

"He's accusing Magus of stealing the tribe's Star!" the professor said.

But to this outburst, the sorcerer merely pulled his thin lips back into a truly gruesome smile of dozens of small sharply tipped teeth.

Najib took a hesitant step away, but Magus made his intentions clear when he stretched out the hand holding the giant blue sapphire toward the warrior, then spoke to him in Arabic.

"What'd he say?" demanded Carl in a breathy whisper.

The professor didn't answer him right away, so Thatcher urged, "Professor Nutley? Can you please translate for us?"

The professor shook his head, clearly troubled. "Magus is claiming to have come across a German band of looters in Larache and discovered they'd stolen this from a tribe in the badlands. He says he's gone to great lengths to return the Star of Lixus to its rightful owners out of the goodness of his heart."

"If that mingy-looking bloke has goodness, then I'm the King of England!" sneered Carl.

The group waited in silence while Najib weighed what Magus was saying against his anger at being unseated and humiliated in front of his men. Then, finally, the Jichmach warrior snatched the sapphire out of Magus's extended hand and pointed toward the north. "*Allez-vous-en!*" he yelled.

"He's demanding that Magus leave," explained the professor.

But Magus didn't move. Instead, he tossed the pouch of gold coins up and down in his hand temptingly. Then he spoke to Najib, his voice high and grating on Ian's already frayed nerves.

"Magus is asking how much for the children," the professor explained, worry edging its way into his voice.

Najib stomped the ground again, obviously still irritated by his loss of face. But then, as the sorcerer continued to talk to him, he pointed to the pouch and yelled something.

Again the professor didn't translate right away, so Ian gently reminded him. "Sir? Could you tell us what he said?"

The professor met his eyes, and Ian thought for a moment that he wasn't going to explain. The older man looked at Thatcher and Perry, who both nodded, so he continued. "Najib is asking for the entire contents of the pouch in exchange for the children."

Ian gasped and turned back to Magus, knowing already what the answer would be.

The crack that was Magus's mouth spread wide, showing double rows of those fangs. *"Bien,"* the sorcerer said with a nod, and tossed the pouch with the gold at Najib. Then he calmly walked up the hill, straight for their group.

Ian felt a cold trickle of sweat make its way down his back. He knew that if he, Theo, and Carl were handed over to one of Demogorgon's offspring, they would most certainly be dead before morning.

"We're done for," moaned Carl, his voice squeaky and frightened as he too watched Magus approach them. Ian's mind began to race. He thought perhaps they could all make a run for it. He wondered if Najib would send his warriors after them now that they technically belonged to Magus. But before Ian could make a decision, the silence of the night was sliced by a great cry from the northwest and thundering hoofbeats.

Without warning, and seemingly appearing out of thin air, a horde of cloaked warriors rode into their camp, their scimitars raised and high-pitched cries reverberating across the lands.

Ian crouched low and held Theo tightly, trying to figure out what was happening. He looked up just as one of the Jichmach tribesmen who had been guarding them was cut down by an invader on horseback.

And then, he heard Perry shout above the noise, "It's the Jstor!"

Ian squinted into the dark, finally spotting none other than Raajhi on his black stallion as he raced into the middle of the surprised and scrambling Jichmach. Ian jumped to his feet, pulling Theo with him. To his right, Perry yelled out, "Let's run for it!"

Ian gripped Theo's arm tightly and bolted after Perry, who was practically dragging the professor along on the mad dash through the maze of tents, warriors, and chaos. Ian could see that Thatcher had yanked Carl up by the shoulder and was running to catch up to his brother, but as they skirted around warriors, scimitars, and horses, a tribesman came charging at their group, his scimitar raised directly at Thatcher's head. Ian shouted, "Look out!" and Thatcher barely had time to dive out of the way, pulling Carl with him.

Ian didn't see the peg in the ground securing the tent until he tripped over it, tumbling to the earth and taking Theo with him. Quick as a flash, he scrambled to his feet. "You all right?" he shouted to her in a panic as he helped her back up.

"Yes, yes!" Theo answered, her eyes large and frightened. But when Ian turned to look for Thatcher and Carl, they were nowhere to be found. He'd nearly run all the way back to where he'd last seen them, but stopped when he heard Perry shout, "Ian! Theo! Stay with me!"

With one more anxious look around, Ian turned, then ran with Theo to catch up to Perry and the professor. They wove through the maze of tents and the fighting warriors, who seemed to be closing in on them. In fact, they barely managed to escape the blows of two fighting tribesmen as they rounded one tent. There was no easy way out of the mess of battle, and finally Perry steered the professor into the cover of a tent, with Ian and Theo ducking in after them.

The interior was dimly lit by a small lantern in the corner, and Ian looked nervously at Perry and the professor. "What do we do?" he asked, breathing heavily.

"We need to get to Raajhi!" said Perry as he searched the tent.

"I believe he's a little preoccupied at the moment," said the professor, bent over at the waist, huffing and puffing with effort. The old man took a few moments to catch his breath, then added, "For now we'll need to stay down and keep quiet until the Jstor defeat the Jichmach."

"But what if they don't?" said Theo, tears of fear in her eyes. "What if it's the Jichmach who win?"

Ian looked at her and noticed that Theo was gripping the crystal at her neck. "We'll need to escape," he said firmly. "Somehow we need to get out of here."

Suddenly, the flap door of their tent was ripped aside and everyone jumped. Ian saw Perry lurch at something on the ground and, to Ian's amazement, come up with Najib's scimitar. The schoolmaster raised the heavy sword with both hands above his head, but just before he was to bring it down on the intruder, up through the flap popped Jaaved. *"Bonjour!"* he said happily. Then he saw Perry with the scimitar and quickly hopped over to stand next to Theo.

"Jaaved!" Theo gasped, throwing her arms around their guide. "Oh, I thought you were lost!"

Jaaved smiled uncomfortably and raised his finger to his lips. "Shhh," he whispered. *"Il faut attendre encore un peu avant de pouvoir nous échapper."*

"He says we must wait here quietly for a bit before we

can escape," the professor translated. He and the boy spoke between themselves; then the professor turned to the others and explained, "Jaaved says that if we can make it to the hills, there is a group of caves that he knows well. Though we should wait for the fighting outside to die down before we attempt it."

But the chaos outside wasn't dying down. The war cries and screams and the metallic sound of scimitar on scimitar echoed horribly through the camp until the front flap of their tent was flipped up again and in the doorway was a bloody Najib, looking crazed and terrible and still holding the borrowed scimitar. Theo screamed and Ian pulled her behind him while Perry, still clasping Najib's own sword, rose from his crouched position to meet the tribesman.

"On guard!" Perry yelled, holding the scimitar out in front of him and taking up a defensive fencing stance.

Najib growled and charged at Perry while Ian scooted himself and Theo as far out of the way as he could. Perry swung the scimitar with amazing skill and the schoolmaster managed to fend off Najib's downward thrusts, but the larger man beat him back into the rear of the tent with the force of his blows.

Worried that Perry was outmatched, Ian looked around him for anything that might help his schoolmaster, but the only thing he could find was the holster that the tribesman carried his sword in. Ian hauled up the buckle and whipped it at Najib, striking the man in the head. It was all the advantage Perry needed, and he wasted no time thrusting his sword forward into Najib's chest before yanking it back out.

The tribal leader howled once, then crumbled to the ground, gripping his bloody wound even as his eyes glazed over and he slumped lifeless and still.

Panting heavily, Perry stepped over Najib's body.

Ian rushed to his schoolmaster's side. "Are you hurt?"

"It's nothing," Perry said as he examined a long and nasty gash on his sword arm.

"But, sir!" Ian said, wincing when he saw the wound. "You're cut!"

"Leave it for now, Ian," said Perry, still breathing heavily. Then he turned to Jaaved and with a wave of the sword, he said, "We need to go, Jaaved, *now!*"

Though Perry had spoken in English, Jaaved must have understood the man's urgency, because with a nod he motioned them all to the front of the tent. Ian braced himself and gripped Theo's hand tightly again, ready to dash out into the melee still raging outside. But just as he sensed that Jaaved was about to bolt, another figure halted at the opening, one that sent dread straight through Ian's heart.

"Good evening," said Magus, bowing low and stepping through the entrance. "I'm so glad to find two of my purchases together in one place."

Perry stepped in front of Ian and Theo. Again, he took up his fencing stance and announced, "These children are subjects of His Majesty the King of England! They are not commodities to be bought and sold by the likes of you!"

Magus showed his jagged, fanglike teeth and whispered harshly, "Oh, but we are not in England, young man. We are in the badlands of Morocco, and when in Rome . . ." His voice trailed off ominously.

Quick as a flash, Perry whirled around and sliced through the side of the tent with the scimitar, creating a large tear. "Jaaved!" Perry commanded. *"Allez!"* Glancing at Ian, he said, "Go with Jaaved. The professor and I will join you later!"

Ian didn't hesitate. He dashed with Theo and Jaaved through the hole in the tent.

Outside, all around them, were screams from both man and horse and the clanging of metal. Ian felt dizzy with all the chaos, but he grabbed Theo's hand and tore after Jaaved, who was running away, ducking low and keeping to the cover of the surrounding tents.

They wound their way through the camp and the hordes of fighting men. And it was clear to Ian that most of the dead were Jstor. It seemed the Jichmach were too much for them, and Ian winced as he watched Jaaved run between the bodies of his brethren.

After a few more close calls with scimitars, horses, and warriors, the trio reached the edge of the encampment, shaken and distraught. With one last worried glance over his shoulder, Jaaved led them quickly away and into the darkness beyond.

THE SEEKER

Ian, Theo, and Jaaved ran for their lives, hiding when they could behind outcroppings of boulders, getting ever closer to the foothills. Finally, they made one final dash and reached the relative safety of the caves.

Ian could see as they approached that there were several dozen openings along a large expanse of rock that shot straight up. He followed Jaaved as he ducked into one, and pulled Theo along inside after the Moroccan boy.

Ian collapsed on the ground, panting like a dog on all fours, and Theo dropped to her knees beside him, holding her side. Ian's feet throbbed so painfully from the running and the rocky terrain they'd just covered, he wondered if they would ever return to normal.

He gasped, "We should move as far into this cave as possible. I don't want that Magus character or one of those Jichmach tribesmen finding us." Jaaved looked at him quizzically, and Ian pointed to the back of the cave.

As they made their way deeper into the cavern, the light from the moon outside became dimmer and dimmer and the group had to feel their way along, whispering so as not to lose track of one another.

Finally, when they had crept well away from the opening and were deeply nestled in the blackness of the back of the cave, Ian announced, "We should be safe here," and he gave Theo a small tug on her blouse. She dropped to the cold stone floor and Jaaved took her cue and sat beside Theo. Ian also dropped and leaned his head back against the cave wall, straining to hear any sounds. He could no longer hear the commotion from the camp, and he felt that the quiet was somehow eeriest of all.

As time passed Ian became aware of first Theo's and then Jaaved's heavy breathing and he knew that exhaustion had won out against them. But try as he might, and as tired as he was, Ian could not doze off. In his whole life he had never, ever felt so exhausted, yet his mind was full of the nightmare from that evening. He had no idea what had happened to Carl and Thatcher or to Perry and the professor in the face of the powerful Druid sorcerer.

Eventually, however, in the wee hours of the morning, his mind finally allowed him the briefest moment of silence, and he was mercifully able to close his eyes and fall into a troubled slumber.

Ian awoke soon after dawn. He blinked blearily as the sun's rays reached him all the way in the back of the cave, and he stared numbly about. In the dimness he could just make out Theo's head leaning on his shoulder and Jaaved next to her, curled up on the cave floor.

Ian yawned and rubbed his eyes. He was still sore and

tired, but now he was thirsty and hungry too. Carefully, he laid Theo gently on the ground, giving her his shirt for a pillow. He shivered in the coolness of the cave and moved carefully toward the mouth, keeping in the shadows lest someone had made his way into the cave while they were sleeping.

No one was about, so he continued forward until he was at the opening and could clearly see across the hills. Smoke billowed from their campsite, and in the dirt he could just discern the figures of the dead lying on the ground. A wave of emotion swept over him; the professor, Perry, Thatcher, and Carl might well be among the casualties. He turned away miserably and walked back to Theo and Jaaved, then sat down heavily. He hadn't ever felt so sad before, and he struggled to hold back the anguish that wanted to pour out of him.

Wordlessly, Jaaved got up and walked past him. Ian didn't try to stop him. Jaaved had family at the camp, and Ian couldn't blame him for wanting to see for himself if any of his fellow tribesmen had survived.

Ian sat and waited patiently for Jaaved to return. Just as he was beginning to get concerned, Jaaved appeared again in the cave's entrance. And to the lifting of Ian's spirits, he carried with him the two backpacks that had been taken from them at Jifaar's house, along with two canteens of water and a satchel of food. The Moroccan boy, however, was wearing a look of such deep sorrow that Ian couldn't help feeling bad for him.

"You went to the camp," he said as Jaaved set the backpacks down.

Jaaved didn't respond, and Ian hadn't expected him to. Instead, Jaaved handed Ian one of the canteens and made a motion to drink. Just as Ian took the canteen from him, he saw a horrible burn on the bottom of Jaaved's palm. "Blimey!" said Ian loudly.

"What's the matter?" asked Theo, startled out of her sleep.

"Jaaved's hurt," Ian said as he took the boy's hand in his and turned it gently up to inspect. Then he took the canteen and poured a bit of water on Jaaved's wound.

"Let me see," said Theo as she got up and came over to look at it. "Oh, heavens!" she exclaimed.

"I know," said Ian, looking in sympathy at Jaaved. "That must have hurt," he added, making an expression like he was in pain so that Jaaved knew he felt bad for him. "You must have picked up something hot?"

But Jaaved didn't understand and he cocked his head at Ian.

Ian mimed touching his finger to something that burned, and Jaaved nodded. The Moroccan then pantomimed holding a sword out in front of him before opening his hands wide and shaking the one he'd injured as if he'd touched something hot. Ian nodded as he grasped what Jaaved was showing him.

"What do you think happened?" Theo asked, puzzled by their game of charades.

"I think he was trying to pick up a sword that had been burned in one of the fires and it was hotter than he thought," said Ian.

Theo reached for Jaaved's hand to inspect his wound

again, then gasped. "Ian!" she exclaimed. "Look at the wound closely!"

Ian peered down at Jaaved's burn and immediately noticed that the horrible bumpy blister marring Jaaved's palm had a distinct shape to it. As Ian squinted closer, he realized that it was in the form of a diamond, just like the one on the hilt of Raajhi's scimitar. "The mark from your premonition!" he said, gazing at Theo in amazement.

Theo was pumping her head up and down, but Jaaved was eyeing the pair of them as if they were ridiculous to be so happy about his wound. He roughly yanked his hand away from Ian and started to turn his back on them. But Theo moved quickly to Jaaved's side and took his hand in hers. She pantomimed wrapping it in a bandage, then turned to Ian and said, "Can you help me tear off a bit of cloth from my blouse to wrap his hand?"

Ian looked from her dirty but otherwise unmarred shirt to his own shirt, which was in tatters, still lying crumpled on the floor where he'd set it for Theo's pillow. With a smirk, Ian picked up his shirt and tore off a length, then handed it to her so that she could wrap it around Jaaved's hand carefully.

Ian then put his tattered shirt back on and turned back toward the opening of the cave.

"He went to the Jichmach's camp to bring us back some supplies," Ian explained to Theo when he saw her gaze fall on the backpacks.

Theo's eyes lit up. "Did he find the professor? Or Thatcher and Perry? Carl?"

Ian looked at Jaaved. He was aware that their guide knew their companions by name, and when the Moroccan faced them again, Ian's heart sank at Jaaved's grief-stricken face. He felt like he'd just been kicked in the stomach. He watched Jaaved dully as their guide turned away from them and began busying himself by digging around in the backpacks. After a few moments he pulled out Ian's pocket torch and compass amd handed them to him, but Ian felt little joy at the return of his possessions. Next Jaaved dug into his own small sack and produced three portions of smoked meat, offering one each to Theo and Ian.

Theo took hers without looking at it and Ian saw small tears trickling down her cheeks.

Jaaved looked at Theo when she began crying, and it seemed to undo him. He moved to the back of the cave, sat down, then leaned his back against the wall and pulled his knees up close before he hid his chin in his chest and was lost in his emotion. Theo crept close to him and the two cried together.

As Ian watched them, he found that he was breathing hard and had a very difficult time swallowing. He knew he should go over and at least try to comfort Theo, but his own grief was suddenly so heavy that he couldn't do it. He wasn't able to sit there and be strong in the face of the loss he felt, but he also realized that it wouldn't do to break down in front of the others. So wordlessly he walked past the pair, deeper into the rock enclosure.

"I'll be back," he said hoarsely before switching on his torch and moving even farther into the cave. When he was far enough away that he was certain Jaaved and Theo couldn't hear him, he clicked off his light, letting the darkness of the cave envelop him, and cried bitter tears.

A long while later, when Ian was spent of his emotions, he sat on the floor and looked out at the darkness hopelessly. He wondered how he and Theo were ever going to find their way back to Delphi. And if they did, how would they explain what had happened? Who would believe such a story? How would they explain what had become of Thatcher, Perry, the professor, and Carl?

He sat dumbly and stared at the blackness for a long time, clicking his light on and off, his thoughts bleak and his spirit crushed. Finally, he clicked his pocket torch on one final time, preparing to get back to Theo and Jaaved, when he noticed something peculiar caught in the light's beam. On the wall opposite him and down to his right, he noticed dark squiggles and lines. Ian got to his feet, moved to the opposite wall, and looked closely at the shapes, tracing them with his finger. "Incredible," he said, taking one step back so that his light could better illuminate the wall. "I can't believe it!" he nearly shouted before turning to race back down the path he'd taken. He found Jaaved and Theo sitting back to back, staring listlessly into space, much like he'd just been doing. "Jaaved! Theo!" he called excitedly. "Come quick! I've got to show you something!"

They scrambled to their feet and hurried after him. The deeper into the cave they went, the more narrow the opening became. Ian managed to find the exact spot he'd been sitting in when his torch had lit on the writing. "Look,

Theo!" he said as he shone his light onto the wall. "Does it seem familiar to you?"

"It's just like the writing in the cavern back in Dover!" Theo said, pressing her hand to the wall.

"Exactly! Come on. I'll bet you there's something at the end of this cave! Maybe there's another silver box with a scroll, and maybe we can trade the box for enough money to get us home!"

Jaaved gave each of them a confused look but followed dutifully as Ian and Theo made their way deeper into the cave. Before long Ian was ducking low, and then so was Jaaved, and finally Theo was bent over. "Ian," she said to him. "This tunnel keeps getting shorter and shorter!"

"Yes, but see that?" Ian said, pointing at the wall to his right. "Someone wrote that, Theo. And I'm sure it's a marker to keep going."

The threesome continued on, soon reduced to crawling, and abruptly they came to a sharp fork in the tunnel and the cave headed off into two directions. The one on the right appeared to be easier to travel; there was a dip into what looked like a larger cavern with more headroom. The one on the left became narrower still.

"Which way?" Theo asked as she crawled up next to Ian.

"Well, right seems most likely. I mean, I can't imagine that anyone would choose to go into such a narrow space when something roomier is at hand."

Ian moved toward the right and Jaaved yelled out, "*Non!*"

Both Ian and Theo turned to look at Jaaved, who was pointing toward the left tunnel. "*Allez à la gauche!*"

"He wants us to go to the left," said Theo.

Ian hesitated only a moment, but two things came back to him: Laodamia's words from the prophecy about the Seeker guiding them deep in stone, and Theo's vision of the boy with the diamond mark. He decided to trust Jaaved, and with a shrug he led the way into the narrower tunnel.

The threesome were able to crawl a while longer before the ceiling forced Ian to lay flat on the ground and pull himself along with his arms, which was difficult, as he was trying to hold the torch out in front of him to guide them with some light. "I must be daft," he said, panting, irritated that he'd listened to the Moroccan. "There's no way someone would have come this way, Jaaved! We should have gone to the . . ." Ian's voice trailed off, because in front of him, the floor sloped drastically downward and a huge cavern opened up.

"Oh, my," he heard Theo say from behind. "Ian! Look at that!"

Excitedly, he squirmed his way forward and half rolled, half crawled into the cavern. As he stood, he flashed his torch all around and gasped. Everywhere his torch beam touched, it glinted off treasure.

In his amazement, Ian had almost forgotten about Theo and Jaaved until Jaaved's yelp broke the silence. *"Trésor!"* their guide yelled, and ran to a hill of gold on the floor.

Theo too went to a pile and happily picked up huge fistfuls of gold coins. "Ian! We're rich!" she squealed. "We can get back to England now!"

Ian sat down heavily on the ground, dumbstruck. They could buy passage back to England, and with this much treasure, he could ensure that he and Theo would never be separated. He could purchase them a house to live in, even hire a governess to look after them until they became old enough to take care of themselves. All the hopelessness he'd experienced that morning seemed to fade away as he looked at Theo dancing atop a mound of gold.

A smile formed on his lips just as his torch noticeably dimmed. "Bugger!" he muttered, shaking the light as it flickered again. "Theo! Jaaved!" he said, turning to them. "Grab as much of the treasure as you can carry and hurry after me. The light on my torch won't last much longer, and we've got to be out of this tunnel before it dies completely!"

Theo hurriedly bent down and began stuffing her shirt with gold coins. Jaaved stood with a confused look on his face as he watched Theo, until Ian pointed to his torch, which flickered again. Jaaved suddenly seemed to understand. He turned and began grabbing fistfuls of gold and jewels himself.

Ian held his small torch in his mouth while he grabbed as much as he could. Glancing to his left, he was caught completely by surprise. Moving over to one of the rocky ledges, he couldn't believe what he saw: a silver box identical to the one he'd left at the keep. It had to be another of Laodamia's. He set the gold in his hands down quickly and grabbed the box, gazing at it in the dimming light of his torch. Making a snap decision, he shoved the box into the waistband of his trousers and gathered up his two handfuls of gold again, tying them in his shirttails, then shoved fistfuls into his pockets. He wanted to carry out as much gold as he could, but as his torch gave yet another flicker, Ian realized they should really make their way out of the darkness while they still had light. He gazed longingly at all the gold they would be leaving behind and tried not to be bitter. Instead, he focused on getting them safely back out before his torch died for good. "Come on, you two," he said. "Let's head back."

Ian held his torch between his teeth again and crawled along on his forearms, as his fists were full of gold. The skin on his arms became so raw that he winced with each painful reach forward, but he refused to leave behind any coin he'd carried out. Soon they'd made it to where they could crawl along on their hands and knees, and Ian's heart raced when his light dimmed even more. Squinting in the grayness of the tunnel, he felt a note of relief when they came to the fork. He moved even faster and grunted to Theo and Jaaved, hoping they understood the need to hurry.

Just as they made it to the point of being able to crouch low on two feet again, Ian's torch went out completely and plunged them all into absolute blackness. He opened his mouth and spit his light to the ground.

"What do we do?" Theo asked from behind him, her voice anxious.

"Put your hand on my back, and have Jaaved do the same. I'll go slowly, okay?"

"Okay," said Theo.

"Okay," said Jaaved.

Ian stopped. "What did he say?" he asked, turning to look back into the blackness behind him, thinking that maybe he had misheard Jaaved.

"I said okay," Jaaved repeated.

Ian and Theo both gasped in surprise. "Jaaved!" Theo said. "You spoke English!"

"I did?" he said. "When?"

"Just now!" Ian said, then realized that the Moroccan boy must have been lying all this time. "When did you learn to speak English?" he asked carefully.

Jaaved didn't respond right away, but after a moment he said, "I never learned to speak English. You must be speaking French!"

Ian shook his head in frustration but decided to argue about it later. At the moment they had more pressing issues. "Fine, have it your way," he said impatiently. "Just follow closely behind Theo."

They were in the dark for quite a while, but finally Ian could see the shapes of their surroundings. Eventually, there was a small bead of light ahead, and he knew they weren't far from where they'd started. He breathed a sigh of relief when they reached their backpacks and water canteens.

"How are we going to get the rest of the treasure out?" Theo asked him, holding up her two kneesocks, which she'd cleverly loaded with gold.

"We're not," he said, smiling at her ingenuity as he unloaded his hands and his pockets. "We've got to get home, and we've got enough here to do that. Oh!" He interrupted himself as he pulled the silver box from his trousers. "Theo, look at what I found in the cavern!"

"It's another box!" she exclaimed. "Just like Laodamia said we'd find!"

Ian nodded. "And I think it might hold the Star." Flipping

the box over, he began turning each of the feet, hoping that this box opened like the others. He found the right ball on the second try and unscrewed it, revealing the key. With shaking fingers he inserted it into the small keyhole at the front of the box and it opened with a pop. But inside all he saw was another scroll and a small bronze sundial.

"What is it?" Theo asked over his shoulder.

"Just another scroll," he said, disappointed. "And a sundial."

"A sundial?"

"Yes," he said, holding it up for her to see.

"How peculiar."

"Quite," he said, setting it back into the box with a sigh.

"No sign of the Star?" she asked.

"Not unless the sundial is the Star," said Ian. He was starting to grow weary of Laodamia and her riddles. He closed the lid, locked it, and returned the ball to the bottom of the box. "Seems we're all out of missing gemstones with magical powers."

Theo gave him a sympathetic look but said nothing. Instead, she focused on Jaaved, who was distracted by the treasure he was unloading. Ian saw with a bit of humility that Jaaved's pile was bigger than his.

"That's a pretty good haul, Jaaved," Ian said to him.

"That *is* good," Theo agreed, then looked at Ian and a smile spread across her face. As if she'd just realized it, she turned round and showed them a huge knot in the tail of her blouse. She undid the knot and an enormous pile of treasure slipped out onto the ground. Adding to what was in her socks, it was as much as Ian's and Jaaved's combined.

"*Mais . . . quel énorme trésor là!*" exclaimed Jaaved, pointing to her pile.

Ian gave him a weary look, out of patience for his silly language games. "You can drop the act, Jaaved," he snapped. "We know you can speak English."

Jaaved cocked his head at Ian, confusion on his face. "*Qu'avez-vous dit?*"

"We know you can understand us, Jaaved," Theo said, more gently. "It's all right; we're not mad."

"Speak for yourself," muttered Ian, thoroughly irritated that Jaaved had duped them.

"*Je ne comprends pas!*" said Jaaved, standing up and pointing to them. "*Parlez-moi comme vous avez fait dans le tunnel!*"

"What's he so mad about?" Ian asked Theo.

"I don't know," she replied. "Jaaved, why won't you speak English? You know we can't understand French."

Jaaved glared at her and stomped his foot. Bending low and grumbling to himself, he gathered up his pile of treasure and shoved it into his pockets. "If you won't speak to me like you did in the tunnel, then you may find your own way back!"

"We *are* speaking to you like we did in the tunnel!" insisted Theo. And just like that, everyone stopped talking and looked at the last handful of treasure in Jaaved's palm. There, in his bandaged palm, was the biggest opal Ian had ever seen. The iridescent stone shone blue, orange, yellow, and green, and at the center of the stone was a cluster of red flakes that reflected the light brilliantly. Most startling of all, however, was that the stone was shaped into a five-pointed star.

"The Star of Lixus!" Theo gasped.

"It gives him the power of language!" said Ian, putting the final pieces of Laodamia's riddle into place. "Jaaved, give me the opal, and when it's in my hand, say something in your native tongue, not in French but in Arabic!"

Jaaved handed over the stone and said, "Hello, Ian, it's a lovely day for a camel ride."

Ian scowled. It hadn't worked. "No, you're just speaking English again," he said, but he noticed a look of shock on Theo's face. "Ian!" she gasped. "You just spoke Arabic!"

"I did?" he asked.

"Now you're back to English!" she said.

"I don't understand you, Theo," said Jaaved, looking confusedly from Ian to Theo.

"What's not to understand?" asked Ian.

"You did it again!" Theo exclaimed. "This time you spoke French!"

Ian thought back to how he had responded to Jaaved. It was odd, but there had been just a slight change in the way his brain thought out the words and his lips had formed them. "Jaaved," he said excitedly, "after I give the Star to Theo, I want you to ask her what her favorite book is."

"All right," said Jaaved, and Ian handed the Star to Theo. As Theo held the stone, Jaaved asked his question in French, and Theo responded in French, with a perfect accent.

Ian looked at her, stunned. "That was brilliant!" he said. He took the Star from Theo, gave it back to Jaaved, and asked, "You can understand us, right?"

"Yes, perfectly," Jaaved answered.

"Brilliant!" Ian repeated. "How do we get back to your boat?"

"We've got to cross the valley again, and go back the way you came."

"How dangerous will it be?"

Jaaved looked grim. "Very. We have only the water in the canteens, and this meat. The journey will take two days on foot. I've been to the Jichmach camp. Only a few of my tribesmen survived the fight, and from the tracks I found, I know they are headed back to our lands. The surviving Jichmach have gone deeper into their lands to bring more warriors to help collect their dead and gather up the remaining supplies."

"I'm so sorry about your family," Theo said, and patted Jaaved's arm.

He nodded and pressed his lips together. "My grandfather was badly injured. I had to leave him and seek out help from my tribe. While Raajhi led us to the Jichmach, my aunt was dispatched to the river to care for my grandfather. I wish to go back to him as soon as possible."

Ian hesitated before asking his next question, and even when he found the courage, his voice would not rise above a whisper. "Did you see any sign of Carl or our schoolmasters and the professor?"

Jaaved's face fell. "The tent they were in was burned to the ground. I saw two bodies there. And there was no sign in the campsite of Carl or Thatcher but I did not stay long. . . ." Jaaved paused. "My uncle was among the dead, along with my cousin, Mahir. Once I saw them, I focused only on getting what had not been destroyed in the battle."

Theo turned her face away from them, and Ian knew she was weeping again. He nodded to Jaaved and tried to clear his throat of the lump that was stuck there. "Right," he said, picking up one of the backpacks. "We should carry the treasure, of course, and only what is absolutely necessary for the two-day journey, and we should travel at night until we can get clear of the valley. Let's repack these and get some rest. We'll set out right after nightfall."

Shortly after dusk, Jaaved woke Ian and Theo from their fitful sleep. It was cold on the floor of the cave, and Ian had been so anxious and uncomfortable that he'd gotten very little rest.

Wordlessly, he and Jaaved put on the backpacks, and Theo carried their food and canteens. They crept to the mouth of the cave and looked about at the long shadows, listening for the slightest sound. The desert world was silent, so they stepped out of the mouth of the cave and crept along the hillside. Then they heard a noise that stopped them cold.

A howl, long and horrible, echoed across the valley and reverberated against the rocks and into the caves. Ian and his companions flattened themselves to the ground, waiting for the beast to show itself.

After several moments Ian carefully lifted his head and looked behind him at Jaaved and Theo. "I knew it was too much to hope that the beast would've moved on from us. We'll need to keep to the shadows as much as possible," he said.

"Maybe we should wait for daylight to cross the valley," Theo proposed. "The beast doesn't seem to like daylight."

"But the Jichmach do," said Jaaved. "Our choice is to risk being hunted by the beast or face certain death at the hands of the Jichmach. I expect them back here to claim their dead within the next hour or two, and have no doubt, their hearts will thirst for revenge. Out in that valley, we're sure to be spotted by the warriors if we wait until daylight."

Theo shivered. "Jaaved's right. We should cross the valley tonight."

Ian got to his feet but crouched low; the other two followed suit. "We'll have to plan every move," he said, his eyes scanning the valley in the dimming light. "We'll need to go from cover to cover. Like when we made it to the caves from the campsite. And we'll start there," he said, pointing to a large boulder. "We should sprint for that and hide. Then we'll pick the next place and so on."

He looked over his shoulder to get their approval, and both of them nodded. Ian turned back to focus on the boulder. His palms were slick with sweat but he forced his voice to be calm for the sake of his friends. "All right, then, after me, you two," he said, and sprinted to the boulder. He crashed against it and dropped down low. Jaaved and Theo were right behind him, panting hard. "Good job," he said when they were all together. "Now let's look for the next spot."

Theo pointed to some low bushes. "There, Ian!" she said. "That's not very far away and we should be able to make it."

Ian smiled and gave her a reassuring squeeze on the shoulder. "Follow my lead," he said before dashing off.

And so they continued like that for most of the night, running in short bursts from cover to cover. Sometimes they hid behind bushes, sometimes rocks, and once they hid behind a termite mound. An hour or two before dawn, they'd made it nearly out of the valley, and Ian was starting to feel much better about their chances. But as he scanned the terrain ahead, looking for the next place of cover, something in the dark moved. He pulled his head back from the opening in their hiding place between two large rocks, his breath catching in his throat.

"What is—" Theo started, but Ian put a hand over her mouth and shook his head.

Moving in close, he whispered, "The beast," and pointed up over the rock. Theo's mouth dropped open wide and she gripped his tattered shirt in fear. Jaaved looked alarmed; he knew that Ian had seen something but he didn't know what. Ian mouthed, *The beast,* and Jaaved nodded gravely.

Ian then pulled Theo close and pressed them both into the rock, shielding her as best he could. He could feel her trembling and he wondered if she could sense his heart hammering against his chest. A smell that made him want to gag—sulfur mixed with wet dog and rotting meat—came to their nostrils then. Ian shut his eyes and tried to hold his breath as the awful smell grew stronger. Within moments he heard the labored panting of the beast drawing near.

Ian wondered how close the deadly creature was to them. He prayed it would simply pass by their hiding spot. But all hope of that fled when a horrible howl sounded right by them.

Theo put her hands over her ears and leaned hard into Ian's chest while Jaaved put his face to the rock and covered his head with his arms. But Ian forced himself to keep his eyes open and wait for the beast's next move, expecting that at any moment it would leap over the rock they hid behind and tear them all to shreds.

As the howl died away, Ian realized that the ground beneath them was vibrating. For a moment he thought it was just his imagination, but he soon realized that along with the vibration came a pounding so great that it began to echo about the valley.

Then, on the other side of the rock where they crouched, there came a loud snort, followed by an enormous shadow that blocked out the moon before dropping just a few meters away. Ian gasped when he realized he was looking at the hackles of the beast as it raced away from them.

He had only a moment to consider how vulnerable a position he was in as the vibrating earth and the thundering sound of galloping horses grew into a terrible crescendo of noise. Then, suddenly, horses began leaping over their boulder, landing with tremendous tremors. Dozens of horses flew overhead only to charge away after the beast. Dust and sand were kicked up, filling Ian's nose, eyes, and mouth with grit while the thunder of hooves filled his ears, until finally, the last horse had cleared the boulder and was pounding away.

Ian felt a strong tug on his arm and he looked up, dazed, to see Jaaved. "We must go!" he urged. "We must hurry before they look back and see us!"

Realizing that Jaaved was right, Ian scrambled to his feet, pulling Theo up with him. The three made a mad dash across what was left of the valley, their legs pumping as fast as they could, closer and closer to the hilly terrain with plenty of cover just a quarter mile away.

With hearts racing, Ian, Theo, and Jaaved made it to the edge of the rocks, through the narrow opening of the valley, and down the path before dropping to the ground, exhausted. It was only when he'd caught his breath a little that Ian noticed for the first time the unmistakable sound of a horse snorting directly above his head.

HOMEWARD BOUND

Terrified that one of the Jichmach had found them, Ian sprang to his feet. He looked up at the rider, his mouth set firmly, and raised his fists, prepared to go down fighting. But to his astonishment, a smiling sooty man sat bareback on the white stallion before them. "I never thought I'd see the likes of you three again!" the man said happily before jumping down and moving to Ian. Ian realized that the man underneath all that soot was Perry.

"Schoolmaster Goodwyn!" Theo shouted, and barreled into Perry's chest. Ian had never been so glad to see someone in his life.

Perry hugged Theo fiercely. "My young Miss Fields," he said softly. "I thought we'd lost you to those barbarians."

"That's Najib's horse!" gasped Ian, recognizing the warrior's stallion. "Wherever did you find him?"

"Not far from here," came another voice, and Ian saw that there was another horse on the path, this one ridden by the professor. "We made it out of the valley about six hours ago and bedded down in the bushes over there. When we woke up, we saw the horses on the path. It took us a little while to catch them, but we finally managed it. And that's when we saw you three making your way over to us."

"I daresay, we thought for certain that horrible beast was going to gobble you up and I very nearly raced out to try to rescue you when I saw that band of Jichmach coming across the valley," added Perry.

"They flew right over our heads," said Theo. "We were almost trampled!"

Perry smiled, the white of his teeth bright against the soot on his face. "I know," he said, and stroked her hair. "I thought the professor was going to have a heart attack. Thank heavens you weren't hurt."

"And what happened to you two?" Ian asked. "The last we saw of you, you were squaring off against Magus the Black."

"Ghastly man—if you can call him that," sniffed the professor, spitting into the dirt for emphasis. "He came right for Perry the moment you three dashed out of the tent. I've never seen anything so frightening, and that includes the beast."

Perry nodded. "It was like looking straight into the face of the devil," he said, and Ian would swear he saw his schoolmaster shiver. "But just before he closed in on me, something crashed into our tent. To be honest with you, I'm not even sure if it was one of the invaders or one of our captors, but *someone* came barreling into the tent, and he was on fire."

Ian saw Theo blanch.

Perry nodded. "Yes, a horrible sight, that. But it saved us

in the end. The tent caught fire and that distracted Magus while the professor here dragged me clear before the whole tent went up in smoke. We managed somehow to get to the foothills and then we hid in one of those caves until the battle was over."

"We hid in a cave too!" said Theo. "And we found treasure!"

"Treasure?" asked the professor, nudging his horse forward.

"Yes! And Jaaved found the true Star of Lixus! Show him, Jaaved."

Jaaved opened his bandaged palm and the professor gingerly got down off his horse and hurried over. "My word," he breathed, eyeing the opal closely. "It is as beautiful as the legend said it would be."

"And it's as magical as Laodamia told us it would be," added Ian, proud that they had discovered the lost gem. "Do you remember the line in the prophecy that said, 'Language now is not unknown'?"

The professor nodded. "Yes, I remember."

"Well!" said Ian, with as much drama as he could muster. "Jaaved can understand and speak English with it!"

The professor looked amazed and glanced at Jaaved. "Really?" he asked. "Is that true?"

"Yes, Professor," Jaaved answered with a huge grin. "I can understand everything you've said."

Ian delighted in seeing both the professor and Perry gasp in surprise.

"My word!" said Perry. "He's even speaking without a noticeable accent!"

"Try talking to him in another language," Ian suggested to the professor. "I bet he'll be able to understand that too."

The professor eyed Ian skeptically. "You think so?" he asked, then turned to Jaaved and said something to him that sounded like a chicken clucking.

Jaaved laughed and said something back, making the identical clucking noises. "That's remarkable," said the professor. "Simply remarkable!"

"What did you say to him?" asked Theo.

"I told him an ancient Phoenician joke involving a mule and a monkey. He told me it was very funny, also in Phoenician."

"Speaking of Phoenicians . . . ," said Theo, poking Ian with her elbow. "Show the professor the box you found."

Ian reached into his pack and pulled out the silver box and handed it to the professor, who took it from him gingerly. "You found this along with the Star?"

Ian nodded. "It's identical to the other one, don't you think?"

The professor squinted in the moonlight. "It certainly seems so," he agreed.

"If I may propose a theory, sir, I believe that Laodamia arranged for this box to make it to Adrastus, who hid it for us along with the Star. Which also made me wonder about something," said Ian.

"What's that, lad?" asked the professor, still eyeing the box.

"What happened to Adrastus after the Carthaginians conquered Lixus?"

The professor looked at Ian thoughtfully. "The legend says that he escaped to his boat near Larache and attempted to return to Greece; however, his boat was thought to have sunk, because he was never heard from again."

"I wonder if Adrastus really did set sail," Ian said. "I mean, the portal is close to Larache's harbor. Maybe the Phoenician general discovered it, and perhaps Laodamia gave Adrastus charge of not one, but two boxes—one to be placed here in the cave in Morocco, the other in a cavern back in Dover." Ian had been thinking on this theory ever since he'd discovered the writing on the wall of the cave where they'd hidden from the Jichmach.

"That would be an extraordinary coincidence," said the professor, "but given what we've witnessed recently, not out of the realm of possibility."

"Yes, but you have to agree, sir, that the timing is rather close," Ian said, pressing his point. "What I mean to say is that you determined that the script from the cavern back in Dover was from around 400 BC, and wasn't that near the time this general Adrastus was here in Morocco?"

The professor looked at him curiously. "Yes, Ian," he agreed.

"Well, we found the same Greek scribbling on the wall of the cave we hid in after leaving the Jichmach's camp," Ian explained. "And I swear to you, sir, the writing looks to have been made by the same hand."

The professor eyed him with interest. "Most curious, in-deed, my young lad," he admitted.

"Maybe the scroll inside the box will give us a clue!" said Theo.

The professor's soot-streaked eyebrows jumped. "There's another scroll inside?" he asked.

"Yes," Ian said, motioning to the box. "I opened it up earlier, before we knew Jaaved had hold of the Star, thinking that it might have been hidden inside. Would you like to see it?"

But Perry laid a hand on Ian's shoulder. "I'd rather we get as far away from here as possible," he said reasonably. "Let's save the box and its contents for when we get home."

"Yes, of course," said Ian. "Theo and I have collected enough treasure to get all of us to England, anyway, and there'll be plenty of time to look at the scroll once we're back in Larache. Jaaved said that he can see us safely to our boat in Lixus and sail us downriver to Larache, where we can figure out how to get home."

Perry nodded. "Excellent," he said, but Ian saw that his eyes drifted back to the valley and clouded over with worry. "We were hoping when we first spotted you that we'd see Carl and my brother too. Did you happen to catch sight of them?"

Ian didn't answer his schoolmaster. Instead, he deferred the question to Jaaved, who shook his head sadly and said, "I went back to the camp to retrieve what I could this morning. They were not among the dead that I saw, but I don't know what became of them."

Perry's mouth formed a thin line and he cleared his throat. Ian didn't know what to say, and in the silence that followed, it seemed no one else did either. After a few moments, Perry squared his shoulders and said in a voice barely above a whisper, "Very well. Let's be on our way, then. Theo and Jaaved, you can ride behind the professor. Ian, you're with me."

The group made excellent progress and were lucky enough with Jaaved's help to find a small watering hole for the horses and their canteens. After a short rest they mounted up again and pushed on through the hot sun, sometimes riding, sometimes walking to give the horses a break. By nightfall they could make out the lost city in the distance and Ian felt tears of relief sting his eyes.

Theo and the professor were having a rough go of it, however. Both of them looked weary to the bone and in need of some proper rest, so as the moon rose, Perry finally stopped the group and found them a place off the dirt path to bed down for a short reprieve. "I'll take the first watch," he said. "Ian, I'll wake you in a few hours. Then, Jaaved, it will be your turn until dawn."

Ian felt Jaaved shaking him far too soon, and as he sat up and looked wearily about, he realized the first rays of sun were already snaking their way across the eastern horizon. He stood and shook out the stiffness, realizing much to his relief that his feet weren't suffering nearly as much as they had been the last several days.

They made it to Lixus by midmorning and urged their mounts quickly down the hills toward the river. Jaaved, however, was greeted by an unwelcome sight. He jumped from his horse and ran frantically toward a large pile of burned wood next to the charred ruins of Jifaar's little house.

"Oh, my," breathed Perry, and he clicked his tongue, sending his mount into a canter that the other horse followed. They pulled to a stop next to Jaaved, and Ian quickly dismounted and hurried to the side of the boy, who had dropped to his knees and was openly weeping in front of the large pile of burned wood.

"What's happened?" Ian asked. "Jaaved? Tell us what's wrong!"

But Jaaved simply continued to wail inconsolably and shook his head.

"What is it?" Ian asked, turning to Theo, confused. "Why's he so upset?"

The professor softly explained, "It's a funeral pyre, Ian," pointing to the burned remains of the piled wood.

"Funeral pyre?" Ian repeated. "For whom?"

"For Jifaar," said the professor quietly.

Ian gasped and Theo began to cry as well. And everyone fell silent as Jaaved wept.

When his sobs finally subsided into gurgly hiccups, Ian put his arm around his friend and said, "Why don't you come back to England with us, Jaaved? Theo and I don't have much in the way of family either, and the keep where we live is a better spot for you than under the thatch of some fat sailor in Larache."

Jaaved gulped and looked at Ian, his soft brown eyes still moist with tears. "Thank you," he said, choking. "I'd like that."

Perry cleared his throat. "Yes, Jaaved, of course you're welcome to join us, but I'm afraid the way home won't be easy." Ian wondered at first what Perry was talking about, but then he saw that his schoolmaster was pointing toward the dock. "Our boat is gone," he said gravely.

Ian's heart sank. What more could go wrong?

"How are we going to get home if we don't have a boat?" Theo moaned. "And for that matter, aren't we on the wrong side of the river? How are we going to get our horses across *that*?"

Ian's spirits sagged even lower as he looked across the eight-hundred-meter expanse of the Loukkos River.

"There is another way," said Jaaved with a sniffle. "We can go up the river and take the bridge my people built. It will put us near the pass of Avanclair." He pointed to the southeast. "It's steep, but the horses can make it and we can still be in Larache the day after tomorrow."

"Why didn't we come that way before?" asked Ian.

"By boat is better," said Jaaved. "Easier. You'll see."

And Ian did. They reached the bridge and then the pass about an hour later and began to hike up the slope of the pass on foot—the grade was too steep to ride the horses.

The trek was long and difficult, and later that evening as the group made camp and Jaaved passed out the last of their rations of dried meat, everyone ate in gloomy silence, knowing that this would be their last meal for at least the next two days.

They camped that night under an overhang of rocks. An uneasy feeling had crept up Ian's backbone shortly before they'd stopped for the night. He didn't know if it was his physical discomfort or if it was something in the atmosphere, but one look at the faces around him told him that every one of his companions felt the same. Even the horses stomped their feet.

Dawn broke the next morning, and Ian, who had been awake well before, stood and stretched with a groan. His legs and back ached terribly and he could only imagine what the professor must be feeling as he helped him up.

The day passed with very little conversation, the foul mood permeating their little group like a bad cold. But by nightfall they came to a crest and Jaaved announced, "From this way forward it is all downhill. It will be easier but still difficult. We should rest until daylight to be sure of our footing."

There was no shelter for them that night and they huddled together in the cold, sharing the three blankets they had. Again, Perry took the first watch and Ian took the second. Toward the end of Ian's watch, when his eyelids were beginning to droop and his shoulders had slumped, he heard something in the distance that snapped him into wakefulness.

Theo sat up from where she was lying and looked at him. "What was that?" she gasped.

Ian stood and eyed the pass behind them. "I don't know," he whispered.

"Was it the beast?" she asked him anxiously.

"No," he said to her, but the standing hair on his arms told him differently. "Go back to sleep, Theo. There's only a few hours till dawn, and I'll make sure you're safe until then."

Theo settled back down but Ian knew she lay awake like he did for the rest of the night.

At first light the exhausted group was up and moving again, but at least their path was downhill now. The professor suffered greatly, his sore knees giving out almost constantly. Perry finally had no choice but to put him on the white stallion and hope for the best. The steed did a remarkable job keeping its footing with the extra weight on its back.

As the sun began to drop into the west, they caught their first glimpse of the sea. "There!" Perry said excitedly, pointing to the north. "The ocean! We're close now, my friends!"

The ground had leveled off significantly and the six of them were once again on horseback. They had to stop several times, however, as their horses were nearly as weary as they were, and because there hadn't been anything for them to eat along the pass, the hungry steeds gobbled up the grass that seemed to be growing more lush the closer they got to Larache. "I wish I could eat grass," said Ian, looking at the horses feasting. For emphasis his stomach gave a loud growl.

"We'll get something to eat the moment we reach the city," Perry promised. "And then we'll work on booking our passage to Spain."

"But the boat won't be leaving for another six days," said Theo, and Ian realized with surprise they'd only been gone eight days. It had felt much longer.

"Not to worry," said Perry confidently. "I have a suspicion that in Larache, if you flash enough gold bullion about, you can charter a private craft up the coast and across the Strait of Gibraltar."

Jaaved nodded. "That is correct," he said. "And I know of a wealthy shipowner at the docks who could take us safely to Spain in his private yacht. But his price is quite steep."

Ian's spirits rose. He longed for the comforts of home, and if he couldn't get to England right away, Spain was at least Europe and a good place to start.

"We'd best be off," said the professor. "It'll be nightfall soon, and I would very much like to sleep in a real bed this evening."

When the moon was just beginning to rise, the utterly exhausted band found themselves on the main road leading to Larache. They stopped at the first inn they came to and the professor went inside to see about food and lodging. He'd told Ian on the road before they'd reached the city that he intended to keep their treasure a secret and hoped to sell their horses for a nice bit of cash.

While Ian, Jaaved, Perry, and Theo waited outside the inn, Ian rubbed the muzzle on the great white stallion and thanked him for being such a good horse. The professor soon reemerged with the innkeeper, who inspected the steeds, scowling at their condition and shaking his head as if he were unhappy. Ian could sense that it was all for show; he knew that the horses were fine animals and worth a great deal to the likes of the innkeeper, who could probably sell them for a lot more than he would offer the professor.

Finally, the professor and the Moroccan reached an agreement. Money was exchanged for the horses; then the professor came back to the group and announced proudly, "I've managed to get a good price for them, if I do say so myself. The innkeeper is preparing two rooms for us and we're welcome to have some supper in the dining hall while he gets them ready."

The professor led the way back inside and Ian felt his legs wobble with effort. He was dizzy in anticipation of a substantial meal and could hardly believe that one was so close at hand.

They took a seat at a long table in one corner of the dining hall and immediately a woman in a set of robes and a veil came out and began serving them from a large platter of fruit, vegetables, and lamb. Ian filled his plate, trying hard to resist the urge to shove all of it into his mouth at once.

Instead, he forced himself to take small bites and savor the flavor. At one point, he realized that Theo was giggling, and when he turned to look at her, she said, "You're moaning!"

Ian blushed as he swallowed the bite of lamb he'd been eating. "It's delicious," he said; and he caught his schoolmaster smiling good-naturedly at him. As Ian was exchanging a smile, he happened to catch sight of someone across the room openly staring at them. He wasn't too concerned about it—after all, they must look a bit unsightly after their long ordeal—but the man then waved at them, as if he wanted them to come over.

Ian turned to the professor. "Sir, that man is trying to get our attention."

The professor turned and nodded politely at the stranger but did not attempt to talk to him. "He's probably just curious about the likes of us, Ian," he said, turning back to the table. "Come on now, eat your supper."

But the stranger persisted. "You there," the man called to

them in English, and Ian caught that he seemed to be point-ing at Perry. "A word with you!"

Ian froze, unsure about the accusatory tone in the man's voice. Around the table he noticed everyone else had stopped eating too. The professor sighed heavily and whis-pered, "I'll take care of this, Perry. Sit tight with the chil-dren."

"You!" the man said again, and this time it was clear he was talking to Perry. "You are so rude that you will not ac-knowledge me?"

Perry smiled and gave the man a little bow of his head. "I'm sorry," he said. "But we are very tired and just want to eat our dinner."

"Did you find your way to the shore?" the man de-manded, and got up from his table to walk over to them.

"Excuse me?" Perry said.

"This morning, when you asked me for directions to the shore. Do you not remember me?"

Perry squinted at the man. "I never asked you for . . ." His voice trailed off. With a gasp, Perry jumped up from the table and hurried around to the stranger. Gripping his linen tunic, he said, "A man who looked like me asked you for directions this morning?"

"Yes!" said the man, obviously startled by Perry's reac-tion. "It was you, was it not?"

"Was he alone?" Perry asked with wide eyes.

"No," said the man, scratching his head in confu-sion. "You were with a young boy. I think it was him." He pointed to Ian.

Ian's mind finally made the exciting connection. "He's talking about Thatcher and Carl! They're alive!"

Perry let go of the man's tunic and swept a hand through his sooty hair. "If you please, sir, you seem to be talking about my brother, and I'm afraid we've become separated. Can you tell me where you saw this man and the young boy?"

The man squinted at him again, as if he were trying to accept that he'd been talking to someone else earlier in the day. "I spoke to this man who looked very much like you at the fountains. He and the young boy were drinking from them like common animals."

Perry gave him a shaky smile. "They would have been very thirsty," he said.

"Yes, well, I told them that it was very improper and that if they wanted to drink, they should find a well."

"A well?"

The professor cut in. "It is the equivalent here, Perry, of a public drinking fountain. Please continue, sir, with your story."

"Well, they didn't know where the nearest well was, so I led them to one and then they asked me if I could direct them to the shore on the west side of the city. They said that they'd been lost wandering the streets, and seemed to be going in circles."

"But they were all right, overall?" Perry asked anxiously. "They were unhurt?"

"Yes," said the man. "Except that they both looked very hungry and were obviously thirsty, they were fine. The boy seemed a bit dizzy, though."

"Dizzy?"

"Yes. He was so thin, you know, and I suspected he was very hungry, so I bought the boy and the man a wedge of cheese and some bread. They seemed very grateful."

"As are we," said the professor, and Ian saw him discreetly hand the man several bills for his trouble. "Thank you for caring for our friends."

The man smiled, and with a small bow, he took the money and his leave of them. "We've got to find them," said Perry, turning to the group.

"They must be headed back to the cave," said Ian. "I'll bet they're hoping we'll head there if we're still alive as well."

"Jaaved," said the professor, "can you take us to the beach where you first found us?"

"At the Mother's Cradle?" Jaaved asked.

"Yes," said the professor.

"Of course," said Jaaved. "It's not far."

Ian quickly gathered up his pack and a few handfuls of lamb to eat on the way. After the professor explained to the innkeeper that they would need one more room upon their return, they set off at a brisk pace.

It was dark and the streets were nearly empty as they made their way through the maze that was Larache. And even though they had come a long way and were physically exhausted, the small bit of nourishment coupled with the news that Thatcher and Carl were alive gave Ian a surge of energy.

Finally, they came to a small cul-de-sac lined with wooden houses and dirt yards and Jaaved pointed to a set of stairs between two of the houses. "That stairwell will lead us to the beach," he said. But as he looked behind them into the darkness, a strange expression crossed his face.

"What is it?" Ian asked their guide.

"I'm not sure," Jaaved answered, staring into the dark. "But I think someone is following us."

Ian turned and looked back toward the streets. "Who could be following us?" he asked nervously.

Jaaved shook his head. "I don't know, but I don't think we should wait to find out. We need to hurry."

Ian's nerves urged him down the stairs, but every time he glanced back, he caught his schoolmaster also looking over his shoulder. Ian was now convinced that something was tagging along after them in the darkness.

When they reached the bottom of the staircase, Perry pointed to the Mother's Cradle, barely discernable in the moonlight ahead. "There!" he yelled. "We're nearly there—" His voice was drowned out by a horrible howl that Ian knew all too well.

Theo screamed and grabbed Ian's hand while he looked up and down the beach, waiting for those thundering paws. "To the rocks!" the professor yelled, and with a wave he hurtled forward as if he were a young man again.

For a split second, Ian hesitated, but his schoolmaster gave both him and Theo a rather firm push and said, "Go! Make it to the top of the rocks and you should be safe! The professor and I will catch up!"

Ian, Theo, and Jaaved ran for it, passing the professor. The trio struggled in the sand until they got to the water's edge, where the beach was firmer, and then they plunged doggedly ahead. Ian felt Theo losing ground quickly and he slowed only as much as he needed to grab her hand and tug her along. He could hear Perry behind them, encouraging the children on as he helped the professor, who seemed to be lagging farther and farther back.

Ian and Theo reached the large outcropping first and he wasted no time lifting her up onto the first boulder before ordering her to keep climbing. He then turned and waited for Jaaved, who was not far away. Farther down the beach he saw the professor and Perry struggling to reach the outcropping. He heard Perry yell, "Get over the rocks, Ian! Help Theo and Jaaved, but don't wait for us!"

Ian was just about to follow orders, but as he was coaxing Jaaved the last few strides, two large shadows lurched out of the darkness far down the beach. Ian's heart sank when he saw the unmistakable shapes of the beasts racing along the water's edge, closing in on Professor Nutley and Perry like sharks after injured seals.

"Hurry!" Ian shouted. "Professor Nutley! *You've got to hurry!*"

Above him Theo screamed and Ian realized she had stopped climbing and was looking back toward the beasts. Jaaved must have noticed something was wrong too, because he had stopped and was looking over his shoulder. Ian knew that Jaaved could see the beasts, but that didn't stop the boy from dashing back to Perry's side to help with the professor. Ian watched Jaaved lift the old man's legs while Perry grabbed the professor's middle and the pair attempted to move awkwardly down the beach.

"We've got to help them!" Theo shouted, and she began

to edge back down the rock. Ian knew he had to get Theo to safety.

"Get up there!" he yelled at her, leaping next to her and forcing her to a higher boulder.

"But, Ian!" she wailed. "They'll be torn to pieces!"

Ian looked toward the safety of the flat section of the Mother's Cradle. He shrugged quickly out of his backpack and launched it as hard as he could, and with satisfaction he saw it land on the boulder just below the cradle. "Move up there!" he ordered, his tone sharp.

But Theo was resistant. "They need us!" she yelled back.

Ian was as angry as he'd ever been with her and he roughly pushed her to the next perch. "I'll help them if you get yourself to the cradle!" he promised.

Just then there was a thud in the sand to Ian's left, and he turned to look in alarm, but to his shock and surprise he saw that what had dropped beside him was Carl. "Get her clear!" Carl yelled over his shoulder. "Thatcher's just on the other side! I'll hold them off!" Carl raised the Phoenician short sword he must have recovered from the Jichmach, and charged down the beach, mimicking the Jstors' high-pitched war cry.

Theo and Ian locked eyes for a moment before she said, "I promise I'll keep going, Ian. Now, *please,* go help them!"

Ian gave a quick nod, then dropped to the ground and picked up several large rocks before racing after Carl, who was dashing as fast as his skinny legs could carry him, still howling the horrible off-key war cry.

As Ian flew down the beach, he saw Jaaved and Perry struggling mightily under the weight of the professor. Carl had just about reached them, and Ian thought that his friend might stop to help, but to his distress, Carl ran right past, ignoring Perry's labored yell: "Stop, Carl!"

As Ian came abreast of his schoolmaster and Jaaved, he was torn between helping them and going after Carl, who Ian feared might have gone completely mad. "Go!" panted Perry with a nod over his shoulder toward Carl. "Stop him before he gets himself killed!"

Ian took off again but couldn't seem to gain ground on Carl, who was growing ever closer to the beasts. Ian could see that one of the beasts was much smaller than the other, and this creature was far out in front of the larger one. Ian was at least thankful that he wouldn't have to fend off both of the brutes while he attempted to save Carl.

Still, Ian's friend wasn't making it easy on him. Carl charged at the first beast, his sword extended and his cry slicing the night. Ian knew that his chum would never defeat the hellhound, and as the distance closed between them, he curled his fist around a rock he'd picked up and drew back his right arm, feeling his muscles stretch as he took careful aim.

He was by far the best pitcher in cricket at the orphanage and most of Dover, for that matter. Very few players had gotten a hit off him, and he put all his skill into setting up the shot he was about to throw. He wound up, looked the closest beast dead in the eye, and fired his rock with such effort that his shoulder gave a jolt of intense pain.

To his immense relief the throw was true and straight and struck the animal right between the eyes. The hellhound gave a great yelp, lost its footing, and tumbled head over heels, kicking up sand and surf as it barreled into Carl, dragging him into the sea.

Ian cried out in alarm as he dove into the water after his friend.

Carl sputtered and floundered in the surf before going completely underwater, but Ian managed to grab his leg and pull him away from the creature as it shook its big ugly head and tried to get to its feet amid the waves and its own disorientation.

"Come on!" Ian yelled, hauling Carl back to the beach. "The other one is coming!"

Sure enough, the larger beast was thundering down on them, its white fangs snapping and its paws pounding along the shore.

Carl, who was soaked and a bit disoriented himself, gave a nod and the two boys ran for the rocks. Carl had managed to keep his sword, and Ian saw the tip of it rising and falling beside him while Carl pumped his arms wildly, keeping up with Ian's longer stride, and even gaining ground.

To Ian's relief he could see Thatcher helping the professor up the rocks, with Perry and Jaaved pushing from the rear. Behind them Ian could hear the larger beast closing in, and his feet felt the vibration of the terror almost within striking distance. Ian knew they had only seconds left before the beast would pounce on them, and he dug in with everything he had, willing his feet to move faster and faster. And little by little he began to move past Carl, only to reach back and grip his friend's shirt, half tugging, half jerking him forward as Ian leaned into his stride and gained a few precious steps.

A moment later they both leapt together and landed on

the first boulder before scrambling quickly up to the second and third, panic fueling their efforts.

Ian made it up to the next series of rocks quickly, but Carl was lagging behind, his sword making it difficult for him to climb. "Let it go!" Ian yelled over his shoulder. But stubborn Carl only gripped his sword more tightly and jumped to a boulder farther away from Ian. "Carl!" Ian yelled, pulling himself up one more level. "Let the blasted sword *go*!"

But Carl wouldn't. Instead, he jumped laterally, taking him even farther away from their group and cornering him on a ledge that even the smaller beast could leap to.

Ian wanted to scream in frustration but continued to scramble up the rocks and soon got to the next boulder, nearing the top of the Mother's Cradle, where he sensed he'd be safe. The climb was far too slippery for the beasts, and Ian reasoned that the higher the group could get, the safer they'd be.

He clambered up one more rock and stole a glance behind him. The larger beast was struggling to gain purchase on the slippery rocks, and couldn't get close to him, but the smaller beast, who seemed to have recovered from his head wound, was loping down the sand, making a beeline for poor Carl.

Meanwhile, Carl stood terrified with his back flat against the rock where he'd inadvertently stranded himself. The ledge above him was beyond his reach, and he couldn't move right or left, as both directions would bring him closer to the beast at the base of the rocks. It might be that the smaller beast would catch him, or the larger one would tire of chasing the group up the boulders and turn on him. Either way, Ian knew that his friend was doomed.

Desperately, Ian looked above him. The professor had just gained the top rock of the Cradle, and Thatcher was helping his brother and an exhausted Jaaved up onto the ledge. "Ian!" Thatcher shouted down to him. "Come on, lad! It's not safe there! Keep climbing!"

Ian looked back at Carl and their eyes met. There was no way for Ian to help his mate in time, and Carl knew it. Raising his sword in salute, Carl gave him a nod, and the understanding that he was done for passed between them. The courage he showed in the face of imminent death broke Ian's heart. "*No!*" Ian yelled fiercely. "Carl, you've got to try to climb! Drop your sword!"

But Carl was no longer listening. The smaller beast was just down the beach. With a sickening feeling, Ian could see the evil look of satisfaction on its face as it moved in for the kill.

Under Ian there was a *snap!* and the hot breath of the larger beast brushed against his feet. He looked over his shoulder and saw the beast's snout just below him. The monster was clinging to the rock, its red eyes glowing. Ian scrambled up another level and turned back to look for Carl. Part of him couldn't bear the thought of watching his brave friend fall victim to the beast, and he wanted to turn away, but another, stronger part of him knew that Carl didn't want to die without witness.

Then, to Ian's astonishment, just as the smaller beast stopped at the base of the rock and prepared to leap up, Theo dropped one of the straps of a backpack just above

Carl's head. The clever girl was also looping the other strap around a cone-shaped rock jutting out from the ledge she was standing on. With her body she then braced it to keep it in place.

"Carl!" Ian shouted with a hammering heart. "Look up!" Carl did just as the smaller beast crouched. As if in slow motion, Ian watched as his friend and the beast both leapt into the air. In the nick of time, Carl managed to grab the backpack and curl himself up, away from the snapping jaws of the beast. The hellhound missed his legs by centimeters and knocked its head against the rock where Carl had just been standing. The blow sent the beast back to the sand for another round of shaking its giant head.

Ian watched anxiously as his friend dangled in the air, holding on for dear life, his sword still gripped tightly in his hand as he wound his arms awkwardly through the strap and curled his body as far away from the beast as he could get. Theo, meanwhile, was holding her end of the pack down around the rock as best she could, but it was quickly slipping upward.

Ian knew she wouldn't be able to hold it much longer, and the larger beast, which was still after him, had only to turn its focus away from Ian and it would realize that it could take Carl out in a heartbeat.

Ian looked up the rock and saw Perry and Jaaved still helping the professor while Thatcher waved at Ian to hurry. "Thatcher!" Ian shouted up the rock. "You've got to help Theo and Carl!"

Thatcher looked at what Ian was pointing to and

shrieked in horror. "Get up here now!" he shouted to Ian as he scrambled over the rock toward Theo.

But Ian knew he had to keep the larger beast occupied and away from Carl. Reaching into his pocket, he grabbed a few of the stones he'd stuffed there earlier, and instead of going up the rock, he began pelting the larger beast.

The giant hellhound became enraged. It snapped its evil jaws and clawed toward Ian. "Take that, you mangy cur!" Ian shouted as he pelted it again, right above its snout. "Stupid beasty!" he shouted. "Stupid, hairy, smelly beasty! How do you like that?" He hit the creature again.

Then, out the corner of his eye, he saw the smaller beast give a final shake of its ugly head and focus again on Carl. Ian crept further up the rock, just out of range of the larger hellhound, so that he could track the smaller one. With mounting worry he watched the smaller beast creep over to the rock and, crouching low, aim for his dangling friend again. Ian's eyes darted upward to see how close Thatcher was, and although his schoolmaster was hurrying as fast as he could toward Theo and Carl, Ian knew he would never make it in time.

Quickly, Ian looked about and found a nice-sized rock wedged in the outcropping. He dug it out, wound his arm back, and let it fly, nailing the crouching beast right on the ear as it leapt into the air. The rock was large enough to throw the creature off, and for the second time, it crashed into the outcropping, narrowly missing Carl.

Ian whooped as the hellhound bounced off the boulder and fell to the sandy ground. To add to Ian's jubilation, the smaller beast attempted to leap toward Ian, but its judgment was severely off and it missed him, colliding with the first beast, sending them both tumbling to the sand below, where they snapped and snarled at each other.

Ian didn't wait for the two of them to reconcile. Instead, he shinnied up the rocks, making it to Jaaved and Perry, who grabbed his hands and pulled him over, though not before he was able to steal a glance toward Carl, who had himself also just cleared the rocks, thanks to Thatcher.

"We've got to get off here!" yelled Perry. "It's only a matter of time before they figure out how to climb up. Professor, can you make it down?"

Ian saw with alarm that the professor looked gray with fatigue, and he suddenly seemed much older than Ian had ever remembered him looking. "I'll make it," he said wearily.

Turning to Ian, Perry said, "Thatcher's been to the cave. Apparently, right before he heard our shouts on the other side of the rocks, the portal in the cave opened and he was able to see that Caphiera's ice wall is gone. The way back is clear, lad! We've got to get through to Dover before it closes again!"

Ian nodded and the group scrambled down the rocks, Perry and Thatcher helping the professor along while the children made it with relative ease. "I thought for sure you were dead meat," Ian said to Carl as they leapt down to the sand.

"Makes two of us," said Carl with a grin.

"Children!" Thatcher shouted from above them. "Run to the cave! Get yourselves through before the wall closes. If we get shut out, get word to the earl to send passage for us home!"

Ian, Carl, Jaaved, and Theo all nodded, and grabbing his pack, Ian led them at a run toward the cave. But suddenly, Ian heard a faint splashing between the noise of the crashing waves. He turned to look back at the dark sea, and squinting, he saw something large and blacker than the surrounding ocean bobbing in the water. He slowed to a stop, knowing that whatever was in the water wasn't good. Carl, Jaaved, and Theo stopped too and trotted back to him.

"Come on, Ian!" Theo insisted. "We've got to get through before the wall closes!"

"What's that?" Ian asked, pointing just offshore to the black mounds bobbing in the water, coming nearer and nearer.

Jaaved gasped. "The beasts!" he shouted. "They're swimming around the rocks to us!"

"What?" Carl shouted. "Don't they *ever* stop?"

Turning to Carl, Ian gave him his backpack with the treasure and commanded, "Take this and get Jaaved and Theo through the portal and home safely, and no matter what happens, Carl, don't look back!" With that he dashed off toward the boulders, where the professor was being gently lowered to the sand. Ian loaded his hands and his pockets with as many rocks as he could find and ran toward the surf.

"Ian!" he heard Thatcher shout behind him. "Come back! What's gotten into you?"

"The beasts!" Ian called over his shoulder. "They're swimming right for us! Get the professor to the cave. I'll hold them off!"

As he ran closer to the surf, Ian could clearly see the hellhounds in the moonlight paddling through the waves. Their giant snouts were raised high and their glowing red eyes bobbed in the water. He knew he had to try to give everyone time to reach the cave, and to do that he had to stall the beasts' progress as much as he could. Ian wound his arm back and aimed right for those glowing red eyes, but adrenaline caused him to miss his first throw, sending his rock skipping over the nearest beast's head.

To Ian's surprise, Thatcher suddenly appeared at his side. Winding his own arm back, Thatcher let loose a rock that skipped once and hit the larger beast right in the snout. It yelped, then growled, and a little hope rose in Ian's chest. "Keep throwing!" Thatcher said. "We've got to give the others time to get through the portal!"

Ian and Thatcher threw a volley of rocks, shells, and sand—anything they could get their hands on—at the beasts.

Finally, Thatcher looked over his shoulder and saw that Perry nearly had the professor into the mouth of the cave. "Best to run for it," he said to Ian, and the two bolted toward the cave. Behind them they could hear the growl of the beasts and the splashing take on a frantic pace, but they didn't pause to look back. Ian knew they'd make the cave ahead of the beasts, and if the portal wall was open, they could get to the tunnel and race for the stairs. He'd worry about the beasts charging after him once he made it back to British soil. For the moment he put all his concentration into making it to the cavern.

But just as he and Thatcher were in that final sprint, a figure, tall and cloaked, stepped from the shadows, blocking their entrance. Ian and Thatcher swerved to avoid crashing into it and both of them tripped and fell into the sand.

"So we meet again," said an eerie, high-pitched voice, sending a chill up Ian's spine. Scrambling to his feet, Ian faced the figure. In front of him stood the Druid sorcerer, Magus the Black. "I see you've made the acquaintance of two of my pets," he said. Behind him, Ian could hear the pounding of paws, large as dinner plates, closing in.

Thatcher was a little slower in getting to his feet, but after pulling himself up, he shouted, "Out of our way!"

But Magus only laughed, the sound like hot metal hitting water. "Now, now," said Magus, wagging his finger at Thatcher. "Temper, temper." He waved his hand and Thatcher fell back to his knees, gripping his stomach in agony. Ian hurried to his schoolmaster and tried to help him to his feet, but Magus waved his hand again and Ian fell, curling up into himself. His insides felt as if they were on fire. "My pets always did like their meat cooked," said Magus, his voice breaking through Ian's agony like an ice pick.

But before Magus could continue, there was a loud gasp that wasn't from Ian or Thatcher, and Magus the Black fell to his own knees, gripping his rear end. Instantly, the pain in Ian's insides stopped and he lay there panting and dazed.

"Leave them alone!" he heard Carl shout, and Ian caught a glimpse of his friend standing over Magus, the tip of his sword dark with blood.

Arms curled under Ian's shoulders and he was lifted to

his feet. "Run!" Thatcher gasped, and Ian did. He, Carl, and Thatcher raced around Magus, who was still holding on to his buttocks.

"We've got to make it!" shouted Carl as they tore into the cave and threw themselves forward.

As they hurtled across the line in the stone that marked the wall, Ian fell to his knees, his abdomen growing hot again. Carl fell too, then Thatcher, and the three crawled on until the pain became too intense. Ian was aware of paws thundering into the cavern and a great howl echoed along the walls. He rolled to the side, hugging his stomach, writhing in pain, as a dark shadow passed over his head and landed nearby. Then there was a great scraping sound, and when it ended, the pain in his insides disappeared entirely.

He lay there gasping for breath and realized that Carl was on his knees, struggling to stand. "Ian," he sputtered. "Get up!"

But Ian knew he couldn't. That second assault had taken everything out of him. In the back of his mind, he knew that the shadow that had passed over him was the beast, and its hot breath was right now blowing down at him from just a foot or two away, but he was too drained of energy to care. "I can't," he gasped. "Save yourself, Carl." Then the world grew dark.

THE GARDENER'S TALE

I an awoke to a chaos of noise, shouting, and confusion. He picked his dizzy head up from the lap it was resting on, and saw an awful sight unfolding below him. He realized with a jolt that he was on the stairs leading down to the portal, and below him, at the base of the steps, the smaller of the beasts stood menacingly, growling at Perry, Thatcher, Jaaved, and Carl. His friends and schoolmasters were moving around the beast in a circle, yelling at the hellhound while they held it off with any weapon they could find. Thatcher had the long stick that Carl had first brought down to the tunnel; Perry had the shield from the soldier encased in the wall; Carl had his short sword; and Jaaved had the professor's walking stick.

Even in his dazed state, Ian could see that the beast was having a hard time concentrating as it struggled to focus and blood dribbled from its right ear. The several knocks to the head it had received seemed to have severely wounded the creature. He also saw that it moved lethargically, probably worn out from all the running and swimming, and Ian realized with hope that their band might be able to hold it off until help arrived.

"He's awake!" shouted Theo.

"Ian?" said the professor, off to his left. "Ian, my young man, you must get up and make your way out of here! The others will do their best to hold off the beast until we get to safety, but we cannot leave you in this state."

Ian groaned while he got shakily to his feet. "Theo, Professor, you two go," he insisted. "Get some men from the castle. Tell them to bring their guns. I'm going down to help them keep it occupied."

"Don't be ridic—" Theo began, but Ian turned to her with a look of such intensity that she didn't finish.

"Go!" he shouted at her, and he stumbled woozily down the stairs to join the others while they yelled and called and chanted at the beast.

Perry banged his fist on the copper shield, creating an awful racket, which made the beast shake its head and growl low. "It can't handle the noise!" shouted Perry when Ian came to stand next to him. "Every time we yell, it gets confused!"

Ian bent and picked up a nearby rock, then threw it as hard as he could at the ugly matted creature. He smiled when it hit the creature squarely on the nose. The beast yelped and shook its head, then turned toward Ian. Peeling back its lips, the hellhound snarled and crouched low. Perry pounded on the shield again to distract it, but the beast paid him no heed. Somehow it managed to focus only on Ian.

"Yah!" said Thatcher as he poked the beast with his stick. "Take that!"

The hellhound snarled at the schoolmaster but quickly focused back on Ian, who took a wary step away, regretting the stone he'd just lobbed. The way the beast was looking at him, he could tell that the brute was about to pounce.

"Ian!" shouted Thatcher as he jabbed his stick at the beast again. "Run!"

Ian took another unsteady step backward just as the beast gave a terrific growl and leapt into the air. Ian's breath caught; his vision filled with the beast flying directly toward him, its hideous jaws opened wide.

Inches from death and paralyzed in fear, Ian was suddenly shoved violently sideways and he crashed to the floor while a horrible and deafening yelp pierced the night like a knife.

He rolled quickly to one side and tried to get to his feet, but he was in such terrible shape it took him a moment. Finally managing to stand, he looked at where he'd just been. There lay the beast, its mouth open, red-tinted drool dripping onto the tunnel floor, its eyes glazed over lifelessly.

The beast was dead! But just as he was about to shout for joy, he noticed a thin, bony arm sticking out from under the hellhound. "Oh, no," he gasped. Thatcher and Perry were already pulling at the beast and trying to shove it off poor Carl.

The beast was terrifying even dead, its sulfuric stink almost too horrific to stand. And when the two men finally managed to roll it over, Ian's heart sank once again. Carl's sword was buried deep within the creature's furry flesh, but poor Carl was left flat on the ground, pale and limp. Ian rushed to Thatcher, who bent down to pick up the unconscious boy.

"We must get him help," said Thatcher, lifting Carl gently in his arms. "Hurry, to the castle!"

Everyone raced up the stairs and ran toward Castle Dover.

Ian led the way through the woods and to the path leading to the castle. They were just about to enter the back gate when it opened and none other than the earl appeared, along with several of his armed men and Theo. Ian was startled to see him, as he hadn't realized he was in residence. "Where's the beast?" the earl demanded when he reached them.

"Dead, back at the tunnel," said Perry, coming up beside Ian; then the schoolmaster pointed behind him to his brother, holding Carl. "The boy killed him single-handedly, but the poor lad is in terrible shape."

"Here," said the earl more gently as he passed his rifle off to one of the men and held his arms out for Carl. "Give him to me. We've already sent for the doctor. Professor Nutley collapsed inside."

The earl took Carl carefully and hurried back through the gate and up to the castle, where a bustle of activity was taking place. Servants rushed about, gathering blankets and basins of water. Ian followed the earl anxiously as he carried Carl into the drawing room and laid him gently on the couch. Ian stood there, staring down at his friend, feeling helpless and afraid. Carl seemed to be breathing, but not well, and there was a ragged sound to his inhalations that Ian knew was dire. Theo came to his side and placed her hand in his. "Come," she said softly. "Let them tend to him."

Ian followed her to sit by the fireplace. He gazed around the room dully. Theo sat next to him, reaching out to hold his hand now and again, but even she couldn't ease the knot of worry and sadness that tangled up his insides. Jaaved sat across from them and stared at his surroundings with large brown eyes but he didn't seem to notice much that was going on around him.

A doctor arrived in short order and was shown to Carl's side. The children were then urged to the dining hall, where large bowls of steaming cabbage soup and huge chunks of freshly baked bread were placed in front of them. Even though Ian's stomach rumbled with hunger, he couldn't manage more than a few sips of soup and a nibble or two of bread.

No one disturbed them as they sat in the dining room. Before they'd left the drawing room, Ian had caught the earl motioning Perry and Thatcher away as soon as the doctor had arrived. Ian wondered how the earl would react to their incredible tale. It occurred to him that he might not believe them, were it not for the awful condition they were all in.

He glanced down at himself and—if his best mate hadn't been in the other room fighting for his life—would have laughed at how he must appear. Perry and the professor had been a mess as well, covered in soot, and all their faces were freckled, red, and blistered, as if they'd spent several days in the sun, which in fact they had.

After a long while, servants came in and removed their

mostly untouched dinners. The maid who cleared his plate clucked unhappily at him, but as he looked up at her, she seemed to catch herself and placed a gentle hand on his shoulder instead.

Just as Ian was about to pull himself away from the table, there was a commotion in the front hall, Madam Dimbleby's voice rising above the fray. "I demand to know where my children are!" she insisted. "Landis said they've been attacked by that awful beast again! Take me to them immediately!"

A moment later she was bustling into the dining hall, her face tense until she saw them, and then she let out a gasp and her hand flew to her mouth. She stared with wide, disbelieving eyes, first at Ian, then at Theo, and finally at Jaaved. Ian saw that her gaze lingered the longest on the foreign-looking boy. She blinked furiously, as if she were trying to place the face with a name.

"His name is Jaaved," Theo said quietly. "He's an orphan, from Morocco."

Madam Dimbleby's eyes darted to Theo, and she opened her mouth as if to speak but no sound came out. Instead, she leaned against the doorway and simply stared at them. Finally, she seemed to gather her composure and came into the room to sit down next to Ian. Taking his hand, her eyes roved his sunburned face and tattered clothes and she said, "Ian, dear, please tell me, what *on earth* has happened to you in the last few hours?"

But Ian found that he couldn't speak. He was suddenly completely overcome by his exhaustion; his many aches, pains, cuts, and bruises; his hunger and thirst; and most of all his intense worry over Carl. He could only stare back at her, his eyes welling and then overflowing with tears. Even so, he tried to open his mouth to talk, but no sound came out. Finally, he shook his head, unable to communicate anything other than his misery.

And to his immense relief, Madam Dimbleby seemed to understand. She looked deeply into his eyes and nodded. "All right, lad," she said softly, stroking his hair. "It can wait. Let's get you upstairs for a bath and a soft bed, shall we? I believe the earl would not object if you all stayed the night here, away from prying eyes and questions."

Ian nodded and wiped his nose on his tattered sleeve. Save for Carl's recovery, there was nothing he could think of that would be better.

It was a long time before Ian woke. But when he did, he rolled over and blinked against the light coming through curtains he didn't immediately recognize. His mind seemed to want to place him at the keep, but the view from where he was lying was all wrong. And then, as if his brain were a train that had slowly left the station, it began to pick up steam, and all that had happened came flooding back.

He wanted to curl away from the assault of those memories and would have attempted to go back to sleep were it not for two things that he realized with a jolt: that according to the sun's position through the window, it was late afternoon, and that the earl was sitting next to his bed, wearing a smile and watching him closely. "It's about time you woke up, lad."

Ian sat up stiffly and winced. He was very, very sore and

the sudden movement sent little tremors of pain through several body parts. "I'm sorry, my lord," he said with a groan as he prepared to throw back the covers and get out of bed.

"Now, now," said the earl, placing a gentle hand on the bedsheets to stop him from leaving. "The doctor has suggested that you take a few days to regain your strength, and allow those feet to heal. And seeing that Schoolmasters Perry and Thatcher agree you've been through the greatest ordeal, you're to remain here for another day or two at least."

Ian sat back against his pillow, relieved and grateful. "Thank you, my lord."

"How are you feeling, lad?" the earl asked him.

"Better, thank you. Just a bit hungry is all."

The earl smiled. "I'll send for some supper as soon as we're finished talking," he said. "First I want to hear your version of what happened. I've already heard from Schoolmasters Goodwyn, Miss Fields, and this bright young boy, Jaaved, but now I think I shall like to hear your story."

So Ian told him, as succinctly as possible, about everything that had happened from the time he and Carl had discovered the portal and the bones in the wall to when they'd met the earl on the garden path, with his poor friend so close to death. Ian dropped his chin and had a hard time meeting the earl's gaze.

"Carl will recover, Ian," the earl assured him.

Ian lifted his chin, hope welling up in his chest. "Really?" he asked. "Can I see him?"

The earl crossed his legs and sat back in his chair. "No, lad, I'm sorry. He's been taken to hospital."

Ian's jaw dropped. "Hospital?" he asked in alarm. "When will he be released?"

"A week," said the earl. "Several of his ribs were broken, and one of them punctured his lung. It was a very close call there and a lucky thing we're not far away from some of Britain's finest doctors. I met with them myself this morning, and they assured me that, barring any unforeseen complications, Carl will make a full recovery."

Ian nodded solemnly. "I need to give him my thanks," he murmured. "He saved my life, you know."

"And according to all accounts, you saved his, Theo's, Thatcher's, Perry's, and the professor's," said the earl. "It seems that all of you joined together to leave no man behind."

Ian hadn't looked at it that way, and he was grateful for the earl's perspective. "And how is the professor?" he asked, remembering the gray pallor of the old man.

"In hospital as well, but also expected to make a full recovery. He'll be right as rain soon enough, which is a good thing, as I'll need to talk to him about this mystical portal on my property as soon as possible."

"I'm sorry I disobeyed orders not to go exploring again," Ian said, lowering his face once more. He hated disappointing the earl.

The earl was silent for so long that Ian finally looked up, thinking that he'd really bungled it this time, but when he looked into the older man's eyes, he could swear he saw indecision there. Finally, the earl seemed to make up his mind and he leaned forward again and began talking softly to Ian.

"My young Master Wigby," he said. "What do you know about your delivery to Delphi Keep?"

Ian's brow furrowed. "My lord?" he said, having no idea what the earl was asking.

The earl appeared to struggle for the right words. "What I mean to say is . . . has anyone ever told you how you came to my orphanage?"

"Er . . . ," Ian said, still very confused. "No, my lord, they haven't." The earl frowned, and Ian thought he'd given the wrong answer, so he added, "But that could be my fault. I've never asked."

The earl grunted and sat back again with a sigh. "I suppose someone should tell you the story sooner or later," he said. "And in light of these recent events, I believe it is probably my responsibility after all."

Ian was trying to follow the earl's words, but it seemed that his patriarch was talking in circles. "Thank you, my lord, that would be nice."

"You see," the earl began, "thirteen years ago last month, one of my gardeners was taking an afternoon nip of bourbon out beyond the castle's walls. According to his story, he heard something like the sound of a baby crying coming from that patch of woods where you discovered the portal. So, my gardener ventured into them and found a stone structure which obscured a set of stairs.

"He told me that as he approached, he stopped hearing the cries of the baby and thought it must have been his imagination, but then he heard shouting, and so he went down the stairs to investigate."

Ian's heart had begun to pound. He knew that what the earl was telling him was about to change his life forever, and he focused on every nuance and syllable.

"When my gardener reached the last step, he saw that he was in a tunnel and he swore to me on his life that at the end of the tunnel he saw a series of things which were quite troubling: The first was that a beautiful woman clad in the finest silks and holding tightly to a newborn babe was crawling along the tunnel floor, and my gardener could see that the end of the tunnel opened up to a hot breeze, desert sand, and palm trees. He also swore that in the distance he could hear shouting from men in a language he didn't recognize and he distinctly heard the approach of galloping horses.

"Then," his patriarch continued, "the woman lifted her babe up to my very stunned gardener as if she was begging him to take the infant. He claims that he rushed to her and she pushed her child into his hands but refused to let him help her any further. He says that she only allowed him to get her to her feet before she stumbled back down the tunnel, in the direction of the approaching men on horseback. He said he stood there in a daze for several seconds and the beautiful lady turned once to look back at him and pointed to the babe. She said the name Ian and then, as if by magic, a wall appeared out of nowhere and shut off the woman and the approaching men on horseback from his sight."

Ian could feel the first trickle of a tear as it slid down his cheek. "My mum," he said hoarsely. "She was from the portal?"

The earl nodded gravely. "So it appears, Ian," he said.

"Where is your gardener?" Ian asked with sudden urgency. "I've got to talk to him! I've got to ask him what she said . . . what she looked like . . . why she gave me away!"

But the earl laid a gentle hand on his arm to calm him. "I'm afraid, my young lad, that he is no longer here."

"What happened to him?" Ian demanded. He had to find out more.

"I dismissed him," said the earl sadly. When Ian's jaw fell open, the earl explained, "You have to understand, Ian, my gardener had been known to nip at the bottle more than was healthy, and I kept him on solely because he'd been in my family's employ for many years before his drinking became a problem. But when he showed up in my library, claiming some fantastic tale to be true with a real baby in his arms, I'm afraid I thought the worst of him. I thought he had stolen the child in a drunken haze and couldn't remember where the babe had come from so he'd invented this outlandish story. I dismissed him immediately, and reported what had happened to the authorities, hoping to find your parents, but there were no reports of a missing baby anywhere in Kent. And so, I delivered you to the keep until such time as your mother could be located or we found a home for you and, barring that, I would provide you with food and shelter at the orphanage until your sixteenth birthday."

Ian sank into the pillows, utterly crushed. It was horrible to hear these details about his mother but not be able to know anything more about her or where she'd come from or who she might have been. And because she had come through the portal, he knew he was likely never, ever to know who or what or why or where.

And that was what sapped the hope right out of him. His mother would never appear at the orphanage to claim him. He would never be able to trace her through records or a search of the countryside. His past was lost to him forever, and he realized that knowing for certain that it was out of his reach was far worse than simply assuming it might be.

The earl seemed to understand, because he squeezed Ian's arm and said, "I'm terribly sorry, lad, but that's all I know."

Ian nodded dully. What else was there to say? They sat there in silence for a while as Ian did his best to accept what he'd just heard. Finally, with a deep sigh he said, "Thank you for telling me, my lord."

The earl smiled sadly. "I felt that it was important for you to know."

Ian nodded again and his stomach gave a low growl.

The earl's smile broadened into a happier one. "All right, lad, I've kept you long enough. Time to get some food into you, and I must pack for my journey in the morning."

"Where are you going?" Ian asked curiously.

"To London," the earl said, getting to his feet. "Given the fact that all of you are claiming that Searle is dead, and yet we've found no trace of him either in the tunnel or in the surrounding woods, I've got to meet with an investigator."

Ian gasped, remembering how Searle had died at the feet of Caphiera. "I feel terribly responsible about that," he said to the earl.

"You shouldn't," said the earl. "But I'll still need to look into this to the full extent of my resources. I've already got a man working to locate this couple, the Van Schufts, and get to the bottom of this mess. Did you know they came back to the orphanage looking to adopt again?"

Ian's jaw fell open. "Your aunt told us they would!" he exclaimed.

The earl nodded gravely. "That doesn't surprise me. Lady Arbuthnot is usually correct about these things. Madam Dimbleby reported that the couple arrived at the keep shortly after you dropped her off and went on to the portal. She said that she was very stealth in sending them away, but I'm concerned about their efforts to find you and Theo. I'll be looking far more carefully into the background of anyone who wants to adopt one of my children from now on."

"Thank you, my lord," Ian said gratefully. He hated the thought of that couple making yet another attempt to get at them, and he wondered if Searle's showing up with Caphiera meant that they worked for her.

"My man Binsford will be up with your dinner shortly," said the earl. "In the meantime, there is someone who's been pestering me all afternoon to see you."

"Who's that?" Ian asked as the earl made his way to the door.

Instead of answering, the earl held the door open and waved someone in from the hallway. A moment later Theo bounded into the room, looking much better than she had in days. "Ian!" she squealed, and hurried to his bed and plopped down on the end of it. "I'd begun to worry about you."

The earl left them with a wave, closing the door behind him.

"What time is it?" Ian asked her.

"It's nearly five o'clock in the afternoon!" she said, taking up the chair the earl had just vacated. "Are you feeling better?"

"Yes," Ian said. "Just hungry."

"Well, you still look awful," Theo said with a playful smile. "Best to take the doctor's advice and stay in bed for another day or two."

"That's what the earl said."

"Well, he's right. Did you hear about Carl?"

"That he was in hospital and will be all right? Yes, I heard."

"And the earl asked you for your version of events, I expect?"

"Yes, he did."

Theo nodded. "He's asked each of us separately, and we've all told him much the same story, so he has no choice but to believe us, especially since we've brought Jaaved back. Did the earl tell you that yesterday was still the same day?"

Ian furrowed his brow. "I'm sorry, what?" he asked.

"Time held still for us! We passed through the portal and time progressed, but when we tucked back through, we arrived just a few hours later than when we'd left. Yesterday was Saturday, the same day we went to London."

"How is that possible?" he asked.

Theo shrugged. "I don't know, but it is uncanny, isn't it?"

"I don't ever want to go through that portal again," said Ian. "I'm through with caves and tunnels and big hairy beastly things."

Theo smiled and patted his hand. "Well, at least there's one less beast to worry about. Perry and Thatcher took the

541

earl back there so that he could see it for himself, and do you know what they found?"

"What?"

"Just a pile of fur," said Theo. "That, and the skeleton in the wall had been put back to its original position, imbedded within the stone, as if the wall had never let go of it, and all evidence of Caphiera's icy deathtrap is also gone. There's not even an icicle left."

Ian shivered. "She was a ghastly creature."

Theo agreed and they talked amicably for a bit until there was a knock on the door and Binsford appeared with a tray of food. Ian barely mumbled his thanks before diving in to the generous portions of roast beef and creamy potatoes. While he ate, Theo filled him in on the earl's reaction to Jaaved, which was quite humorous, given the magical gem in Jaaved's possession. She also said that Jaaved had been assigned Searle's old bed back at the keep, and he was being introduced to the rest of the orphans as they spoke.

During their talk, Ian thought about telling Theo the story of the gardener, but he decided to keep it to himself. He knew he'd tell her eventually, but he felt he needed time to sort the pieces out and try to make sense of them. His mind kept drifting back to the part about the gardener's hearing approaching men on horseback, and this disturbed him in a way he couldn't fathom. He sensed that his mother had been trying to save him by handing him off, but that also meant that she had gone back to face the approaching danger alone, weakened, and likely very scared. Now that he knew a little, he ached to know more by finding the gardener, but didn't know if he could. Until he could figure out where to start looking he would keep quiet about it.

Theo stayed with him until he'd finished his supper and began to grow drowsy again, which he thought was absurd, because he'd slept all the night before and much of the day, but Theo reminded him of how little sleep he'd gotten in Morocco. And with a peck on the cheek, she left him to get some rest. He drifted off just as she closed the door to his room, his dreams filled with a beautiful woman with long brown hair, offering him up to an old man with a garden hoe.

A few days later, after Ian's feet had healed and his body had recovered, he returned to the keep. He was very glad to be home, though when he went upstairs to his cot and saw the empty bed where Carl slept, he couldn't help the achy feeling in his heart.

But his spirits were lifted later that day when Madam Dimbleby pulled him aside and said, "The doctors have declared Carl well enough to receive visitors. He is asking to see you and Theo, so I have arranged for Schoolmasters Thatcher and Perry to accompany you to the hospital."

The tenseness that Ian had carried ever since seeing the beast on top of Carl seemed to lift at that moment. "That's brilliant, ma'am!" he said. "I'll go tell Theo straightaway!"

But Theo already seemed to know when she met him in the hallway of the girls' dormitory. She announced, "I've just had a vision; we're going to see Carl tomorrow!"

Ian laughed, realizing that there was no getting anything past her. "We should bring him a present," he said.

"I know just the thing," said Theo with a mischievous look in her eye. "Leave it to me, Ian."

The next morning Ian, Theo, Thatcher, Perry, and even Jaaved set off to the hospital to visit Carl. They found him already receiving guests as Professor Nutley sat by the boy's bedside in a wheelchair, still looking a bit peaked but overall in good spirits.

"Well, well," the professor said as Ian and the others marched in. "If it isn't my traveling companions. About time you lot showed up."

At the professor's ribbing, Thatcher smiled easily and joked, "We had to make sure we wouldn't need to arrange for your funeral, sir." And Ian found himself laughing heartily for the first time in ages.

"And thank goodness," said Perry, joining in on the fun. "Those can be such a bother."

Around him Ian heard the chuckles and laughter of the rest of the group, except for Carl, whom Ian noticed gave only a short laugh, then held his side in pain. Theo strode right next to him and climbed onto the bed, mindful of the various tubes jutting out of Carl's arm. "How are you, then?" she asked him directly.

"A bit knackered," Carl admitted weakly. "But I think I'll make it."

"Well, you'd better," said Theo sternly. "Or else, who will inherit this?" She held a small blue booklet out to him. Ian stepped forward, curious about what she was up to, while Carl took the book and prepared to open it. Before he did, though, Theo handed a similar blue book to Ian.

"What's this?" he asked her.

Before she could answer, he heard Carl exclaim, "Gaw, blimey!" as he stared into its pages.

"See for yourself," said Theo with a happy grin.

Ian opened his booklet, which he saw was imprinted with the gold embossment of the Bank of Brittan on the cover, and inside were two columns, one headed "Deposits," the other headed "Withdrawals." Under the first column was a sum so large that Ian had to blink three times before his eyes could fully take in the digit.

"*Ten thousand pounds!*" shouted Carl. "How can that be?"

Theo smiled and looked at Ian, who was just as confused and astounded as Carl. "It's from the treasure," she explained. "With the earl's help, I took the bulk of what Ian and I got from the cave in Morocco and divided it by three. The earl sold it off at auction yesterday and made these deposits from the proceeds in our names. Jaaved also had the earl cash in his treasure, and he's got his own account now too."

Ian was at a loss for words. His mind had been so preoccupied by the story the earl had told him of the gardener and the woman who might have been his mother that he'd almost managed to forget about the treasure completely. "Theo . . . ," he said, looking up at her with a heart filled to bursting as he realized they would never, ever have to worry about making ends meet when they left the keep.

"Oh, but there's more," Theo said, and Ian's eyes widened.

"More?" he asked, holding up the booklet. "You mean this isn't all of the treasure?"

"Not quite," she said, motioning to Jaaved, who stepped forward then and said in perfect English, "I have something for you as well." He handed two small pouches with long bits of cord to Carl and Ian. "For you to wear," he said, and Ian noticed for the first time that Theo was already wearing hers.

Ian peeked inside at something small, triangular, and luminescent. Tipping the pouch, he let the thing drop into his palm. It was one of the points from the Star of Lixus.

"Jaaved!" he said in astonishment. "You've cut up the Star!"

Jaaved nodded. "The power of the stone has not lessened, though," he said. "It carries through each point even when it's separate from the center star."

" 'Break the Star to serve you best,' " said Theo, quoting Laodamia's prophecy.

Jaaved nodded and handed Ian a second pouch. "These are the other points. I think you should be the one to hand them out."

"To whom?" Ian asked.

"It is not for me to say," Jaaved replied with an easy smile.

"Perhaps the answer lies in here," Theo said, pulling out the silver treasure box they'd found in the cavern with the Star.

Thatcher inhaled sharply. "You found another box?" he asked.

"Yes," Ian answered. "We found it in the cavern with the gold."

Thatcher stepped forward and extended his hand. "May I have a look?" he asked. Theo glanced at Ian, who nodded, and she gave it to him. Thatcher inspected it, but Ian could tell he wasn't happy to see it.

"I've already looked inside," Ian said. "There's another scroll in there and a rather curious-looking sundial."

Thatcher's frown only deepened. "Yes," he said, "I rather expected that if we found another box, there'd be more instructions."

The professor seemed to notice Thatcher's unease and he asked, "Something troubling you, Master Goodwyn?"

Thatcher looked up. "I think we shouldn't translate the new scroll," he announced. "In fact, I think we should take this box, dig a hole, and bury the thing for good." Ian's eyes widened in surprise. That was not at all the attitude he was expecting from his schoolmaster.

Beside him, Perry barked in laughter. "You're joking!" he said.

"Not in the slightest," Thatcher said gravely. "Look here. These riddles from Laodamia have nearly gotten each one of us killed, and several of us have been gravely injured. While I'm delighted to see the children recover a bit of treasure from their exploits, after what we've been through, I hardly think it worth it to continue putting ourselves in harm's way."

"But we've no choice!" Theo said loudly. "We simply *must* follow the Oracle's prophecy!"

But Ian was having his own doubts, and the more he

thought about his schoolmaster's reasoning, the more he thought it might be good to quit while they were still all alive. "Theo," he said, "I think Schoolmaster Goodwyn is right." Theo whirled around and stared at him with large, disbelieving eyes. "We've got our treasure, and with it we'll never have to worry about the future. What more do we need?" he argued.

"We'll never have to worry about the future?" she repeated, her voice rising to a high, screechy pitch. "Have you gone *daft?*"

"Er," Ian said, wondering what he'd said to make her so upset.

"Ian," she snapped, as if he were a slow-witted git, "don't you realize that Demogorgon does not care if *you* don't want to follow Laodamia's prophecy? He clearly believes that you and I are part of his undoing, and he will not allow his evil offspring to quit until we are dead or they have been destroyed!"

"And there's that end-of-the-world bit to worry about," added Carl. When Ian looked at him, Carl shrugged apologetically and added, "Sorry, mate, but I'm with Theo. I'd much rather go down fighting than turn a blind eye and hope for the best."

Theo beamed at him and Ian turned to the grown-ups for their take on it. "The lass is right," said the professor with a chuckle. "I see that all Oracles have a bit of wisdom beyond their years. I believe we must translate the scroll and follow Laodamia's instructions. We've already gotten a taste of Caphiera and Magus. I think the only way to protect ourselves from them and the other two sorceresses is to know what's coming next. And the only way to know *that* is to translate the scroll."

Ian faced Perry. "Sir?" he said. "What do you think?"

Perry ran a hand through his hair and smiled grimly. "You know, a fortnight ago I'd have thought this whole thing was complete madness," he said, then rubbed his arm where he'd received the wound from Najib. "But I'll never take that attitude again. I agree with the professor, Theo, and Carl. We should find out what the scroll says."

That left Thatcher and Ian to decide, and the whole room fell silent as Ian focused on his other schoolmaster. "Sir?" he said at last.

Thatcher was turning the silver box round and round in his hands, his brow low and his look troubled. After another moment his gaze traveled up to meet Ian's. "All right, lad," he said, extending the box to Ian. "I'm in. Let's find out what the great Oracle Laodamia has in store for us next."

Ian took the box and walked it over to the professor. Placing it in his lap, he said, "When you're better, sir, we'd appreciate it if you would translate the scroll for us."

"By all means, lad," said the professor, patting his hand. "By all means."

ACKNOWLEDGMENTS

The concept of this novel would never have existed were it not for my grandfather Carl Laurie, who, when I was a little girl, told me of being orphaned at the tender age of five and brought up in the most inhospitable of conditions within a poorly run and underfunded orphanage in the South of England. There, from the ages of five to fourteen, he was routinely starved and beaten, barely clothed, and hardly cared for.

I carried the burden of knowing that my grandfather had suffered such cruelty for nearly thirty years before it occurred to me to rewrite a portion of that history as homage to such a charming, courageous, and sublimely elegant man. Thus, this story and all its sequels are for you, Granddaddy. May you rest in peace and know that I love you . . . eternally.

Thanks also to: Jim McCarthy, the single greatest agent in the universe, who read the first one hundred pages and encouraged me with boundless enthusiasm to carry on. Krista Marino, my phenomenally talented editor, who applauds my efforts while pushing and challenging me in such magnificent ways (and I'm truly a better writer for it). Pam Bobowicz, assistant editor, whose advice and comments have proven invaluable. Vikki Sheatsley, cover designer extraordinaire! Publisher Beverly Horowitz, who works tirelessly behind the scenes to ensure that I am well supported and cared for. Antonio Javier Caparo, for his powerful and intriguing cover art, which both mystifies and fascinates. And everyone else at Delacorte Press for their supreme efforts and energy on behalf of this story. Also Grahame Baker-Smith, thank you for your beautiful vision—it was quite an inspiration.

Elizabeth Laurie and Mary Jane Humphreys, every bit as beautiful and elegant as their father, and who remain my most avid supporters, confidantes, and friends. (Love you, Aunties!) Inga Brault, my childhood best friend, who may find herself at times reflected in the character of Theo. Thomas Robinson, for his help with French translations. Karen Ditmars, who reads every first draft and always makes me feel like a rock star. And the rest of my family and friends, too numerous to name here, but you know who you are. Thank you for your love, support, and most importantly, your inspiration. I'm forever in your debt.

Finally, I would like to acknowledge that I have taken some small liberties with historical fact, mythology, and even geography. I have done so not to deceive the reader, but solely for the purpose of convenience to this story. My hope is that you will recognize this as a work of pure fiction—and forgive the license.

ABOUT THE AUTHOR

When Victoria Laurie was eleven, her family moved from the United States to England for a year. She attended the American Community School at Cobham, and one day, while on a class field trip, she caught her first glimpse of the White Cliffs of Dover. Her trip to the cliffs, her year abroad, and her grandfather's stories of his childhood as an orphan left such an indelible impression on her that when she turned to a career as an author, she was compelled to write this story.

You can visit Victoria at www.oraclesofdelphikeep.com.